Modi's Vision to Empower Women

Modi's Vision to Empower Women

Editor
Punam Kumari

Published by
PRABHAT PRAKASHAN PVT. LTD.
4/19 Asaf Ali Road,
New Delhi-110 002 (INDIA)
e-mail: prabhatbooks@gmail.com

ISBN 978-93-5562-892-3
Modi's Vision to Empower Women
Ed. Smt. Punam Kumari

Edition
First, 2024

Paperback Price
₹ 500.00 (Rupees Five Hundred only)

Printed at
R-Tech Offset Printers, Delhi

Dedicated
to all the incredible women of Bharat,
whose potential, efforts, and
endeavors are paving the way for Nation
to become a Viksit Rashtra by 2047.

Preface

India has seen a massive shift in the role and impact of women throughout its territory in the last one decade. From agriculture to aeronautics, from business fields to battle-fields, from classrooms to corporate rooms and from playgrounds to Parliament, women have consistently been at the forefront to redefine the narrative of gender equality in the country.

This compilation of different articles is a strong testament to the indomitable spirit of the Indian woman. Here we have attempted to explore the arduous path taken by Indian women, their struggles, their triumphs and their enormous contribution in shaping a new horizon for the country. Hence, this is not just a reflection of the evolving clout of women in the contemporary Indian society, but is also a celebration of the achievements made by women in diverse fields. From challenging the societal norms to driving a fast economic growth, from advocating a perception shift to defying the age-old conventions, every chapter of the book is a tribute to *nari shakti* (women's power) which is on a roll ever since the new dispensation took charge at the Centre.

"*Women are the largest untapped reservoir of talent in the world*" – says Hillary Clinton.

Let alone the underdeveloped countries and regions on this earth, the cerebral power and talent of women, even in developed countries of the world, often go untapped. This has been one of the most unsavoury home-truths since ages.

But now, finally, India is witnessing a tectonic shift on this front in India.

The different chapters of the book provide an incisive glance into this paradigm change taking wings in the country. From grassroots leaders and activists to corporate executives and entrepreneurs, women in every domain who have dared to dream are challenging the status quo and have emerged victorious against all odds. As we delve into the narrative of the extraordinary women's power, the chapters remind us of the cultural and socio-economic diversity that defines India.

"*Women's empowerment is very crucial to our growth. Days of seeing women as home-makers have gone; we have to see women as nation-builders*" – says Prime Minister Narendra Modi.

True to his vision for the country, a law to reserve 33 per cent of seats in the Indian Parliament was passed in September 2023. What's more, in recent times, there has been a phenomenal surge in the involvement of women in governance and administration. The presidency of Hon'ble Draupadi Murmu stands as a testimony to this hard-earned empowerment which is further spruced up by her tribal identity and background.

The present government at the Centre, among the many other schemes to empower the female force, is all set to unleash the entrepreneurial capacity of women and aims to create three crore female entrepreneurs referred to as '*Lakhpati Didi*' at the grassroots level. These women entrepreneurs are well supported to achieve an annual income of Rs. one lakh or more. The 'Drone Didi' scheme is introduced to revolutionise agricultural practices and enhance the rural yield, focusing in particular on transforming the role of women in the agricultural sector.

While we celebrate the progress that has been made in the country in the last decade, we also highlight the work that still needs to be done on this front.

It stands to reason that empowered women contribute to the economic growth of the country by participating in the workforce at different levels. They also play a crucial role in breaking the cycles of poverty by improving the health, hygiene and education of their immediate families. What's more, empowered women actively participate in the decision-making processes of their community, leading to a progressive and prosperous society. In a nutshell, women empowerment in India is the key to realising the full potential of this bounteous country.

I would like to express my deepest gratitude to all the women contributors of this book for working very hard to make this compilation a grand success. Your courage, your determination and your perseverance as women are bright and inspiring. Very cordially, I also thank the readers for joining us on this remarkable journey. I wish and pray that the contents of this book ignite a fire inside you and inspire you to dream big and work hard for the country and for your own success.

Together, let us celebrate the new and emerging power of Indian women and together, let us strive hard to create a brighter future for the country as a whole.

Sincerely,

—Punam

Contents

Preface 7

1. Legislative Equality—Assessing the Women's Reservation Bill in India 13
—Prof. Punam Kumari & Ankesh Bhati

2. *Shakti* Unleashed—Women March Ahead in a New India 28
—Prof. Anamika Sinha

3. *Nari Shakti* in Uttarakhand 43
—Prof. Vijeta

4. The Growing Role of Meditation at the Foundation for Skill Development in Young Women Pursuing Higher Studies 66
—Prof. Richa Sawant

5. Accelerating Women Empowerment: A Reconnaissance of Government Policies and Initiatives 74
—Dr. Manorama Tripathi & Shipra Awasthi

6. Triple *Talaq* Unravelled: Assessing Judicial Dynamics and Government's Perspective in Contemporary India 97
—Dr. Geetika Sood

7. *Atmanirbhar Bharat* and the Predicament of Women 120
—Dr. Beena Agarwal

8. Girl Child's Education: Reflection on Last Few Decades, Current Trends and Future Outlook 129
—Ms. Ruby

9. *Viksit Bharat* and Role of Women in Science 137
—Dr. Poonam Mehta

10. Women Empowerment—Growing Economy 146
—Dr. N. Lavanya

11. Advancements in Women's Health: From Medical Breakthroughs to Empowerment Initiatives 152
—Dr. Kalpana Dubey

12. A Decade of Women's Rights—Towards a Legal System from a Female Perspective 173
—Nikita Upal

13. Empowering Girls and Youth through Welfare Schemes in the Last Decade 196
—Dr. Richa Sahay

14. Towards Self-reliance and Sustainability: A Journey of Women Empowerment through Ecofriendly Measures 241
—Dr. Shivani Jha

15. Empowering Indian Women through Financial Inclusion: A Policy Review of Select Government Initiatives 252
—Dr. Geetanjali Batra, Shabana Noori & Anjali R. Meena

16. Rural Women: A Decade of Upliftment, Empowerment and Societal Change 266
—Dr. Ritu Saraswat

Government of India Schemes for Women 281

Notes on the Contributors 291

1
Legislative Equality—Assessing the Women's Reservation Bill in India

—Prof. Punam Kumari & Ankesh Bhati

"Nari Shakti Vandan Adhiniyam is not an ordinary legislation. It is a proclamation of the new democratic commitment of New India. It is a very big and very strong step towards building a developed India with Sabka Prayas in the Amrit Kaal."[1]

—Hon'ble PM Shri Narendra Modi

Introduction

India, the world's largest democracy, has historically witnessed a stark under-representation of women in its legislative bodies. This lack of parity not 2only undermines democratic ideals but also hampers inclusive policymaking and development.

The year was 1996, when the Women's Reservation Bill was introduced first time in Lok Sabha. It was a time when the temple of our country's democracy didn't even have 8% female members[2]. That bill lapsed due to the dissolution of Lok Sabha, and the three later attempts in 1998, 1999 and 2008, also met a similar fate. But, on the historic date of September 19, 2023, when the proceedings of the special session of the Indian Parliament started in the new Parliament building, the atmosphere was different, there was a firm and unanimous resolve among the Parliamentarians to clear the long awaited fair share of the Nari Shakti of Bharat in representation in the legislature, which got reflected in passage of the Nari Shakti Vandan Adhiniyam with almost unanimous approval in both the houses of the Parliament in the next couple of days.

A Glance at the 106th Constitutional Amendment Act[3]

To assess the Women's Reservation Act from multiple dimensions, it is first necessary to understand the provisions of the Act.

The 106th Constitutional Amendment Act 2023, reserves one-third of all seats for women in the lower house of the Parliament (Lok Sabha), State Legislative Assemblies and the Legislative Assembly of the National Capital Territory of Delhi, including those reserved for women from Scheduled Castes and Scheduled Tribes (which is equal to one-third of the total seats reserved for women). The reservation will be implemented after the publication of the census conducted following the Act's commencement and will remain in force for a 15-year period, with potential extension to be determined by parliamentary action. For inserting these provisions in the Constitution, the Nari Shakti Vandan Adhiniyam amended the Article 239AA and inserted Articles 330A, 332A and 334A.

This phased approach, with its built-in opportunity for review and extension, reflects a practical understanding of societal and political realities. It allows for adaptation based on the experiences of the initial years, offering valuable feedback for potential tweaks or extensions. Moreover, by linking the effective date to the upcoming census, the Act ensures that the reserved seats will accurately reflect the evolving demographics of the population, further strengthening its representative character. This pragmatic approach strikes a delicate balance between immediate action and long-term vision, paving the way for a progressive and sustainable transformation of India's political landscape.

Spatial and Temporal Analysis of Women's Participation in Legislatures[4]

The temporal analysis shows that, for around 3 decades from 1950s to 1980s, the percentage of female members in the Lok

Sabha hovered around a mere 5%. Paradoxically, in this phase itself, India saw its only female Prime Minister till date. However, the lesser participation of women in politics in this phase can be largely attributed to the patriarchal nature of society. But, at the same time, right from the beginning, Lok Sabha heard some powerful female voices on the floor of the house. This included voices of powerful female leaders like Subhadra Joshi, Anasuyabai Kale and Vijaya Lakshmi Pandit.

From the mid-1980s, for around 2 decades, the percentage of female members in the Lok Sabha hovered around 8%. This was a phase when, gradually, more and more women were coming into the public sphere. This was enabled by emphasis on female education and women empowerment. However, the participation of women in politics at national and state level was still suboptimal which gets reflected in single digit percentage of female members in Lok Sabha. Even though at grassroots level, the participation had increased due to 73rd and 74th Constitutional Amendment Acts in 1992 which mandated reservation of at least 1/3rd seats for females.

The 15th Lok Sabha, for the first time in history, saw more than 10% female members which increased to more than 11% in the 16th Lok Sabha and to more than 14% in the 17th Lok Sabha (2019-2024). This gradual increase is attributed to the women-centric policies of the Modi Government and to internet revolution which is increasing awareness among women.

Also, one very significant development in this recent phase was that, for the first time Lok Sabha got a female speaker - Meira Kumar - during 15th Lok Sabha. This trend continued during the 16th Lok Sabha when Sumitra Mahajan became the speaker of the house.

The chart shown below depicts the share of women members in each Lok Sabha since independence (in %). Dashed line shows the 33% mark which will be reached in 2029 after the Nari Shakti Vandan Adhiniyam comes into effect.

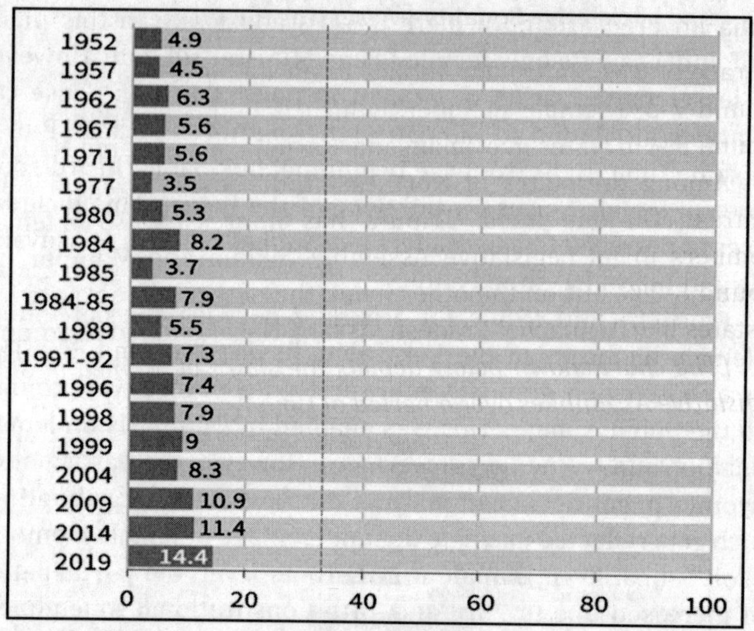

[Source: The Hindu, Delhi Edition, September 25, 2023]

Now, coming to the spatial analysis among Legislative Assemblies of states/UTs, here we observe a large variation in the extent of participation of women in politics among different states. But, the overall trend is of improvement in the percentage share of female members in Legislative Assemblies in almost all the states/UTs.

In North India, a stark difference is seen among the states in terms of percentage of female members in Legislative Assemblies. States like Chhattisgarh and West Bengal have around 14% female members in their Legislative Assembly which is much higher than the national average of 8%. On the other hand, Himachal Pradesh has mere 1.5% female members in its Legislative Assembly which is much lesser than the national average. Rajasthan, Uttar Pradesh, Bihar, Jharkhand, Delhi, Punjab and Haryana show a fair participation of women in politics with 11-12% of female legislators in their Legislative Assemblies when compared to national average.

In South India, almost all the states have a lesser percentage of female members in their Legislative Assemblies than the national average of 8%. States like Andhra Pradesh, Kerala and Goa, have around 7-8% female members which is better as compared to around 5% in states like Telangana, Karnataka and Tamil Nadu.

Among the states of Northeast India, there is again a big contrast. On one hand, Tripura has impressive 15% female members in its Legislative Assembly, Sikkim and Manipur has around 8-9%, but on the other hand, the percentage is quite low in states like Arunachal Pradesh, Assam, Nagaland and Mizoram.

(The chart shown below depicts the share of Women in State Legislative Assemblies over a period of time.)

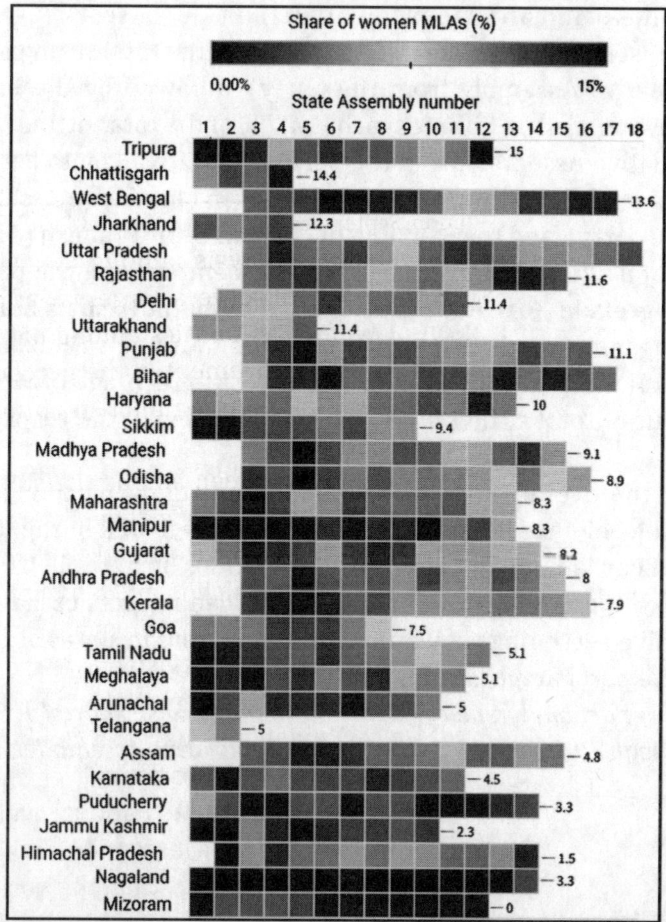

[Source: The Hindu, Delhi Edition, September 25, 2023]

When we see across party lines in India, we observe that women are just 13.5% of the sitting MPs of the largest political party, Bharatiya Janata Party, in the Lower House. In the second largest party in the Lower House, Indian National Congress, this number is 14.5%. The biggest number of women MPs in the house is from Biju Janata Dal, which is around 42% of total sitting Lok Sabha MPs from the party, followed by the Trinamool Congress - around 41% of total sitting Lok Sabha MPs from the party.

Just like that, a party-wise study of the State Legislative Assemblies of Indian states shows that the TMC in West Bengal has the highest share of women MLAs (15.3% of the total sitting MLAs in Legislative Assembly from the party), followed by the Indian National Congress in Chhattisgarh (14.7% of the total sitting MLAs in Legislative Assembly from the party), Bharatiya Janata Party in Rajasthan (13.7% of the total sitting MLAs in Legislative Assembly from the party), and the Samajwadi Party in Uttar Pradesh (12.6% of the total sitting MLAs in Legislative Assembly from the party). The Congress in Karnataka (only 3%), the Bharat Rashtra Samithi in Telangana (only 3.4%) and the Dravida Munnetra Kazhagam in Tamil Nadu (only 4.5%) have the lowest percentage of women MLAs out of total sitting MLAs from the parties in the respective states.

So, the overall trend shows that the leading parties at the national level have lesser percentage of women MPs in the lower house of Parliament. In Legislative Assemblies of States in Eastern India like West Bengal and Odisha, the leading parties have an impressive percentage of women MLAs, whereas in states of South India, the percentage is suboptimal.

The chart shown below depicts the party-wise share (in %) of women legislators in Lok Sabha and in Legislative Assemblies.

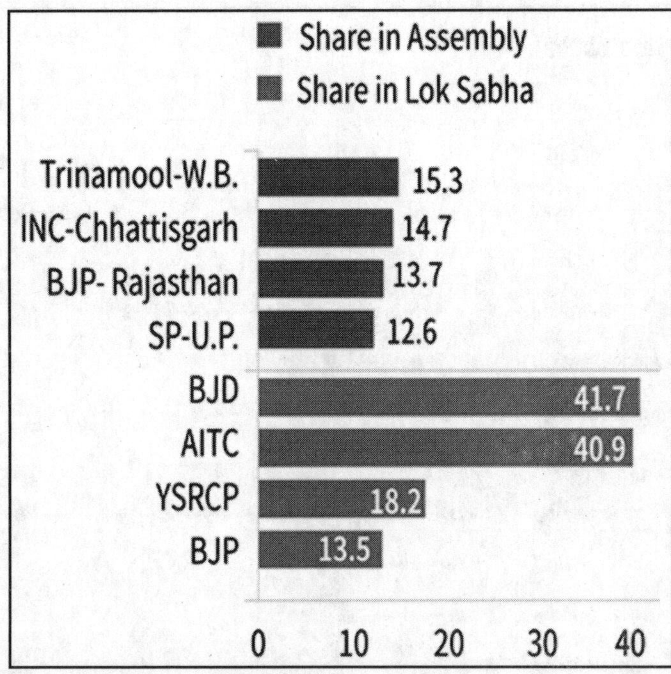

[Source: The Hindu, Delhi Edition, September 25, 2023]

The percentage of women members in India's Parliament is among the very lowest in the world. When compared with BRICS nations, including the 5 newly added members - Saudi Arabia, Egypt, UAE, Iran, Ethiopia - India has the second-lowest percentage of women parliamentarians i.e., 15%, just above Iran which is 6%. Over the past 3 decades, South Africa, Ethiopia and Argentina have made significant changes in terms of women representation in their national legislatures. Women representation in national legislatures of Nordic countries like Sweden and Norway has always been on the higher side. This can largely be attributed to the higher levels of gender equality and human development in those countries. India's condition in this regard will improve significantly once the Nari Shakti Vandan Adhiniyam comes into effect. This also highlights the importance of this legislation.

The chart shown below depicts the change in percentage of women members in Parliaments of various countries (in %) from 1990 to 2023.

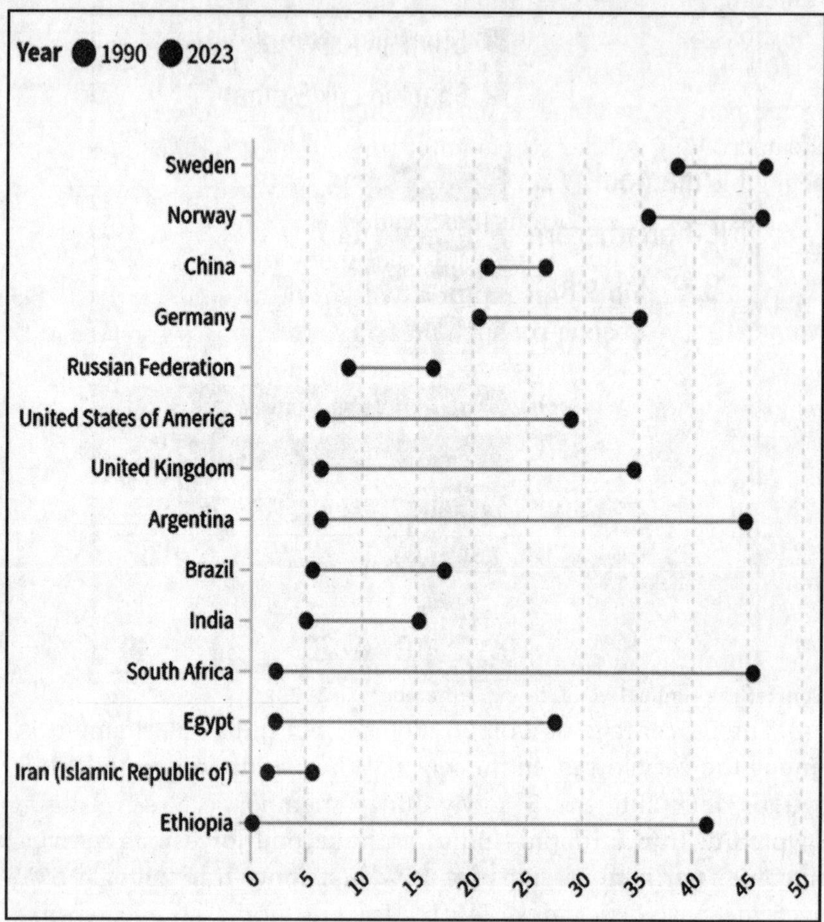

[Source: The Hindu, Delhi Edition, September 25, 2023]

Significance of the Nari Shakti Vandan Adhiniyam

For decades, India's parliament has mirrored a stark reality: the underrepresentation of women. While presence of women in the Lower House of the Parliament has gradually risen from a mere 5% in the 1st Lok Sabha to around 15% in the 17th, this falls far short of the global average of 26.7% and even the Asian average of 21%.[5] In fact, India languishes at 143rd among 193 countries, a position even lower than its neighbors like Nepal and Bangladesh.[6] This concerning deficit stems largely from the reluctance of major national parties, excluding the Trinamool Congress and Biju Janata Dal, to field women candidates. In the 2019 general election, a meager 13% and 12% of candidates were women for the two biggest parties,[7] highlighting a disconnect with the narrowing gender gap in voter turnout, which now stands at a negligible difference.

Learning from nations like Sweden, Norway and South Africa, can be incorporated, where internal party quotas have spurred significant female representation, with over 30% of seats held by women. In the absence of such measures in India, the Nari Shakti Vandan Adhiniyam emerges as a beacon of hope.

Beyond parliament, the picture remains bleak. State assemblies average a mere 8% female representation, with states like Mizoram having just 2 or 3 women legislators.[8] This political marginalisation significantly impacts India's global standing, evident in its abysmal ranking of 127th among 146 countries in the 2023 World Economic Forum's Global Gender Gap Report.[9]

However, amidst these challenges, a silver lining appears. The Nari Shakti Vandan Adhiniyam, as mentioned by the Union Finance Minister Nirmala Sitharaman, holds immense potential to unlock women's political empowerment. This landmark legislation is more than just a legal document; it's a transformative journey signifying a shift in societal perspectives. No longer passive recipients, women are poised to become active participants and influential shapers of the nation's destiny.

The success story of gender quotas can be gleaned from India's impressive 46% female representation in local urban and rural bodies, a direct result of the landmark 73rd and 74th Constitutional Amendment Acts.[10] This not only stands as the most advanced gender quota policy globally but also represents the largest empirical study in the field of politics, encompassing millions of women representatives. It serves as a powerful testament to the positive impact of quotas on political and governance equality.

India's journey towards an inclusive parliament is far from over. But the Nari Shakti Vandan Adhiniyam, coupled with the inspiring example of local governance, offers a glimmer of hope. This is not just about numbers; it's about dismantling systemic barriers and unleashing the collective power of women to shape a brighter, more equitable future for India. It provides the robust mechanism that has potential to empower India's Narishakti in the true sense and give them their rightful share in the Lok Sabha and the legislative assembly of the states, though after a long wait.

Empowering women at the grass-root level through reservations for female Sarpanch in Gram Panchayats have yielded positive results. These women leaders have prioritised issues that directly impact voters, like sanitation, education (especially Anganwadis) and healthcare. By tackling these crucial public services, women have not only saved time they previously spent on chores like fetching water or caring for children, but have also gained opportunities for income generation, either through home-based work or outside employment. Furthermore, female leaders often focus on public safety and gender-inclusive urban planning, which potentially increases women's physical mobility and their access to wider job opportunities located beyond their immediate vicinity.

The enactment of the Bill carries significant weight in empowering women and promoting the advancement of gender equality within Indian society. Unfortunately, a multitude of discriminatory practices and oppressive systems continue to plague the lives of Indian women. These include, but are not limited to, the abhorrent practice of female foeticide, the detrimental social custom of child marriage, the persisting issue of dowry-related violence, the pervasive problem of domestic abuse, the heinous crime of sexual assault and harassment, the barbaric practice of honor killings, the abhorrent act of human trafficking and the enduring issue of wage disparities. The legislation seeks to address these challenges by establishing an enabling environment where women can confidently voice their grievances and assert their rightful entitlements. Furthermore, this initiative aims to catalyse a greater participation of women in the public sphere, fostering their leadership roles and dismantling the prevailing patriarchal norms and stereotypes that impede their full potential.

Affirmative action for women is imperative to better their condition since the majority of political parties in India are inherently patriarchal. It would also help overcome the entry barriers like money and muscle power, for women leadership at the state and national level. Women representation in the decision-making process is essential to address problems like lower female labour force participation, increasing crime rates against women, etc. Evidence from the reservation at local level: According to assessments by Oxfam India, reservation for women at local level led to a visible increase in the reporting of crimes, improved access to basic amenities like drinking water, schools, etc.[11] The Act can enable greater participation of women in policy-making at the national and state level.

Are there any Inadequacies in the Provisions?

Some genuine and healthy criticisms came from the opposition benches during the debate on the bill in the house.

Firstly, the delimitation exercise is supposed to be held in 2026, this pushes the earliest year of implementation to the 2029 general elections. Opposition members asked why the provisions can't be implemented right from 2024 itself. But it is truly said, "better late than never". After implementation, there will be at least 181 elected women MPs in the Lower House of the Indian Parliament. At present there are only 82 women parliamentarians in the Lok Sabha which is only 15% of its total members. How surprising it is that the share of women parliamentarians has never exceeded the 15% mark in over 70 years of India's electoral history!

Secondly, demands were raised for reserving the seats for Muslim women and women belonging to Other Backward Classes. However, this was the major bone of contention and a major reason because of which the earlier 4 attempts failed as there is fragmentation in opinion on this particular matter among the parties. So, the ruling party ensured that this time the bill does not meet the same fate because of the same reason.

Thirdly, one more valid concern that was raised by the opposition benches was that the bill provides for rotation of seats after every delimitation exercise as against after every general election to the Parliament or State Legislative Assemblies. This can mean that the aspiring male candidates of a reserved constituency can't contest elections for a long period from their constituency.

Fourthly, there can possibly be disparity across states, because the Act provides for reservation of 1/3rd seats across all Lok Sabha seats, as against the provision of reserving 1/3rd seat in each State/UT as mentioned in 2008 Bill.[12]

Fifthly, it was pointed out by some of the opposition members that the Bill does not contain any provision for reservation for women in the Rajya Sabha and the Legislative Councils. The Geeta Mukherjee Committee (1996) had recommended providing reservation for women in Rajya Sabha and Legislative Councils as well.[13] However, since the members of these houses are indirectly elected with some nominated members from various fields, it is not much convincing to make the process further complicated.

And lastly, some MPs of parties from South India such as DMK expressed their concern that, when delimitation will be carried out, South Indian States can possibly face repercussions for their implementation of family planning measures, it will be like punishing them for their good work. Leaders of South Indian States have always maintained that if delimitation will happen on population census, it will reduce their proportion in the houses of the Parliament.

An Assessment of the Challenges that may come up in Future

One concern surrounding quotas for women in legislative bodies is the potential impact on merit and representation. Critics argue that simply basing candidacy on gender could lead to under-qualified individuals being elected, potentially hindering the effectiveness of government. They raise the possibility of women being chosen due to external influences rather than their own abilities, or lacking the necessary experience and vision for the role.

As seen in Panchayati Raj Institutions in some states, there has been a trend of "Sarpanchpati" and "Mukhiyapati" unofficially wielding the real power on behalf of their wife and using female just as a token to contest elections, there exists a looming risk of tokenization of female candidates and emergence of a similar trend of "Vidhayakpati" and "Sansadpati". Additionally, quotas could unintentionally contribute to existing biases, portraying women as needing special measures to compete rather than being capable on their own merits.

Political power dynamics are fluid, and the bill's long-term success hinges on its adaptability to changing political contexts. Addressing potential loopholes and manipulation of the reservation system requires robust legal frameworks and vigilant oversight mechanisms. Also, there is a risk that the period of 15-years proposed in the Act can be extended for political gains.

Another apprehension is that reservation of seats for women in legislature can restrict voter's choices and can run counter to the idea of self-determination. However, proponents counter that reservations, seen in various democracies, correct historical imbalances and expanded female representation ultimately broadens voters' options. Recognising both sides is crucial, as informed debate and careful implementation can pave the way for a more inclusive and representative democracy.

Navigating the Road Ahead

Timely implementation of the Act is of utmost importance. For this, time bound conduct and publication of the census data and delimitation exercise should be done. Any delay in these exercises would delay the implementation of the Act.

Legislation getting passed is only half the task done, the equally important task at hand is capacity building, which can be done by involving civil society and other institutions for training and mentorship of women leaders at local level to ensure their effective mobilisation at state and national level.

While ensuring minimum representation through quotas is crucial, we must move beyond mere numbers. Fostering a supportive political environment, dismantling patriarchal mindsets and providing equal access to campaign resources are vital to nurturing a critical mass of women leaders who raise not due to quotas, but sheer merit and public support. This requires political parties to actively include women in key decision-making roles, promote their visibility in the media, and challenge internal biases that hinder their advancement.

Leveraging the technology can be a game-changer. Online platforms can provide accessible training programs for aspiring women leaders, connect them with mentors and experienced politicians and facilitate knowledge sharing and networking. Digital campaigns can break down geographical barriers, increase transparency and mobilise rural women, allowing them to actively participate in political processes. This can revolutionise political engagement and create a more inclusive democratic space.

Collaboration across the political spectrum is essential. While differences in opinion are inevitable, but finding common ground on the issue of gender equality is vital. Establishing institutional mechanisms to monitor the Act's implementation, ensuring fair and transparent candidate selection processes, and fostering a culture of dialogue and cooperation can pave the way for a united front against the challenges that lie ahead. The era of Nari Shakti has come, the force is going to be unstoppable, and this legislation is going to bring about a paradigm shift in the political landscape of India.

Embracing a Brighter Future

For centuries, the corridors of power have echoed with a singular melody: the voices of men. But at the dawn of a new era, a transformative chorus has risen. It swells with the strength of countless dreams, fuelled by the unwavering spirit of women striving for equality, taking inspiration from the greats like Rani Lakshmi Bai and Savitribai Phule.

The Women's Reservation Bill, a symphony of justice long in the making, has finally found its crescendo – a triumphant declaration that no longer shall half the population - Aadhi Aabadi -

be silenced in the halls of power. This is not just a legislative win, it's a revolution at the heart of democracy, a promise whispered in the wind: a brighter future where Nari Shakti, the feminine force, takes its rightful place in the orchestra of progress.

The journey towards true legislative equality remains long and arduous. However, the Nari Shakti Vandan Adhiniyam offers a beacon of hope. It is the impulsive force that can finally shatter the political glass ceiling for women. The challenges are not insurmountable, by addressing the challenges head-on, engaging in capacity building and fostering a supportive political environment and sustained commitment to gender equality, India can leverage this legislation to build a brighter future where women's voices are heard loud and clear in the halls of power.

References

1. Hon'ble PM Shri Narendra Modi while addressing the women at Nari Shakti Vandan-Abhinandan Karyakram on 22nd September 2023
2. Statistical Report on General Elections, 1951 To The First Lok Sabha, Election Commission of India
3. The Gazette of India, No. 36, Published on Sept. 28, 2023
4. Data and Charts under this heading have been taken from Trivedi Centre for Political Data - Indian Elections Dataset, Election Commission of India, Inter-Parliamentary Union, and The Hindu, Delhi Edition, September 25, 2023
5. https://www.ipu.org/impact/gender-equality
6. https://data.ipu.org/women-ranking?month=12&year=2023
7. Statistical Report on General Elections, 2019, Election Commission of India
8. https://pib.gov.in/PressReleasePage.aspx?PRID=1809217
9. https://www.weforum.org/publications/global-gender-gap-report-2023/digest/
10. https://pib.gov.in/PressReleasePage.aspx?PRID=1988601
11. Oxfam Report on India
12. https://prsindia.org/billtrack/womens-reservation-bill-the-constitution-108th-amendment-bill-2008-45
13. https://static.pib.gov.in/WriteReadData/ebooklat/Flip-Book/constfiles/files/basic-html/page153.html

□

2

Shakti Unleashed—Women March Ahead in a New India

—Prof. Anamika Sinha

We often discuss the gold hidden in Indian lockers and households, which, if unearthed, would make a difference to the state of India's economy. Seldom do we discuss the hidden talent of women in our economy or the poor state of empowerment and inclusion of women in the formal economic system or corporate career.

When Hon'ble Prime Minister Narendra Modi announced the Atmanirbhar Bharat campaign on 12 May, 2020 and allocated Rs. 20 lakh crore or 10 per cent approximately of India's GDP to fight the COVID-19 pandemic and create a better and more self-reliant India, the role of women in this campaign and their progress in this effort remained undeniable and obvious. There are five pillars of *atmanirbhar* or self-reliant India – economy, infrastructure, governance, vibrant demography and demand and seven sectors in which reforms are to be made. Gender and equity for all genders at workplaces definitely is an important area of focus. Through this article we highlight that whenever women have been given the opportunity to prove their worth, including careers and areas which have traditionally been ruled by men exclusively, they may have taken a longer ramp space in terms of time, mentoring and support but they have always given a 131 per cent plus performance. The names of women who are remembered for their contributions have remained quintessential beyond time and memory.

We bring defence and aerospace research, entrepreneurship and STEM careers which are considered male-dominated and which are thus assumed as non-friendly for women to excel in. We present success stories of some successful women to highlight and inspire men and women to support the cause of women and their inclusion in all sectors and industries, as well as roles.

As per Atmanirbhar Bharat, the key areas of reform are supply chain reforms in agriculture, including women-farmer-producer organisations as a key initiative to formalise the women workforce which otherwise has remained ignored despite its contribution to the field. This would be a small step towards making visible an otherwise covert contribution, like rational tax system (led by a female Finance Minister), simple and clear laws (continuous and firm assertion by lawyers like Mithan Jamshed Lam, Cornelia Sorabji, Anna Chandy, Violet Alva, Fathima Beevi, Leila Seth, Indira Jaising, Indu Malhotra since years), capable human resource and capability building and strong financial system to complement the initiative. The current government has the highest women representation ever, thus highlighting that women are capable of breaking the glass ceiling and being an important contributor to the economy and social reforms.

Complementing the initiatives taken by the government and supported through changing social narratives, many women have taken a leap frog to add to the quantum jump made in the economy and towards building of roads, railways, airports, bridges, expressways and technology-driven options as seen in defence, aerospace and science and technology. This article is not about mentioning success or failure stories, but only for indicating some names to inspire action in favour of women at work.

Women who Broke the Glass Ceiling and made a Mark in Defence Forces

Before the call for atmanirbhar Bharat, Mrs. J. Manjula was appointed the first female Director General of Defence Research

Development Organisation in 2015 and it seemed as a prelude to her contribution towards Atmanirbhar Bharat in the defence sector.

The Indian Armed Forces devised an assertive approach in 2021 to deal with national security challenges and took several initiatives towards empowering women in the Services. Permanent Commission of women officers was implemented in the Armed Forces. Several women Army schools and exclusive women's batches at National Defence Academy were announced. Women, starting from Sarojini Naidu in the Independence movement coupled with the contribution made by Indian nurses in the World War and in medical hospitals to the recent promotion of former Flag Officer Punita Arora as the first woman in the Indian Armed Forces to the rank of Lieutenant General in the Indian Army and Surgeon Vice Admiral in the Indian Navy, are worth mentioning for their different roles. It may be fair to say that Punita Arora was an early entrant to the otherwise male-dominated workforce. In 1964, when women joined the Armed Forces through AFMC, she was the first one to seek entry. From then on more and more women have broken the glass ceiling and changed the narrative of the Armed Forces through their achievements. Some significant names and their contribution to the nation are as follows:

Padmavathy Bandopadhyay is the first Indian woman Air Force officer to specialise in aviation medicine and the first woman to conduct scientific research at the North Pole and the first woman to be promoted as Air Vice Marshal. She is the second woman in the Indian Armed Forces to be promoted to a three-star rank. She was awarded the Vishisht Seva Medal for her meritorious work during the 1971 Indo-Pak conflict.

Lt. Col. Mitali Madhumita is the first Indian woman to receive a gallantry award for her courage during operations in Jammu & Kashmir and in the northeast region of India.

Squadron Leader Nivedita Choudhary is the first Air Force officer to climb the Mt Everest and the first woman to achieve this feat.

Role of Women in Aerospace

Before the clarion call for Atmanirbhar Bharat, it was way back in 1965 that physicist and astronomer Vikram Sarabhai started the aerospace programme in India. In 1983, the missile technology programme was launched to achieve self-reliance in air defence and space.

It is pertinent here to discuss some of the notable women who played a role in aerospace before the Atmanirbhar programme was launched.

Sarla Thakral was the first women in 1947 to fly an aircraft. Prem Mathur was the first female commercial pilot. Captain Durba Banerjee was the first woman commercial pilot to be employed by the Indian Airlines.

Air Marshal Padmavathy was the first woman officer in the Indian Air Force to pass out from the Defence Services Staff College of India.

Flying Officers Gunjan Saxena and Sreevidya Rajan were the first women pilots to fly fighter jet planes in the combat zone during the Kargil war.

Avani Chaturvedi, Bhawana Kanth and Mohana Singh were the first women to fly supersonic fighter jet planes.

Women Scientists in Research Organisations

Mrs. J. Manjula was appointed as the first woman Director General (Electronics Systems) in the Defence Research and Development Organisation in 2015. She has played a major role in DRDO's electronics and communications systems cluster and thus done her bit to make India *atmanirbhar*. She said in a video interview that her team in DRDO has worked on integrated early warning system, LRDE and many women scientists are working on the in Uttam Radar Project under LRDE, Light Combat Aircraft Mark II. She also said that SAR or system aperture radar has mainly women scientists and technologists employed. The other projects where women are contributing are Kautilya (satellite payload development) or advance alighting system. They are also working on airborne early warning system software development and payload development

1. Jessy Thomas is Director General (Aeronautics) at Defence Research Development Organisation and was engaged in the indigenously made Agni missile, LCA, AWC and TAPAS.
2. Ms Suma Varughese and Rajalakshmi were Project Directors at Aerospace Surveillance Warning and Control System, the erstwhile Centre for Airborne Systems.
3. Ms Shashikala Sinha is an Indian scientist and Project Director in Endo-Atmospheric Interceptor Missile Advanced Area Defence Programme. Ms Pamela was recruited by Mr APJ Abdul Kalam and was the key person in development of the Brahmos ssonic missile, She says she was given absolute freedom to work and was encouraged to put in her best. Ms U.V.V. Krishna Veni was instrumental in developing the electronics intelligent subsystem for manned and unmanned flight control software.

   Ms Asha Garg, the project director, has been instrumental in light combat aircraft software development. She said in a video interview that due to Bengaluru (Bangalore) being an IT hub, the Air Force keeps losing manpower after training them but plenty of women are continuing to contribute their bit. She talked about women striking a balance between workplace and home and contributing to completing their mission. Ms Padmavati as Group Director of visual management system at DRDO worked on open architecture software for light combat aircraft (LCA). She talked about Light Combat Aircraft Tejas, which has carried out 4,200 sorties and that now India is self-reliant or *atmanirbhar* in manufacturing any aircraft indigenously. India has also developed the technology for air—to-air refuelling. Ms V. Sundari, who is Group Director at DRDO in weapon delivery system has worked on on Avionis weapon system and Light Combat Aircraft, besides developing air-to-ground and-air-to-air weapon delivery systems. She says that design development, testing and certification onboard have been carried out indigenously and that women scientists have contributed towards manufacturing many indigenous tools for analysis and algorithm.

Ms Gracy Phillip, Regional Director of LCA programme, has developed indigenous verification, certification, airborne-embedded system for LCA in Jaguar and Mirage at the Indian Space Research Organisation/Council of Scientific and Industrial Research and National Aeronautical Laboratory.

Ms T.K. Anuradha, Director, SATCOM programme of Indian Space Research Organisation and firstwoman Project Director at ISRO headquarters has contributed towards the geostationary satellite's design, configuration of satellites for communication and remote sensing, etc. programmes.

Ms Lalitambika, Director, the space programme of Indian Space Research Organisation has devised the autopilot for PSLV and GSLV (satellite launch vehicles).

Dr. Latashree, senior principal scientist at NAL has worked on flight dynamic modelling.

4. Dr. M. Sujata, senior principal scientist is responsible for failure analysis and accident investigation of LCA 900 engines and radar.

Role of Women in Science and Technology

Under the able guidance of Jitendra Singh, Hon'ble Minister of State for Science and Technological Advancement, , three important programmes for women in science and engineering were announced. The first is the Industrial Research Fellowship for Women which will provide opportunities for young women researchers to work in the industry for short and long periods. The programme will have two components, viz. industrial internship for six months in industry for girls who have submitted their Ph.D. thesis and the other is industrial fellowship for three years after acquiring Ph. D./M. Tech./M. Pharm. or an equivalent degree. This new programme will be a one-time grant for women scientists.

Second, the senior women scientist fellowship programme is proposed to provide dignity to senior women scientists who perform well in research but are not in regular employment due to various circumstances. The programme will benefit these scientists in age group of 45-60 years and who have completed at least two independent research projects and possess an excellent track record. Under this programme, a five-year project will be given to women scientists along with fellowship and other research grant. The projects are grouped under six subject areas – Physical and Mathematical Science, Chemical Science, Life Science, Earth & Atmospheric Science, Engineering & Technology, Science & Technology for Society.

The third programme of overseas fellowship for women will encourage research scholars and young women scientists to upgrade their skills in various countries. The programme will serve Ph.D. scholars of age group 21-35 years and young faculty of age 27-45 years through its two components, viz. Women Overseas Student Internship and Women Overseas Fellowship, respectively. This three to six-months' overseas visit will include a monthly stipend, return airfare, health insurance, contingency, etc. All the three programmes are in line with Prime Minister Narendra Modi's efforts to introduce programmes that are pro-people, pro-poor and pro-women, thus maintaining women's dignity and health. Several initiatives include Navodaya Women's Schools and other mechanisms to promote education for women.

Some key beneficiaries and exceptional performance by women are as follows: Dr. Tessy Thomas, known as the 'Missile Woman of India' is the first woman scientist to head a missile project in India.

Dr. (late) Kalpana Chawla, the first woman scientist to undertake space journey in space shuttle, Columbia.

Dr. Gagandeep Kang is the first microbiologist to get elected as a Fellow of the Royal Society.

Dr. Aditi Pant, an astrophysicist, has done remarkable work in the field of astronomy.

Dr. Rukmini Bhaya Nair, has contributed significantly to

linguistic and computational science.

Dr. Indira Hinduja has made remarkable contribution in reproductive technology and *in vitro* fertilisation.

Dr. Sounya Swaminathan has worked in the World Health Organisation as a clinical scientist and a paediatrician. Dr. Anita Goel, a nanotechnologist, is the founder-owner of the firm called Nanobiosym and is a renowned physicist and entrepreneur.

Debjani Ghosh is president of the National Association of Software and Service Companies (NASSCOM) and has been a prominent figure in the Indian IT industry.

Arati Prabhakar is a former Director, Defence Advanced Research Projects Agency with an electrical engineering degree.

Women and Entrepreneurship

The Government of India has launched several schemes that would benefit the women as listed below:

1. Mudra Yojana or the Pradhan Mantri Mudra Yojana provides financial support to micro and small enterprises, including women entrepreneurs through NBFCs and MFIs.
2. Stand Up India scheme for women belonging to Scheduled Caste and Scheduled Tribe. Loans up to Rs. 10 lakh and Rs. one crore for setting up a green-field enterprise are granted under this scheme.
3. Stand up India scheme is designed to promote entrepreneurship between the marginalised members of the society, especially women, Scheduled Castes (SC) and Scheduled Tribes. Bank loans ranging from Rs. 10 lakh to one crore are granted to at least one borrower from the aforementioned groups per bank branch for setting up a green-field enterprise.
4. Mahila Coir Yojana, launched by the Ministry of Micro, Small & Medium Enterprises, encourages women to take up coir-based business activities. Financial assistance and training are provided to women entrepreneurs.
5. Annapurna Scheme is a loan disbursement scheme run by the Bharatiya Mahila Bank (now merged with State Bank

of India) to support women entrepreneurs in the food catering business. It provides working capital to finance the purchase of kitchen equipment, utensils and other essentials.

6. The Udyogini Scheme offers financial assistance to women entrepreneurs in the form of capital for starting small businesses and enterprises. It is implemented by various financial institutions.
7. Stree Shakti package for women entrepreneurs is a scheme aimed at supporting women entrepreneurs by providing them with easy access to credit. It includes features like lower interest rates and a composite loan to cover both the loan and the working capital.
8. National Mission for Empowerment of Women (NMEW) aims to empower women socially and economically. It supports initiatives related to skill development, livelihood and entrepreneurship.
9. Trade-Related Entrepreneurship Assistance and Development (TREAD) is a scheme run by the Ministry of Micro, Small & Medium Enterprises which provides support to women entrepreneurs through training, counselling and financial assistance for setting up business ventures.
10. Support to Training and Employment Programme for women (STEP) is run by the Ministry of Women and Child Development that aims to provide skills, training and employment opportunities to women, including support for entrepreneurship.

Some key successful stories in this domain are in the field of beauty and personal care where names like Vandana Luthra of VLCC fame, Shehnaz Hussain for beauty care products, Vineeta Singh for sugar cosmetics and others like Ritu Kumar and other fashion designers are extremely popular. Some names in the field of technology worth mentioning are:

1. Kiran Majumdar Shaw who is a pioneer in biotech innovation and owns Biocon Limited which is evaluated

at more than Rs. 4,000 crore.

2. Rupa Patel is the CEO of Vocalid which creates personalised, natural sounding voices and is a path-breaking innovation in speech technology.
3. Debjani Ghosh is president of the National Association of Software and Service Companies and has played a key role in development of the IT industry in India.
4. Nivruti Rai is the country head of Intel India and vice president of data platform groups.
5. Anu Acharya is the CEO of map my genome, which deals in genomics and is an expert in bioinformatics. Her contribution to personalised medicine is remarkable.
6. Gitanjali Rao has earned international recognition for her work in science and technology and has won the TIME award for her innovation in devising an instrument that detects lead in water and diagnoses opiod addiction.

Women CEOs in Indian Industry

Women occupy high positions in the Indian industry though some sectors have higher representation of women than others. For example, the banking and financial industry has some famous names like Chanda Kochhar at ICICI Bank, Shikha Sharma at Axis Bank and Arundhati Roy at SBI. The three top private and public sector banks are all chaired by women. Besides Kalpana Morparia of JP Morgan, Naina Lal Kidwai of HSBC Bank, Ranjana Kumar at NABARD and Manimekhalai of Union Bank are names worth mentioning.

In the banking sector itself, the wrong arrest of Chanda Kochhar was unfortunately a muscular display of power by the CBI. Way back in the 1990s, Prof. Beverly Skeggs had remarked that if a woman errs, then the expectations and punishments are harsher. This makes difficult for women to break the glass ceiling. If they match the masculine energy of the system, then they are treated as "not women enough" and thus have to work doubly hard to prove their efficiency.

Overall India ranks third globally for women reaching high

posts and have left a mark across different spheres, including manufacturing where Revathi Advaithi from Flex group leads in technological innovation and strategic direction. Sharmistha Dubey, CEO of Match India, leads in mating/dating online community, like Tinder, OKCupid, Hinge and Plentyoffish. Reshma Kewalramani heads the pharma giant Vertex; Sonia Syngal heads the fashion MNC, the Gap; Jayashree Ullal heads Vertex, the computer network company; Anjali Sud heads Vimeo, video online aggregating firm and Priya Lakhani heads the AI FirmCentury tech.

The names and achievements of women are unlimited as many women have been able to break through the social shackles and create a mark, though there is still scope for doing much more globally.

Challenges that Women Face

From the above success stories it is evident that when given an opportunity, women are able to rise to the occasion. These success stories act as inspiration and evidence in favour of what women can do, provided the society, policy makers and government are willing to create workspace for women in traditional and emerging IT industry. Most of the successful women have mentioned the support of their near and dear ones in their successful careers and these include:

1. Supportive family: Husbands, in-laws and parents. Progressive leadership and values of the organisation that help to bring out the best in women.Grit and determination and inherent passion of women by playing different roles, such as mother, wife and other gendered roles.
2. Presence of a mentor or guide who acts as an inspiring mind.

For creating an Atmanirbhar Bharat, the empowerment of women in the traditionally male-dominated sectors remains a critical frontier. The Indian societal fabric presents formidable challenges that impede women from ascending to the upper echelons of defence, STEM careers and technological entrepreneurship.

Socialisation plays a pivotal role in perpetuating gender norms. Girls from an early age are often subjected to societal expectations that prescribe traditional roles like becoming homemaker and caregiver that restrict their aspirations and choices. Women further face challenges where balancing professional aspirations with societal expectations of fulfilling familial roles add an extra layer of complexity. Deep-seated stereotypes and resistance within families and communities hinder women from pursuing careers that deviate from conventional norms. Thus educational systems from early age must sensitise girl students to inclusive practices and habits. Sexual safety and exploitation and focus on good values must be an equal part of the education content as much as skills or vocational components. Mass media campaigns that question the gender-based stereotypes and build awareness should be started. Flexible school, college and work schedules and ease in rejoining after dropping out at any stage must be encouraged. The two most critical junctures that affect a woman's career are menstrual and hormonal cycle. Amajor change around Class 8 regarding puberty-related issues and body changes daunt the girls. One witnesses maximum dropouts at that stage from schools. The other is around 24-34 years when mid-career transitions occur with childbirth and child care responsibilities increasing for women. Around 45-55, menopause and senior leadership transitions take place. This is the time when demands on the woman from her physiology, life stage and family responsibilities are highest and care and support is needed by them.

Providing opportunities through schemes and granting parenting leave, child care leave, mentoring, sponsorship including provision of a creche and other facilities become essential. Changing the narrative of who and what a good leader is by displaying understanding and empathy will benefit the women and the society. Ample space should be provided for women to speak what they think, feel and want as this will surely lead to a better working space for women. Employee resource groups need not begin at multinational job portals alone, but be part of the basic social fabric which can be strengthened through the existing Anganwadi and ASHA workers. Tolerance for bullying, harassment, micro aggression and discrimination must end and reverse victimisation must stop. In the recent incidence of a successful entrepreneur in the tech space murdering her four-year old child throws some interesting narratives on the social media.

It need not be said that women are more empathetic about motherhood, mental stress and are more forgiving and kind, while men are aggressive and rude. Though thes differences can neither be denied nor changed, but gender equality at workplaces is an important factor in changing the environment at workplaces that are often unwelcoming and unsafe. Lack of adequate representation of women or the freedom to voice their views leaves unaddressed many nuances of their inclusion in the system.

In order to change this narrative or norms, behaviour need to be changed at home and society and the definition of merit itself needs to be looked at through multiple lenses, including the gender lens. This is more so as men and women don't begin with equal opportunities as seen when time out for a boy is different from time out for a girl, expressions of masculinity and feminism and role expectations are different. Biologically a woman's body is geared for childbirth and child nurture, thus there emerges a systemic barrier. With biological processes of menstruation, the workplace expectation may also realign. There is already a backlash on women's employment due to maternity leave policies and sexual harassment prevention and redressal policies. These conversations, though intimidating for a certain section of the society are the only method for giving an equal share of voice to women. Otherwise the historic perpetuation of privileges will continue where men with better access to opportunities and meritocracy can continue to rise on the pretext that this is fair. Diversity always carries a cost, increased conflict, lack of tolerance and acceptance for different individuality, ideation and processes. However in the long run, it pays to have diverse thought processes. Cases like the Amazon retail when the entire shop floor had to be broken and redesigned as the shop floor was designed for women with children shopping in the afternoon by men who were 6 feet tall. The shelves were way higher than what the end consumer was comfortable with. This led to financial losses. Likewise, Shoppers Stop misjudged its business opportunity on home stop as they calculated the number of households and not the fact that Indian households do not buy household items for more money unless it is a wedding or the occasion of death. If the team had female advisors, these grave business mistakes could have been avoided.

Addressing these challenges is imperative for fostering a truly Atmanirbhar Bharat. It requires a concerted effort to dismantle gender stereotypes, promote supportive familial and societal structures, ensure workplace safety and eliminate biases that hinder the equitable participation of women in defence, STEM and tech entrepreneurship. Only through such transformative measures can India truly harness the full potential of its women and achieve self-reliance across diverse sectors.

Access to Formal and Informal Spaces

Most women are not part of the old boys' clubs, commonly known as 'drink or smoke zone' or gossip sessions held outside office hours. These informal spaces are where most business decisions are taken. From data quest to Swiggy, many business ideas germinated over a drink between a few friends under frustrating circumstances of job loss and giving vent to feelings over the state of affairs. For the same reasons, women find it difficult to find mentors and advocates. There are very few women on the top and those who are there are often routed in the group dynamism which are owned by the men. In the absence of role model in women, if a man mentors or champions for a woman, there are sexual connotations ascribed to the woman. This dissuades both men and women to seek complimenting mentoring relations at work. This starts during the mid-career transitions, where even women do not support their women counterparts for fear of withdrawal of support from the men counterparts.

Conclusion

To summarise, there are many challenges to women emerging as leaders in their respective fields, especially when it comes to masculine careers which have traditionally been seen as male careers. However, with the right mind set, government policies, support from the elite leaders and thought leaders, a larger and near equal representation of the women at corporate workplaces is possible. Family support, social support and financial support is needed to change the existing mind set on what is merit and who can and should be the leader.

References

1. https://www.oneindia.com/india/from-atmanirbhar-bharat-to-women-s-empowerment-a-year-of-reforms-for-defence-ministry-3353984.html?story=2e
2. https://economictimes.indiatimes.com/news/company/corporate-trends/for-atmanirbhar-bharat-its-important-to-take-women-along-jahnabi-phookan-ficci-flo/articleshow/76343281.cms?utm_source=contentofinterest&utm_medium=text&utm_campaign=cppst
3. https://www.drdo.gov.in/video-gallery/women-aerospace
4. India ranks third globally in terms of the proportion of women.
5. http://timesofindia.indiatimes.com/articleshow/81319402.cms?utm_source=contentofinterest&utm_medium=text&utm_campaign=cppst
6. https://dst.gov.in/dr-jitendra-singh-announces-several-programmes-increase-participation-women-science
7. Adler, N.J. (1999), Global Leaders: Women of Influence. In: G. Powell (Ed.), Handbook of Gender & Work, Thousand Oaks, CA: Sage.
8. Babic, A. and Hansez, I. (2021). The Glass Ceiling for Women Managers: Antecedents and Consequences for Work-Family Interface and Well-being at Work, Frontiers in Psychology, 12: 677.
9. Gupta, V. and Krishnan, V.R. (2004), Impact of Socialisation on Transformational Leadership: Role of Leader Member Exchange, South Asian Journal of Management, 11(3): 7-20.
10. McKie, L. and Jyrkinen, M. (2017), My Management: Women Managers in Gendered and Sexualised Workplaces, Gender in Management: An International Journal, 32(2): 98-110.
11. McEldowney, R.P., Bobrowski, P. and Gramberg, A. (2009), Factors Affecting the Next Generation of Women Leaders: Mapping the Challenges, Antecedents and Consequences of Effective Leadership, Journal of Leadership Studies, 3(2): 24-30.
12. Vijay, D. and Nair, V.G. (2022). In the Name of Merit: Ethical Violence and Inequality at a Business School, Journal of Business Ethics, 179(2): 315-337.

□

3

Nari Shakti in Uttarakhand

—Prof. Vijeta

Uttarakhand, nestled in the lap of the Himalayas, captivates with its breathtaking natural beauty. Majestic snow-capped peaks, serene valleys, lush forests and pristine rivers adorn its landscape. The state boasts of picturesque hill stations like Mussoorie, spiritual havens like Rishikesh and Haridwar and divine pilgrimage sites of Kedarnath and Badrinath. Its rich biodiversity, vibrant culture and tranquil ambiance make Uttarakhand an enchanting destination, inviting travellers to immerse themselves in its unparalleled splendour.

Women in Uttarakhand embody strength, resilience and cultural richness that have been integral to the region's identity and progress. Upholding a significant role in both rural and urban spheres, the women have contributed significantly to the socio-economic fabric of the state. Traditionally, the society has revered women here as is evident in the region's cultural practices and folklore that celebrate the valour and fortitude of women. They play a pivotal rolesin household, the community and local governance structures. In recent decades, strides have been made to empower women further, thereby enabling their participation in various fields.

This paper traces the progress made by the women of Uttarakhand in the past decade as seen in the framework of the Human Development Index.

Sex Ratio

The overall sex ratio of Uttarakhand is 963 females per 1,000 males while the national sex ratio is 1,020 females per 1,000 males. The state government has implemented various policies and initiatives aimed at improving the sex ratio and addressing gender imbalance issue in the state. Here are some key policies and efforts:

1. **Beti Bachao, Beti Padhao (BBBP) Campaign:** This national campaign was launched in 2015 to address the declining child sex ratio and to promote the value of the girl child. The programme focuses on preventing gender-biased sex-selective elimination, ensuring survival and protection of the girl child and ensuring her education and participation.
2. **Awareness Programmes:** The state government has undertaken extensive awareness programmes aimed at changing societal mindsets and promoting the importance of gender equality. These programmes involve campaigns, workshops, seminars and community-engagement initiatives to educate people about the value of the girl child. These are: ***Nanda Devi Kanya Yojna*** The 'Hamari Kanya Hamara Abhiman' scheme, formerly known as Nanda Devi Kanya Yojana, is a state government endeavour to focus on providing financial security for girls' future education and addressing the issue of female foeticide. Under this programme, every eligible girl child receives a deposit of Rs. 15,000 in her name. The initiative reflects a commitment to empower and support the education of girls while simultaneously working to curb gender-based discrimination. This scheme underscores the government's dedication to fostering a conducive environment for the education and well-being of the female child in the state.
3. ***Dishayenan*:** An initiative for career counselling of adolescent girls focuses on raising awareness in remote districts. The programme aims to inform adolescent girls about diverse career options across various fields through

collaboration with professional institutions. By providing valuable insights, it empowers young girls in remote areas to make informed decisions about their future careers. The initiative reflects a commitment to bridging information gaps and ensuring that adolescent girls have access to information needed to explore and pursue diverse career paths, thus fostering empowerment and informed decision-making in remote communities.

In addition, several projects have been launched under the Sarva Shiksha Abhiyan (Education for All) programme to address the gender-based gap in children's education. The Department of Education has established the following:

Early Child Care Education Centres, which aredesigned to improve the enrolment and retention of females in elementary schools (Verma, 2016). *National Programme on Education for Girls at Elementary Level (NPEGEL):* Since education falls under the jurisdiction of both Central and state governments, the nationwide initiative has also been put into action at the regional level in specific districts and blocks since 2003.

Kasturba Gandhi Balika Vidyalaya (KGBV) derives its validity from the emphasis found in the national policy documents as well as in international discourse that refers to bridging the gender gap.

Innovative Scheme for Adolescent Girls: To create and foster interest in education, girls are imparted training in craft so as to produce useful items which are essential in their daily routine. Additionally, they are provided with empowerment strategies including personal growth, confidence-building exercises and education focused on practical skills.

Financial Incentives: Various financial incentives have been introduced to encourage the birth and education of the girl child. Schemes offering scholarships, cash incentives and other benefits have been implemented to support families in raising and educating their daughters. The various schemes are: *Gaura Devi Kanya Dhan Yojana:* The Chief Minister of Uttarakhand, T.S. Rawat has named a scheme Nanda Gaura Devi after the mother of Bahuguna, who launched the Chipko movement in the state. This initiative, known as the Gaura Devi Kanya Dhan Yojana, underscores the significance of knowledge and structured learning for girls. It aims to eliminate traditional notions that prevent girls from pursuing education. The scheme, a progressive endeavour in Uttarakhand, seeks to empower and motivate young girls to pursue higher education. Specifically designed to offer crucial financial assistance, it targets girls from economically-disadvantaged backgrounds, encompassing various categories like Scheduled Caste, Scheduled Tribe, Other Backward Castes and the general category.

Nanda Devi Kanya Yojana, is a state government initiative that ensures financial stability for the education of girls and combats female foeticide. Qualified girls under this scheme receive Rs. 15,000 which is deposited in their names, reflecting the government's commitment to empowering young girls and fostering education while addressing gender-based challenges.

4. **Women Empowerment Initiatives:** Efforts to empower women through education, skill development and employment opportunities have been the focus. By enhancing the status and role of women in society, the government aims to shift traditional attitudes towards gender and promote a more balanced sex ratio. Some of the women's empowerment schemes are:

At the moment, there are two types of programmes in operation in the state. One is the Mahila Samkhya which is a significant project of the Government of India, currently funded by the Department of International Development (DFID), United Kingdom. The other includes the following state-funded schemes:

Mahila Samkhya (Education for Women's Equality), which aims at women's development and empowerment and its pilot phase was initiated in 1989 across six Indian states, with financial support from the Dutch Government, through the Education Department of the Ministry of Human Resource Development. It was introduced in Uttarakhand in 2002 and is presently operational in numerous districts across the state including Pauri, Tehri, Uttarkashi, Nainital, Udham Singh Nagar and Champawat. The basic objectives of Mahila Samkhya are:

- As it is focused on genderit develops a societal environment that fosters tolerance and respect for women.
- It strives to make education readily available to women and girls who are socially and economically marginalised.
- It seeks to stimulate and advance discussions on gender within society.
- It advocates for collective participation in decision-making processes and pursuit of equal rights and opportunities to foster a more egalitarian society.
- It endeavours to enhance the involvement of females in both formal and informal educational settings.

Department of Women's Empowerment and Child Development runs women's empowerment programmes in the state. While the ICDS programme is managed by the department, the women's empowerment programmes are fully managed by non-governmental organisations (NGOs).

Uttarakhand Mahila Samekit Yojana (an integrated scheme for women): This initiative was created in response to the unique challenges that women in Uttarakhand encounter in their daily lives. A registered society was set up within the Department of Women's Empowerment and Child Development known as the Uttarakhand Women and Child Development Society.

The scheme's key goals include simplifying of women's life; providing training for women's self-employment and effecting change in issues which are gender-related; accelerating women's participation in Panchyati Raj institutions; encouraging the use of technology to lighten the burden of women's backbreaking work; encouraging the use of better sources of energy for cooking and providing assistance to women in order to eliminate gender inequality.

It is intended that 80 per cent of the beneficiaries would belong to the SC/ST and the BPL (below poverty line) groups.

Swayam Siddha Pariyojana: Assisted by the Ministry of Human Resource Development, Government of India, this programme is being implemented by the Department of Women's Empowerment and Child Development since 2001 in Uttarakhand. The objective of this scheme is to set up small enterprises by making credit accessible to the Self-Help Groups (SHGs).

A major characteristic of this programme is the partnership between the state government and the NGOs and which is implemented through the SHGs.

The programme also envisions formation of federations at the block, district and state levels to facilitate the functioning of the SHGs.

State Women's Commission: Established in 2003, the State Women's Commission was created to address issues related to gender disparities and violence against women, while also offering legal counselling services. At the state level, the Commission comprises a president, vice-president and secretary, with one member selected from each district. The commission operates on a three-year tenure and its budget is allocated by the Department of Women's Empowerment and Child Development.

5. **Healthcare Services:** Improving access to quality healthcare services, especially for maternal and child health, is crucial. Ensuring better healthcare facilities and services for women and children helps in reducing maternal mortality rate and promotes the well-being of both mothers and daughters. The following organisations are engaged in healthcare services:*Sparsh:* The main objective of the state-funded scheme is to create awareness about personal hygiene and health among the adolescent girls of Uttarakhand and promote personal hygiene habits. Under the scheme, at the initial level, sanitary napkins are distributed at subsidised rates through *Anganwadi* centres of Dehradun, Pauri Garhwal, Pithoragarh and Almora. Provision of reward money has been made for *Anganwadi* workers, so that women can also be economically empowered.

Janani Shishu Suraksha Karyakaram (JSSK): Launched by the Government of India on June 1, 2011, the aim is to support over 12 million pregnant women utilising government health facilities for delivery. The programme not only benefits pregnant women but also encourages those opting for home deliveries to choose institutional ones. The initiative reflects a commitment to ensure that every pregnant woman in need, accessing government facilities, receives JSSK benefits. All states and Union Territories are implementing the scheme, thereby fostering the government's aspiration for widespread coverage and enhanced maternal and child healthcare services.

6. **Strict Enforcement of Laws** against gender-based discrimination, female foeticide and infanticide is crucial. Strong measures to prevent and penalise illegal practices are essential in changing societal norms.

These policies and initiatives are part of a comprehensive approach to address the issue of skewed sex ratio of 962/'000 and promote gender equality in Uttarakhand. While these efforts have had some positive impacts, yet achievement of a significant and sustainable improvement in the sex ratio requires continuous commitment, monitoring and evaluation of these programmes over time.

Significant efforts have been made to improve healthcare, access to medical facilities and overall well- being in Uttarakhand. These efforts have generally contributed to improvement in life expectancy, not just for women but for the population as a whole.

Life Expectancy: Traditionally, advancements in healthcare, education, economic opportunities and public health awareness tend to positively impact life expectancy. Uttarakhand, like many other states in India, has been focusing on these areas, especially in rural and remote regions, to enhance the quality of life and increase life expectancy for its population, including for the women.

Factors contributing to potential improvement in life expectancy for women in Uttarakhand include:

1. ***Better Healthcare Access:*** Improved access to healthcare facilities, maternal and child healthcare services, immunisation and awareness programmes.
2. ***Health Infrastructure Development:*** Investment in healthcare infrastructure, including hospitals, clinics and health centres, particularly in remote or under-served areas.

3. ***Public Health Initiatives:*** Awareness campaigns, health education programmes and initiatives focused on women's health issues and prenatal care.
4. ***Improved Socio-economic Conditions:*** Better living standards, increased literacy rates and economic empowerment of women can positively impact health and life expectancy.
5. ***Government Policies:*** Implementation of policies aimed at improving overall health indicators and reducing gender disparities in healthcare.

Increased life expectancy of women in Uttarakhand signifies improved healthcare, better living standards and enhanced overall well-being. It leads to stronger family structures, increased community engagement and contributes to economic growth. A longer life span allows women to participate actively in education, workforce and decision-making processes, thus fostering societal development. With improved health and longevity, women can offer guidance, support and contribute significantly to the welfare of future generations. A higher life expectancy for women also reflects societal progress, affirming gender equality efforts and promoting a more inclusive and empowered society in the state. These efforts and factors generally contribute to improvement in life expectancy.

Aiming for betterment in healthcare and life expectancy in the state residents, the following healthcare programmes and schemes have been introduced in the state:

Reproductive and Child Health: To ensure fair reproductive and child health (RCH) services and overall healthcare, a dedicated effort is underway with the aim of addressing regional disparities and fulfilling the objectives outlined in state and national policies. This involves enhancing access to high-quality services through improved and reinforced infrastructure and adopting a comprehensive approach that includes collaboration with private and civil society organisations. The strategy encompasses heightened public health investment, reduction in gender discrimination and active participation of elected representatives and the community at large.

NRHM – National Rural Health Mission: The National Rural Health Mission (2005-2012) was officially inaugurated in Uttaranchal on 27 October, 2005 with primary focus on fortifying primary healthcare by implementing grassroots-level public health initiatives that emphasise community ownership.

This initiative has led to the establishment of several programmes, including initiatives for providing medical care to Below Poverty Line (BPL) population through the Uttaranchal State Illness Assistance Fund and mobile health vans, like TIFAC (Technology Information Forecasting and Assessment Council) and Sehat Ki Sawari (Mobile Health Clinic) in Chamoli and Tehri. districts. Additionally, the mission introduced the Universal Health Insurance Scheme for the BPL population, aiming to enhance healthcare accessibility and coverage for the economically disadvantaged.

Janani Shishu Suraksha Karyakaram (JSSK): Launched by the Government of India on 1 June, 2011, it is anticipated to have a positive impact on over 12 million pregnant women seeking delivery services at government health centres. The primary objective of this initiative is to encourage institutional deliveries by providing essential benefits. The scheme aims to extend its reach to pregnant women in need, fostering the hope that every eligible woman visiting a government institutional facility will receive the advantages outlined in JSSK.

The following are the complimentary entitlements offered to pregnant women:

1. Free and cashless delivery.
2. Free C-section procedures.
3. Free drugs and consumables.
4. Free diagnostics.
5. Free provision of a nutritious diet during the stay in health institutions.
6. Free availability of blood when needed.

Maternal Health Programme: In an effort to deliver reproductive and child health (RCH) services and broader healthcare equitably, a mission-oriented approach is being pursued. The primary goal is to address geographical disparities and fulfil the objectives outlined in state and national policies. This involves enhancing access to quality services through improved infrastructure by employing a comprehensive strategy in collaboration with private and civil society organisations. It also entails increased investment in public health, the mitigation of gender discrimination and active involvement of elected representatives and the community at large.

Technical Objectives, Strategies (or interventions) and Activities:

1. Reduce Maternal Mortality Rate (MMR) of 315 (as per state survey) to below 100.
2. Reduce Infant Mortality Rate (IMR): Targeting a reduction from the existing rate of 44 (according to SRS 2008) per 1000 live births to 28.
3. Reduce Child Mortality Rate (CMR): The objective is to bring down the present CMR of 17 to below 15.
4. Reduce Total Fertility Rate (TFR): The goal is to decrease the current TFR of 2.55 to 2.1.
5. Increase Modern Contraceptive Prevalence Rate (CPR): The strategy aims to boost the current modern CPR of 55-70 per cent.

These technical objectives, strategies and activities collectively contribute to the overarching mission of enhancing maternal health and reproductive well-being.

Literacy Rate

Uttarakhand has been making progress in improving the literacy rate, especially among women, over the past decade. However, the precise and updated data specifically covering the entire past decade (from 2012 to 2022) might not be readily available or officially published yet.

In the 2011 Census of India, the literacy rate in Uttarakhand was around 79.63 per cent, with the female literacy rate slightly lower than that of males. As of 2023 update, the literacy rate has been 78.82 per cent.

Over the years, the state government and various organisations have been implementing initiatives and programmes aimed at enhancing literacy rates, especially among women. These efforts include:

1. *Educational Initiatives:* Implementation of various educational programmes focusing on girls' education, adult literacy programmes and initiatives to promote education in rural and remote areas.
2. *Girls' Education Programmes:* Special programmes and incentives aimed at encouraging girls to attend and complete school by offering scholarships, free education and mid-day meal schemes.
3. *Adult Literacy Campaigns:* Campaigns targeting adult women to improve their literacy and numeracy skills to enable them to actively participate in social and economic activities.
4. *Awareness and Advocacy:* Increasing awareness about the importance of education for girls and women and advocating for equal access to education.

The heightened literacy rate among women in Uttarakhand fosters economic growth, better health practices and enhanced decision-making. Educated women contribute to family income, prioritise healthcare and actively participate in community development. Their literacy cultivates empowered decision-makers, promotes children's education and challenges gender disparities. With increased knowledge, women gain confidence, reduce vulnerability and play pivotal roles in preserving their cultural heritage. Ultimately, heightened female literacy not only empowers individuals but also creates a more equitable and prosperous society, propelling the state towards sustainable development and inclusive progress.

Education

Uttarakhand has been striving to improve educational opportunities for women over the past decade. Efforts have been made to increase enrolment, retention and overall access to education for girls and women in the state.

While specific and updated data specifically covering the entire past decade (from 2012 to 2022) might not be immediately available, various initiatives and trends have contributed to the educational improvement of women in Uttarakhand during this period:

1. *Increased Enrolment:* Efforts have been made to increase the enrolment of girls in schools at primary, secondary and higher education levels. Schemes and incentives have been introduced to encourage families to send their daughters to school.
2. *Focused Government Programmes:* The Uttarakhand government has launched specific programmes and initiatives aimed at promoting girls' education by including scholarships, free education schemes and incentives for girl students.
3. *Improved Infrastructure:* Investments in educational infrastructure, including schools and colleges, have been made to provide better facilities for students, thus facilitating better access to education for girls in rural and remote areas.
4. *Awareness and Advocacy:* Awareness campaigns about the importance of education for girls and women have been conducted to change societal mindsets and encourage communities to support female education.
5. *Skill Development and Vocational Training:* Initiatives have been taken to provide skill development and vocational training programmes for women, enhancing their opportunities for employment and economic independence.
6. *Promotion of Higher Education:* Efforts to increase access to higher education and technical/professional courses for women have been undertaken to empower them with diverse career opportunities.

Some initiatives, by the state government, aiming at enhancing the literacy rate and the quality of education in the state are as follows:

Saakshar Bharat Programme in Uttarakhand: Saakshar Bharat, initiated on 8 September, 2009, by the Prime Minister of India on International Literacy Day, is a centrally-sponsored scheme under the Department of School Education and Literacy, Ministry of Human Resource Development (MHRD), Government of India. This scheme is designed to promote and strengthen adult education for those who have missed the opportunity for formal education and have surpassed the standard age for such learning.

Saakshar Bharat encompasses adults aged 15 and above and offers comprehensive programmes in basic literacy, post-literacy and continuing education. The approach involves a volunteer-based mass campaign, exploring alternative methods for adult education. Jan Shiksha Kendras (Adult Education Centres) (AECs) are established to coordinate and manage all programmes within their territorial jurisdiction. Saakshar Bharat has been operational since 1 October, 2009.

The primary target is to provide functional literacy to adults aged 15 years and above. Supplementary goals include encompassing adults in basic education programmes and an equal number in vocational (skill development) programmes. The programme places special focus on women, Scheduled Castes (SCs), Scheduled Tribes (STs), minorities, other disadvantaged groups and adolescents in rural areas of select districts. The overall objective is to bridge gaps in education and empower marginalised sections of the population through tailored literacy and skill development initiatives.

Women's Literacy and Education Programme by UK Seva Nidhi Paryavaran Shiksha Sansthaan: The programme was aimed to educate 600 women within a three-year period starting in 2011. However, the initial target was surpassed by the second year, ultimately reaching close to 1,600 women. Out of this total, 1,289 women successfully attained literacy, as confirmed through formal assessment and evaluation. The programme's success in exceeding its goal was attributed to the direct demand for literacy from the women themselves. As a result, mobilisation was not a significant challenge and the programme smoothly transitioned to operating the centres with strong community support.

The curriculum was meticulously developed in collaboration with partner organisations and experienced field workers. Understanding the specific nature of the demand for literacy proved to be a crucial challenge that influenced the curriculum's structure. Factors such as language, awareness, women's perceived need for literacy, the time they could dedicate to attendance, existing knowledge patterns and past experiences with literacy campaigns by other organisations played a vital role in designing materials for adult female literacy.

To meet the diverse needs of illiterate and semi-literate women, a set of three workbooks was created, ensuring that each woman could benefit from the programme. An initial primer for illiterate women gained popularity in the villages. Following the literacy programme, a post-literacy campaign was implemented, showcasing a comprehensive and sustained effort to address the educational needs of women beyond the initial attainment of literacy.

Kishori Shikshan (Adolescent Education): This programme, specifically designed for girls aged 11-20 years, places prime emphasis on life skills and gender equality. Adolescent girls are organised into groups, engaging in workshops that address various issues pertinent to their lives and in the village context. The initiative extends to government schools, involving collaboration with teachers and principals.

These programmes are structured to cultivate an understanding of crucial topics, such as self- development, emotions, gender and caste dynamics, challenges encountered by adolescent girls, violence against girls and women, dowry laws, the government's Right to Information (RTI) provisions and the role of community cooperation and cohesion. Additionally, the programmes actively encourage girls to enhance their educational status. For those who have dropped out, there is a concerted effort to motivate them to re-enrol in schools, ensuring that every girl not only attends, but also continues her education. The comprehensive approach of the programme aims to empower adolescent girls with essential life skills and promote gender equality while addressing various challenges they may encounter.

Standard of Living

Several initiatives and improvements in various aspects have been taken to enhance the standard of living for women in Uttarakhand over the past decade. While precise and updated statistics covering the entire past decade (from 2012 to 2022) might not be immediately available, several factors and initiatives indicate positive advancements in the standard of living for women:

1. *Economic Empowerment:* Efforts made to enhance economic opportunities for women through various means, such as skill development programmes, entrepreneurship initiatives and providing access to credit and resources for income generation.
2. *Healthcare Access:* Improvement made in healthcare infrastructure and services, particularly maternal and child healthcare, to ensure better access to healthcare facilities and reduce maternal mortality rates.
3. *Education:* Enhancement in educational opportunities for girls and women, leading to increased literacy rates and improved access to education at different levels has helped to empower them with knowledge and skills.
4. *Women's Rights and Empowerment:* Advocacy and awareness campaigns focus on women's rights, gender equality and empowerment to promote a more supportive and equitable environment for women in the state.
5. *Government Welfare Schemes:* Implementation of various government welfare schemes and programmes specifically targeting women, such as financial aid, healthcare benefits and social security measures, has been carried out.
6. *Infrastructure Development:* Investment in infrastructure development, including roads, electrification and

sanitation, is contributing to an overall improvement in living conditions for women in rural and urban areas.

7. *Cultural Shifts:* Changes in societal attitudes and perceptions regarding the role and status of women, have resulted in increased opportunities and acceptance for women to participate in various spheres of life.

Quality of Life

Efforts have been made in Uttarakhand to improve the overall quality of life for women over the past decade. Several factors contribute to enhancing the quality of life in the state:

1. *Healthcare Access:* Initiatives taken to improve healthcare facilities, access to maternal and child healthcare, immunisation and awareness programmes aimed at improving overall health outcomes for women.
2. *Education:* Increased access to education and literacy programmes promotes girls' education and ensures equal educational opportunities for girls and women across rural and urban areas.
3. *Economic Opportunities:* Efforts made to empower women economically through skill development programmes, vocational training, entrepreneurship initiatives and employment opportunities.
4. *Women's Safety:* Measures and campaigns focus on ensuring women's safety, combating gender-based violence and enhancing awareness about women's rights and legal support.
5. *Social Empowerment:* Efforts made to promote women's participation in decision-making processes, community involvement and advocacy for gender equality and women's rights.
6. *Infrastructure Development:* Investments made in infrastructure development, including transportation, sanitation facilities and electrification, thus contributing to an improved quality of life for women in both rural and urban settings.

7. *Government Welfare Schemes:* Implementation of various government welfare schemes are targeted at women's empowerment, providing financial aid, healthcare benefits and social security measures.

Education has been a cornerstone of this empowerment. Women here have increasingly pursued education, with initiatives ensuring improved access to schools and higher education. Rising literacy rates have catalysed women's participation in diverse professions, transforming them into educators, healthcare professionals, entrepreneurs and civil servants.

Economic empowerment has been another significant stride. Women in Uttarakhand have engaged in agriculture, animal husbandry and various cottage industries. They also actively participate in tourism- related activities, showcasing indigenous crafts and cultural practices while contributing to the state's economy.

Healthcare access has improved, albeit challenges persist in remote areas. Efforts to enhance maternal and child health, immunisation programmes and awareness campaigns have positively impacted women's well-being. However, there's a continued need to bolster healthcare infrastructure and services to ensure comprehensive care for women across the state.

Despite progress, gender disparities and societal norms remain challenges. Issues such as gender-based violence, unequal opportunities and limited decision-making roles persist. Addressing these challenges necessitates sustained efforts to dismantle barriers and foster gender equality.

The women here continue to be the custodians of local traditions, art forms and cultural heritage. They play an indispensable role in preserving and promoting the rich cultural tapestry of the state.

Festivals, folk-music, dance and craft are woven into their daily lives, reflecting the vibrant heritage of Uttarakhand.

In governance, women have made considerable strides. Through local self-government bodies, like *gram panchayats*, women have assumed leadership roles, contributing to community development and decision-making processes. Their involvement signifies a shift in societal attitudes and recognising women's capabilities in governance.

Efforts by the government and NGOs have been instrumental in empowering women through skill development programmes, entrepreneurship initiatives and legal support mechanisms. These initiatives aim to enhance opportunities for economic independence and societal integration.

Some initiatives by the state government aimed at enhancing the quality of life as well the standard of living are as follows:

*Uttarakhand Women Integrated Development Scheme*aims to alleviate the burden on women and foster self-reliance. Assistance is extended to self-servicing institutions, government/semi-government organisations, cooperative societies, self-help groups funded by banks, municipal bodies, district/region/*gram panchayats*, public undertakings and colleges, universities and research institutes. Currently, there are 54 projects under this scheme, operated by self-servicing organisations dedicated to women's empowerment.

Ujjwala: The Ujjwala scheme is implemented to reintegrate women involved in activities deemed immoral and provide them with shelter. Ujjwala Griha is actively operating in the Champawat district, offering support and rehabilitation to women seeking a transition to mainstream society.

STEP: The STEP (Support to Training and Employment Programme for Women) scheme is executed with the objective of providing self-employment training to women in traditional enterprises, such as agriculture, animal husbandry, dairy, matting, horticulture, etc. Training is carried out in collaboration with non-governmental organisations (NGOs), aiming to empower women economically through skill development.

Protection of Women through Domestic Violence Act: Under the Protection of Women from Domestic Violence Act, women officers are given priority for nomination as protection officers. Non-governmental organisations (NGOs) have been selected as service providers in all the districts. Additionally, all district hospitals,

Community and Primary Health Centres and A.N.M. sub-centres have been designated as Medical Facility Centres. Protection officers and service providers undergo training facilitated by the Judicial Academy at Bhowali, Nainital, ensuring a comprehensive and informed approach to addressing issues related to domestic violence.

Udyogini refers to female entrepreneurs and this programme has been introduced by the government to promote the well-being and progress of women entrepreneurs in India. The initiative targets illiterate women, aiming to enhance their skills as producers and deepen their understanding of the markets they engage in while enabling them to thrive in competitive environments. Registered under the Indian Societies Registration Act, 1860, Udyogini is dedicated to delivering tailored, high-quality business development services. The ultimate goal is to empower women to increase their income, secure improved education and health services for their children, with particular emphasis on the well-being of girls.

Uttarakhand Mahila Samekit Vikas Yojana: (UMSVY) was designed as a testing ground for experimenting with ideas tailored to address the specific needs of women in mountainous regions. The initiative aims to leverage the strengths of mountain-dwelling women and develop suitable schemes that can benefit them, with particular focus on enabling fuller participation in various aspects of human endeavour.

When proposing projects for funding consideration from UMSVY, certain key principles must be adhered to. These include commitment to sustainability, ownership, inclusiveness and accountability, with a strong emphasis on achieving tangible results. Projects should be incremental and synergetic, meaning that they should recognise and incorporate all available funds and resources in the project area. Ideally, these projects should build upon or integrate with existing programmes to maximise impact and effectiveness.

Uttarakhand Start-Up Ecosystem: Through an official government notification, the state has clearly defined the category of 'women entrepreneurs' as a means of identifying and providing support to startups through various schemes and incentives. Uttarakhand boasts a robust startup ecosystem, offering significant opportunities, incentives and support to emerging businesses.

According to the Uttarakhand Star-Uup Policy of 2018, startups are entitled to a monthly allowance of INR 10,000 for a duration of one year. For startups operated by individuals from marginalised groups, such as SC/ST, women, physically challenged individuals, or those belonging to Category-A regions as per the MSME Policy of 2015, this allowance is increased to INR 15,000. Additionally, the policy outlines marketing assistance, providing support of up to INR 5 lakh for the marketing and publicity of innovative products. For businesses operating in focus sectors or run by individuals from SC/ST, women, physically challenged individuals, or Category-A regions as per the MSME Policy of 2015, this marketing assistance is increased up to INR 7.5 lakh.

Small Industries Development Organisation (SIDO) organises a diverse range of programmes, including entrepreneurship development programmes specifically designed for the advancement of women. An exemplary woman entrepreneur of the year is acknowledged and rewarded with a special prize, recognising her noteworthy achievements and contributions in the entrepreneurial realm. Furthermore, the office of DC (SSI) has established a women's cell dedicated to offering coordination and assistance to women entrepreneurs who encounter specific challenges in their endeavours. This initiative aims to provide targeted support to address the unique issues faced by women entrepreneurs.

Uttarakhand Mahila Parishad (Uttarakhand Women's Federation): Established in 2001 at Almora, Uttarakhand Mahila Parishad (UMP) emerged through collaborative efforts of partner organisations and rural women. The primary goal of UMP is to serve as a state-level organisation fostering collective action to attain gender equality and justice. Operating across the nine hill districts of Uttarakhand, UMP comprises 490 groups with around

16,000 rural women as active members.

At the village level, all women become members of a unified group known as the '*mahila sangathan*' or Whole Village Group (WVG). The emphasis is on ensuring inclusivity, transcending caste, class and other disparities, with the aim of uniting all women into a cohesive group where a sense of bonding and solidarity prevails. Each WVG elects a female president and, in some cases, a secretary also to facilitate effective organisation and representation.

Research Project: In 2013, an ICSSR sponsored two-year research project on disaster and gender was entrusted to USNPSS, addressing two themes:

1. Gender issues in the development of ecologically fragile zones, a case study of the village communities in Uttarakhand, and
2. *Gender and Disaster*: Women affected by disasters and their coping strategies in Uttarakhand.

Knitting and Sewing Programme by Uttarakhand Seva Nidhi Paryavaran Shiksha Sansthaan: Following the June 2013 disaster in the Ukhimath area, numerous women expressed interest in weaving and learning to operate knitting machines during local village meetings. Responding to this demand, discussions were held with a local village group, called HGVS, and a decision was made to procure six knitting machines for the region. The inaugural training programme on knitting machines commenced in April 2014 at HGVS, Ukhimath, where 20 women received training. After completing the two-month training, three of them were chosen to become trainers. Subsequent training programmes on knitting machines were conducted in various villages with the assistance of these new trainers. By

February 2015, six training programmes had been successfully completed, benefitting a total of 90 women. Notably, 12 women invested in their own knitting machines, incorporating knitting as a part- time profession to supplement their income.

In the year 2014-15, HGVS acquired additional five knitting machines. Three of these machines were purchased by using the proceeds from the fruit processing unit and marking a sustainable and ongoing process.

Moreover, tailor training programmes, lasting from three to six months, were organised for adolescent girls and women in Ganai Gangoli, Pawwadhar (district Pithoragarh) and Danya (district Almora). These initiatives aimed to empower and skill women in various aspects of tailoring.

The future for Uttarakhandi women holds promiseand is marked by ongoing initiatives to bridge gender gaps, promote inclusivity and provide a conducive environment for their holistic development. Continued focus on education, healthcare, economic empowerment and gender equality is pivotal for further progress and for unlocking the full potential of Uttarakhandi women in shaping the state's future.

References

- Divya (2023), Gaura Devi Kanya Dhan Yojana: Empowering Education for Girls. Https://Vakilsearch.Com/Blog/Gaura-Devi-Kanya-Dhan-Yojana/.
- Government of Uttarakhand (n.d.), National Health Mission, Government of Uttarakhand. Https://Nhm.Uk.Gov.in/Pages/Display/114-Janani-Shishu-Suraksha-Karyakram-(Jssk).
- India Census (2023), Uttarakhand Ratios. Https://Www.Indiacensus.Net/States/Uttarakhand/Sex-Ratio.
- Initiatives taken by Uttarakhand State: Save the Girl Child Scheme, especially in the context of BBBP (n.d.).
- Janani Shishu Scheme (n.d.).
- JSSK, Government of India (n.d.).
- Maternal Health, UK Government (n.d.).
- NRHM. (n.d.).
- Objective_Sanitary_Napkin, Sparsh, 1 (n.d.).
- Reproductive and Child Health (n.d.).
- Saakshar Bharat Programme in Uttarakhand (n.d.).
- The Indian Iris Dakshay (2016), Schemes for Women Welfare: Uttarakhand. Https://Www.Theindianiris.Com/Schemes-for-Women-Welfare-Uttarakhand/.
- Udyogini Programme (n.d.). Https://Udyogini.Org/. Retrieved on 28 November, 2023, from https://udyogini.org/
- UK Scheme - Kishori Shikshan (n.d.). Https://Www.Sevanidhi.Org/Education_adolescent.Html. Retrieved on 28 November, 2023, from https://www.sevanidhi.org/education_adolescent.html
- UK SIDO (n.d.). Https://Sheatwork.Com/Government-Schemes-

Incentives-for-Women- Entrepreneurs-in-Uttarakhand/. Retrieved on 28 November, 2023, from https://sheatwork.com/government-schemes-incentives-for-women-entrepreneurs-in- uttarakhand/

- UK Women's Federation (n.d.). Https://Www.Sevanidhi.Org/Empowerment_mahilaparishad.Html. Retrieved on 28 November, 3023, from https://www.sevanidhi.org/empowerment_mahilaparishad.html
- uk.gov.in (n.d.), Uttarakhand Demography, Dept. of Economics and Statistics.
- UKSNPSS Knitting and Sewing Programme (n.d.). Https://Www.Sevanidhi.Org/Livelihood_kbittingsewing.Html. Retrieved November 28, 2023, from https://www.sevanidhi.org/livelihood_kbittingsewing.html
- Uttarakhand Disaster of June, 2013: Relief & Rehabilitation Work in Ukhimath Area by USNPSS, Almora, A Brief Report (n.d.).
- Uttarakhand MSVY (n.d.). Https://Wecd.Uk.Gov.in/Pages/Display/154-Uttarakhand-Mahila-Samekit-Vikas-Yojanaand Policies. Retrieved November 28, 2023, from https://wecd.uk.gov.in/pages/display/154-uttarakhand-mahila-samekit-vikas-yojanaand policies
- Uttarakhand Start-up Ecosystem (n.d.). Https://Www.Startupindia.Gov.in/Srf/Reports1/Uttarakhand_State_Report_07-06-2022.Pdf. Retrieved on 28 November, 2023, from https://www.startupindia.gov.in/srf/reports1/Uttarakhand_State_Report_07-06-2022.pdf
- Verma, K.K. (2016), Women Empowerment in India: A Study of Uttarakhand, In: Motherhood International Journal of Multidisciplinary Research & Development: Reviewed, Referred in International Research Journal, vol. I.
- Women's Literacy Programme - UKSNPSS (n.d.). Https://Www.Sevanidhi.Org/Education_womensliteracy. Html. Retrieved on 28 November, 2023, from https://www.sevanidhi.org/education_womensliteracy.html

□

4

The Growing Role of Meditation at the Foundation for Skill Development in Young Women Pursuing Higher Studies

—Prof. Richa Sawant
Centre of Russian Studies,
SLL&CS, Jawaharlal Nehru University

It has been observed over the past decade that the number of young women taking admission in higher educational institutes has risen steadily. A report in the national daily newspaper dated 30 August, 2021 states, "The latest report of the UP Higher Education Directorate sent to the state government said 27 state universities and 7,391 degree colleges of UP in 2020-21 session have a total of 50,21,277 students enrolled in them, out of which 62.95% are women. The count of men 18,60,220 (37%), they added."[1]

"Four years ago, in the academic session 2017-18, there were a total of 55,74,638 registered students in UP's higher educational institutions and the number included 27,77,137 women amounting to 49.81% as compared to 27,97,501 (50.18%) men. Thus, the percentage of girls enrolling for higher education has increased by 13% from 2017-18 to 2020-21."[2]

These figures are indeed very commendable and the news is heartening for all concerned. For women especially, education is a means of overcoming the hurdles due to socioeconomic factors. It is axiomatic that the economic, social and political progress of a country is founded on how educated its women are. "... Education and learning can support habits, skills and values conducive to social co-operation and participation. Good quality institutions, a highly-skilled labour force and the prevalence of norms and networks facilitating social cooperation ... can potentially enhance strategies to renew the natural environment."[3]

It is noteworthy, that in the XXI century, in addition to the traditional courses in various streams, the present generation needs to master a different set of skills in order to have the competitive edge and develop holistically. These skills can be broadly categorised into three groups - Learning and Innovation skills, Life and Career skills, and Information, Media and Technology skills. Learning and Innovation Skills include the skills of communication and collaboration, critical thinking and problem solving to name a few. Life and Career Skills include, among others, the skills of leadership and decision making, initiative and self-direction as well as social and cross-cultural skills. Information, Media and Technology Skills include media literacy as well as ICT Literacy.[4]

Mastering these skills is vital as the students have to be prepared for a new global economy, with new areas of coverage and emphasis on innovation and creativity, on mastering information technology. The 18 December, 2006 issue of *TIME* magazine is devoted to the question of 'How to Build a Student for the 21st Century'. "This is a story about ... whether an entire generation of kids will fail to make the grade in the global economy because they can't think their way through abstract problems, work in teams, distinguish good information from bad, or speak a language other than [their own]."[5]

For young women mastering these skills comes with its own set of challenges. For instance, it may seem that one of the skills, i.e. communication, both oral and written, is where the women excel, as they understand its value. However, this is a vast area with many genres. Young women are adept in the genre of informal written communication. On the other hand, written communication in the formal context is a skill that must be learnt, by many, from the beginning. Many universities have introductory classes on academic writing, as well as on communication in the field of administration and business.

The genres of oral communication in the informal as well as formal contexts pose problems too. If one takes a close look at what entails adequate oral communication, one finds that it has two equal components – the skill of listening as well as of speaking. Women have been taught to listen from childhood, to be obedient. It is emphasised, that listening expresses empathy and compassion and indicates that one is genuinely interested in the conversation and values it.

Young women, however, have not been encouraged to express their opinion, whether inside the house or with acquaintances. They also hesitate to speak out or voice their doubts in the formal setting of the classroom. Thus, a complete half of the skill of oral communication is unknown territory. If young women do not learn to respond and participate in a conversation, then the wrong message is conveyed which can result in a loss. The inability, in many, to speak is a hurdle that needs to be overcome, especially as they begin a new phase in life in higher educational institutions and later in the professional world.

Having a voice, both literally and metaphorically, requires having belief in oneself, one's ability to understand and respond to the various aspects of the world we live in, and the premise that one has the right to express opinion.

The self-confidence required to participate in a conversation, a wide-ranging discussion or for public speaking can be nurtured through the practice of meditation. The educational and humanitarian movement 'The Art of Living' emphasises that meditation gives the youth, especially young women, the edge to cope with the everchanging scenario of modern life. The benefits are manifold resulting in "... a calm mind, focussed attention, good concentration power, clarity of thoughts and feelings, balanced emotions in stressful situations, improved communication skills..."[6]

"Meditation frees you from within, which allows you to shed the inhibitions and barriers that prevent effective communication. Finding peace within yourself gives you the confidence necessary to master communication."[7]

The 'Art of Living' and various similar organisations have

been organising lectures and workshops in higher educational institutions since many years to strengthen the practice of meditation amongst the students. The aim is to provide the students with academic as well as life skills. Well-grounded young women have the potential to become change agents leading to the overall welfare of the family and community.

One of the most highly sought after skills in the XXI century is that of conflict management. We face conflicts or disagreements in all aspects of life. Disagreements are a result of an extreme difference of opinion, a personality clash or even structural problems in an organisation. As more women rise to the upper echelons of management in various fields, the skills of resolving conflicts become all the more essential. The training for conflict resolution must be given in institutes of higher education.

Young women need to master this Life and Career skill. As it has been observed, there isn't a set formula as each situation would demand one or a combination of management styles. The authors of the study 'The Relationship between Mindfulness and Conflict Resolution Styles among Nurse Managers: A Cross-sectional Study' opine: "The following management styles helped women in integrating, obliging, dominating, avoiding, and compromising. *Integrating or accommodating conflict resolution style* is a problem-solving style in which women demonstrate a high level of concern for self and others... In *dominating* or *competing conflict resolution style*, the person has great concern for self and low for others. In *avoiding conflict resolution style*, there is a low concern for self and others. The person following the *compromising* style is at a moderate level of concern for self and others. Meditation practices by women helped in gaining internal clarity – which made their conflict resolution management efficient and effective."[8]

The difference of opinion among members of an organisation is generally perceived negatively. However, a book, *Conflict Management* by Yasmyne Ronquillo; Vickie L. Ellis; Tammy J. Toney-Butler provides a wonderful insight that, "Conflict can, in fact, be positive if it is managed properly. Conflict can promote team-building skills, critical thinking, new ideas, and alternative resolutions. Conflict management is a crucial competency that leaders must possess, for the success of the team, group, unit, or employees they lead".[9]

Conflict management is based on how skilled the mediator is at communicating, as well as on how good he or she is as a leader. *Conflict Management* classifies the various types of leaders as the transformational leader, the laissez faire leader, the lean or servant leader, the authoritarian leader, the transactional ;eader and the visionary ;eader. These names are a good reflection of the characteristics that each type possesses. The transformational leader brings about a transformation in the values and beliefs of a member of the organisation so that they align with those of the organisation. The laissez faire type of leadership puts the onus on the members of the organisation to propose new projects and set the trajectory for future growth, while being responsible for the decisions taken as a group. Mediating sometimes requires one to be a lean or servant leader, when the well-being of the others is at the forefront. It is similar to the accommodating conflict resolution style mentioned earlier. The authoritarian leader does not take the opinion of team members while making decisions, which reflects a lack of trust in their capabilities. The decisions are based solely on the leader's views and ideas. This style of management is detrimental as it doesn't promote a healthy atmosphere for any growth in the workplace, but may be used in extraneous situations. The transactional kind of leadership is based on the rewards and punishment model, where the members are either given various incentives and perks for completing tasks well or face disciplinary action for failure or negligence of duties. The visionary leader works towards a common vision or goal and has the interests of the team at heart. This type of leadership promotes team-building and empowerment for future growth.

Indian philosophy elaborates that the solution to all external problems do not come from external interventions. They come through internal clarity which is a result of meditation, the practice of turning your attention inwards. It provides clarity about oneself, about one's personality and traits. Having a clear understanding of one's nature, positive and negative characteristics would help young women in choosing the type of leadership that is best suited to them, as well as the kind of leadership that should be practiced in a specific context.

In an article 'A 10-Minute Meditation to Help You Solve Conflicts at Work', Monique Valcour writes: "Practicing loving-kindness meditation yields two substantial benefits for increasing relational agility. First, it helps you to become much more aware of yourself and of how you relate to the other person. You learn to recognize thoughts (such as 'I don't trust him') when they enter your mind and to let them go without judging or reacting to them. This prevents you from being ensnared by thoughts that can trip you up when you're navigating a high-stakes conversation. Second, the meditation exercise helps to cultivate greater awareness of and compassion for the other person."[10]

An article in the journal, *Psychiatry,* titled '6 Effects of Heartfulness Meditation Programme on Perceived Stress and Satisfaction with Life of Female Students' states: "A growing body of literature on meditative practices, including mindfulness, yoga, and other forms, have shown to ... be beneficial in improving emotional intelligence, leadership skills, ability to focus, developing higher levels of self-actualisation, and performing under stress..."[11]

The role of meditation in the sphere of education has grown steadily over the past decade. The Faculty of Yoga and Alternative Medicine in the University of Lucknow offers undergraduate and postgraduate programmes in Yoga which includes the study of meditation. The Faculty has also been organising workshops on yoga and meditation on a regular basis since 2015.[12]

The King Georges Medical University, Lucknow collaborated with The Maharishi University, Lucknow in 2018, to tackle issues related to anxiety, depression and stress amongst the students and faculty members through transcendental meditation.[13]

The practice of meditation enables students not only to become centred, but also, as a natural continuation of the process, work towards sustainable student reforms and community citizenship. Allahabad University in 2022 began conducting free classes on yoga and meditation, both in online and offline modes. As a university official states: "... teachers, students, officers and employees of AU will also be learning the scientific method of meditation and will also get acquainted with the effective form of Yoga as per the Indian tradition of knowledge."[14]

The Centre of Professional Courses Aligarh Muslim University, in offers P.G. programme in Fitness and Yoga Studies which includes the study of asanas, pranayama and meditation.

The Maharishi University of Information Technology, Noida has been offering courses on Transcendental Meditation to students from all streams since 2001.[15]

Established in 2008, and accredited with NAAC A grade, The Teerthankar Mahavir University, Moradabad has a dedicated yoga and meditation Centre

The Department of Physical education of the Shiv Nadar University organised a course on Yoga Nidra or Deep Meditation in 2022.[16]

The University Grants Commission has asked colleges and Universities to encourage students to practice meditation. As one can read on their website, "The higher educational institutions and their affiliated colleges or institutions are requested to encourage students and faculty members to take benefit of this program by introducing to meditation as a solution for positive mental health."[17]

Thus, to conclude, it has been observed over the past decade that the number of young women taking admission in Higher Educational Institutes has risen steadily. It is noteworthy, that in the XXI century, in addition to the traditional courses in various streams, the present generation needs to master a different set of skills in order to have the competitive edge and develop holistically. These skills can be broadly categorised into three groups – Learning and Innovation skills, Life and Career skills, and Information, Media and Technology skills. As more women rise to the upper echelons of management in various fields, the skills of communication and resolving conflicts become all the more essential. For young women mastering these skills comes with its own set of challenges. The self-confidence required to excel in these areas can be nurtured through the practice of meditation. Indian philosophy elaborates that the solution to all external problems do not come from external interventions. They come through internal clarity which is a result of meditation.

References

1. https://www.hindustantimes.com/cities/lucknow-news/women-students-now-far-outnumber-men-in-uttar-pradesh-colleges-universities-says-high-education-department-report-101630263161290.html accessed on 05.11.23
2. Ibid.
3. The Well-being of Nations, 2021, The Role of Human and Social Capital. Education and Skills, OECD.
4. https://www.oecd.org/site/educeri21st/40756908.pdf accessed on 05.11.23
5. Ibid.
6. URL: https://www.artofliving.org/in-en/meditation accessed on 10.11.23
7. https://www.ncbi.nlm.nih.gov/books/NBK470432/
8. https://www.ncbi.nlm.nih.gov/pmc/articles/PMC9709178/
9. https://www.ncbi.nlm.nih.gov/books/NBK470432/
10. https://hbr.org/2015/04/a-10-minute-meditation-to-help-you-solve-conflicts-at-work accessed on 02.12.23
11. Effect of heartfulness meditation program on perceived stress and satisfaction with life of female students, Front. Psychiatry, 2 November, 2023 Sec., *Public Mental Health*, vol. 14, 2023. https://doi.org/10.3389/fpsyt.2023.1214603 accessed on 10.11.23
12. https://udrc.lkouniv.ac.in/Department/DepartmentDetail/History?dept=65 accessed on 5 December, 2023.
13. https://timesofindia.indiatimes.com/education/news/kgmu-maharishi-university-join-hands-to-drive-away-depression-stress/articleshow/63241294.cms
14. *Hindustan Times*, 15 November, 2022, https://www.hindustantimes.com/cities/others/now-free-yoga-meditation-lessons-for-allahabad-university-students-teachers-and-staff-101668530767196.html accessed on 21 November, 2023.
15. https://muitnoida.edu.in/about-the-university accessed on 19 December, 2023.
16. https://snu.edu.in/events/department-of-physical-education-is-organizing-the-yoga-nidra-deep-meditation-program/accessed on 15 December, 2023.
17. https://news.careers360.com/ugc-asks-colleges-universities-host-sessions-on-meditation-mental-health Accessed 24 November, 2023.

□

5

Accelerating Women Empowerment: A Reconnaissance of Government Policies and Initiatives

—Dr. Manorama Tripathi & Shipra Awasthi

"Women empowerment is crucial to India's growth. Days of seeing women as 'home-makers' have gone; we have to see women as nation builders!"

—**Narendra Modi**[1]

Introduction

In the 2011 Census, the female population in India was recorded at 48.5% of the total population. In the evolving societal landscape, the significance of women empowerment cannot be overstated. Hon'ble Prime Minister Narendra Modi emphasised the importance of women empowerment during the 82nd edition of Mann Ki Baat: The Constitution of India includes provisions dedicated to promoting women's empowerment and preventing discrimination in society. Article 14 addresses the principle of equality before the law, while Article 15 empowers the State to enact special provisions for the benefit of women (NITI Aayog, 2022).[2] Despite women making up nearly 50% of the global population, India has displayed an uneven sex ratio, with the female population being relatively lower than that of males (Hazarika, 2011).[3]

In 2021, India experienced a slight improvement in its ranking on the Gender Inequality Index (GII), with a score of

0.490 compared to 0.493 in 2020. The GII assesses disparities in achievements between women and men in three key dimensions: reproductive health, empowerment and the labour market (Bhagat and Goli, 2023).[4] India's recent support for the ambitious 2030 Sustainable Development Goals (SDGs) signifies a pivotal shift in the development trajectory. This endorsement aims to tackle fundamental challenges like poverty, inequality and violence against women, emphasising their crucial role in the global achievement of these goals (National Policy for Women, 2016).[5]

In India, statistical data indicates that women constitute 30 to 45% of the total recipients of doctoral degrees (All India Survey on Higher Education (2020-21). The average involvement of women in research and development activities in India stands at 18.6% (Research & Development Statistics, 2023).[6] At the university level, the proportion of female teaching staff is approximately 37%, while at the college level, it is around 43% (All India Survey on Higher Education 2020-21).[7]

The notion of women's empowerment was initially introduced during the 1985 International Women's Conference at Nairobi, where it was characterised as the reassignment of social power and control over resources to benefit women (Panucha and Khatik, 2005 in Lakshmi and Khanna, 2019).[8] Women's empowerment is influenced by factors, such as educational access, workplace flexibility, allocation of resources and opportunities for social and economic advancement (Charlier and Caubergs, 2007 in Agarwal, and Kaur, 2023).[9]

Empowerment can be described as a "multifaceted social process that enables individuals to exert control over their own selves (Pathania, 2017).[10] Women's empowerment involves elevating their status through avenues such as education, employment, awareness, literacy, etc. It entails embracing ideologies, respecting diverse points of view and providing women the freedom to pursue their desired goals. In support of this, Prime Minister Narendra Modi, has implemented numerous initiatives and campaigns to safeguard, empower and educate women (Kumar, M. Nitish, nd).[11] Empowering women involves providing them with the tools to achieve economic independence and self-reliance and foster positive self-esteem to enable them to confront challenging situations. Additionally, empowered women should actively engage in development activities and contribute to decision-making (Hazarika, 2011).[3]

NARI SHAKTI IN WORKFORCE

FEMALE LABOUR FORCE PARTICIPATION RATE HAS INCREASED IN RECENT YEARS

Year	(in %)
2017-18	23.3
2018-19	24.5
2019-20	30.0
2020-21	32.5
2021-22	32.8
2022-23	37.0

Source: Periodic Labour Force Survey (PLFS), NSSO

Source: Times of India, 31.01.2023

The government is aiming to increase women's involvement by improving working conditions. The following measures have been taken:

- Conducting reviews and audits of pay structures to verify the absence of any discriminatory practices.
- Procurement practices can be adjusted to encourage the participation of businesses led by women.
- Suggesting a balance between employment and care-giving responsibilities for both men and women.
- Companies and MSMEs are encouraged to establish women hubs, comprising hostels, dormitories and shared working facilities.
- Establishing creches and senior-care facilities, along with the nationwide implementation of creche protocols that define standards, administrative panels and inspection procedures.
- Construction and road-sector workers are entitled to

26 weeks of maternity benefits for up to two deliveries. In the case of more than two children, adoption, or commissioning mothers, a 12-week paid maternity leave will be granted.

- Employers are instructed to ensure a secure environment for female workers during night shifts, including arranging transportation for pick-up and drop off (Times of India, 2024).[12]

Two female scientists from the Indian Space Research Organisation led the Chandrayaan-2 lunar mission from its inception to its completion in 2019. The collaboration between the National Institution for Women and the United Nations (UN) India Business Forum has resulted in the establishment of UN-India NITI Aayog Investor Consortium for Women Entrepreneurs. This initiative aims to further support female entrepreneurship and create a conducive environment for women, working in conjunction with Changing India (NITI Aayog) Investment. As per the report, just 25% of women are either employed or actively seeking employment in contrast to 82% of males. As per the *World Wages Report*, 2018/19 by the International Labour Organisation (ILO), India exhibits the highest average gender wage gap among the 73 countries scrutinised, standing at 34.5% (Singh, 2023).[13] India's female labour force participation has increased from 23.3% in 2017-18 to 37% in 2022-23, attributed to the participation of rural women, with unemployment declining from 5.6% to 2.9% (Ministry of Statistics and Programme Implementation, 2023).[14]

In the fiscal year 2024-25, the Women and Child Development Ministry has received a budget allocation of Rs. 26,000 crore, marking a 2.52% increase compared to the previous budget. The highest funds have been allocated to Saksham Anganwadi and POSHAN 2.0, amounting to Rs. 21,200 crore. The Mission VATSALYA (Child Protection Services and Child Welfare Services) was allocated Rs. 1,472 crore. The Mission VATSALYA scheme is being executed with the aim of establishing a secure and nurturing environment for the holistic development of children requiring care and protection (*The Economic Times*, 2024).[15]

The objective of the chapter is to highlight the various welfare schemes of the Government of India, initiated to encourage and support women in different fields.

Family responsibilities, such as childbearing and raising children, as well as caregiving for elderly parents, often limit women's involvement in formal employment and senior leadership positions. To address this issue, the government is actively working to enhance women's participation in the workforce and formal employment sectors. Various rules and policies have been introduced to create a women-friendly working environment.

The G20 New Delhi Declaration emphasises the fundamental importance of gender equality, with women's empowerment playing a significant role in achieving the SDG 2030. The government is dedicated to advancing women's leadership and participation across sectors, focusing on reducing the gender gap in labour force participation, ensuring equal access to quality education, promoting inclusive employment, addressing care-work imbalances, eliminating gender-based violence, enhancing women's financial inclusion and challenging gender stereotypes (G20 New Delhi Leaders' Declaration, 2023).[16]

The Central Government addressed the gendered impact of the pandemic by introducing cash transfer programme under PM Garib Kalyan Yojana (PMGKY) for women holding PM Jan Dhan Yojana accounts. The goal of the programme was to facilitate women to have control over their finances and access financial services identified under the PMGKY initiative. During April 2020- June 2020, the Central Government transferred INR 1500 to women PMJDY accounts (National Portal of India).[17]

Initiatives of the Government of India

Several initiatives were taken by the government to empower women in various ways:

MUDRA Yojana (Micro Units Development and Refinance Agency Ltd) is a scheme introduced on April 8, 2015, offering loans up to Rs. 10 lakhs to women entrepreneurs without requiring any collateral. It is categorised as MUDRA loans under PMMY and the these financial loans are extended by Commercial Banks, RRBs, Small Finance Banks, MFIs, and NBFCs (Mudra).[18] Under this scheme, financial assistance has been extended to 8 crore people, which will provide employment opportunities to 8-10 crore more people. It has been reported that from 2015 to 2018, PMMY created 12 crore jobs. During 2022-23, 6.23 crore loans worth Rs. 4.56 lakh were disbursed. It is worth noting that 69% of the loans were given to women entrepreneurs (Employment News, 2024).[19]

Nari Shakti Puraskar: Annually conferred by the Ministry of Women and Child Development of the Government of India, this award recognises individuals, organisations, or institutions that actively contribute to the advancement of women empowerment (Kumar, M. Nitish, nd).[11]

Pradhan Mantri Ujjwala Yojana 2.0 – Swachh Indhan Behtar Jeevan: The Ministry of Petroleum and Natural Gas (MoPNG) launched in 2016 a flagship scheme, PMUJ, with an aim to extend the facility of LPG to the rural and deprived households who used firewood, coal and cow-dung cakes. Under this scheme, 10.35 crores connection have been released to the people living below the poverty line. The scheme provides a financial help of Rs. 1600 for each connection which includes a cylinder, pressure regulator, booklet and a safety hose (Ministry of Petroleum and Natural Gas).[20]

Mahila Coir Yojana & Coir Vikas Yojana: Under the scheme of coir Vikas Yojana, is the skill upgradation and Mahila Coir Yojana. The scheme extends opportunities for employment to women, trains them and provides spinning equipment at subsidised rates. Under this scheme, the trainer and trainee get a stipend of Rs. 6000 and Rs. 1000, respectively. The Coir Board facilitates 75% of the cost of motorised ratt on motorised traditional ratt as a one-time subsidy to rural women artisans in coir fibre-producing areas.

Coir Vikas Yojana is an umbrella scheme of the Coir Board for the development of the coir industry across the country under the National Institute for Micro, Small and Medium Enterprises and the organisation of the Ministry of Micro, Small and Medium Enterprises (Ministry of Micro, Small and Medium Enterprises).[21]

Maternity Leave for Women: In accordance with the Maternity Benefit Amendment Bill of 2017, female employees now have the right to 26 weeks of paid maternity leave, marking a significant increase from the previous 12-week duration. This change plays a vital role in empowering working women in India. Implementing of maternity benefits allows women to effectively balance their reproductive and professional responsibilities (Care Health Insurance, 2023).[22]

The Ministry of Women and Child Development is implementing a range of schemes and programmes with the aim of integrating women into all sectors of the country, thereby working towards their empowerment, such as:

Mission Shakti Scheme: The government has launched Mission Shakti, an integrated programme for empowering women through safety, security and social and financial inclusion during the 15th Finance Commission period, 2021-22 to 2025-26. The government aims at nation-building through convergence and citizen ownership.

Mission Shakti has two components – Sambal and Samarthya. The Sambal Scheme includes One Stop Centre (OSC). Women Helpline (WHL), Beti Bachao Beti Padhao (BBBP) and Nari Adalats, which are women groups to moderate and resolve disputes and facilitate gender equality within families and in society. The Samarthya consists of Ujjwala Homes, Swadhar Greh and Working Women Hostel, National Creche Scheme for children of working mothers and Pradhan Mantri Matru Vandana Yojana (PMMVY). It also includes hubs at national, state and district levels for Empowerment of Women (Ministry of Women & Child Development, 2022).[23] The Mission Shakti (Mission for Protection and Empowerment for Women) has been granted Rs. 3,145.97 crore (*The Economic Times*, 2024).[15]

One Stop Centre and Universalisation of Women Helplines: The Ministry of Women and Child Development (WCD) administers two schemes from the Nirbhaya Fund: the One Stop Centre and the Universalisation of Women Helplines. The One Stop Centres, commonly referred to as Sakhi Centres, are designed to offer a comprehensive range of integrated services under one roof for women affected by violence, including domestic violence. These services include police facilitation, medical aid, legal assistance, legal counselling, psycho-social counselling and temporary shelter (Press Information Bureau, 2022).[24]

Pradhan Mantri Matru Vandana Yojana (PMMVY): The maternity benefits programme was introduced in 2017. Under this programme, a cash incentive of Rs. 5000/- is transferred to pregnant and lactating mothers' bank or post-office accounts for the first living child (Press Information Bureau, 2022).[24] As many as 3.21 crore women covered under PM Matru Vandana Yojana and more than Rs. 14 thousand crore were given (*Employment News*, 2024).[19]

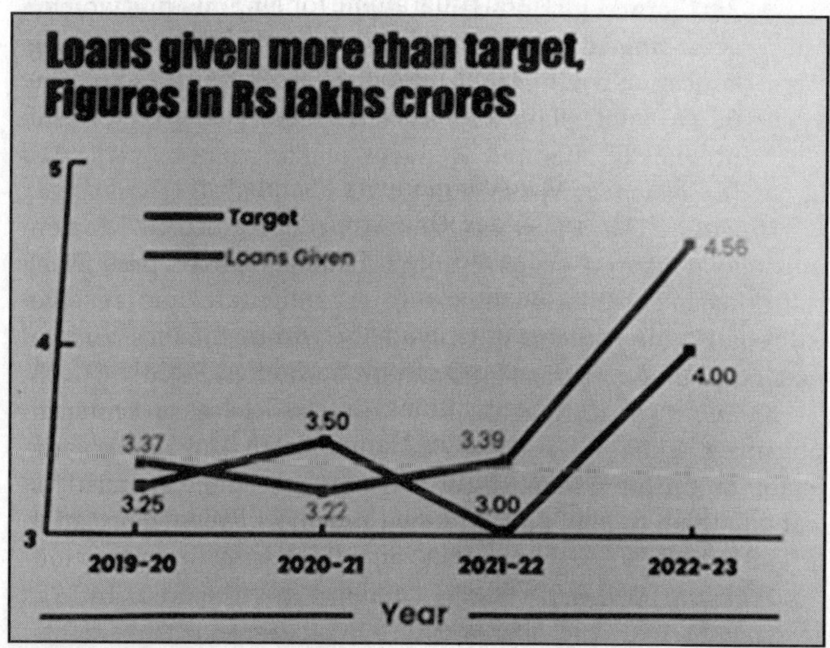

Source: New India Samachar, 2024

Beti Bachao Beti Padhao Andolan: This programme was launched in the Panipat district of Haryana on 22 January, 2015, initiated with an initial fund of Rs. 100 crores. https://www.niti.gov.in/empowerment-women-through-education-skilling-micro-financing. It was initiated with the primary objective of addressing the declining birth rate of female children resulting due to female child abortion. The focus is on providing them the invaluable gift of education, which serves as a support system across all facets of life (Press Information Bureau, 2022).[24]

- More than 4 crore Sukanya Samriddhi Yojana accounts have been initiated, with approximately Rs. 1.5 lakh crore deposited. Additionally, there has been a notable rise of over 15% in the enrolment of girls aged 10 and above in education, attributed to the implementation of the Beti Bachao, Beti Padhao initiative.
- 12.28 crore girls' enrolment in school education in 2021-2022 for primary to higher secondary classes.
- 2.01 crore girl students enrolled in higher education according to the All India Survey 2021-2022 on higher education conducted for the first time.
- 69.75 lakh plus women have been assisted on the previously operated women's helpline since April 2015 (*Employment News*, 2024).[19]

Ujjwala: The Ujjawala Scheme is being executed as a centrally-sponsored scheme with the objective of preventing trafficking and facilitating the rescue, rehabilitation, reintegration and repatriation of victims involved in trafficking for commercial sexual exploitation (Press Information Bureau, 2022).[24]

Swadhar Greh Scheme is being executed as a centrally-sponsored scheme to provide institutional support and rehabilitation for women facing challenging circumstances and enabling them to lead their lives with dignity (Press Information Bureau, 2022).[24]

Working Women Hostel scheme is executed by the government with the aim of offering secure and conveniently situated accommodation for working women. The scheme includes providing daycare facilities for their children, whenever feasible, in urban, semi-urban, or even rural areas where employment opportunities for women are available (Press Information Bureau, 2022).[24]

Rajiv Gandhi National Creche Scheme: There is a national crèche scheme for children of working mothers in place under which employees in the organised sector are bound to provide daycare facilities to the children of their women employees. The number of functional crèches in the country during 2019-2020 was 6,458 (Government Schemes for Women Empowerment in India, 2024, 2023).[26]

Mahila Shakti Kendra (MSK) was launched by the Government of India in 2017. This campaign aims to empower rural women through active community participation and foster an environment where they can realise their full potential (Kumar, M. Nitish, nd). The programme functions at different tiers, including national, state and district levels, with the government's objective being the establishment of 920 Mahila Shakti Kendras in the 115 most underdeveloped districts (Government Schemes for Women Empowerment in India-2024, 2023).[26]

Mahila Police Volunteers Scheme is a centrally-sponsored scheme that seeks to create a link between police authorities and local communities, ensuring police outreach in handling crime cases (Government Schemes for Women Empowerment in India-2024, 2023).[26]

Mahila E-Haat: An online platform initiated by the Ministry of Women and Child Development enables women entrepreneurs to display their products to potential buyers via mobile and internet connections. The initiative aligns with the 'Make in India' programme and encompasses a diverse range of products, including clothing, fashion accessories, home decor, pottery, toys and various others (Government Schemes for Women Empowerment in India-2024, 2023).[26]

STEP (Support to Training and Employment Programme for Women): The objective is to provide skill development training to women and create avenues for employment. This government-backed initiative provides financial assistance to institutions and organisations for conducting training programmes (Government Schemes for Women Empowerment in India, 2024, 2023).[26]

Hub for Empowerment of Women (HEW): To enhance awareness regarding the ministry's schemes and the government's initiatives for women's welfare and development, national, state and district-level Hubs for Empowerment of Women (HEW) have been sanctioned under the new Mission Shakti. These hubs aim to facilitate the convergence of schemes and programmes for women at different levels, promoting an environment where women can realise their full potential. The HEW component provides support for guiding, connecting and assisting women in engaging with various institutional and programmatic setups for their empowerment and development (Schemes for Welfare of Women, 2022).[27]

Deendayal Antyodaya Yojana Rural Livelihood Mission (DAY-NRLM) has been introduced to eliminate poverty and uplift the status of the poor by extending them self-employment opportunities for sustainable and diversified livelihoods. The programme focuses on improving the lives of rural women through financial and social inclusion and sustainable livelihoods. The mission aims to facilitate more than 10 crore rural households. It has mobilised rural women into 81 lakh self-help groups (India's Gender Budget, 2023).[28]

Mahila Samman Savings Certificate was introduced in April 2023 for two years, till March 2025. A woman, the guardian of a minor girl child, may open an account under this scheme. The minimum deposit amount is Rs. 1000 and the maximum deposit amount is Rs. 2 lakh. The scheme offers a fixed interest rate of 7.5 % per annum (India's Gender Budget, 2023).[28]

Lakhpati Didi Yojana/Scheme was introduced on 23 December 2023. Under this scheme, the resources of Department of Agriculture and Farmers' Welfare (DA&FW), Department of Rural Development (DoRD) and Department of Fertilisers (DoF), Women Self-Help Groups and Lead Fertiliser Companies (LFCO) will be used. The grant will bear 80% of the cost of the drone. Following the implementation of the scheme, approximately 10 crore women are benefiting from it and engaging with self-help groups (Lakhpati Didi Yojana/Scheme, 2024).[29]

Jal Jeevan Mission (JJM) was introduced in August 2019. There are more than 19.24 crore rural families in India until August 2019 and only 3.23 crore had tap connections. Under this mission, 10.53 crore approximately in 1,99150 villages have been given tap connections. It is very beneficial for women of the rural areas. As per the WHO estimates, provision of tap water saves more than 55 million hours per day of the time women spend on household needs. It has been reported that JJM has the potential to create jobs for more than 282 crore people. Further, there are 2,111 testing laboratories for drinking water. It is estimated that 23.36 lakh women have been trained to test water samples through field test kits (*Employment News*, 2024).[19]

Pradhan Mantri Jan Dhan Yojana (PMJDY): Launched in August 2014 with 1.5 crore accounts, the scheme provides a debit card to each account holder. This debit card ensures an insurance cover of Rs. 1 lakh for every economically disadvantaged family, offering financial security during crises. By August 2015, the Jan Dhan accounts had surged to 17.9 crore, thus experiencing a threefold increase to approximately 51 crores by November 2023. Notably, 28.29 crore accounts were specifically opened for women (Employment News, 2024).[19]

The government is executing various schemes and programmes to support, rehabilitate, empower, educate and provide employment opportunities for destitute women, such as:

National Health Policy (NHP) 2017: The government introduced the comprehensive Ayushman Bharat Programme in September 2018, comprising two main components: health and wellness centres and the Pradhan Mantri Jan Arogya Yojana (PMJAY). The Jan Aarogya Yojana extends coverage to impoverished and vulnerable families and is expected to enhance women's accessibility to healthcare services (Schemes for Welfare of Women, 2022).[27]

The Indira Gandhi National Widow Pension Scheme offers financial support to widows from Below Poverty Line (BPL) households. As a sub-scheme under the National Social Assistance Programme (NSAP) of the Ministry of Rural Development, the scheme provides a monthly widow pension of Rs. 300 to eligible widows aged 40-79 years. Upon reaching the age of 80, the pension amount is increased to Rs. 500 per month (Schemes for Welfare of Women, 2022).

The National Social Assistance Programme (NSAP) is a centrally-sponsored scheme that is fully funded and aimed at identifying and providing basic financial support to destitute individuals by the states and Union Territories. Within NSAP, senior citizens (60 years and above), widows (40-79 years) and disabled persons receive central assistance ranging from Rs. 200 to Rs. 300 per month as pension (Schemes for Welfare of Women, 2022).

Stand Up India scheme was initiated by the Government of India on 5 April, 2016, with the objective of fostering entrepreneurship among women, Scheduled Castes (SC) and Scheduled Tribes (ST). These demographic groups are perceived to encounter substantial challenges, including lack of guidance, mentorship and timely access to credit. The scheme facilitates bank loans ranging from Rs. 10 lakhs to Rs. 1 crore, ensuring that each branch of Scheduled Commercial Banks extends support to at least one Scheduled Caste/Scheduled Tribe borrower and one-woman borrower for establishing new enterprises in the trading, manufacturing and services sectors (Schemes for Welfare of Women, 2022).

Several other initiatives taken by the GoI to empower women in various ways:

*The **Science and Engineering Research Board (SERB)***, a statutory body under the Department of Science and Technology (DST) has introduced the SERB-POWER (Promoting Opportunities for Women in Exploratory Research) programme. This initiative is a research funding scheme specifically designed for women, offering financial support through SERB-POWER Research Grants and SERB-POWER Fellowship (SERB India Home Page).[30] Since the challenges faced by women researchers differ significantly from those of their male counterparts, it becomes imperative to uplift women scientists through initiatives, such as SERB's POWER scheme. The SERB's POWER research grant (SPG) scheme, within this programme, aims to offer financial support to women affiliated with State-funded universities, private institutes, colleges, NGOs and similar institutions (Agarwal and Kaur, 2023).[9]

The University Grants Commission has developed a portal called Saksham to empower women by extending access to information about opportunities available for women in higher education, redressal mechanisms to address their problems and various policies and initiatives implemented to empower women (UGC-Saksham).[31]

Swami Vivekananda Single Girl Child Fellowship for Research in Social Sciences: The University Grants Commission (UGC) offers a fellowship programme designed for single girls pursuing research in the field of Social Sciences. The primary objective is to offset the direct expenses associated with higher education, particularly for those girls who are the sole female child in their families. The financial support provided through the scheme includes: fellowship at Rs. 25,000 per month for the first two years and Rs. 28,000 per month for the subsequent duration; also contingency fund at Rs. 10,000 per annum for the initial two years and Rs. 20,500 per annum for the remaining period and assistance of Rs. 2,000 per month for Escort Reader in the case of candidates with disabilities (PWD) (myScheme, Ministry of Education).[32]

Drone Scheme for Women Self-Help Groups (WSHG) in Agriculture: The government has approved an outlay of Rs. 1261 crore for two years; under this scheme, drones will be provided to 15,000 women self-help groups to provide rental services to farmers over a three-year period from 2023-24 to 2025-26 (Ministry of Rural Development, 2023).[33]

The ***Indo-US Fellowship for Women in Science, Technology, Engineering, Mathematics and Medicine (WISTEMM)*** programme aims to provide Indian women researchers to undertake collaborative research in leading institutions in the USA to augment their research capacities and capabilities. It encourages research and fosters capacity building for Indian women students and scientists in various forefront areas of Science, Technology, Engineering, Mathematics, and Medicine (STEMM) (*Indo-U.S. Science & Technology Forum*).[34]

The University Grants Commission has introduced a scheme of post-doctoral fellowship to women candidates, who have completed their Ph.D. but are unemployed. Every year, 100 candidates are considered under this scheme with the goal of propelling the innate talents of female candidates to pursue advanced studies and research (UGC, post-doctoral fellowship to women candidates).[35]

Safe City Project: The initiative was implemented by the Ministry of Women and Child Development in 2018, in collaboration with other stakeholders. The project's objective is to create a safe and secure atmosphere for women in the city, encompassing their residence, workplace and travel. The budget for this initiative has experienced an eightfold increase compared to the revised 2022-23 budget, surging from INR 165 crore to INR 1300 crore (India's Gender Budget, 2023).[28]

Samarthya Umbrella Scheme was introduced by the Ministry of Women and Child Development in 2021. This includes women empowerment programmes, such as the Pradhan Mantri Vandana Yojana and Swadhar Greh, receiving a budget allocation that is 33 per cent higher than the revised estimates of the 2022-23 budget (India's Gender Budget, 2023).

Other schemes collectively constitute approximately INR 45,000 crore.

- Saksham Anganwadi and Poshan
- Flexible pool for RCH and health system strengthening
- National Health Programmes and Nation Urban Health Missions
- Samagra Shiksha Scheme
- Samarthya scheme for women empowerment

Swachh Bharat Mission was launched in October 2014 and aimed at making the country open-defecation free by constructing 100 million toilets across the villages. During the second phase of SBM, started in February 2020, efforts are being made to provide adequate solid and liquid waste management, including plastic waste management. In August 2022, more than 96.622 villages obtained the status of ODF plus status (Ministry of Jal Shakti, 2022).[36]

Vishwakarma Yojana: Under this scheme, the government wants to help the artisans of 18 traditional crafts and has allocated an amount of Rs. 13,000 crore for 2023-2028 (*Employment News*, 2024).[19]

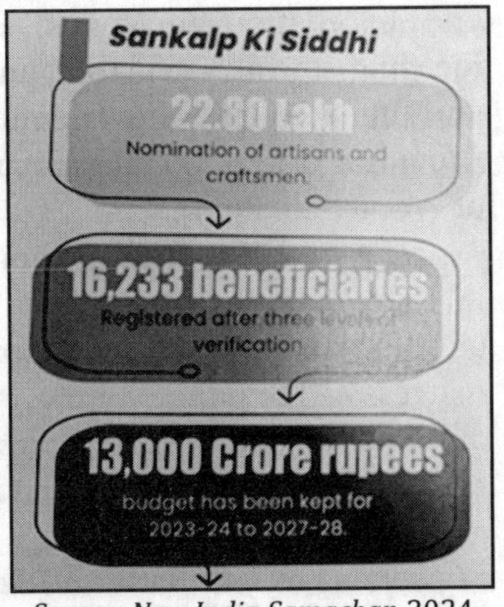

Source: New India Samachar, 2024

Palna Scheme: Provision for Anganwadi-cum-crèches has been introduced by the Ministry of Women and Child Development. Another goal of this component would be to oversee the adherence to the provisions outlined in Section 11A of the Maternity Benefit Act, particularly concerning the establishment's obligation to set up crèche facilities. The Ministry of Labour and Employment has notified/mandated that any establishment having 50 or more employees shall have the facility of a crèche (Ministry of Women and Child Development).[37]

PM Aawas Yojana: This initiative is significantly contributes to the empowerment of both the impoverished and women. Over the past nine years, around 4 crore solid and permanent houses have been allocated to underprivileged families with approximately 70 per cent of these houses are registered in the names of female beneficiaries (Ministry of Housing and Urban Affairs).[38]

WISE-KIRAN: The government is offering numerous scholarships and fellowships for women in STEM through the comprehensive scheme known as 'Women in Science and Engineering – KIRAN (WISE-KIRAN)' by DST. The primary objective of the WISE-KIRAN Scheme is to enhance gender equality in the science & technology sector by integrating more female talent into the research and development domain through diverse programmes. These initiatives include the Women Scientist Scheme designed for women scientists with career gaps, the 'Consolidation of University Research through Innovation and Excellence in Women Universities (CURIE)' programme focusing on infrastructure and research facilities development and the 'Indo-US Fellowship for Women in STEMM (WISTEMM)' providing international exposure to women scientists (Promotion of Women in Stem).[39]

HimmatPlus App for women was reintroduced on 6 February, 2018 by Delhi Police. The app is now available in both English and another language. It was launched to facilitate women to send a distress call to police control room, COP. The latest version of the app incorporates a special functionality for scanning QR codes of taxi, TSR and e-rickshaw drivers. Throughout the year, the app garnered 66,946 downloads, with 46,111 individuals successfully registering on the platform (Best Practices in Delhi Police).[40]

Life360 App is a personal security smartphone app designed for family communication, location sharing and alerts. Users can share their locations with each other through the app. Once installed on a phone, Life360 enables the administering phone to establish geo-fences, outlining specific chosen areas (LIFE360).[41]

Sashakti (Self-defence Training): Girls and women receive self-defence training to equip them with the skills needed for self-protection and to empower them in repelling potential aggressors. Specialised self-defence training teams are established within the Special Police Unit for Women & Children and at the district level. Delhi Police has achieved recognition in the *Limca Book of Records* for training more than 9,98,216 women through 5,172 programmes conducted under this scheme since 2002 (Best Practices in Delhi Police).[40]

Viksit Bharat@2047 (Voice of Youth): The Prime Minister has announced a vision to turn India into a developed nation over the next 25 years. He has emphasised the importance of human-centric development and equality. The key components of his vision are sustainable development infrastructure, new-age skills, artificial intelligence and innovation. The initiative will offer a platform for the youth of the country to contribute their ideas to the vision of Viksit Bharat @2047 (Ministry of Education).[42]

The Muslim Women (Protection of Rights on Marriage) Bill, 2017: It was presented in Lok Sabha by Ravi Shankar Prasad, Minister of Law and Justice, on December 28, 2017. The Bill renders any pronouncement of *talaq*, whether in written or electronic form, null and void (i.e. not legally enforceable) and deemed illegal (Ministry of Law and Justice, 2017).[43]

Prevention of Sexual Harrasment (POSH) Act within the 'Women at Workplace Act' was implemented in India in 2013 to tackle the issue of sexual harassment (SH), targeting women in professional settings. This legislation mandates that every employer must institute Internal Complaint Committees (ICCs) responsible for probing SH complaints and ensuring that suitable measures are taken against the offender. The implementation of the POSH Act has been a pivotal measure in enhancing the workplace environment for women, fostering gender equality and promoting respect in professional settings (Prakash *et al.*, 2023).[44]

Women Empowerment and Sustainable Development Goals (SDGs): Gender equality is essential for attaining sustainable development and it hinges on a fair allocation of resources. The empowerment of women plays a pivotal role in realising sustainable economic growth, fostering social development and ensuring environmental sustainability. Rooted in principles that promote solidarity across generations, women's empowerment is a crucial factor in these interconnected goals (Pathania, 2017).[10] Achieving gender equality stands as a pivotal factor, crucial for the comprehensive advancement of society and the realisation of all other UN SDGs, as evidenced by the inclusion of 54 gender indicators out of a total of 232 (Basnet, 2018).[45]

Achieving the empowerment of women and girls within the framework of sustainable development requires more than just a dedication to these objectives. Hence, initiatives for sustainable development must emphasise the recognition that women and girls face an increased risk of being marginalised or excluded (a global voice for women).[46]

The empowerment of women is essential for instigating positive transformations across Sustainable Development Goals (SDGs). Empowered women serve as catalysts for advancing progress, influencing areas such as poverty, health, gender equality and environmental sustainability. Women's empowerment and SDG targets can be catered by the following: quality education, gender equality, health and well-being, clean energy and environmental conservation, decent work and economic growth, and peace, justice and strong institutions. The challenges women encounter in achieving the SDGs are limited access to education, gender pay gap, violence and gender-based discrimination, lack of representation in decision making, reproductive rights and limited access to healthcare, unequal land and property rights, stereotypes and social norms, limited access to financial services (Mahila Housing Trust towards responsible urban development).[47]

Conclusion

Women's empowerment in India is a continuous and multifaceted journey that includes several initiatives and schemes implemented by the government. The aim is to facilitate, support and enhance the status and rights of women. The collaborative efforts from different bodies and stakeholders will bring lasting changes and provide opportunities for women to contribute meaningfully to the progress of the nation.

References

1. Narendra Modi. https://twitter.com/narendramodi/status/424901312401002496?lang=en
2. NITI Aayog, 22 May, 2022. https://www.niti.gov.in/empowerment-women-through-education-skilling-micro-financing. (accessed on 30 January, 24).
3. Hazarika, D. (2011). Women empowerment in India: A brief discussion, International Journal of Educational Planning & Administration, 1(3): 199-202.
4. Bhagat, L and Goli, D. (2023). How empowered are Indian women?

https://thewire.in/women/womens-day-graph-numbers (accessed on 30.1.24).

5. National Policy for Women, 2016: Articulating a Vision for Empowerment of Women, Ministry of Women and child Development, GoI, May 2016. https://wcd.nic.in/sites/default/files/draft%20national%20policy%20for%20women%202016_0.pdf (accessed on 30.1.24).
6. Research & Development Statistics at a Glance, 2022–23, Ministry of Science & Technology, GoI, March 2023. https://dst.gov.in/sites/default/files/R%26D%20Statistics%20at%20a%20Glance%2C%202022-23.pdf (accessed on 30.1.24).
7. All India Survey on Higher Education (AISHE) 2020-21, Ministry of Education, GoI. https://aishe.gov.in/aishe/viewDocument.action?documentId=352 (accessed on 30.1.24).
8. Lakshmi, G.S. and Khanna, J.V (2019). Women Empowerment in India, Journal of Emerging Technologies and Innovative Research, 6(2): 208-214.
9. Charlier, S.; Caubergs, L. The Women Empowerment Approach: A Methodological Guide; Commission of Women and Development, 2007. https://www.nsf.gov/crssprgm/advance in Agarwal, M. & Kaur, P.J. (2023). Impact of Selected Schemes of SERB: Empowering Indian Women in R&D Spectrum, ACS Omega, 8(45): 42006-42013.
10. Pathania, S.K. (2017). Sustainable development goals: Gender equality for women's empowerment and human rights, International Journal of Research, 5(4): 1-15.
11. Kumar, M. Nitish, nd. Women Empowerment. https://static.mygov.in/indiancc/2021/05/mygov-10000000001983178197.pdf (accessed on 30.01.24.)
12. Times of India, 31.01.24 (accessed offline on 31.01.24).
13. Singh, S. (2023). Women Empowerment in India: A Critical Analysis, Universal Research Reports, 10(1):, 69-74.
14. Ministry of Statistics and Programme Implementation, 9 October 2023 https://pib.gov.in/PressReleaseIframePage.aspx?PRID=1966154 (accessed on 04.02.2024).
15. The Economic Times, 1 February 2024. https://economictimes.indiatimes.com/news/india/women-children-in-budget-2024-25-marginal-rise-in-allocation-for-wcd-ministry/articleshow/107325705.cms?from=mdr (accessed on 04.02.2024).
16. G20 New Delhi Leaders' Declaration, 9-10 September 2023, New Delhi. https://www.mea.gov.in/Images/CPV/G20-New-Delhi-Leaders-Declaration.pdf (accessed on 04.02.2024).
17. Pradhan Mantri Garib Kalyan Package (PMGKP), National Portal of India. https://www.india.gov.in/spotlight/pradhan-mantri-garib-kalyan-package-pmgkp (accessed on 04.02.2024).
18. Mudra. https://www.mudra.org.in/ (accessed on 31.1.24).
19. Employment News, 3-9 February, 2024 (accessed offline on 04.02.24).

20. Ministry of Petroleum and Natural Gas. https://www.pmuy.gov.in/about.html (accessed on 31.1.24).
21. Coir Vikas Yojana - Skill Upgradation and Mahila Coir Yojana, Ministry of Micro, Small and Medium Enterprises. https://www.myscheme.gov.in/schemes/cvy-sumcy (accessed on 30.1.24).
22. Maternity Leave Rules in India, 2023, Care Health Insurance, 10 October, 2023. https://www.careinsurance.com/blog/health-insurance-articles/maternity-leave-rules-in-india (accessed on 30.1.24).
23. Mission Shakti, Ministry of Women & Child Development, 14 July 2022. https://wcd.nic.in/sites/default/files/Mission%20Shakti%20Guidelines%20for%20implementation%20during%2015th%20Finance%20Commission%20period%202021-22%20to%202025-26_1.pdf (accessed on 31.1.24).
24. Press Information Bureau, Ministry of Women and Child Development, Government of India. 04 February 2022. https://pib.gov.in/Pressreleaseshare.aspx?PRID=1795471 (accessed on 30.1.24).
25. New India Samachar (fortnightly), 4(13): January 1-15, 2024, New Year Special Issue, Press Information Bureau, New Delhi. (accessed offline on 02.02.24).
26. Government Schemes for Women Empowerment in India - 2024, 07 December 2023. https://fi.money/blog/posts/list-of-women-empowerment-schemes-in-india (accessed on 30.1.24).
27. Schemes for Welfare of Women, Press Information Bureau, Ministry of Women and Child Development, 22 July 2022. https://pib.gov.in/PressReleasePage.aspx?PRID=1843808 (accessed on 30.1.24).
28. India's Gender Budget, 2023, 15 February 2023. https://www.studyiq.com/articles/indias-gender-budget/#:~:text=The%20project%20seeks%20to%20create,crore%20to%20INR%201300%20crore (accessed on 30.1.24).
29. Lakhpati Didi Yojana/Scheme: Transform Your Finances with this Empowering Initiative, 28 January 2024. https://awbi.in/lakhpati-didi-yojana-scheme/ (accessed on 31.1.24).
30. SERB India Home Page, https://serb.gov.in (accessed on 30.1.24).
31. UGC, Saksham: Measures for Ensuring the Safety of Women and Programmes for Gender Sensitisation on Campuses. https://www.ugc.gov.in/pdfnews/5873997_SAKSHAM-BOOK.pdf
32. myScheme, Swami Vivekananda Single Girl Child Fellowship for Research in Social Sciences, Ministry of Education. https://www.myscheme.gov.in/schemes/svsgcfrss (accessed on 30.1.24).
33. Drones to Self-Help Groups, 19 December 2023, Ministry of

Rural Development. https://pib.gov.in/PressReleaseIframePage.aspx?PRID=1988271#:~:text=The%20Government%20of%20India%20has,application%20of%20fertilisers%20and%20pesticides (accessed on 30.1.24).

34. Indo-U.S. Science & Technology Forum (IUSSTF). https://iusstf.org/indo-u-s-fellowship-for-women-in-stemm-wistemm- (accessed on 30.1.24).
35. UGC, Post-Doctoral Fellowship to Women Candidates. https://www.ugc.gov.in/pdfnews/7347918_pdfw.pdf (accessed on 30.1.24).
36. Open Defecation-free Villages, Ministry of Jal Shakti, 04 August 2022. https://pib.gov.in/Pressreleaseshare.aspx?PRID=1848437 (accessed on 03.2.24).
37. Palna Scheme, Ministry of Women and Child Development. https://wcd.delhi.gov.in/sites/default/files/WCD/universal-tab/palna_scheme_under_mission_shakti.pdf
38. Pradhan Mantri Aawas Yojana, Ministry of Housing and Urban Affairs. https://pmaymis.gov.in/(accessed on 03.2.24).
39. Promotion of Women in STEM, Ministry of Science & Technology, 2023. https://sansad.in/getFile/annex/260/AU1723.pdf?source=pqars#:~:text=WISE%2DKIRAN%20Scheme%20is%20primarily,Consolidation%20of%20University%20Research%20through (accessed on 30.1.24).
40. Best Practices in Delhi Police. https://delhipolice.gov.in/doc/Best_practices-English.pdf (accessed on 30.1.24).
41. Life360. https://www.life360.com/intl/ (accessed on 30.1.24).
42. Viksit Bharat @2047: Voice of Youth, 11 December 2023, Ministry of Education. https://pib.gov.in/PressReleaseIframePage.aspx?PRID=1985077#:~:text=Viksit%20Bharat%20%402047%20is%20the,environmental%20sustainability%2C%20and%20good%20governance (accessed on 30.1.24).
43. The Muslim Women (Protection of Rights on Marriage) Bill, 2017, Ministry of Law and Justice, 2017. https://prsindia.org/billtrack/the-muslim-women-protection-of-rights-on-marriage-bill-2017#:~:text=2,The%20Muslim%20Women%20(Protection%20of%20Rights%20on%20Marriage)%20Bill%2Cenforceable%20in%20law)%20and%20illegal (accessed on 30.1.24).
44. Prakash, N., Lakhera, G., Berlien, R. and Thoti, K.K. (2023). Role of POSH (Prevention of Sexual Harassment) of Women at Workplace Act in Making Workplace Better for Women: An Empirical Study, Journal of Informatics Education and Research, 3(2).
45. Basnett, B.S. (2018). UN Women's Evaluation of Gender in the SDGs. https://www.jstor.org/stable/pdf/resrep21676.pdf (accessed on 31.1.24).

46. Women's Empowerment and Its Link to Sustainable Development: A Cross-cutting and Integrated Approach, A global voice for women, Soroptimist International.
https://www.soroptimistinternational.org/wp-content/uploads/2016/12/soroptimist-international-csw60-written-statement-final.pdf (accessed on 30.1.24).
47. Role of Women in Achieving Sustainable Development Goals (SDGs), Mahila Housing Trust towards Responsible Urban Development. https://www.mahilahousingtrust.org/role-of-women-in-achieving-sustainable-development-goals-sdgs/ (accessed on 30.1.24).

□

6

Triple *Talaq* Unravelled: Assessing Judicial Dynamics and Government's Perspective in Contemporary India

—Dr. Geetika Sood

Abstract

Triple *talaq* faces several challenges, primarily centred around issues of gender equality, women's rights and legal implications. Some key challenges include gender inequality. The practice of triple *talaq* is often criticised for perpetuating gender inequality. Its instantaneous nature places significant power in the hands of husbands, leaving wives vulnerable and without sufficient legal safeguards. Frankly speaking, triple *talaq* is a procedure of an instant divorce under Islamic law followed by Muslim men in India. It allows a Muslim husband to legally divorce his wife by pronouncing '*Talaq, talaq, talaq*' three times. It can be pronounced in oral or written or electronic media, like e-mail, SMS or WhatsApp. Recently, in a landmark ruling, the Supreme Court of India declared triple *talaq* unconstitutional, stating that it violated the fundamental rights of Muslim women. The practice allowed Muslim men to divorce their wives by uttering the word '*talaq*' three times rapidly, without the wife's consent. This research paper delves into the complex dimensions of triple *talaq* in Islamic family law, focusing on its historical evolution, theological basis and legal implications. The Government of India has taken a stand against the practice of triple *talaq* and enacted legislation to address concerns related to gender equality and women's rights. In 2019, the Indian Parliament passed the Muslim Women (Protection of Rights on Marriage) Act, criminalising the practice of instant triple *talaq*. Research underscores the evolving landscape, emphasising the intersection of tradition and modern legal principles, and the imperative for human rights protection in divorce proceedings. With primary focus on India, the study explores constitutional challenges that led to the enactment of the Muslim Women (Protection of Rights on Marriage) Act in 2019. Comparative case studies from Muslim-majority countries offer insights into diverse global responses and reforms. Additionally, the outcome will contribute to the discourse on triple *talaq*, offering insights into its evolution, global perspectives and the ongoing struggle for gender justice within Islamic family law in India and suggestive futuristic planning to eliminate this menace permanently.

In simple words, this paper scrutinises the evolution of triple *talaq*, encompassing Talaq-ul-sunnat and Talaq-ul-biddat, along with the contentious issue of instant triple *talaq*. A pivotal focus is placed on the Shayara Bano case, offering a critical analysis of its constitutional implications and legislative responses, notably the 2019 Act, aimed at rectifying the discriminatory nature of triple *talaq*.

Introduction

This research paper provides a thorough examination of triple *talaq*, a controversial practice within Islamic family law, with focus on its historical evolution, theological foundations and legal implications. Emphasising the Indian context, the paper delves into constitutional challenges, ultimately leading to the enactment of the Muslim Women (Protection of Rights on Marriage) Act in 2019. Comparative case studies from Muslim-majority countries enrich the analysis, offering diverse perspectives on legal responses and reforms. The introduction traces the historical roots of divorce in Islam, highlighting Prophet Mohammed's reforms to address challenges posed by unregulated divorce powers in pre-Islamic Arabia. The paper underscores the Quranic condemnation of *talaq* and Hadith, establishing a foundational understanding for the subsequent exploration of triple *talaq*. A critical examination of triple *talaq's* interpretation in the Holy Quran reveals the divergence between its practice and the Quranic spirit, challenging its theological and legal validity. This section provides insights into the theological debates surrounding triple *talaq*, questioning its alignment with Quranic principles.

Subsequently, a comparative analysis takes place, examining the various approaches taken by Pakistan, Bangladesh, Sri Lanka, Egypt, Tunisia and other nations in addressing the issue. By using this comparative approach, the study highlights efforts made by different countries to eliminate or modify triple *talaq* and sheds light on the global trend. Aligning these legal developments with modern justice ideas and human rights norms continues to be the main focus. This comparative analysis is a crucial part of the larger conversation because it broadens the scope of the analysis beyond the Indian context and provides insights into the various international strategies used to handle the technicalities of triple *talaq*. The landscape of Muslim personal laws in India has witnessed significant evolution, particularly in relation to marriage, divorce and women's rights. The *Shariat*, rooted in the teachings of Prophet Mohammed and the Quran, governs Muslim personal laws, but India's diverse legal framework is undergoing reforms. This paper examines pivotal court verdicts that have shaped the discourse on triple *talaq*, a controversial divorce practice. Amidst ongoing reforms, the judiciary has played a crucial role in addressing gender inequities and safeguarding the rights of Muslim women. The examination begins with the landmark Shah Bano case in 1985, traverses through subsequent legal developments and culminates in the celebration of Muslim Women's Rights Day, marking the enactment of laws against instant triple *talaq*. These court decisions underscore the judiciary's commitment to justice, equality and constitutional principles, while also shedding light on the challenges and suggestions for further legal reforms in the realm of Muslim personal laws in India.

Development of Term 'Divorce' in Islam

Although divorce is accepted in Islam, it is seen as a necessary evil. According to the Hadith, *"Of all the permitted things, talaq is the most offensive with God."*[1] *Talaq*, an Arabic term meaning the 'undoing of or release a knot', is used in Islamic jurisprudence to signify the release of a woman from the marriage tie, denoting divorce. In legal terms, it involves the dissolution of marriage through the annulment of its legality by the husband's declaration. The term has evolved to mean 'freedom from the bondage of marriage', as used in the Qur'an and the traditions of the Prophet. *Talaq* and its variations are legal terms, emphasising the technical meaning acquired through usage.[2] The term 'divorce' is often used interchangeably with '*talaq*', which, in legal terms, has two senses: a narrow sense limited to separation through specific words by the husband, and a broader sense covering all separations initiated by the husband. In pre-Islamic Arabia, husbands had unlimited divorce power, allowing repeated pronouncements of *talaq*. They could even swear to abstain from intimacy without formal consequences, accuse wives of adultery and leave them without legal responsibilities. This unregulated authority posed societal challenges. Abdur Rahim identified four pre-Islamic Arab methods of marriage dissolution: *talaq, ila, zihar* and *khula.* If a woman fully separated from her husband, she could remarry after the *iddat* period, often linked to determining potential child paternity. Despite not being strict, cases existed, such as a pregnant wife remarrying under an agreement. Islam, led by Prophet Mohammed (PBUH), disapproved of these customs, aiming to transform a semi-barbaric society into a civilised one. While impossible to abolish entirely, reforms allowed divorce under specific conditions, introducing a three-period process to encourage reconciliation. Mohammed granted women the right to seek divorce for valid reasons, emphasising the detestable nature

---

1 Furqan Ahmad, *Triple Talaq: An Analytical Study with Emphasis on Socio-legal Aspect*, Regency Publications, 1994.

2 P.V. Kane, *History of Dharam Shashastra 619-23*, Bhardarkar Oriental Research Institute, Poona, Vol. II, 1975.

of divorce before God due to its impact on marital happiness and children's education.

It is worthwhile to mention here that the practice of *talaq* is strongly condemned in the Holy Qur'an and Hadith and viewed as a highly disfavoured act with widespread consequences. Beyond affecting the involved parties, it significantly impacts society and has economic implications in contemporary times. The repercussions extend to children, influencing their upbringing and overall progress in the absence of one parent. In essence, the general effects of *talaq* are detrimental, with rare instances where it brings peace to the separated parties.[3]

Historic Background to the Practice of Triple *Talaq*

In Islamic law, the husband possesses a more extensive authority to initiate divorce compared to his wife.[4] *Talaq*, a divorce initiated by the husband without the wife's consent, exists in two forms: *Talaq-ul-sunnat* and *Talaq-ul-biddat. Talaq-ul-sunnat*, following Prophet's traditions, includes *Talaq ahsan* and *Talaq hasan*. Talaq *ahsan*, the preferred form, requires a single pronouncement during the wife's purity, followed by a three-month abstention period, with revocability before completion. *Talaq hasan* involves three pronouncements, each a month apart, finalised after the third. *Talaq-ul-biddat*, recognised only by Sunnis, involves three instant pronouncements during the wife's purity, with Shias not acknowledging this form. *Halala* applies when a husband has divorced his wife through three pronouncements, as mandated in triple *talaq* scenarios, like *Talaq hasan* and *Talaq-ul-biddat.*[5] In Islam, marriage is viewed as a civil contract based on mutual consent, unlike Hinduism's eternal sacrament. Triple *talaq*, a form of Islamic divorce, was deemed unconstitutional, particularly instant triple *talaq* (*talaq-e-biddah*). This practice allows a Muslim man by uttering '*talaq*' thrice to divorce his wife.

---

3 Basant K. Sharma, *Hindu Law 77*, Central Law Publications, Allahabad, 3rd edn., 2007.

4 Dr. Zeenat Shaukat Ali: *Marriage and Divorce in Islam; An Appraisal*, p. 200, 1987, Jaico Publishing House, Bombay.

5 *The Hindustan Times*, PTI report, July 9, 1993, New Delhi.

Despite being disproved in classic Islamic jurisprudence, the triple *talaq* still remains an effective or valid form of divorce. It occurs when a husband says '*talaq*' three times, triggering a waiting period called '*iddat*' during which the couple can reconsider. Reuniting during *iddat* doesn't require a new marriage contract, but after its completion, remarriage follows the '*nikah*' process. The All India Muslim Personal Law Board (AIMPLB) recognises eight forms of divorce in Islam, including triple *talaq*. However, many Muslim-majority countries, such as Pakistan, Iraq, Iran, Bangladesh and others, have abolished the practice, recognising its infringement on the fundamental rights of Muslim women due to its irreversibility and lack of reconciliation opportunities. The triple *talaq*, or merely uttering a word or instant divorce is not explicitly mentioned in Islamic *Sharia* or the Qur'an, though it has been a long-standing custom. This practice, prevalent since the eighth century AD, creates legal disputes. Ironically, proponents claim it is beyond court jurisdiction, yet its consequences are arbitrated in court. Women in Islam have the option of seeking '*khula*', returning the dowry or including it in the marriage contract. No Quranic verse authenticates triple *talaq* and Prophet Mohammed condemned it as detrimental. Caliph Umar initially allowed it administratively, later deemed valid by Hanafi jurists, setting a concerning precedent. Challenges arise when husbands falsely claim triple *talaq* to evade legal responsibilities. Courts, like the Bombay High Court, require proof of the *talaq* stages, relying on Quranic principles. Despite being recognised mainly by Sunni Muslims, triple *talaq* faces criticism and protests, particularly for its impact on Muslim women's lives. The Hanafi School, influencing over 90 per cent of Indian Sunnis, has followed triple *talaq* for centuries, contributing to ongoing socio-legal issues.

Meaning and Definition of Triple *Talaq*

Generally speaking, triple *talaq*, a system of divorce in Islamic law as practiced in India, involves the unilateral termination of a marriage contract through the husband's pronouncement – a power granted by Allah. This practice is prevalent among Hanafi

Muslims, particularly in India and has faced criticism for its potential exploitation. The concept has been examined through comparative case studies, revealing its complexities and prompting discussions on the need for reforms to align it with the true spirit of Islam. Within the framework of Hanafi law, *talaq-ul-biddat*, also known as triple *talaq*, is recognised despite lacking classical jurisprudential approval. This form of divorce provides simplicity for the husband, allowing three pronouncements in a single sitting, but it has been regarded as irregular. Sunni law acknowledges *talaq-ul-biddat*, even though it violates Quranic procedures. In cases like *Rashid Ahmad v. Anisakhatoon,*[6] when triple *talaq* or *talaq-ul-biddat* is pronounced by the husband, it becomes immediately irrevocable. Children born after such dissolution are considered illegitimate. Despite a Supreme Court ruling declaring it unconstitutional, reports indicate that the misuse of triple *talaq* continues. This practice encouraged requests for legislative action to penalise the offenders and enforce the court's decisions effectively. Since the last few years, there has been a shift in judicial approaches toward progressive interpretations of Muslim law. The Supreme Court's landmark judgement, particularly in the Shayara Bano case,[7] in which her husband Rizwan Ahmed granted her divorce under *talaq-e-biddat*, is worth mentioning. She filed a petition in Supreme Court asking the court to declare practices of *nikah halala* and polygamy illegal and unconstitutional. The court held that these practices violated fundamental rights guaranteed by the Constitution as triple *talaq* is not an essential practice of Islam. But still it is followed in the society since a long time and is not protected under Article 25 (1) of the Constitution of India. If any marriage is broken without the consent of the women, it will constitute gender inequality and is a violation under Article 14. The Shariat Act of 1937 was passed before the Constitution of India was enacted, hence it was considered as pre-constitutional law (Art 13(1)) as in this case the doctrine of eclipse and severability will be applied. Despite the legal rulings, instances of arbitrary divorces persist, indicating a gap between

---

6 Rashid Ahmad vs. Anisa Khatoon, 1932, 59 IA 21 (Alld): 1932, PC 25.

7 Shayara Bano vs. Union of India, [(2017) 9 SCC 1].

legal pronouncements and on-the-ground realities. The Apex Court had urged the Central Government to legislate on debatable concept of triple *talaq* within six months of the Shayara Bano case[8] judgement. This underscores the ongoing challenges in ensuring the effective implementation of legal decisions and protecting the rights of Muslim women. The evolving judicial landscape reflects a growing commitment to advancing the rights of women within the perspective of Islamic law.

Practice of Triple *Talaq*: Insights from the Holy Quran

The Holy Quran does not explicitly state that pronouncing triple *talaq* at once constitutes three divorces. In verses '229' and '230', divorce for mutual incompatibility is allowed, with a limit of two divorces to prevent impulsive separations. Reconciliation is possible after two divorces, but a third pronouncement becomes irrevocable unless the woman who is divorced marries another man.[9] The verse uses the term '*marrataan*' (two times), which some interpret as repetition of the term '*talaq*' or specifying the figure of divorces. According to this interpretation, saying '*talaq, talaq, talaq*' or declaring 'three *talaqs*' would imply three divorces. However, the correct understanding is that '*marrataan*' does not refer to repeating the word '*talaq*' but rather denotes giving *talaq* for the second time.[10] Shams Pirzada, in the book, *Triple Talaq in the Light of Quran and Sunnah*, examines the Arabic term '*marrataan*', clarifying that it signifies "on another occasion after the first time." This clarification challenges the misunderstanding that the term involves a simple verbal repetition.[11] *Talaq-e-biddat,* deemed the most sinful form of divorce, stands in clear violation of both the letter and spirit of the Quran and it was expressly forbidden by the Prophet (PBUH).[12]

---

8 Ibid.

9 Abdullah Yusuf Ali, *The Quran,* translated into English (Goodwords Publication , New Delhi, 14th ed., 2016.

10 Shams Pirzada, *Triple Talaq in the Light of Quran and Sunnah* (Dara dawat ul Quran Publications, Mumbai, 1996.

11 Ibid.

12 Asghar Ali Engineer, *Islam, Women and Gender Justice 134-135,* Gyan Publishing House, 2nd ed., 2003.

The significance of Quranic verse '230' lies in advocating restraint for husbands, discouraging sudden divorces driven by anger.[13] Despite this, the prevalent cases of triple *talaq* often arise from the husband's sudden anger or trivial reasons. *Talaq-e-biddat*, deemed the most sinful form of divorce, contradicts the Quranic spirit and was disallowed by the Prophet (PBUH).[14] It's evident from Quranic verses that triple *talaq* doesn't adhere to clear commandment of the Holy Quran and lacks validity in Muslim Personal Laws.

Shayara Bano Case *vis* a *vis* Constitutionality of Triple *Talaq*

In Shayara Bano case,[15] the Apex Court unequivocally invalidated triple *talaq*, asserting its unconstitutionality. The court underscored that the 1937 Act[16] acknowledges and upholds all *talaq* forms, explicitly including triple *talaq* for Indian Sunni Muslims. It further held that any inconsistency with constitutional provisions renders the law void under Article 13(1)[17] and Article 13(3)(b).[18] The constitutional legitimacy of triple *talaq* faces

---

13 Supranote 9.

14 Supranote 12.

15 Shayara Bano vs. Union of India [(2017) 9 SCC 1].

16 Section 2 of the the Muslim Personal Law (*Shariat*) Application Act, 1937 provides: Application of Personal Law to Muslims: Notwithstanding any custom or usage to the contrary, in all questions (save questions relating to agricultural land) regarding intestate succession, special property of females, including personal properly inherited or obtained under contract or gift or any other provision of Personal Law, marriage, dissolution of marriage, including *talaq, ila, zihar, lian, khula* and *mubaraat*, maintenance, dower, guardianship, gifts, trusts and trust properties, and *wakfs* (other than charities and charitable institutions and charitable and religious endowments), the rule of decision in cases where the parties are Muslims shall be the Muslim Personal Law (*Shariat*).

17 "All laws in force in the territory of India immediately before the commencement of this Constitution, insofar as they are inconsistent with the provisions of this Part, shall, to the extent of such inconsistency, be void."

18 Article 13(3)(b) of the Constitution of India provides that "laws in force include laws passed or made by Legislature or other competent authority in the territory of India before the commencement of this Constitution and not previously repealed, notwithstanding that any such law or any part thereof may not be then in operation either at all or in particular areas."

scrutiny under Articles 14[19], 15[20] and 21[21]. In case of *Smt. Sumaila vs. Aaqil Jamil*[22], the Allahabad High Court adjudged the husband's triple announcement of *talaq* or divorce as wrongful, mentioning violation of the statutory principles protected in these articles, emphasising the pillars of equality, non-discrimination and also the right to life and personal liberty. In defence of triple *talaq*, AIMPLB[23] maintains that its validity persists, acknowledging its theological and legal standing despite being deemed sinful. The argument extends beyond a solo case, with instances like *Jiauddin Ahmed vs. Anwara Begum*[24] also asserting the unconstitutionality of triple *talaq*. The constitutional guarantee of religious freedom in Article 25[25] encounters limitations in the form of Article 14 and Article 15(1) due to the discriminatory nature of triple *talaq*. Despite conflicting with the principles of equality, the statutory acknowledgment of triple *talaq* under the 1937 Act introduces a constitutional quandary, governed by Article 13.

---

19 Article 14 of the Constitution of India reads as under: "The State shall not deny to any person equality before the law or the equal protection of the laws within the territory of India."

20 Article 15(1) of the Constitution of India reads as under: "The State shall not discriminate against any citizen on grounds only of religion, race, caste, sex, place of birth or any of them."

21 Article 21 states: "No person shall be deprived of his life or personal liberty except according to a procedure established by law."

22 Smt. Sumaila vs. Aaqil Jamil and Ors , 2017, SCC 1325.

23 All India Muslim Personal Law Board (AIMPLB) is a non-governmental organisation in India that represents the interests of Muslims in matters of personal law. It was formed in 1973 with the objective of protecting and promoting the application of Islamic personal law among Muslims in India. The AIMPLB is primarily concerned with issues related to marriage, divorce, inheritance and other personal matters governed by Islamic law, known as *Shariah*. The AIMPLB has been involved in various significant cases and debates, including those related to the Muslim Women (Protection of Rights on Divorce) Act, the Shah Bano case, and the triple *talaq* issue. It has also played a role in advocating for the preservation of Muslim personal laws and resisting attempts to introduce a uniform civil code in India.

24 Jiauddin Ahmed vs. Anwara Begum, Criminal Revision No. 199 of 1977.

25 Article 25 guarantees the freedom of conscience, the freedom to profess, practice and propagate religion to all citizens.

The Muslim Women (Protection of Rights on Marriage) Act, 2019

The enactment of the 2019 Muslim Women (Protection of Rights on Marriage) Act was prompted by the prevalent exercise of prompt triple *talaq* (*talaq-e-biddah*) among Muslim husbands, causing hardships for divorced Muslim women. This practice involved the immediate and unilateral pronouncement of '*talaq*' three times, leading to instantaneous termination of the marriage. Passed by the Parliament of India, the Act received the President's assent on July 31, 2019 and became effective from August 1, 2019. The Act's primary aim is to safeguard the rights of married Muslim women, prevent the arbitrary and immediate termination of marriages through triple *talaq* and provide financial support and custodial rights for the affected women and their dependent children. Following are the key provisions of the Act: Invalidation of Talaq,[26] Penalty for Talaq Pronouncement,[27] Financial Support,[28] Custodial Rights,[29] Offence to be cognisable and compoundable.[30]

Gender Justice *vis* a *vis* Ban on Triple *Talaq* in India: Legal Considerations

In India, the illegalisation of triple *talaq* represents a decisive moment influenced by a blend of governmental, social and juridical

26 Section 3 of the Act declares any form of *talaq* pronounced by a Muslim husband – whether spoken, written, electronic, or in any other manner – as void and illegal.

27 Section 4 of the Act states that a Muslim husband who pronounces *talaq* in violation of the Act may face imprisonment for a term extending up to three years, coupled with a fine.

28 Section 5 of the Act provides the subsistence allowance and states that the Act ensures that a married Muslim woman, upon whom *talaq* is pronounced, is entitled to receive a subsistence allowance for herself and her dependent children, the amount of which is determined by the agistrate.

29 Section 6 of the Act provides that in the event of pronouncement of *talaq*, a married Muslim woman is entitled to custody of her minor children.

30 Section 7 of the Act states that police can act on the complaint of the affected woman or her relatives, offences can be settled with Magistrate's permission and the bail is granted if the Magistrate finds reasonable grounds after considering the affected woman's views.

factors. In a study, 92 per cent of the Muslim women in India said they would like to see triple *talaq* abolished.[31] Legal challenges – such as *Shayara Bano vs. Union of India*[32] – brought triple *talaq's* discriminatory nature to light and sparked discussions about how it conflicts with fundamental rights guaranteed by Articles 14 (right to equality) and 21 (right to life and personal liberty) of the Indian Constitution. The global trend of some Islamic countries reforming or doing away with triple *talaq* coincides with this judicial examination. The political environment was crucial, as more people realised how important it was for the empowerment of women and gender justice. The need for change was heightened by international scrutiny and debates concerning human rights. The need for legislative action was increased by the Supreme Court's assertive approach, which was based on fundamental constitutional foundations. In response, the Muslim Women (Protection of Rights on Marriage) Act, 2019 has been enacted by the Indian government. Factual evidence and government figures were vital in forming the narrative. The incidence of triple *talaq* and its adverse effects on numerous women were highlighted by empirical research. The Act, a significant piece of legislation, demonstrated India's dedication to justice and gender equality in addition to making the practice illegal. Supported by the real-world reality of the suffering brought on by the practice, it was a substantial step towards harmonising personal laws with constitutional goals in mind.

Triple *Talaq*: Worldwide Comparative Overview

Globally speaking, many Islamic nations have barred the practice, including Pakistan and Bangladesh, although it is technically legal in Sunni Islamic jurisprudence. Husbands can file for divorce immediately in Muslim communities by saying '*talaq*' three times. This practice, known as triple *talaq*, has drawn criticism for giving preference to men. This hasty approach

---

31 BYJU's Exam Prep., Triple *Talaq* Bill, available at: https://byjus.com/free-ias-prep/triple-talaq-bill-upsc-notes/ (last accessed on 28/12/2023)

32 (2017) 9 SCC 1.

ignores the complexity of interpersonal interactions and is occasionally motivated by emotional outbursts. The Supreme Court's position, declaring it to be beyond the bounds of law, highlights how it violates the right to equality (as stated in Article 14) and is discriminatory towards women. Justifications for maintaining this practice as a religious right are insufficient to support it. Triple *talaq* is a family law practice that has attracted a lot of attention globally and prompted differing legal reactions in various nations. This comparative investigation seeks to illuminate the many strategies that different countries have employed to deal with the controversial problem of prompt and irrevocable divorce. The analysis explores the complex terrain of triple *talaq*, including everything from divergent legal systems to cultural variations and provides insights into how various jurisdictions handle the meeting place of Islamic custom and modern legal theory. This study aims to unravel the complexity of triple *talaq* by exploring the worldwide landscape and offering a comprehensive understanding of its effects on marital relations and the pursuit of gender justice. In Pakistan and Bangladesh, the male files for divorce by serving a written notice on the 'arbitration council', a copy of which he also gives to his spouse. Conversely, Afghanistan views a divorce that is finalised in three sittings as invalid. Interestingly, India banned instant triple *talaq* along with 22 other nations. By enacting the Muslim Family Law Ordinance in 1961, Pakistan accomplished a major milestone by abolishing triple *talaq*. Comparably, the Marriage and Divorce (Muslim) Act, 1951 of Sri Lanka, as amended in 2006, forbids the practice explicitly.[33] By reinterpreting the divorce laws in Egypt in 1929, the country made a groundbreaking move.[34] Egypt was

33 Press Trust of India, *India's Muslim Neighbours among 23 Countries that have Banned Triple Talaq,* available at: https://www.hindustantimes.com/india-news/india-s-muslim-neighbours-among-23-countries-that-have-banned-triple-talaq/story-J8b9HkOCwdMAIWyscwxZMK.html (last accessed on 28.12.2023).

34 Jagran Josh, *What is Triple Talaq and List of Countries where it is Banned,* available at: https://www.jagranjosh.com/general-knowledge/muslim-countries-where-triple-talaq-is-banned-1490788669-1 (last accessed on 28.12.2023).

committed to harmonising its legal system with Islamic values, as demonstrated by this action. The institution of marriage is within the jurisdiction of the State and the judiciary in Tunisia, according to the 1956 Code of Personal Status.[35] This stops husbands from divorcing their wives verbally on their own without giving an adequate reason. The Sri Lankan Marriage and Divorce (Muslim) Act, 1951 is considered an excellent piece of legislation regarding divorce, specifically triple *talaq*, by some Islamic scholars, despite the fact that Sri Lanka is not a Muslim-majority country.[36] This statute states that a husband must inform the local Muslims who hold authority, as well as his family, the elders and other Muslims, if he wishes to file for divorce from his wife. This clause promotes re-examination, reconciliation and careful contemplation before granting a divorce.[37] The Indonesian laws pertaining to divorce include the Marriage Law (Law No. 1 of 1974) and the Government Regulation No. 9 of 1975, which regulates the law. According to these regulations, a court order is required before a divorce can be formally granted. Informal agreements between spouses are not legally recognised as grounds for divorce.[38] Muslim nations, such as the UAE and Qatar, support Taimiyah's stance on triple *talaq*, ranging from Iraq to Indonesia. Even farther, the 1956 Code of Personal Status of Tunisia mandates that divorces be granted by a judge. When attempts at reconciliation are unsuccessful, divorce is granted by the courts after they look into the matter. After adopting this rule, Algeria instituted a 90-day time for reconciliation.

An important turning point in legal history of India was reached in 2017 when the Indian Supreme Court ruled in a historic decision of *Shayara Bano vs. Union of India*[39] that instant triple *talaq* was illegal. This action is in line with the positions of other nations that have abolished the practice of instant triple *talaq*, including Tunisia, Cyprus, Turkey and more. Due to the realisation that this

35 Ibid.
36 Ibid.
37 Ibid.
38 Ibid.
39 (2017) 9 SCC 1.

practice has repercussions for human rights and the constitution, many countries have passed laws protecting people against hasty and arbitrary divorces, creating a more equitable legal system.[40]

Triple *Talaq*: Response of Judiciary through Landmark Verdicts

The *Shariat* law, which has its roots in the precepts of the Prophet Mohammed and the teachings of the Quran, governs Muslim personal laws in India. Muslims in India abide by these individual or personal laws, which are defined or assured by the Constitution of India in Article 25 which talks about the Right to Religion. In contrast to numerous Islamic nations that have updated *Shariyat* legislation, India is still undertaking reforms, particularly in relation to marriage, divorce, inheritance and family dynamics. Although constitutional rights usually take precedence over ordinary laws, personal laws are not always subject to this law. Significant rulings have been rendered by the Apex Court to protect Muslim women's rights in relation to marriage and divorce. In the historic case named, *Mohd. Ahmed Khan v. Shah Bano Begum and Others*[41] also referred to as the 'Shah Bano Case', deals with the controversial 'triple *talaq* verdict'. The significance of this case in the fight for the independence and the rights of Muslim women in India cannot be overstated. A major turning point in the struggle against gender inequities was reached when the fearless protagonist, Shah Bano, opposed the triple *talaq* practice. Shah Bano bravely challenged the system that was controlled by men despite of criticism from the side of her husband and social pressure too. But, after facing all these challenges, she was successful in changing the system; thus her tenacity and hard work paid off. The Shah Bano case from 1985 is still seen as a turning point in the legal history of Muslim women's

40 Press Trust of India, *India's Muslim Neighbours among 23 Countries that have Banned Triple Talaq,* available at: https://www.hindustantimes.com/india-news/india-s-muslim-neighbours-among-23-countries-that-have-banned-triple-talaq/story-J8b9HkOCwdMAIWyscwxZMK.html (last accessed on 28.12.2023).

41 1985 SCR (3) 844.

rights since it sparked discussions regarding the power of the Supreme Court in these kinds of cases. Shah Bano Begum was a Muslim woman whose husband used the triple *talaq* system to divorce her. The problem started when she turned to the Code of Criminal Procedure for maintenance moderately than the limited assistance provided by Islamic personal laws. This brought to light the tension that exists between Indian laws regarding lifetime maintenance and Islamic law, with certain limitations.

The petitioner in the Shah Bano case said that the Articles 14 and 21 of the Constitution of India were violated by the Muslim Women (Protection of Rights on Divorce) Act, 1986 making it illegal. Despite being a source of inequality, the respondent argued that personal laws did not violate these constitutional provisions. In an attempt to prevent the Act from being invalidated, the Supreme Court interpreted Section 125 of the CrPC to give Muslim women the same maintenance rights as women of other religions. After analysing the Act, the Court came to the conclusion that it is mandatory for a Muslim husband that he must maintain or support his ex-wife for the rest of his life, but he must give her the full amount during the *iddat* period. This ruling struck a balance between the demands of proponents of women's rights and the Muslim community. The ruling maintained Muslim women's right to maintenance in the face of criticism and subsequent manoeuvring by politicians. The case of Shah Bano is still remembered as a turning point in the battle of equality and justice against religious personal laws. In *Danial Latifi and Another vs. Union of India*[42] (post the revolutionary Shah Bano case), the Muslim Women (Protection of Rights on Divorce) Act, 1986 was enacted by the Parliament to report the unrest in Muslim individual or personal law. According to Section 3(1)(a) of the Act, a divorced woman is entitled to reasonable provisions and maintenance during the '*iddat*' period. Daniel Latifi challenged this act, asserting its unconstitutionality and violation of Articles 14 and 21.

In the instant case, the petitioner argued that the Muslim Women (Protection of Rights on Divorce) Act, 1986 is

42 (2001) 7 SCC 740.

unconstitutional and suppresses Muslim women, violating Articles 14 and 21. The respondent countered, asserting that personal laws are a legitimate reason for divorce and do not breach Article 14. The Court, employing a cautious approach, upheld the Act by interpreting it to provide Muslim women with maintenance similar to women of other religions under Section 125 of CrPC. The Court examined Section 3(1)(a) and determined two separate obligations for the husband: to make a reasonable arrangement and to pay maintenance. The decision reflected tensions between actors in the Muslim community and women's rights activists. The Court, aware of potential social backlash, strategically avoided questioning the constitutionality of the Act and focused on interpreting Islamic personal law to balance gender equality for Muslim women. The Daniel Latifi case exemplifies the Court's delicate handling of Muslim personal law claims post the Shah Bano case.

In 2016, in the case of *Shayara Bano vs. Union of India*,[43] Shayara Bano, having faced a divorce through triple *talaq*, challenged not only this practice but also polygamy and *nikah halala*, asserting their unconstitutionality. The Supreme Court, primarily addressing triple *talaq*, ruled it as unconstitutional under Articles 14 and 13(1) of the Constitution. The Court declared the Muslim Personal Law (*Shariat*) Application Act, 1937 void insofar as it recognised triple *talaq*, emphasising that the arbitrary nature of the practice violated the principle of equality. This landmark decision has brought hope and encouragement to women challenging such discriminatory practices. Shayara Bano's public interest litigation (PIL) has sparked crucial debates on women's rights, providing optimism for those who have endured the repercussions of these practices. While awaiting the final judgement on the broader issues, the case signifies a positive step towards addressing gender injustices. The ongoing discussions underscore the importance of sustained advocacy to ensure that legal decisions contribute to the overall empowerment of women and are not misused for political gains.

---

43 (2017) 9 SCC 1.

Other Judicial Pronouncement that deals with Triple *Talaq* Cases in India

Sayid Rashid Ahmad vs. Anisa Khatun[44]

The husband divorced his wife in her absence but in presence of the witnesses and then after four days he executed *talaqnama* stating that he had divorced his wife in an abominable form. Later on, they started living together as husband and wife as there was no proof for the compliance of doctrine of *halala*. The five children were born to the couple and the husband treated them as legitimate. The trial court held that the triple *talaq* given by the husband has dissolved the marriage and any child born out of this marriage is not legitimate. The privy court also held that the marriage is dissolved.

Mst. Fuzlunbi vs. K. Khader Vali[45]

The Andhra Pradesh High Court ruled that the husband cannot pronounce triple *talaq* out of mere whims or caprice; instead, he must provide a legitimate reason.

Mst. Zohara Khatoon vs. Mohd. Ibrahim[46]

The Patna High Court decided that merely saying '*talaq*' three times in one sitting is insufficient to establish a valid divorce. In order to apply for divorce, one must provide a valid reason.

Jiauddin Ahmed vs. Anwara Begum[47]

This case addressed the arbitrary nature of divorce under Muslim law, even though it was not specifically regarding triple *talaq*. According to the Supreme Court, the husband needs to prove to the judge that he has a good basis to file for divorce.

Nazeer vs. State of Karnataka[48]

This triple *talaq* case, which was primarily criminal in character, is noteworthy because of the court's observation on the lack of legal protections for Muslim women.

---

44 AIR 1932.
45 AIR 1981 AP 71.
46 AIR 1981 Pat 28.
47 AIR 1981 SC 721.
48 AIR 1992 SC 196.

Shamim Ara vs. State of UP[49]

The Supreme Court underlined the necessity of significant legal reform in Muslim personal law, particularly in regards to matters concerning arbitrary divorce.

Neelam Katara vs. Union of India[50]

The Supreme Court made several notable remarks regarding the arbitrary nature of triple *talaq* and the necessity for legal reform in this case, which was primarily a criminal case.

Imrana vs. State of Uttar Pradesh[51]

This case touched on issues of triple *talaq* and the need for legal clarification, raising concerns about the legality of marriage following an alleged incidence of rape by the husband's father.

Ahammedkutty vs. Neelakandan[52]

According to a ruling by the Kerala High Court, a marriage cannot be dissolved by simply pronouncing *talaq* three times without fulfilling the requirements outlined in Islamic law.

Masroor Ahmed vs. State (NCT of Delhi)[53]

In the said case, it was noted that the position of Muslim women under customary law is deplorable. Muslim women organisations have strongly condemned Customary Law for its adverse impact on women's rights. They advocate for the application of Muslim Personal Law (*Shariat*) to elevate women to their rightful position. The enactment of Muslim Personal Law is seen as a measure that would bring clarity to mutual rights and obligations, ensuring certainty and benefiting society.

Nashim Akhtar vs. Ghulam Mohiuddin[54]

The Allahabad High Court highlighted that the authority to declare triple *talaq* is not unqualified and ought to be used sparingly and for a valid reason.

---

49 (2002) 7 SCC 518.
50 (2003) 6 SCC 342.
51 AIR 2005 SC 3133.
52 2007 (4) KLT 673.
53 2008 (103) DRJ 137 (Del.).
54 AIR 2014 All 46.

Shabnam Hashmi vs. Union of India[55]

The Supreme Court stressed the requirement for reform and female equality in Muslim personal law, even though it had nothing to do with triple *talaq* specifically. Triple *talaq* has been the matter of historic rulings by the Supreme Court of India and several High Courts, which have largely shaped the conversation and supported the idea that it should be declared illegal. In tackling the complications of triple *talaq*, promoting gender justice and realising the necessity for legislative changes within Muslim personal law, the Indian judiciary has done a good job. All of the rulings demonstrate the judiciary's dedication to protecting Muslim women's rights, guaranteeing equality and preserving constitutional principles. Triple *talaq* is a discriminatory practice that has been eradicated in India in a large part because of the change of legal perspectives prompted by these significant incidents. Muslim Women's Rights Day, observed annually on August 1, commemorates the enactment of the law against triple *talaq* in India. The law, implemented on August 1, 2019, criminalised the practice of instant triple *talaq*. Celebrated nationwide, this day holds significance as it marks the second anniversary of the law's implementation under the Protection of Marriage Rights Act of 2019. The Supreme Court had declared the practice of triple *talaq* unconstitutional in August 2017. Subsequently, in December 2017, the government introduced the Muslim Women (Protection of Rights on Marriage) Bill in Parliament. Despite facing opposition, the Bill was successfully passed in both the Lok Sabha and the Rajya Sabha in July 2019. The legislation, a crucial milestone, not only criminalised instant triple *talaq* but also prescribed a three-year jail term for violators along with fines. Landmark cases like *Shah Bano Begum*[56] and *Shayra Bano*[57] played an essential or major role in laying the base for the Triple *Talaq* Bill. Shayra Bano's writ petition sought the Supreme Court's declaration of *talaq-e-biddat*, polygamy and *nikah-halala*

---

55 (2014) 4 SCC 1.
56 1985 SCR (3) 844.
57 (2017) 9 SCC 1.

as unconstitutional, citing violations of Articles 14, 15, 21, and 25 of the Constitution. The celebration of Muslim Women's Rights Day reflects the positive impact of legal reforms on the lives of Muslim women in India, marking a major step towards gender justice and equality.[58]

Concluding Observations: Thus, India, a democratic country strives for growth, needs to emphasise and address the mistreatment of the Muslim women. A just interpretation of Islam is required, and the judiciary and legislature are essential to bringing this happen. Given the sizeable Muslim community, it's critical to adapt to the changing circumstances and take personal law reforms into consideration. To truly advance society, the All India Muslim Personal Law Board ought to recognise gender equality. Differentiation has influenced identity politics, which must conform to global gender equality norms. Managing these distinctions and promoting inclusive group politics can be facilitated by embracing inter-sectionality. To guarantee that the rights of Muslim women are respected, it is time for reform and unity. Amidst the complex landscape of Muslim personal laws, it is also the duty of enlightened individuals and the informed public to work for fairness in the community and to promote knowledge about the fundamental rights of Muslim women. In the purview of gender equality, in particular, the notion of inter-sectionality provides a comprehensive perspective by recognising and addressing the various elements influencing women's experiences. Articles 14, 15, and 21 of the Constitution may not always capture women's equality, but the debate over the elimination of triple *talaq* represents a major advancement for feminist politics. The government has demonstrated a commitment to reform as evidenced by its admirable efforts to criminalise triple *talaq* and pass laws protecting married Muslim women.

---

58 Sumit Arora, *Muslim Women's Rights Day 2023: Date, Significance and History,* available at: https://currentaffairs.adda247.com/muslim-womens-rights-day-2023-date-significance-and-history (last accessed on 28.12.2023).

Following the Indian government's decision to abolish triple *talaq*, some important suggestions for future action include revising the Uniform Civil Code to give more consideration to personal laws, enforcing monogamy universally, penalising unilateral divorces, abolishing polygamy and *nikah halala*, establishing statutory authority to supervise polygamy cases, encouraging efforts at reconciliation before divorce, defining fair grounds and procedures for divorce, categorising and codifying Muslim law in accordance with Quranic principles, requiring marriage registration and making sure that the Supreme Court's decision declaring triple *talaq* unconstitutional is implemented effectively. The aforementioned ideas seek to enhance the status of women, promote parity and institute a just and responsible legal structure for the Indian Muslim population.

Legislation prohibiting triple *talaq* should consider women's financial stability. The State needs to empower women in negotiations, give marital preservation top priority and provide financial support to impacted women and children in the event that the spouse is imprisoned. Comprehensive legal reforms also require the enactment of appropriate legislation and the discussion of a Uniform Civil Code. Triple *talaq* was declared illegal, which was a long-awaited win for women who had been subjected to its abuse and a major step forward for both the legislative and the judiciary. In the past, the word '*talaq*' was frequently said orally, in written form, or by electronic means, disregarding the rights of Muslim women. It was also used carelessly and as a tool. Like divorce under Hindu law, *talaq* should never be used lightly and should only be used as a last resort. Although it is prohibited, current trends show that people are still using it illegally, which emphasises the necessity for strict enforcement and public awareness campaigns in order to eradicate this practice.

Religious organisations criticise the ban on triple *talaq*, claiming that it interferes with *Sharia* customs, without taking into consideration that it is a great step towards ending the suffering of Muslim women who always suffer and are subject to instantaneous *talaq*. Obstacles include poor literacy rates among

Muslim women, limited knowledge of their legal rights and the possible absence of familial support during judicial proceedings. Even if the prohibition addresses a long-standing problem, clauses like criminalisation need to be carefully thought through and discussed. The fight against unfair practices against the women in all religions and in society at large should also be involved in the endeavours.

It is worthwhile to mention here that the Indian government had taken a stand against the practice of triple *talaq* and enacted legislation to address concerns related to gender equality. In 2019, the Indian Parliament passed the Muslim Women (Protection of Rights on Marriage) Act, criminalising the practice of instant triple *talaq* under Indian constitution. Under this law, pronouncing triple *talaq* in any form – spoken, written, or electronic – is considered illegal and can lead to imprisonment for the husband. This law also includes provisions for financial support and custody arrangements for the affected women. These provisions are outstanding for gender justice and against the practice of triple *talaq*. But at the same time, it is also important to mention here that these words should be implemented in the letter and spirit. This is the right time when Indian government is showing its concern for all the sensitive issues and definitely the time will come when Republic of India will be one of the most acknowledged nations of the world, known for its hidden potential, Thus, it will be write to quote here;

"Make each day Women's Day because the achievement of gender equality is everyone's responsibility."

□

7
Atmanirbhar Bharat and the Predicament of Women

—Dr. Beena Agarwal

Human life is a consistent synthesis of the ideals of 'self and society'. According to the concept of the *Bhagwad Gita* the realisation of self-dignity is the highest human virtue that leads to the elevation of human soul beyond all hurdles and hazards of the world. This self-realisation strengthens human will to make affirmation of the hidden potentials for the betterment of suffering humanity. Across the globe, the great thinkers like Gandhi, Nehru, Lincoln, Martin Luther, Whitman, Radhakrishnan, Emerson and others have a realisation of human will. Regarding 'self-reliance', Emerson admits, "To believe your own thought, to believe that what is true for you in your private heart is true for all men, that is genius" (Emerson, p. 27). In India, Tagore has also accepted the greatness of individual freedom and the realisation of individuality. He makes a confession:"It is only when he comes to feel the glory of his individuality that man tries to reach greatness even though it means suffering. And it is only when they research greatness, that union among men becomes a reality" (Tagore, p. 143).

Motivated by these universal ideologies of Indian philosophy, Prime Minister Narendra Modi, after a long reflection on the causes of suffering and marginality of Indians, came to a significant conclusion that the notion of 'self-reliance' can ensure human dignity, freedom, better economic standard, skill-centric lifestyle, knowledge and enlightenment, power and prosperity to the citizens of India. It becomes more significant in case of marginalised sections, like rural folks, illiterates, low-caste people, tribals, women and other such communities to strengthen their human spirit to resist the forces of contempt and humiliation.

In this respect, the concept of Atmanirbhar Bharat is not a passing phase of Indian political history in the post-COVID period but a comprehensive ideology of organising and assimilating human resources and human potential to be a leader at the global level. Simultaneously, it is a strategy to organise scattered humanity under a faithful umbrella for a society based on social justice and social care. Every crisis leads to creation and opens the windows for resilience, constructing the vision of acceptance and assimilation against the dark clouds of that crisis. Hence, it is only the horrible shadows of COVID-19 pandemic that encouraged the concept of Atmanirbhar Bharat. It emerged as a mechanism for self-survival against the horrible shades of migration, poverty, hardships, unemployment and unfortunate deaths. The crisis was so bitter that it eliminated the differences of male and female and therefore, women equally came out to bear the burden of life, neglecting the stigma of weakness haunting female anatomy and female psyche. The crisis of human life in the industrial world opened a new chapter in human history where each individual was obliged to carry the burden of existence, defying the barriers of gender discrimination, caste discrimination and class parity existing in society. There are numerous examples in this time of crisis that women accepted it as a self-imposed responsibility to save their children from the horrors of starvation and poverty and supporting their male counterparts to accept the jobs full of challenges to provide economic and psychological support to them. It opened the windows to a new concept of women's role in the process of self-reliance, social order and to break the myth of women as the shadow of male desires. It will not be out of place had women been passive during the COVID tragedy. There might have been massive loss of human life and particularly the children would have been unfortunate sufferers.

Women's realisation of responsibility as wife, mother, daughter and sensitive human being can contribute to construct a society based on human values.

In India since time immemorial, thinkers have emphasised the importance of self-reliance to abolish the existing evils and nurturing the values of higher spiritual living and thinking. It constructs a society in which citizens are equipped to articulate the voice of Divine to complete the process of an emancipated society fighting for the values of freedom and social justice. It is with this aim that Prime Minister Narendra Modi gave a clarion call for Atmanirbhar Bharat. It emphasised on the five variables that construct the paradigms of self-reliant India. These are: (i) Economy, (ii) Infrastructure, (iii) Technology, (iv) Vibrant Demography and (v) Demand.

Income in the mainstream women stretching from tribal community to the elitist class for self-growth can make a contribution to modify the existing economic power structure. It will enhance their quality of life along with the possibility of achieving the anatomy of decision making. The second paradigm is infrastructure and the organisation of infrastructure governed by the power of women will give a new direction to the annals of growth and development. With economic independence and infrastructure, there is a relationship of technological development. Women can learn skills in technological exposure to cope up with all pervasive changes creeping fast in the information society. The fourth paradigm of Atmanirbhar Bharat is 'vibrant demography' and it is more significant to require the decisions and determination of women coupled with awareness for her sex roles to ensure their health and can contribute in controlling the population and promoting the generation of enlightened citizen to reduce the vices of poverty, illiteracy and oppressive sensibility.

Woman is the custodian of family values – nurturing morality, independence and self-dignity among children. A successful and organised motherhood becomes a foundation stone for a systematic family, strong society and consistently being operative for the preparation of a strong nation. Under the concept of

Atmanirbhar Bharat, women, instead of being the shadow of males, will emerge as custodians to protect the interest of their family required to construct a society consisting of intellectually aware citizens to overcome the vices of poverty, illiteracy, evil practices, exploring the values of education and motivating the thirst for knowledge. Illiteracy among women shuts the doors of prosperity and progress. Family is the micro unit of social construct and it works as the foundation stone for national growth. However, to overcome the demon of domestic violence, women must cultivate the culture of economic independence, self-dignity and self-awareness among the members of the family. This contribution of women in the programme of Atmanirbhar Bharat is a vital issue that can be nurtured and realised only through the cumulative efforts of women, leading to sublimation, transformation and effective implementation of the policies pregnant with fruitful consequences.

Women with acceptance of the ideology of Atmanirbhar Bharat can develop a state of psyche, free from the burden of patriarchal conventions. It will ensure women to identify themselves with national pride and national dignity and subsequently motivate them to conceptualise the significance of their potential for better fabrication of national designs required for the all-pervasive development of the nation. It will encourage women to devote their potential, time and energy for the modulation of a society based on self-dignity, self-awareness and self-motivation. These three dimensional approaches of feminine self-dignity, self-awareness and self-motivation will positively ensure empowerment to the woman and this realisation of empowerment will certainly contribute to the paradigm of self-reliance at the national level. Women's absence from the issues of national significance makes them invisible minorities and they remain unaware of the issues of vital national importance. Self-reliance will stir self-awakening among women and associate their belongingness with the idea of national development. The kinship with national issues will be a path for women empowerment and the population of women as sensitive human beings would come out as a strategic force in the security and development of the nation beyond and above the dependency syndrome that subjugates the spirit of nationality itself.

The idea of Atmanirbhar Bharat is inevitably associated with the concept of economic independence. It is a fact universally acknowledged that economic security and independence ensure freedom and dignity of human beings. History is a witness to the fact that the prime reason for women's subjugation is their economic colonialism perpetuated by male designs. With this economic slavery, women are not permitted to exercise their freedom of choice to carve out their own dreams of life based on their potential and sensibility. Domestic violence inflicted on the female body is directly or indirectly a mechanism of the imposition of male autonomy that contextualises in terms of economic power structures controlled by male desires. It results in mental slavery and spoils the dignity of the life of women. With this new concept of self-reliant India, women have been encouraged more and more to enter the mainstream of handling the economic power resources that generates money for self-survival, enhancing the conditions of life and accumulating more and more resources for education and enlightenment. It is high time when women should emancipate themselves from the traditional role of running their home to recognise their humanity. It will help them to come out of their marginalised status and join the mainstream. French critic Simon de Bevouir admits that "woman is not born but becomes one." It shows that womanhood is not a physical and social concept only, but a state of mind and social conditioning. In this regard, every woman can play a significant role in the industrial world ranging from the cottage and home industry to the global market. They can efficiently prove their skills in economic empowerment in the field of handicraft, food industry, bangle-making, knitting and designs, jute industry, traditional embroidery, pottery making, garment manufacturing, colouring, flower arrangement, preparation of clothes, candle manufacturing, preparing milk products, pickle making and so many other creative activities. In these fields, they can prove themselves to be the carriers of inspiration and skill development for others. Though the fact is to be accepted that professional skills are not gender specific, it is evident that in these areas, they can contribute to the programme of making a skilled India. It will essentially provide them the skill of work, inspiration, confidence, realisation of responsibility, opportunity for self-affirmation and social work. The dream of Atmanirbhar Bharat can successfully be carried out when women are motivated enough to convert their hidden potential in economic resources to ensure security for their family and enhance the quality of their lifestyle.

Economic independence is the basis of Atmanirbhar Bharat because economic independence ensures mental freedom to make choices and the affirmation of self-chosen ideology. It is a fact universally acknowledged that women due to their restrictions to economic sources are far beyond the concept of freedom, dignity and affirmation of choices. Economic independence can help women to acquire self-sustenance and self-equipped lifestyle for generating the sources of economy. It is therefore that Prime Minister Narendra Modi used the phrase Atmanirbhar Bharat for national security and sustainable development. Economic independence of women is the primal force to ensure gender equality and break the snares of male domination. With their emergence in the economic power structure, the women can ensure spaces for themselves and side by side exercise their hold on economic resources, gradually contributing to the economic power structure at the national level. Organised planning and strategic management are required to organise the small-scale industry to provide a platform to women to utilise their knowledge, skill, strategy and resources to give a required direction in production. The contribution of women in the manufacturing field can yield fruitful results to prepare an economic structure required to meet the demands of Indian citizens and own self-generated sources. It will reduce the production cost and be of immense use for the weaker sections of the society. The skill economy controlled by women will move Indian society in the direction of self-reliance. The idea of producing through *charkha* as suggested by Mahatma Gandhi can be taken as a manifestation of women's skill and inspire them to work in the direction of self-reliance. With the emerging concept of self-reliance, women can move in the direction of self-affirmation and make space for themselves in their social life. Silence, subjugation and non- or passive resistance, tolerance have been common predicaments of women. Women with the new awakening of their human identity will support their compatriots from the marginalised community to construct the fabric of their own life. It will help them to assert their choices in the selection of skills for promoting the resources for economic independence. It can safely be asserted that the realisation of creative impulse operates as a mechanism to strengthen the will of women to seek space in the social and national order. The real cult of self-reliance can be promoted with the strengthening of the will of affirmation and in this process, women can play a significant role to emancipate society from the psyche of subjugation and decolonise female sensibility from the stress of patriarchal framework. In this regard efforts of women can be instrumental in realising the mission of Atmanirbhar Bharat and with active participation, women will contribute as responsible citizens of an enlightened society.

The concept of Atmanirbhar Bharat is not the negation of existing social order but is a declaration of the possibility of introducing a new dimension of thinking. It is for this reason that the government has encouraged the policy of private and public participation in several schemes for the easy access of both men and women. These schemes are MSME, agriculture, food industry, textile industry, sSkilled India, health sector and so on. The participation of women in economic affairs will open the window to modify the resources essential for independent access of women to financial resources. With the availability of funds, women can carve out strategies to open new manufacturing units or generate small-scale industrial units. The fact is to be accepted that there should be adequate guidance for availing the funds and to utilise them in an appropriate manner to establish their professional identity and seek an outlet for their latent skills.

To fulfil the mission of the Atmanirbhar Bharat the role of women can be of paramount importance in different domains like education, industry, defence, skill development and planning of national development. Women have witnessed the tortures of subjugation in the absence of appropriate education. Women can attain independent space with a relentless quest for education to redeem the pain of illiteracy and ignorance. Education leads to enlightenment and their enlightenment will strengthen their will to participate in the social and national fabric. Proficiency in education will inculcate the required skill to participate in the industrial world. In context of women's 'self', the concept '*atm*' includes the betterment of the family paradigm beyond all conventions. With the cosmic realisation of *atma*, women will inevitably move in the direction of self-growth beyond the restrictions imposed by the patriarchal authority. The liberation of spirit through the impact of education will motivate them to learn the desired skills to earn their bread and butter.

The post-COVID period has promoted the concept of the participation of women in private companies and the corporate world to explore more and more possibilities for their economic growth, growth in the industrial world and the subsequent contribution to the national economy. Gradually, with the call for self-reliant India, the differences are disappearing fast in a holistic perception of life conditions. Women are being inspired to be more and more familiar with the technological advances for their freedom and independence. Their exposure to information technology is wide and deep and consequently large groups of female technocrats are emerging and who are running their own businesses and sharing more and more space in the industrial world. Such a transformation of women's role is widening the horizon for the participation of women in the national growth. The journey of women from the kitchen to the computer has made a radical transformation in the position of women as well as in the economic field. Consequently economy is moving from a state of local economy to national economy. The familiarity with the challenges of information society has made women independent and increased their participation in the corporate world. Women can play a vital role as frontline warriors in strengthening the physical and mental resources of rural women who live in the darkness of ignorance and remain unaware of their position in the family and in the society. In the absence of the will to be self-reliant, they are unable to live as responsible human beings. They survive amid the dark shadows of illiteracy and poverty without realising their skills, knowledge and the significance of a respectable life. Within the cocoon of domesticity, their life becomes a burden and they waste their time and energy in the responsibilities that are no longer respected or acknowledged in the socio-political system operating in the nation. It is a high time when there should be extensive awareness programmes for women to strengthen their will for breaking the bonds of sexual colonialism. It will not be out of place to mention that self-awareness programmes can have a far-reaching effect in inculcating the spirit of self-reliance among women.

References

1. Ralph, W. Emerson, *Essays*, First and Second Series, Eurasia Publishing House (P) Ltd., New Delhi, 1965.
2. Tagore, Rabindranath, *Towards Universal Man*, Bombay: Asia, 1961.

□

8

Girl Child's Education: Reflection on Last Few Decades, Current Trends and Future Outlook

—Ms. Ruby

"When women are educated, their countries become stronger and more prosperous."

—Michelle Obama

One of the vivid memories I have of my childhood is the celebration of Independence Day in a small city of Jharkhand. It used to be quite a well-planned event where a few of the senior boys from the colony would help us prepare to sing the national anthem. Another highlight of the event was a small speech by the 'Didi' of our colony. She used to deliver her speech after her father had made a speech. The pride and sense of achievement used to be evident on this uncle's face. A daughter standing up and delivering a speech on the country, its past and future was indeed a proud achievement. It wasn't a usual scene since most of the girls were groomed to prepare for their wedding! This was indeed a ceiling-breaker!

Those were the days, in the early 1990s! Only a handful of parents were willing to put in any extra effort to get their daughters educated. In most families, the prime purpose of a daughter's education was to make them worthy of finding a respectable groom. While there would be many eligible boys employed in government jobs orundergoing some professional course, the number of girls with similar credentials were very far and few.

However, there were a few families who were able to think ahead of time and against the popular approach of mostly providing girls with basic education. They were striving for more. It was mostly driven by an extraordinary girl child putting extraordinary effort and parents willing to give their best to such gifted ones. However, those were very rare stories we got to hear as a kid, especially about a girl child.

If I reflect on my own case, the unwavering support and guidance I received from my parents, my siblings and a few of the God-sent teachers, it was something not everyone received around me at that time. Studying in a government school where we spent one whole year without the maths teacher, where English was optional and out of a whole class of more than 200 girls, now if I reflect only 10 could go till graduation/post-graduation and make some difference in their lives. The quality of education was not delivered to create a solid future for the kid or for that matter for the nation, especially if kids were studying in government schools.

After school while preparing for professional courses, like medical or engineering, I realised that not only did I miss out on a language which is basic for all future opportunities (in India or abroad) but the kind of syllabus which was followed in the government school was quite inferior as compared to what was being taught in private schools. The chasm which I had to cover to finally crack the engineering entrance exam in a national-level college and post-graduate exam in one of the best MBA institutes in India, still feels quite overwhelming.

Today I see things are a bit better for girls in India since parents have realised the importance of education, self-reliance and a career. The percentage of girls going to higher education or professional courses is much higher. But unfortunately, it is still a matter of parents walking the extra mile to support their little ones. It has not been systematised in a way that everyone in India gets quality education which can help them to be valuable at national/international platforms. It is still a family choice and circumstances.

Growing up or even in professional life, while many looked up at me as a source of inspiration and support, I had my own challenges to face. Though my experiences in school/college time were filled with extraordinary teachers walking extra miles to help me get what I needed to move ahead, sometimes I feel there is so much more we can do to make things better for our next generation, especially in the field of education and in the job sector.

If it's a matter of education and support for a girl child, setting up an infrastructure where she is not only receiving quality education but also getting enough support while navigating through different stages of life, such as childbirth, child care, etc., it is of paramount importance to have a well-rounded education system and supporting government policies to ensure she gets a fair chance to reach her full potential throughout her life span.

In the coming sections, I will take you through some facts, issues and possible solutions I think that can help us provide holistic support to our next generation, especially girls.

State of Education in Government Schools – The Foundation Needs Work!

Education, when tailored toh a country's vision, becomes a catalyst for the nation's development, for a large segment of the population, government schools serve as the primary source of education and can be extremely important in guiding the country towards its goals.

There are a few countries we can look at in order to understand why the government-run schools and programmes are considered best in those respective countries. We can learn from Singapore where the government spends a major portion of the budget on government schools that it is the most preferred school system in the country. Similarly in Germany, multiple course options are available as coupled with vocational training which can train students for real-world jobs and help them become more deployable.

In India as well, to bridge the gap between education and national needs, we have to change the educational curriculum strategically. For example, if India wants to become a centre for the manufacturing or service industries, then changing the curriculum to include the necessary skills will guarantee that students have the knowledge and abilities to make significant contributions in these fields. Vocational education and training must be prioritised, according to the most recent *UNESCO State of the Education Report*. The main advantage of vocational education in India is that it equips students with the information and abilities needed to thrive in their chosen field and gets them prepared to face the demands and obstacles that arise when finding a suitable job.

Not only skill-focused courses should be introduced, also linguistic diversity is appreciated in a country like India, due to globalisation. English has been an important factor in both individual and national development, starting with employability, where a lot of jobs across the globe require proficiency in English. A nation with its population proficient in English, enhances its competitiveness in the global market and also helps in the overall cultural exchange and global communication for the nation.

Along with the language, instead of focusing on mere introductory information of the courses, a holistic approach should be adopted, which includes webinars, interactive way of teaching for different types of learners, including digital e-learning platforms which might not just add to the already given knowledge of the government teachers, but also introduce digital learning in the lives of students, who might not be very comfortable with electronic gadgets, which are now used in a lot of competitive examinations, both national and international.

Providing the basic knowledge of computers and internet gives an added advantage to the overall education of students, who might benefit from not just the internet, later on in life, but also become more employable in the future due to the booming tech industry.

The infrastructure and foundation that the country needs today can only be achieved with a progressive vision and focus which India is experiencing since the past few years. As an NRI living outside India, I can clearly see the potential the country has and the heights it can reach with the right leadership.

Teachers – The Unsung Future Creators!

"Teachers, I believe, are the most responsible and important members of society because their professional efforts affect the fate of the earth"

—Helen Caldicott

"A teacher affects eternity; he can never tell where his influence stops"

—Henry Adams

A profession which is the backbone of any country or human race is still undervalued and deficient in government support and care. Everyone acknowledges the contribution of teachers and the kind of influence they have in nation building, but still, so much has to be done to equip them to be the frontrunner in the nation's success story.

It is very important to provide them with the necessary training on the diverse ways of teaching, the essential digital training and literacy, along with conducting workshops and seminars where teachers can participate and actively learn. Including this in the beginning of their joining and continuing it throughout their job period helps to create a good environment from the early stages.

Along with the intrinsic motivation, we need to give these teachers the necessary incentives and salaries for them to be encouraged to work enough, teachers can form the basic building blocks of education for a child. The need for them to be motivated enough has to come into the picture. Teachers are not only responsible for educating the students, a massive part of their motivation and personality development comes from schools in which they are employed for long. Giving them financial rewards, in terms of merit-based pay or performance bonus, or giving them recognition in terms of awards at the state or national level, forming a hierarchy of teachers in the school and promoting and giving them pay hikes with respect to their contribution, will motivate them to strive for better. Intrinsic and material motivation helps teachers to be better at their jobs and contribute more than they were already contributing.

The teaching profession in India is not considered to be as rewarding as that of engineers or doctors. By making this profession lucrative in terms of pay and work-life balance will attract the youth to work hard towards finding a job in this sector, as they are the ones who build and form the reputation of the school and can affect the quality of education imparted to the students. Giving a substantial amount as salary works as an incentive to do still better by those who are already in this profession and help attract talent from different parts of the country.

Government Policies – Long Overdue

The Beti Bachao, Beti Padhao (BBBP) scheme was launched on January 22, 2015 by Prime Minister Narendra Modi.[5][6] It aims to address the issue of the declining child sex ratio (CSR) and is a national initiative jointly run by the Ministry of Women and Child Development, the Ministry of Health and Family Welfare and the Ministry of Education. The Comptroller and Auditor General of India (CAG) reported that the scheme had failed to meet its objectives. As per the CAG data, the sex ratio has deteriorated in many districts of Haryana and Punjab. [9]In 2021, in Lok Sabha, according to the Parliamentary Committee on the Empowerment of Women, 78.91% funds for 'Beti Bachao Beti Padhao' were spent on ads.

This scheme is a good example of how only good intentions may not be good enough. Good vision coupled with meticulous understanding of grassroot levers can help to address the problem. A thorough understanding of what helps a family to send a girl child to school instead of sending her to take up labour at building sites is essential. What is the reason for not sending a girl child to school? Addressing such an issue and implementing these plans with clear accountability and authority of local bodies might move the needle.

Also, it's crucial to understand that sending them to school is only a very first step. We need a well-woven plan to encourage these school-going girls to complete their school education at least. For this, policies should be comprehensive enough to cover the lifecycle of a girl child. Here are few areas where the government can work to support girl education/empowerment in India:

1. The government should begin with enforcing and incentivising policies to make education compulsory for children in general, and giving financial assistance, tax deduction, stipends and scholarships to girl students and their family, safe means of transport for the parents to feel secure and make them realise the importance the government is giving to every girl child.
2. We often come across cases where girls initially enrol in schools, but leave it on reaching higher classes because of the hefty fees required for them to study at good institutes, or because they get married off or for other various reasons. Girls should be encouraged to go in for higher education where they are confident of being mentored by other successful women in their respective fields. Reservation of seats can be given to women, so as to encourage them to take part actively in this field.
3. Policies to support women returning to work post-childbirth or career break due to any other reason can be introduced by the government so that private companies and corporate houses maintain a fixed percentage of career options for such women who are not discriminated against when they return to their careers.
4. Policies to support flexible work responsibilities and hours for women to balance their work and home-related responsibilities.
5. Campaigns to eradicate stigma attached to women and the choices they make should be launched so that they are not harassed or mistreated at their workplace.

Support Network – Women for Women!

In a country where it's difficult to inspire girls to attend school, a few may manage to overcome all the hurdles and find a professional career though they may be completely unprepared and unsupported for the curveballs life throws on them! Be it childbirth, childcare breaks, there is no or limited support for women returning to work post-career break.

The government can design an infrastructure to support women returning back to work by placing either a proper support system for kids (subsidised preschools like what we find in New Zealand) or provide them with options to come back to work with flexible work and work hours post-career break.

What happens at home also plays a major role in the narrative we want to set for women. Today we want our daughters to succeed and get educated, but seldom treat them with respect at home. The daughter sees how married women are treated at home and resigns herself to her fate in the future. Change begins at home. Men must shoulder the household responsibilities to ensure that so-called gender-specific duties are demolished and women get a fair chance to do what they desire. This is not just to teach the next generation, but also to unlearn the generational curses which have been going on for years and which need to be changed.

Also, in schools and workplaces proper structures should be in place to support women who can then form a network of women engaged in a similar work field and interact with and motivate each other. Such networks should be formed and actively encouraged so that the woman who is facing some problem at her workplace or the girl is confronting in her school does not feel isolated or helpless but receives the necessary healthy feedback by like-minded women.

References

- https://asancup.in/blogs/blogs/how-many-girls-miss-school-due-to-periods
- Beti Bachao Beti Padhao - Wikipedia

□

9

Viksit Bharat and Role of Women in Science

—Dr. Poonam Mehta

Women and men play equally important roles in a society, including the Indian context that will be described in the present article. True *aatma nirbharta* or self-reliance can be achieved when all sections of the society are able to contribute their best in life. The first step towards this is to practice gender equality in any profession by engaging both men and women. While women have been encouraged to take up science as a course of study, it is a known fact that at the professional level, there is a sharp decline. The presence of women students in schools and colleges is high and their level of achievement is also high.

However, participation of women in scientific research is miniscule. The fraction of women who have done Ph.D. in physics and are employed in higher education in India is about 20 per cent, which is very skewed. The important positions in academics also have a very low number of women, but, the fraction in elite institutions, leadership positions and in honour lists plummets much further. The fraction of women scientists to win prestigious awards is woefully low. For instance, if we take the case of Shanti Swarup Bhatnagar Award in Physics discipline, there were only male recipients until 2018. Note that this award was initiated way back in 1958.

Thus, there are very serious leakages in the pipeline from college to university to scientific careers. There can be many reasons for this – marriagable age, the child-bearing age or any of the socially-induced circumstances, which are beyond the control of any individual.

Unfortunately, it is a fact that science (and physics, in particular) is a highly gendered (male-dominated) profession. Traditionally, our society prescribes certain kinds of roles for women and more specifically so in the case of academia. While some fields, such as life sciences and medical sciences, attract a large number of women, it is certainly not the case in pure science disciplines, such as physics and mathematics.

The Government of India along with the Indian Physics Association as well as science academies have taken due cognisance of this issue and launched several programmes to mitigate gender disparity in science and engineering research funding in various science and technology programmes in Indian academic institutions and Research & Development laboratories. Some of these include:

1. Establishment of Chairs by Ministry of Women and Child Development in 2020 named after eminent women in universities aimed to motivate young girls and women towards higher studies.
2. Science Education Research Board (SERB) Women Excellence Award is a one-time award given to women scientists below 40 years of age and who have received recognition, such as Young Scientist Medal, Young Associate, etc. from any one or more of the national academies.
3. SERB – POWER (Promoting Opportunities for Women in Exploratory Research) programme is formulated to mitigate gender disparity in science and engineering research funding in various science and technology programmes in Indian academic institutions and Research and Development laboratories. SERB – POWER is specially designed to provide structured effort towards enhanced diversity in research to ensure equal access and weighted opportunities for Indian women scientists engaged in research and development activities.

4. Department of Science and Technology (DST) has restructured all the women-specific programmes under one umbrella, known as KIRAN (Knowledge Involvement in Research Advancement through Nurturing). KIRAN addresses issues related to women scientists (e.g. unemployment, relocation, etc.) and aims to provide opportunities in research, technology development/ demonstration and self-employment.
5. DST, Government of India and Indo-US Science & Technology Forum (IUSSTF) jointly announced the Indo-U.S. Fellowship for Women in STEMM (WISTEMM) programme which is envisaged to provide opportunities to bright Indian women students and scientists to gain exposure and access to world-class research facilities in Amrican academia and labs.
6. Vigyan Jyoti – DST launched this as a dedicated programme for girl students to pursue their careers in science, engineering and technology. The programme aims to encourage and inspire girl students to pursue higher education and become self-reliant and also offers exposure to girl students coming from the rural background to help understand how to plan their journey from school to college and thereafter from research to a job of their choice in the field of science.
7. Vigyan Vidushi (VV) – a three-week summer school for women students, at the end of their M.Sc. first-year in physics will provide them exposure to advanced physics topics and research opportunities and encourage them to take up research in physics as a career option. The students in this programme will also get an opportunity to be taught, inspired and mentored by eminent women-scientist role models.
8. Lilavati's daughters is a collection of essays on women scientists of India. Lilavati is the 12th century treatise in which the mathematician Bhaskaracharya addresses a number of problems to his daughter, Lilavati. Although

legend has it that Lilavati never married, her intellectual legacy lives on in the form of her daughters – the women scientists of India.

In what follows, we narrate the journey of two female scientists who achieved some level of distinction in their respective careers – one from the pre-Independence era, working in the field of high energy physics and one from the present era who is the first female Shanti Swarup Bhatnagar awardee pursuing active research in the field of quantum information which is believed to be the future of science and technology in the present epoch. They have been able to achieve their goals in the Indian social and academic environment and thus serve as role models for young girls aspiring to be physicists.

Bibha Chowdhuri (1913-1991)

Bibha was born in Kolkata at a time (1913) when higher studies in science in India was still in infancy. She has many firsts to her credit. She was the first woman high-energy physicist of India and the first woman to be appointed as a scientist at the Tata Institute of Fundamental Research (TIFR). She (with Prof. D.M. Bose) was the first to measure the mass of meson using nuclear emulsion, while working at the Bose Institute. This formed the basis of Nobel Prize-winning work of Powell.

Bibha's name was largely forgotten (she was missed in the collection of essays, called *Lilavati's Daughters: The Women Scientists of India*) but thanks to the following recognitions that came very recently (decades after her demise in 1991).

- The first one was by the International Astronomical Union (IAU) whichnamed a star 'Bibha' after her name in December 2019.
- Soon, after, in March 2020, the Ministry of Woman and Child Development, Government of India established 11

chairs after renowned Indian women scientists and the Physics Chair was in the name of Bibha Chowdhuri.

We give a glimpse into the life of Bibha based on an outstanding work by Rajinder Singh and S.C. Roy, who brought back this marvellous talent and inspirational character to the young generations [1, 2].

Bibha studied physics at the Rajabazar Science College of Calcutta University and was the only woman to complete M.Sc. in the year 1936. She joined the Bose Institute after graduating in 1939 and worked with Prof. D.M. Bose. Together, they experimentally observed muons and cosmic rays and published it in *Nature*. Seven years after this discovery of mesons by D.M. Bose and Bibha Chowdhuri, C.F. Powell made the same discovery of pions and muons and further decay of muons to electrons using the same technique as was used by D.M. Bose and Bibha Chowdhuri and won the Nobel Prize.

Bibha left Bose Institute and joined the cosmic ray research laboratory of Prof. P. M. S. Blackett at the University of Manchester in 1945. BC started working on the extensive air showers in cosmic rays at Manchester.

Bibha joined the TIFR in 1949 and was there till 1957 or so. After leaving TIFR, she spent a year abroad and then spent several years at Physical Research Laboratory, Ahmedabad before going back to Kolkata.

Bibha is an icon of inspiration, not only for women aspiring in science, but to anyone in this world, who chooses to fight against the odds in societies and aspires to walk a different path.

Aditi Sen De

Aditi is a professor at the Harish Chandra Research Institute (HRI), Prayagraj. Before joining HRI, she worked for a brief period as an Assistant Professor in the School of Physical Sciences, Jawaharlal Nehru University. Her work is on quantum technologies.

She became the first woman recipient of the prestigious Shanti Swarup Bhatnagar prize in Physics in 2018 and even though the prize was instituted in the year 1958, it took many years to recognise the worth of a female physicist to be awarded this prize. Very recently in 2024, she became the first woman scientist to win the G.D. Birla award.

We give a glimpse into the life of Aditi below [3]. After completing her M. Sc. from the University of Calcutta, she moved to Gdansk, a city in northern Poland, for pursuing her Ph.D. in physics. Her guide, a renowned physicist, Prof. Marek Zukowski, worked on foundations of quantum mechanics and quantum optics. During that period, she was the only female Ph.D. student in the Institute of Theoretical Physics and Astrophysics, University of Gdansk.

She then went to Leibniz University, Hannover as an Alexander von Humboldt postdoctoral fellow in the group of Prof. Maciej Lewenstein. The group had 22 members including two senior scientists. Interestingly, both of them were women and were quite well known in the field. It was extremely beneficial for Aditi to grow there as a scientist.

After that, she joined ICFO, the Institute of Photonic Sciences with Maciej Lewenstein where she stayed for the next four years. During the last two years there, she became a Ramon-y-Cajal fellow (a five-year tenure track position) from the Spanish Ministry of Science and Innovation and during that period, she got a chance to work independently. Coincidentally, she supervised one female Ph.D. student along with Prof. M. Lewenstein.

After she joined HRI, they (along with Prof. Arun K. Pati and Prof. Ujjwal Sen) started the group of Quantum Information and Computation. Since she had worked in a big group, her dream was to establish a group in her field in India. During her Ph.D. and postdoctoral periods, she had collaborated extensively with several scientists, many of whom were famous and established in her field.

When she was looking for a job, she had to face questions like the amount of contribution made in her works, the overall understanding of the subject, etc. These are common questions, but she felt on several occasions, during the interview or colloquia, the questions were asked under the assumptions that she surely would not able to answer. Thankfully, when people got a chance to extensively interact with her including her supervisor, her collaborators, they became confident about her capabilities. It was also asked whether she would be able to manage time between research work and family. Such questions were typically not asked of male applicants. Before she started teaching at HRI, students were also not sure about her knowledge. For example, she had not got any Ph.D. student before she started teaching the courses. When she got a chance to teach, students started coming to her, interacted, discussed and were convinced of her abilities.

Although she faced a lot of negative criticism, she always concentrated on the learning process, enjoyed her research and tried to be as sincere as possible in her research activities and other duties. On the other hand, she took positive criticisms seriously and thishelped her to improve as a human being and as a scientist. She always felt that she had to work much harder to establish herself than her contemporary male colleagues.

Towards gaining confidence in herself, she felt that that had to acknowledge the contributions of several female faculties in India and abroad – she had heard a lot of stories about what they had faced in their career and how they ignored those to go ahead in their career. Such discussions helped her enormously to develop herself. At the same time, she was really happy that in her life, she met several male colleagues and senior scientists who were also eager to discuss the problems that she had been facing and offered their possible solutions. She has seen people who have judged her without interacting with her or knowing her properly. Such a set of people continue to exist. She believes that if she ignores such comments and works hard with sincerity, the works, whether scientific or any other, can give her satisfaction.

The number of female Ph.D. students, postdoctoral fellows, faculties are quite low in number in physics as well as in many other fields. Due to the terribly low female participation in research as well as in institutes/universities, in any gatherings/conferences, people made several discriminatory comments, even unknowingly.

Archetypal discussions about women in the workplace, like women are good at cooking, in arts, in raising children, should be strongly discouraged. While designing certain academic or non-academic programmes, authorities tend to forget that women may also want to participate. In the case of responsible duties, it is typically assumed that women are not capable of doing them. She thinks that spreading awareness about these issues in society, including in the scientific community, is extremely important. The efforts like seminars, discussions, advertisements in media as well as on social platforms about the problems that women face, the possible ways to overcome them are an important step towards making everyone alert. Similarly, conference organisers should consciously take care of the ratio of female speakers/chairs/participants with their male counterparts in conferences. It can be made compulsory that while writing academic reports in institutes, in funding agencies, each enstitute or individual should make a list of the efforts that each has made to increase consciousness, to increase the ratio between male and female participation in conferences, etc. and proper weightage should be given during the evaluation of the projects. Finally, facilities like day-care centres close to the main workplace in all the institutes should be made compulsory which may help female students/ scientists to continue their research career.

References

1. Roy, Suprakash C. and Singh, Rajinder, *Indian Journal of History of Science*, 53.3, 2018, 356-373.
2. Singh, Rajinder and Roy, Suprakash C. (2018-08-30), *A Jewel Unearthed: Bibha Chowdhuri: The Story of an Indian Woman Scientist.*
3. Prof. Aditi Sen De, private communication.

□

10

Women Empowerment—Growing Economy

—Dr. N. Lavanya

Women empowerment can be defined as promoting women's feelings of self-esteem, their ability to determine their own choices and their right to influence social change for themselves and others. Empowering women gives them more authority and control over their own life. The advancement of women's status in politics, society, economy and health is essential and it is crucial for achieving sustainable development. Women's empowerment is a controversial issue in India. Women constitute about 50 per cent of the world's population but India shows an unequal sex ratio, resulting in a relatively low female population compared to males. Even though their social status is concerned, they are not considered equal to men and gender barriers and discrimination are constantly found in the society.

The state of women's empowerment in India is considered in various aspects, such as women's household decision-making authority, financial empowerment and dependency on information from various sources, factors including autonomy, freedom of mobility, political engagement, acceptance of an uneven gender role, media exposure, access to education, knowledge of domestic violence, etc. The Indian government has made several attempts to empower women since Independence. Women's empowerment initiatives have received more popularity throughout several plan periods. Today, the use of sports and physical activity as a strategy for the empowerment of women and girls is gaining popularity on a global scale.

Government Initiatives

Over the past few decades, women professionals have worked enormously with their talent, dedication and enthusiasm. They have contributed massively towards India's economic growth and prosperity. At present, there are 432 million women of working age in India, out of which 343 million are employed in the unorganised sector. In rural India, women have been achieving new milestones despite their social and familial exclusion. Women have asserted their right to financial independence, built businesses from scratch and inspired many among their neighbourhood. In the *panchayat* system, 50 per cent reservation is offered to women while many national programmes, such as the National Rural Livelihood Mission, are providing leadership opportunities to them at the grassroots level. Initiatives like 'Swachh Bharat Mission' and 'Mahatma Gandhi National Rural Employment Guarantee Act' have provided women workforce with supervisory job opportunities.

In terms of start-ups, India is the third largest ecosystem in the world and the third largest in the Unicorn community. However, only 10 per cent of them have been led by women founders. The need of the hour is to mobilise more support – mental and financial – for women entrepreneurs and help them to kick start their journey. Fortunately, the last few years have seen a paradigm shift in the entire process of women becoming business leaders and founding companies. Women's economic empowerment is highly connected with poverty reduction as women also tend to invest more of their earnings in their children and communities.

The World Bank ensures that its projects are structured to foster greater economic participation by women. For example, we have invested over $3 billion over the past 15 years to support state governments to empower poor rural women through self-help groups. These projects have supported 45 million poor women access skills, markets and business development services. Some of them have become successful entrepreneurs and inspiration for others. As a result, evidence shows that these women experience greater food security, better access to finance and higher incomes that benefit their families and communities.

The Skill India Mission, not only provides women relevant skills sought by employers, but it also ensures that training programmes are sensitive to their needs by helping to provide safe transport, flexible schedules and childcare support. In Jharkhand, the World Bank is investing in adolescent girls to help them complete their secondary education and providing mentoring services for them to succeed in the job market. The government has organised various programmes for skills development, subsidised loans for businesses led by women and recent legislation doubling maternity leave and requiring childcare facilities in companies that employ more than 50 people. If implemented and respected, these policies could remove some of the barriers women face and offer a significant boost to India's economy.

Major Issues in Women Empowerment in Economic Development

The way to enhance women's economic empowerment is not just by increasing female employment opportunities, but also by reducing the double-shift burden women face. There is a need for adoption of the 3 Rs. approach, which involves Recognising, Reducing and Redistributing the unpaid care work done by women in all areas of policymaking. This can be done by facilitating women's work as investment in public-sector care infrastructure. Public investment of just 2 per cent of India's GDP in the care economy could not only generate 11 million jobs, but could also increase women's economic and social welfare as they venture out into formal work. It is pivotal to have women-centric and women-friendly policies in place with the aim to encourage and support women entrepreneurship in India. There is also an urgent need to ensure that significant interventions take place to provide easier access to banks and other financial institutions, as well as tax incentives.

The problem is to ensure that women have the same access to these opportunities as men. But once women enter and have the chance to show their skill and knowledge, the impact is obvious through economic development by the empowerment of women. Women are not less capable than men but they need more encouragement and opportunities from the families and societies due to:

1. Economic backwardness
2. Implementation gaps
3. Lack of political will
4. Women as unpaid family workers in subsistence
5. Agriculture
6. Low level of technology and primitive farming practices
7. Poor access to credit and marketing networks
8. Social and cultural barriers, such as executive capacity for household work restricts mobility, etc.

When overcoming these constraints, the country's economy and global economic development will prosper through an enactment which encourages the womean's role in different fields of the economy.

Despite their overall low labour force participation, certain fields and occupations employ many women and in some cases, more women than men. Agriculture is the most common employer of working women, with approximately 55.6 million women (about twice the population of Texas) work in agriculture in rural areas alone. Next most common is manufacturing of textiles, food and other products, which is a significant employer of women in both rural and urban areas. Women are also frequently employed in construction work across both geographies. Other common fields employing women across urban and rural areas in the service sector include education, retail trade and home-based services. The Government of India has worked to implement gender-sensitive policies in certain industries and occupations to increase gender parity. Primarily, these have worked through quotas. The sectors in which there are quotas and women have relatively high participation.

Conclusion

Women's empowerment and economic development are closely interrelated. While development itself will bring about women's empowerment, empowering women will bring about changes in decision-making, which will have a direct impact on development. Contrary to what is claimed by some of the more optimistic policy makers, it is, however, not clear that a one-time inclusion of women's rights will spark a virtuous circle, with women's empowerment and development mutually reinforcing each other and with women eventually being equal partners in richer societies. On the one hand, economic development alone is insufficient to ensure significant progress in important dimensions of women's empowerment; in particular, significant progress in decision-making ability in the face of pervasive stereotypes against women's ability. On the other hand, women's empowerment leads to improvement in some aspects of children's welfare (health and nutrition, in particular) but at the expense of some others (education). Women play a substantial role in the economy of India and their contribution must be recognised with full appreciation. Women must be empowered and facilitated so that their productivity gets increased. Equity between men and women is only likely to be achieved by continuing policy actions that favour women at the expense of men, possibly for a very long time. While this may result in some collateral benefits, the benefits may or may not be sufficient to compensate the cost of the distortions associated with such redistribution. This measure of realism needs to temper the positions of policy makers on both sides of the development/empowerment debate.

As the examples and anecdotes show, success will hinge on collaboration between stakeholders, ranging from government ministries to education providers, to public sector and especially private sector employers down to the actions of each of us. In the end, Indian women themselves will have to play a key role in claiming space for themselves in India's workforce. Let's pledge together to increase women's participation in the workforce and realise a higher level of growth and development for India that is more inclusive and sustainable.

References

1. https://www.ciiblog.in/the-role-of-women-in-indias-economic-growth-story/
2. Kirti Shrinivas, 'Role of Women Empowerment in Economic Growth in India', *International Journal of Recent Trends in Engineering and Research*, Vol. 2, No. 11, 2016, pp. 177-179.
3. Gupta, R. and Gupta, B.K., 'Role of Women in Economic Development', *Yojana*, Vol. 31, No. 18, 1987, pp. 28-32.
4. A Study on Role of Women in Economic Development in India, Angala Eswari, .G. Shanlax, *International Journal of Economics*, Vol. 7, No. 4, 2019, pp. 41-48.

□

11
Advancements in Women's Health: From Medical Breakthroughs to Empowerment Initiatives

—Dr. Kalpana Dubey

"You can tell the condition of a nation by looking at the status of its women."

—Jawaharlal Nehru

Introduction

Women play a significant role in the nation's all-round socio-economic development as women's empowerment results in the empowerment of the family and society. Women's health is one of the prime concerns of the world. As per the World Health Organisation (WHO), health is a state of complete physical, mental and social well-being and not merely the absence of disease or infirmity. Since the Declaration of Alma Ata at the International Conference on Primary Health Care in 1978, great emphasis continues to be laid on protecting and promoting the health of humankind. The national health policy accords high priority to maternal health programmes. Recently, women's health issues have been addressed by various government and non-government organisations. Significantly, women's health is affected not only by biological factors but also by various socio-economic conditions.

Healthcare infrastructure is pivotal in shaping women's empowerment, serving as a cornerstone for individual well-being and societal progress. In the global pursuit of gender equality, addressing and fortifying healthcare systems to meet the unique needs of women is not just a matter of health equity but a crucial component of women's empowerment. This essay explores the intricate relationship between healthcare infrastructure and women's empowerment, delving into key impact areas, challenges and opportunities for fostering positive change.

In the ever-changing landscape of healthcare, the attitudes towards women's physical and mental health have undergone significant transformations over the years. From historical disparities to the present-day emphasis on holistic well-being, societal perspectives have evolved, reflecting a deeper understanding of the complex interplay between physical and mental health.

Historical Perspectives

Historically, women's health was often overlooked or misunderstood, with societal norms relegating them to specific roles and expectations. Limited access to education and healthcare compounded the challenges, leading to a lack of understanding of women's unique health needs. The stigma surrounding women's reproductive health, menstruation and mental health further perpetuated misconceptions, hindering open discussions and comprehensive healthcare approaches.

Women's Health in India

Post-Independence, there was no significant change in women's lives in India. Female infanticide was prevalent and the ratio of girls to boys dwindled. Although India is one of the few countries where males and females have similar life expectancy at birth, the same typical female advantage in life expectancy is not observed later. Women still have high mortality rates, particularly during their childhood and pregnancy. Education for a girl child remains optional. Apart from the biological factors associated with female gender, the women's health is also determined by social, cultural and politico-economic inequalities.

Unfortunately, women's health in India is inherently linked to their social status and cultural norms. Illiteracy, forced early marriage, poor maternal care, poverty, unemployment, hard physical labour, low wages, family responsibilities, domestic violence, gender discrimination at the workplace and inadequate access to healthcare facilities are essential determinants that exert a negative impact on the health status of women in India. India ranks very low in the Global Gender Gap Index and the gender-related health concerns, in turn, manifest in demographic, nutritional, educational and other indicators. Multiple pregnancies and closely spaced births erode the maternal nutritional status, leading to premature birth and low birth-weight infants. Although the overall fertility rate and low birth-weight babies continue to decline as per the Indian National Family Health Surveys (NHS-1, NFHS-2 and NFHS-3), the unsafe termination of unwanted pregnancies negatively impacts women's health.

Major Women's Health Issues

In biological terms, women are different from men and undergo dramatic mental and physical changes as their reproductive system goes through significant changes. Specific health issues are unique to them and deserve special consideration. Despite the progress of our country in every field over the last few years, women's healthcare in India still needs to be addressed. The maternal mortality ratio (MMR) is defined as number of maternal deaths per 100,000 live births during a given time period. Although the MMR in India has declined from 113 in 2016-18 to 97 in 2018-20, certain states, such as Rajasthan, Uttar Pradesh, Madhya Pradesh, Chhattisgarh, Bihar, Odisha and Assam, have very high MMR. Majority of maternal deaths are preventable in nature. Likewise, carcinoma of breast and cervix are the most common malignancies in Indian women. Women are uncomfortable in expressing their reproductive health issues due to the social stigmas around them. Hence, access to quality healthcare and ability to make informed decisions about one's health are fundamental rights that every woman should invariably avail. However, numerous constraints exist that deter women's well-being, including gender-sensitive familial and societal discrimination and poor access to healthcare facilities.

Many factors affect women's health and well-being. Some are physical and social, such as our relationship, work and environment; then there are psychological factors, such as our thoughts, emotions and stress levels. All these factors play a role in our overall health and well-being. We cannot control all of them, but we can influence some. Key factors that affect women's health and well-being are social and economic disparities, gender-based violence and discrimination, lack of access to healthcare, lack of education and poor nutrition can all have an effect. To improve women's health, we must address certain factors.

Essential Factors Affecting Women's Health

1. *Social and Economic Factors*: Socio-economic factors are vital to women's health and well-being. Women on low incomes are more likely to lack access to necessities like food and water, which may have a significant negative impact on their health.
2. *Lack of Education*: Women with higher education are more likely to have better health and greater access to healthcare. They are also less likely to experience gender-based violence.
3. *Poor Nutrition*: Poor nutrition can severely impact women's health. Malnutrition is a common problem in women in many low- and middle-income countries. Lack of nutritious food and water access can lead to various health issues, including anaemia and stunted growth. According to the National Family Health Survey-5, anaemia in adolescent females has increased from 54% (2015-16) to 59% (2019-21).
4. *Lack of Access to Healthcare*: Quality healthcare is essential for women's health. Unfortunately, many women in developing countries lack access to critical services, like maternity care, family planning, HIV/AIDS prevention and

treatment. HIV contributes to a higher rate of maternal mortality and morbidity, as well as other health-related issues.

5. *Gender-based Violence*: Domestic violence and gender discrimination in the workplace are one of the most severe threats to women's health and psycho-social well-being. Globally, it has been found that one in three women will experience physical or sexual violence in their lifetime. It can have a devastating effect on a woman's physical and mental health.
6. *Unsafe Abortion*: Unsafe abortion is a significant public health problem that significantly affects women in developing nations. Lack of access to safe abortion services can lead to avoidable complications, including death. Access to safe abortion services and sex education is essential for reducing the rate of unsafe abortion.

Common Health Concerns in Women

Some of the common health issues that affect millions of women each year are as follows:

1. *Menstruation Problems*: It is pervasive for women to have issues such as heavy, scant, missed or irregular periods. Cramps during periods remain another health issue among women. It has been estimated that about 9 to 14 out of 100 women get heavy periods. Heavy menstrual blood loss may result in iron-deficiency anaemia. Premenstrual Syndrome (PMS) is another problem which affects 47.8% of women worldwide. Symptoms of PMS, viz., abdominal pain, change in appetite, headache, swelling of breasts, anxiety and mood swings occur within a few days of the start of menstruation.
2. *Polycystic Ovarian Syndrome (PCOS)*: It is a common metabolic and endocrine disorder of reproductive age. Women with PCOS have excess male hormone (androgen) and may have infrequent menstrual periods. In India, this disorder is getting prevalent and women with PCOS have

an increased risk of obesity, type 2 DM, heart disease, infertility and acne.

3. *Infertility Issues*: The fertility rate of Indians has come down by more than 50% from 4.97 to 2.3. Currently, the infertility rate is 10-14%, which is higher in urban areas where one out of sixcouples is affected. Various causes responsible for infertility of women are PCOS, abortion, infection, STD, PID, etc. Lifestyle problems, such as smoking, alcohol and physical and emotional stress can also play a significant role in infertility.
4. *Reproductive Health Problems*: Reproductive health in a society forms a crucial part of general health. In developing countries, unsafe sex is a significant risk factor for maternal death. Reproductive health problems are responsible for one-third of the health issues for women between the ages of 15 to 44 years. Most maternal deaths occur due to complications in pregnancy and childbirth and to promote the health of mothers and children, the Government of India, on 15 October, 1997, launched the Reproductive and Child Health Programme.
5. *Sexually Transmitted Diseases (STD)*: STDs are infections that one acquires from having sex with a person who has the infection. It affects both the man and woman but can be more severe for women. It can cause serious health problems for the baby. STDs often go untreated in women as symptoms are less noticeable or are misdiagnosed.
6. *Urinary Tract Infections (UTI)*: Women have a shorter urethra, which enables the bacteria to travel smaller distances before they reach the bladder and start the infection. It is advised not to hesitate to talk to a healthcare professional.
7. *Thyroid Problems*: Thyroid disease is twice as prevalent in women as in men; women generally have hypothyroidism and pregnancy can raise the level of thyroid hormone in the blood. Almost 5-10 per cent of women suffer from postpartum thyroiditis, which occurs within one year after giving birth.

8. *Cancer of the Breast and Cervix*: Each year, half a million die from breast cancer and half a million occur in India. Women should be educated regarding self-examination of the breasts, which, along with mammography, can help early detection of breast cancer. Risk factors involved are family history, the onset of periods or menopause and obesity. Screening tests can detect early cervical cancer and vaccination against HPV needs to take hold.
9. *Menopause*: Menopause is a natural biological process that involves a decrease in hormone production, primarily oestrogen. Menopause can bring various symptoms, like hot flashes, mood swings, sleep disturbance and vaginal dryness. HRT and lifestyle changes help to control symptoms.
10. *Heart Diseases*: Heart diseases in women aged more than 40 years become a significant concern. Oestrogen offers some protection against heart disease, but the oestrogen level declines during menopause. Common heart diseases are heart attack, coronary artery disease, arrhythmia and heart failure.
11. *Osteoporosis*: Menopausal women are at increased risk of osteoporosis, which is characterised by decreased bone density and increased susceptibility to fracture. Women undergo various hormonal changes that can affect the utilisation of vitamin D metabolism. Adequate calcium and vitamin D intake, regular weight-bearing exercises and lifestyle modifications, such as avoiding smoking and alcohol consumption, can help reduce the risk of osteoporosis.
12. *Miscellaneous Issues*: Women face other health issues in India that are equally important matters of concern. Domestic violence, often neglected, is also a health issue because it has a massive impact on women's mental health. Problems such as dowry death, marital sexual abuse and physical cruelty by relatives are still reported in high numbers, which is the root cause of anxiety, depression

and suicidal thoughts in women. Emotional abuse (verbal abuse, shaming, criticism and insult for not having a child) diminishes women's self-esteem and affects their mental well-being. Due to cultural constraints, people still harbour myths about menstruation and the fact is alarming that only 36 per cent of women in India use sanitary napkins. Lack of education and stigma around sexual health is mainly because of the poor literacy of Indian women. Women can take charge of their health by eating a proper diet, seeking adequate screening and maintaining healthy lifestyles, which are the best ways to avoid disease, prolong life and improve the quality of life.

Women's Liberation Movement and Health Awareness

The latter half of the 20th century saw the emergence of the women's liberation movement. This socio-cultural revolution challenged traditional norms and advocated for women's rights, including the right to comprehensive healthcare. This movement spurred increased awareness of women's health issues and the need for more gender-sensitive medical research and treatment. The 1970s and 1980s saw the establishment of women's health clinics, providing specialised care and fostering an environment where women could openly discuss their health concerns, which marked a crucial turning point, with a growing recognition that women's health encompasses more than just reproductive concerns, emphasising the importance of addressing physical and mental well-being as interconnected facets.

This movement was also crucial in dismantling societal barriers surrounding mental health discussions. As women gained knowledge in various aspects of life, including healthcare, mental health became a focal point of the broader conversation. The 1970s and 1980s witnessed the establishment of mental health support networks specifically designed for women. Feminist psychology emerged as a distinct field, recognising and addressing women's unique stressors and challenges. The movement not only advocated for the de-stigmatisation of mental health issues but also emphasised the importance of mental well-being as an integral part of overall health.

There have been remarkable advancements in women's health in recent years, encompassing ground-breaking medical discoveries and empowering initiatives. These developments have enhanced women's healthcare quality and fostered a broader sense of empowerment and well-being. On the medical front, significant breakthroughs have been achieved in areas like reproductive health, cancer treatment and hormonal therapies. Cutting-edge technologies and research have led to more personalised approaches to managing conditions unique to women, offering tailored solutions for issues ranging from fertility challenges to menopausal symptoms.

Reproductive Rights and Family Planning

In the realm of reproductive health, advancements in assisted reproductive technologies (ART) have revolutionised family planning. Techniques, such as *in vitro* fertilisation (IVF) have provided new hope for couples facing infertility issues, offering alternative pathways to parenthood. Moreover, advancements in prenatal screening and genetic testing have allowed for early detection of potential complications, enabling timely interventions to ensure the health of both the mother and the baby.

One significant milestone in evolving attitudes towards women's health was recognising and promoting reproductive rights. Access to safe and legal reproductive healthcare became a central women's health-advocacy tenet. The introduction and acceptance of contraception, family planning services, and the right to choose marked a seismic shift in societal attitudes, empowering women to make informed decisions about their bodies and reproductive choices.

Medical Breakthroughs and Specialised Care

Medical research and technological advancements have been crucial in shaping attitudes towards women's health. Breakthroughs in gynaecology, obstetrics and fertility treatments have provided unprecedented opportunities for women to address reproductive challenges. Improved diagnostic tools and treatment options for conditions, such as breast cancer and gynaecological disorders, have significantly enhanced healthcare outcomes.

Moreover, recognising gender differences in medical research has led to more personalised healthcare approaches. Tailored treatments for conditions like heart disease, which may manifest differently in women than in men, reflect a more nuanced understanding of gender-specific health concerns.

Cancer Research

Cancer research has also witnessed significant strides with improved early detection methods and targeted therapies. For instance, advances in breast cancer research have led to more effective treatments with fewer side effects. Additionally, increased awareness and early screening programmes have contributed to better outcomes in cervical and ovarian cancers.

Mental Health Awareness

Mental health issues were once stigmatised and overlooked, with societal norms, relegating mental health concerns to the realm of taboo and secrecy. The pervasive stigma surrounding mental health, coupled with societal expectations of women to fulfil specific roles, led to the neglect of their emotional well-being. Women grappling with mental health issues were often subjected to societal judgement and misconceptions, hindering both open discourse and adequate mental health support.

However, in recent decades, there has been a notable shift towards de-stigmatising mental health, not only for women but for society at large. Public awareness campaigns led by mental health organisations, celebrities and grassroots movements have contributed to changing societal attitudes. Acknowledging that mental health is essential to overall well-being has prompted a cultural shift towards openness and understanding. The evolving attitudes towards women's health have extended beyond the physical realm to encompass mental well-being.

Advancements in psychiatric research and the development of psycho-pharmacological treatments marked a significant turning point in addressing women's mental health. The discovery of medications that effectively manage conditions such as depression, anxiety and mood disorders provided tangible relief to many women. Additionally, research efforts started recognising gender differences in the manifestation of mental health conditions, leading to more tailored and effective treatments.

Women-specific mental health issues, such as perinatal mental health disorders and eating disorders, are increasingly gaining attention. Initiatives like World Mental Health Day and Mental Health Awareness Month draw attention to the importance of mental well-being and provide platforms for open discussions. Social media has played a pivotal role in amplifying voices, fostering solidarity and reducing isolation among women experiencing mental health challenges.

Empowerment Initiatives

Beyond medical breakthroughs, there has been a growing emphasis on empowerment initiatives to address the holistic well-being of women. Advocacy for women's rights in healthcare decision-making, access to education and participation in research studies has gained momentum. Women's health is increasingly recognised as a medical concern and a critical component of societal progress. Empowerment initiatives also extend to mental health, acknowledging the unique challenges that women may face. Programmes promoting mental well-being, stress management, and resilience have gained traction, fostering a supportive environment for women to prioritise their mental health.

Moreover, advancements in reproductive rights also brought mental health into focus. Recognising the emotional complexities associated with reproductive choices, including pregnancy, childbirth and family planning, paved the way for a more comprehensive understanding of women's mental health needs. Acknowledging postpartum depression and advocating for mental health support during the reproductive years became essential components of women's healthcare.

Despite progress, challenges persist in achieving equitable mental health support for women. Societal expectations, gender norms and the inter-sectionality of identities can contribute to unique stressors for women, impacting their mental health. Additionally, access to mental health services remains uneven, with disparities in availability, affordability and cultural competence.

The stigma surrounding mental health, though diminishing, still lingers, deterring some women from seeking help. Cultural and societal expectations around women's roles as caregivers and nurturers may further complicate the mental health landscape. Addressing these challenges requires continued efforts to promote inclusivity, culturally competent care and awareness campaigns that challenge stereotypes.

There is a growing recognition in the contemporary era that mental health is inseparable from physical health. Holistic approaches to well-being emphasise the importance of addressing both aspects to achieve optimal health. Wellness programmes, mindfulness practices and integrative mental health care models provide a more comprehensive understanding of mental well-being.

Empowerment initiatives in women's mental health focus on the tools and resources that actively prioritise their mental well-being. These empowerment efforts include educational programmes, community support networks and workplace initiatives that promote mental health awareness and self-care. The normalisation of self-care practices, such as therapy and mindfulness, contributes to a culture where seeking mental health support is viewed as a proactive and positive step.

While strides have been made, challenges persist in fully integrating mental health into women's healthcare. Overcoming the remaining stigma and normalising mental health discussions are ongoing tasks. Incorporating mental health education into various sectors, including schools, workplaces and primary care settings, is essential for fostering a society where mental well-being is prioritised.

Technological advancements, such as tele-therapy and mental health apps, provide opportunities to increase access to mental health support. However, ensuring that these resources are inclusive and culturally competent and address the unique needs of diverse populations remains a crucial consideration.

The evolution of attitudes towards women's mental health reflects a journey from silence and stigma to open discourse and advocacy. From historical neglect to contemporary empowerment initiatives, the landscape has gradually shifed towards a more inclusive and understanding approach. As we continue to dismantle barriers, challenge stereotypes and prioritise mental well-being, the evolving attitudes towards women's mental health hold the promise of a future where every woman feels supported, understood and empowered in her journey towards holistic health.

Measures to Improve Women's Health

i. Annual health check-ups (especially in women of reproductive age) to rule out other health problems and anaemia, which affects 50 per cent of women.
ii. Annual cancer screening test to rule out breast and cervical cancer.
iii. Pap smear to detect early cervical cancer.
iv. Mammogram for women having a family history of breast cancer.
v. Human papillomavirus (HPV) vaccination for girls over ten years of age to prevent the risk of cervical cancer.
vi. Maintain a healthy body mass index (BMI) and indulge in physical activities.
vii. Regularly track blood sugar levels and blood pressure to prevent diabetes and heart disease.
viii. Checking for calcium and vitamin D, especially for postmenopausal women.
ix. Taking a balanced diet and nutrition will prevent malnutrition and anaemia.

Challenges and Opportunities in Future

1. *Access to reproductive health services:* One of the fundamental aspects linking healthcare infrastructure to women's empowerment is access to comprehensive reproductive health services. Reproductive rights encompass the freedom to make decisions about one's body, including family planning, childbirth and access to safe abortion. A robust healthcare infrastructure ensures that women have the necessary information, resources and medical support to make informed choices regarding their reproductive health.

Accessible and affordable family planning services contribute to women's autonomy, enabling them to plan the size of their families and the spacing of children. Moreover, access to safe and legal abortion services is essential for safeguarding women's reproductive rights. A well-established healthcare infrastructure with trained professionals and appropriate facilities protects women's health and empowers them to make decisions that align with their life goals and aspirations.

2. *Maternal Healthcare and Safe Childbirth:* Improving maternal healthcare is another critical facet of healthcare infrastructure that directly impacts women's empowerment. High-quality prenatal care, skilled attendance during childbirth and access to emergency obstetric services reduce maternal mortality rates and enhance women's overall well-being. In many societies, women's empowerment is intrinsically linked to their ability to make choices about motherhood and family planning.

A robust healthcare system recognises the significance of maternal health for the individual woman and the broader community. Healthy mothers contribute to the well-being of their families and communities, fostering a cycle of empowerment that extends beyond personal experiences. By ensuring safe and supportive childbirth experiences, healthcare infrastructure catalyses positive outcomes in women's lives.

3. *Preventive and Primary Healthcare:* Beyond reproductive health, the impact of healthcare infrastructure on women's empowerment extends to preventive and primary healthcare

services. Regular check-ups, screenings and vaccinations are essential to maintaining overall health and well-being. An accessible and efficient healthcare system ensures that women can access these services, addressing health issues before they escalate.

Preventive healthcare measures empower women to take control of their well-being, promoting a proactive approach to health maintenance. Early detection of conditions, such as breast cancer, cervical cancer and osteoporosis allows for timely intervention, improving treatment outcomes and preserving women's health. Additionally, primary healthcare services that address common health concerns contribute to increased productivity and quality of life, furthering women's empowerment.

4. Mental Health Support: An inclusive healthcare infrastructure recognises the importance of mental health in women's overall well-being. Mental health support, including counselling, therapy and access to psychiatric services is crucial for addressing the unique stressors and challenges that women may face. Recognising and de-stigmatising mental health issues contribute to fostering a culture of empowerment where seeking help is encouraged.

Moreover, mental health is closely tied to women's ability to pursue education and employment and participate fully in societal activities. By providing mental health resources, healthcare infrastructure supports women in overcoming barriers and challenges, enhancing their resilience and capacity to navigate life's complexities.

5. Challenges and Disparities: Despite the potential of healthcare infrastructure to empower women, numerous challenges and disparities persist. Socio-economic factors, geographical location and cultural norms can create barriers to accessing healthcare services. In many regions, women, particularly those in rural areas, may face challenges, such as limited transportation, insufficient healthcare facilities and cultural barriers that hinder their ability to seek and receive timely medical care.

Gender bias within healthcare systems can also contribute to disparities. Insufficient research on women's health issues, inadequate representation of women in clinical trials and biases in medical treatment can impact the quality and effectiveness of healthcare provided to women. Addressing these challenges requires a multifaceted approach, including policy changes, educational initiatives and community engagement.

6. Opportunities for Positive Change: Efforts to enhance healthcare infrastructure supporting women's empowerment can capitalise on several opportunities. The best approach in enhancing women's healthcare would be to review the tools India already owns but needs to exploit. Technology, for instance, can be leveraged to improve access to healthcare services, especially in remote areas. Telemedicine, mobile health apps and digital platforms can facilitate consultations, disseminate health information and empower women to engage in their healthcare actively.

Healthcare Technology

Technology can be used to reach millions of women nationwide, educate them about their health issues and bust misconceptions. Technology can transform the accessibility and affordability of women's healthcare in the country. By harnessing the power of artificial intelligence, technology can expand healthcare's diagnostic, therapeutic and preventive dimensions. For example, technology can lead to early detection of cervical cancer and favourably impact its cure.

Collaboration, with public-private partnerships, is indispensable for the future of women's healthcare. Furthermore, women leaders need to be incorporated within the healthcare workforce to facilitate critical women-centric interventions and initiate improved patient outcomes.

Health Insurance

Another tool is health insurance that can be crucial in providing preventive care. By providing easy access to health insurance, women's healthcare can be enhanced effectively and rapidly. The majority of women in India, mainly those in rural areas, are not protected by health insurance and, hence, are forced to pay out-of-pocket exorbitant medical expenses. As a result, women tend to delay or decline needed medical treatment, thereby adversely impacting their health and well-being. Health insurance can be made more affordable by offering subsidies or other financial incentives to women who purchase health insurance policies. Currently, only a few insurance providers offer policies explicitly premeditated for women. It will be easier for women to find policies that meet their healthcare needs if more insurers are encouraged to develop policies tailored to their health needs.

Moreover, it is imperative to make women aware of the benefits of health insurance. Governments and private insurance providers should work in collaboration to develop policies precisely customised to women's needs, including those that cover reproductive health and maternity care. Education and awareness campaigns are crucial to create an ambience where women are informed advocates for their health.

Additionally, incorporating a gender-sensitive approach in healthcare policy and research is essential. Such an approach includes:

- Ensuring that medical research includes diverse populations.
- Addressing the distinct healthcare necessities of women.
- Promoting gender-responsive healthcare services.

Empowering Indian Women

Women's empowerment, according to the United Nations, consists of five components: a sense of worth, the right to own and determine choices, the right to have equitable access to opportunities and resources, the right to have the power to control their own lives and ability to influence the direction of social change. The fundamental principle of women's empowerment is enshrined in the Indian Constitution, which, in addition to granting equality, empowers the State to adopt various measures of positive discrimination in favour of women. Apart from the

State's fundamental rights and directive principles, multiple laws have been passed to eliminate gender discrimination and promote gender equality, e.g. the Equal Remuneration Act (1976), the Dowry Prohibition Act (1961), the Immoral Traffic Prevention Act (1956), the Maternal Benefit Act(1961), Medical Termination of Pregnancy Act (1971) and Prohibition of Child Marriage Act (2006). The Pre-conception and Prenatal Diagnostic Techniques (Regulation and Prevention of Misuse) Act (PNDT, 1994) prohibit discriminative gender selection. Similarly, the Sexual Harassment of Women at Workplace Act (2013) protects women from sexual harassment.

Governments can improve women's health by enacting gender-sensitive policies and consolidating health services. Political commitment and community participation are crucial for overcoming the major barriers to implementing women's health programmes. On a positive note, on 22 January 2015, the government launched its most transformational programme for women, namely Beti Bachao and Beti Padhao, aiming for women's security and education. The scheme intends to eliminate the ill-formed perceptions and age-old practices that deter women's holistic development. The immediate effect of the scheme is best illustrated by the improvement in the gender ratio at birth in Haryana state from 871 in 2015 to 914 in 2017. Similar results have also been noticed in other states, such as Rajasthan, Uttar Pradesh, Himachal Pradesh and Andhra Pradesh. The Central and state governments have launched many other similar schemes. For instance, Sukanya Samrddhi Yojna, launched in 2015, encourages parents to build a corpus fund for future education and marriage expenses for their girl child.

Persistent malnutrition is another major hindrance that adversely impacts the health, education and productivity of Indian women. Launched on International Women's Day, 8 March, 2018, by Prime Minister Narendra Modi, the National Nutrition Mission (NNM) aims to provide adequate nutrition to women, adolescent girls and children 0-six years of age for a reduction in stunted growth, under-nutrition, low birth weight and anaemia.

The government has made an annual budgetary provision of Rs. 9,046.17 crores from 2017 to 2020 for the Kuposhan Mukt Bharat Mission.

According to Mahatma Gandhi, "Sanitation is as important as Independence." Unfortunately, even after seven decades of Independence, about 300 million women in India do not have access to clean lavatory facilities and a dignified life. Launched on the auspicious occasion of Gandhi Jayanti in 2014, the Swachchha Bharat movement aims to achieve adequate sanitation and hygiene and freedom from open defecation. Additionally, the Maternity Benefit (Amendment) Bill (2017) protects women's employment during the period of maternity and entitles them to full-paid absence from the workplace to take care of their children. Pradhan Mantri Matritva Vandana Yojna and Pradhan Mantri Surakshit Matritva Abhiyan are other valuable steps towards women's social and financial empowerment. Comprehensive Primary Health Care (CPHC) through Ayushman Bharat Health and Wellness Centres aims for universal and freely accessible preventive, promotive, curative, rehabilitative and palliative services nationwide. Ayushman Health Mela campaigns, tele-consultation services through the eSanjeevani portal, free drug and diagnostic initiatives and provision of mobile medical units have facilitated access to the public healthcare system at the doorstep for the remote population as well.

Development by and for women is at the core of India's vision for inclusive growth. The Union Budget's Nari Shakti initiatives plan to arm women with the necessary tools to steer change and lead from the front towards the building of a great nation.

Conclusion

The interplay between healthcare infrastructure and women's empowerment is a dynamic and intricate relationship beyond addressing physical health concerns. A robust healthcare system safeguards women's health and catalyses empowerment, contributing to their autonomy, well-being and societal participation. To truly advance women's empowerment through healthcare infrastructure, it is imperative to address disparities, challenge biases and seize opportunities for positive change. As societies recognise the importance of investing in women's health, the transformative potential of healthcare infrastructure in fostering empowerment becomes a cornerstone for building a more equitable and inclusive future.

Enhancing women's healthcare in India is a crucial need of the hour and requires a multifaceted approach. Technology, sex-aware care, gender-sensitive mental health services, collaboration in public-private partnerships, women leaders in the healthcare workforce and better awareness and access to insurance and related healthcare facilities are all critical to driving change. Many are already working towards goals; it is time to bring them into synergy.

The reality is that many women are still missing out on the opportunity to get educated, support themselves and obtain the health services they need. That is why WHO is working so hard to strengthen health systems and ensure that countries have robust financing systems and a sufficient number of well-trained, motivated health workers. New global strategies are being developed to ensure women's and children's health. Thus, our objective should be setting targets and catalysing commitments regarding policy, financing and action to ensure that the future will bring health to all women and girls, whoever they are, wherever they live. A significant barrier to women's health is inequality, both between men and women and in women in different geographical regions, social classes and indigenous and ethnic groups. We have to overcome such deep-rooted inequality by providing equal opportunity to healthcare facilities for all women so that they realise their full rights and potential to be healthy.

In conclusion, the advancements in women's health, from medical breakthroughs to empowerment initiatives, mark a transformative era. These developments contribute to women's physical well-being and empower them to take charge of their health, fostering a more equitable and inclusive healthcare landscape. As we continue to witness progress in these areas, the future promises further improvements in women's overall health and empowerment worldwide.

References

1. Kramer, Laura, *The Sociology of Gender: A Brief Introduction*, Rawat Publications, Jaipur, New Delhi, 2001.
2. Chatterjee M., *Indian Women: Their Health and Economic Productivity*, World Bank Discussion paper 109, Washington, DC, World Bank, 1990.
3. World Bank, *Improving Women's Health in India*, Washington, DC, World Bank, 1996.
4. International Institute for Population Sciences, *National Family Health Survey (NFHS)-1*, 1992-93, Bombay, IIPS, 1995.
5. International Institute for Population Sciences, *National Family Health Survey (NFHS)-2*, 1998-99, Mumbai, IIPS, 1998.
6. International Institute for Population Sciences, National Fact Sheet, *India National Family Health Survey (NFHS)-3*, 2005-06, Mumbai, IIPS, 2006.
7. International Institute for Population Sciences (IIPS) and ICF, *India National Family Health Survey (NFHS)-5*, 2019-21. India, Vol. I, Mumbai, IIPS, 2021.
8. Grimes D, Benson J, *et al.*, *Unsafe Abortion: The Preventable Pandemic*, Lancet, 2006, 368.
9. Girija, P.L., Anaemia among women and children of India, *Anc. Sci. Life*, 2008; 28(1): 33-6.
10. Patel, V., Rodrigues, M. and De Souza, N., Gender, poverty and postnatal depression: A Study of Mothers in Goa, India, *Am. J. Psychiatry*, 2002, 159: 43-7.

□

12

A Decade of Women's Rights—Towards a Legal System from a Female Perspective

—Nikita Upal

This book demonstrates the widespread impact of recognising women's rights and its cascading legal and policy implications. I examine these developments in the context of India. Globalisation and the generational shift have changed women's interaction with religion, law and the criminal justice system (CJS).

So, for this chapter, I examine the diverse construction of women's rights from the following perspectives:

Personal Sphere

When it comes to the personal sphere of a woman's body, women's bodies have adhered to the dictates of caste, class, community and religion.[1] From childhood, the female body is gendered and constructed. Perhaps the subject that has witnessed the most transgression is maternity. Transgression by doctors, by the State, is an everyday affair. Targeted towards the vulnerability of women-bearing children, those with reproductive health issues and those who are surrogates.

In this sphere, we will examine the Medical Termination of Pregnancy Act (MTP), 2021 and the Surrogacy Regulation Act (SRA), 2021. Both these amendments have made a pivotal shift.

The MTP Act has extended the time limit to terminate a pregnancy. This shift has been from 20 to 24 weeks. The extension makes women of a specific category eligible for termination of pregnancy up to 24 weeks. This extension under Rule 3 B of the MTP Act includes women who are victims/survivors of sexual violence (rape, molestation, incest), women with disabilities, women with foetal malformation, women in disaster or humanitarian crises and women whose marital status has changed during pregnancy (widowed/divorced/deserted). The move extended limited leeway in obtaining an abortion by technically keeping single and unmarried women out of its ambit.

Recently, the Supreme Court dealt with an appeal from the Delhi High Court. The plea was of an unmarried woman who wanted to undergo medical termination of pregnancy at 23 weeks (Case of *X vs. The Principal Secretary, Health and Family Welfare Department, Government of NCAT, Delhi and Others).*[2] The judgement has expanded the scope for medical termination of pregnancy for women and girls. It also recognised other gender identities, which may require access to safe medical termination of pregnancy. The judgement is also historic in recognising victims of marital rape for the MTP Act. The central part of the judgement, however, stated that all women are entitled to safe medical termination of pregnancies. Thereby, the distinction based on marital status is eliminated. Rule 3B of the MTP Act Rules, which states the upper limit of termination of pregnancy to up to 24 weeks, protected only married women and women who belonged to specified categories and was held to be 'constitutionally unsustainable'[3] as it was discriminatory towards single and unmarried women, and violative of Article 14 (Right to Equality). This has cemented women's autonomy by focusing on the right to life under Article 21 and respecting the dignity and privacy of unmarried women at par with married women.

The case has also significantly contributed to a more harmonious reading of the MTP Act and the Protection of Children from Sexual Offences Act (POCSO). Section 19 of the POCSO Act deals with the provision of mandatory disclosure. It mandates that anyone who knows or has the apprehension of an incident of child sexual abuse has to report it mandatorily. Section 23 of the Act, along with POCSO Rules, 2020, has also recognised the right to confidentiality for victims/survivors of child sexual abuse. The Ministry of Women and Child Development has also established an online portal to file complaints (POCSO e-box)[4] to facilitate reporting, thereby highlighting a move towards accessibility for raising a complaint and also showcasing a move towards a more trauma-informed interaction with children. To further cement institutional response, recently the Supreme Court took *suo moto* cognisance of the rising incidents of sexual abuse of children. The Court appointed V. Giri, Senior Advocate, as an *Amicus Curia.* At the institutional level, the advocate suggested a need for dedicated Forensic Science Laboratories to ensure a dedicated unit for POCSO cases.

On the aspect of confidentiality, it is particularly vital in cases when an adolescent girl who seeks a safe medical termination of pregnancy can avail protection under Rule 3 B and her identity and other personal information will be protected as confidential. Section 5 A of the MTP Act states that all registered medical practitioners are bound by confidentiality.

The MTP Act facilitates aspects of reproductive rights. A significant concern that remains unanswered is intersectionality and the right to motherhood, notably on the rights of women with a disability and the right to motherhood. There is an assumption towards a lack of capability of rearing a child, highlighting a need to revisit the contention of citing disability as a cause for abortion and the associated stigma attached to disability that persuades couples to abort a foetus with abnormalities.

This also closely resonates with the surrogacy law in India. Surrogacy in India had always been the less expensive alternative for prospective parents. In 2002, surrogacy was legalised in India and the industry boomed as an outsourced low-cost provider for foreign parents. An example of this global bio-economy was Anand, in Gujarat.[5] It became a hub for reproductive tourism.

The commercial aspect, however, severely exploited women from examining reproductive autonomy and choice. When it comes to targeted marginalised women, the matter of individual choice is often bridged by their socioeconomic disposition. Caste, class and poverty are relevant indicators for accepting surrogacy. This highlights the divide between the concept of reproductive choice and reproductive justice.

With the passing of the Surrogacy (Regulation) Act, 2021, a positive move in the Act permitted altruistic surrogacy only and outlawed commercial surrogacy. The move eliminates financial incentives towards the surrogate in return for the pregnancy and the child. The Act has also regulated surrogacy by streamlining the surrogacy process with the use of eligibility certificates and fitness certificates. A potential downfall would be the stringent process and the 'gift-giving' relationship that arises due to the surrogacy relationship.[6]

Personal Law

Personal Law has often been reviewed from many perspectives – from secularism, modernism, national unity, community identity and religious freedom to equality. The discourse on gender justice and gender equality, however, is relatively recent. Reform for Personal Law has been challenging due to the intricate web between religion and patriarchy. Issues about women's rights within the realm of marriage, divorce, guardianship, adoption, maintenance and succession often face criticism and public backlash. The undertone for this is that all customary Personal Laws are projected as discriminative towards women.

We will review the growth in the field of Personal law from the gender lens by focusing on two landmark decisions:

i. *Shayara Bano vs. Union of India*[7]: Despite a plethora of decisions over triple *talaq* that have already ensured protection against the practice, the long-standing battle against the practice was put to rest in 2017. The practice of 'triple *talaq*' allowed Muslims to unilaterally dissolve marriage by uttering the term '*talaq*' thrice. The practice also barred women from claiming any provision of maintenance or alimony and left women on their toes, as often the flimsiest scuffle ended up in the pronouncement of '*talaq*'.

The Supreme Court examined whether the practice of '*talaq-e-biddat*' was an essential religious practice, thereby saving it from the rigorous mesh of constitutional law. The five-bench unanimously opined that '*talaq-e-biddat*' is not essentially a practice of Islam. The practice is condemned in Islamic practice and was considered a sin. Its sanction was derived from the Shariat Act and can be constitutionally challenged. The Court relied on the doctrine of manifest arbitrariness, which states that disproportionate, excessive, or unreasonable behaviour hinders fundamental rights and is liable to be held untenable. As it was wrong in theology, it was considered deficient in law. The real challenge was that Fundamental Rights, under Part II of the Constitution, could only be imposed upon the State, not private parties, i.e. husband and wife.

The primary question that needs to be addressed is the supremacy of un-codified Personal Law over Fundamental Rights, paving the path for a robust framework of the Uniform Civil Code.

ii. *Sujata Sharma vs. Manu Gupta*[8]: In 2005, the Hindu Succession Act gave daughters equal rights in coparcenary property. The amendment led to the addition of Section 6(a), which states that a daughter is allotted the same share as is allotted to a son. The concept was relevant within a Hindu Undivided Family (HUF) as traditionally, the term coparcener referred to the male heir of the HUF. These male heirs used to have a claim over all the ancestral property by birth, leaving aside the female heir, thereby making daughters a joint owner of the ancestral property. The move was ground breaking as it brought male and female heirs the right to par with one another. The same was reiterated in 2020 in *Vineeta Sharma vs. Rakesh Sharma.*[9] Despite the amendment, courts applied the law inconsistently due to some contrary interpretations. They stated that daughters could not claim part of the ancestral property in case of the absence of a will before 20 December, 2004 (the date on which the amendment was tabled in the Rajya Sabha as a bill). With the *Vineeta*

Sharma judgement, the Court clarified that irrespective of the date, the claim over ancestral lay, from 2005 onwards, daughters would receive equal shares as the sons. Hence, the cut-off date was eliminated and efforts towards gender equality within the Hindu Personal Law were cemented. This step has empowered women on the economic front.

Judicial interventions further minimised the traditional divide that existed, for instance, regarding the '*karta*' of a HUF. The head of the family, i.e., the '*karta*', within a patriarchal construct, has always been the senior man of the family. He heads the joint family and is the family business and property custodian. Recently, the Delhi High Court declared that the oldest woman of the family can be a *karta.*[10] A *karta* is a legal status that deals with the right to manage the HUF. The judgement echoed that the law and the traditions and practice of Hindu law did not limit a woman's right to become a *karta*.

Employment and Labour-related Laws

i. *Prevention, Prohibition and Redressal of Sexual Harassment of Women at Workplace Act*: The year 2013 was a watershed movement for women's rights. The twin legislations, the PoSH Act and the Criminal Amendment Act of 2013 extended tremendous protection to victims of sexual harassment, both at the workplace and in other places.

Although the *Vishakha*[11] guidelines mandated the establishment of internal committees to deal with allegations of sexual harassment since 1997, its implementations were murky. The irony of its non-implementation is still rampant. This is despite tremendous efforts on the corporate governance front to ensure that companies adhere to this mandate. Some aspects that highlight this are PoSH Act disclosure requirements under the Act, Securities and Exchange Board of India – Listing Obligations and Disclosure Requirements Circulars and Companies Act, 2013. The disclosure covers aspects such as training and awareness sessions conducted, the number of cases and the hearing status in annual reports.

The PoSH Act and *Vishaka's* judgement were in light of a horrific incident in 1992. Bhanwari Devi, a social worker, was a part of the Government of Rajasthan›s effort to eliminate child marriage. She tried to stop the marriage of her nine-month-old daughter and faced much retaliation for registering an FIR.[12] At the same time, she succeeded in stopping the marriage. Members of the village associated the police visit with Bhanwari Devi's attempt to stop the marriage. Later she was gangraped and her husband was assaulted. The situation escalated with the police's callous attitude towards the complaint and the inefficiency in gathering forensic evidence led to unsuccessful prosecution. The lower court acquitted all the alleged accused. On 18 January, 1996, an appeal for the case was filed. Till date, her case is pending before the Rajasthan High Court.[13] Her hope for justice continues. During this ordeal, she has lost her husband. To make things worse, four of the accused have died.

Her case remains to be a dent in the Indian judiciary. Amongst the issues discussed in the case was also what a workplace is. Sixteen years later, when the PoSH Act received the assent, the Parliament proposed the concept of an extended workplace – the move from the traditional office to the workplace has also been streamlined due to the concept of working from home. This also stems from the definition of aggrieved women under Section 2 (a) of the PoSH Act, which states that an aggrieved woman is a woman 'in relation to a workplace'. This even protects women who visit office-related social occasions and work virtually. In the case of *Sanjeev Mishra vs. Bank of Baroda*,[14] the Rajasthan High Court stated that workplace harassment will include online harassment. This is also due to the harmonious reading of the Information Technology Act and the PoSH Act. Under the IT Act, Section 66 E deals with breach of privacy violations and Section 67 A punishes the publication of obscene content. The establishment of cyber-crime cells and digital police has also streamlined the process of online complaints.

The Ministry of Women and Child Development has also successfully created a safety net for women by creating the platform, She-Box,[15] a virtual platform where a woman can raise a complaint. The move towards accepting online complaints highlights the recognition of trauma-informed values to safeguard deposition. This is also highlighted in the case of *Bidyug Chakraborty vs. Delhi University and Ors.*[16] The case has ironed out numerous wrinkles in the context of 'principles of natural justice' in PoSH cases. The Supreme Court held that cross-examination is vital in any disciplinary hearing and is an accused's right. It directed that the identity of a witness need not be revealed. The respondent is entitled to the process of written cross-examination, respecting the sensitivity of such issues.

ii. The recent Maternity Benefit Amendment Act of 2017 has enhanced the period of maternity leave. This period has been enhanced from 12 to a period of 26 weeks. At the Central Government level, childcare leave is also available. The Act has also streamlined recognition of adoption by introducing concepts like 'commissioning mother' (a biological mother who utilises surrogacy for childbearing by implanting her egg into the surrogate) and an adoptive mother. An adoptive mother is entitled to maternity leave for 12 weeks from the date the child is handed over. It has also paved the path for 'work from home' by extending flexible work options for women. The Act also mandated that employers create creche facilities, as in the case of Bahra University, Shimla vs. Dr. Pooja Bhardwaj and Ors.[17] The respondent claimed the salary of maternity leave and the bonus under the Act. In the last month of her scheduled leave, she was denied leave. On a complaint to the local authority and subsequent rejoining, the creche facilities were denied to her. Upon inspection, there was a creche; however, it failed to conform to the National Minimum Guidelines for Setting up a Creche Facility.

The Act has also clarified that contractual employees cannot be denied maternity benefits. In the case of *Annwesha Deb vs. Delhi State Legal Services Authority,*[18] the Court held that maternity benefit is not only a matter arising out of the statutory right or contractual relationship; it is a fundamental right and an integral part of the identity and dignity of women. Thereby, it emphasises a woman's entitlement to maternity benefits by paying the salary and maternity bonus.

The protection extended to women in the workplace recognizes the vulnerable disposition and creates overlapping frameworks to protect women.

Company Laws

Companies Act has witnessed a progressive shift by mandating the recruitment of a female director on its board by a listed company and public companies. The move has acted as a platform to bridge the diversity divide at the highest decision-making level in a corporation. However, having the requisite qualifications, experience and expertise may be a challenge, considering the male-dominated nature of the profession. These barriers escalate with gender bias and stereotypes, family responsibility, particularly childbirth. Hence, creating a 'glass wall' within higher management positions and a 'glass ceiling' makes the jump to the top even more challenging.[19]

The provision ensures companies of a specific category, namely:

1. Listed company
2. Public company
3. A company having paid-up share capital of INR 1 billion
4. A company having a turnover of INR 3 billion
5. Comply with the appointment of a female director within six months of fulfilling these criteria.

The Securities and Exchange Board of India has cemented the same provision – Listing Obligations and Disclosure Requirements. Regulation 17(1) reiterates an optimal blend of executive and non-executive directors, including at least one woman director. The provision also has a strict penalty for non-compliance. Section 172 of the Companies Act applies in case of non-compliance with having a female director. The range of the fine is from INR 50,000 to INR 5,00,000. This has also led to gender tokenism, a 'one-done deal'. It also highlights a 9-5 feminism, the ideal face of globalisation. The move bridges the gap in the corporate sector but fails to protect women in other sectors.

The legal framework and penal consequences have paved the way for gender diversity at the top level. The international framework guiding this principle is the Sustainable Development Goals 2030. We are streamlining national and international initiatives. The move may be slow-paced, but it is in good stead. We are giving women a share in power and reinforcing gender equality.

Criminal Law

A vast body of literature elaborates on the struggle of Indian women in the face of a legal system that was largely silent on women's needs and representation. The last decade, however, has seen a watershed movement in adopting women-friendly laws. Decades of campaigning and protesting for reforms on sexual violence were transformed instantly with the Nirbhaya case[20] in the form of the 2013 Criminal Amendment Act. The gangrape and death of Jyoti Pandey, a medical student, triggered the nation and led to large-scale protests on state inaction towards violence against women.

The Delhi Fast-Track Court tried the case and, under the rarest of rare, held the five men guilty and sentenced them to death. The juvenile involved in the case received a sentence of three years in a reform centre. In an appeal to the Supreme Court, a stay was ordered against four of the convicts. One of the convicts died under mysterious circumstances in detention. It later affirmed the Delhi High Court's stance in awarding the death penalty.

The case also led to the establishment of a Committee for Reforms headed by Justice Jagdish Verma, Justice Leila Seth and Gopal Subramaniam. The committee reviewed feedback from community members and suggested reforms, which led to the passing of the Criminal Amendment Act, 2013. A few other notable cases which added to the discourse of the CLAA were the *Bachpan Bachao Andolan*[21] case, showcasing missing children and the trafficking link and *Saakshi vs. Union of India*[22] in attempting to expand the definition of rape to include all forms of forcible penetration.

These cases added to the discourse of CLAA. They recognised a new set of offences against women, such as throwing or attempting to throw acid, offences relating to sexual harassment such as intent, assault or use of force to disrobe, voyeurism, stalking, trafficking of persons and exploitation of trafficked persons.

Concerning the offence of rape under Section 375, the CLAA highlighted the stance of consent, which was often clubbed with force to dilute prosecution previously. The initial reliance on non-consent and force has ended. Now, there is reliance only on proving lack of consent, irrespective of whether force was used.

The Amendment has also established instances where survivor's lack of consent will be presumed, such as statutory rape. The Amendment also established a framework for rape shield laws, prohibiting the victim/survivor's sexual history. It enhanced the penal consequences under Section 375 for aggravated offences of rape, such as custodial rape and gang rape. Within gang rape, the aftermath of which results in a permanent vegetative state, an enhanced term of imprisonment is not less than 20 years.

It also set procedural guidelines, such as punishment for not extending treatment to victims under Section 357C of theCrPC. This covers victims/survivors of rape, acid attack. To ensure access to medical examination and emergency treatment, it is mandatory for private and government hospitals to provide treatment. Failure to extend this also attracts penal consequences.

Within this sphere, we will examine the effort made towards prohibiting marital rape. However, the stance on marital rape has been wavering from courts and judicial discourse. When it comes to child marriage, the case of *Independent Thought vs. Union of India*[23] is vital. Exception 2 to Section 375 states that a man cannot be charged for the offence of rape, provided his wife is not below the age of 15 years. The CLAA clarifies the age of consent as 18 years. Along with a harmonious reading, the Juvenile Justice Care of Protection of Children Act, Protection of Children from Sexual Offences Act and Child Marriage Restraint Act's stance on the age of consent is 18 years.

Exception 2 to Section 375, however, states that sexual intercourse or sexual acts by a man with his wife, not being under five years of age, is not rape. The case stated the clause as violative of Article 14 (Right to equality), Article 15 (prohibition of discrimination on the grounds of sex, religion, race, caste or place of birth) and Article 21 (Right to life and liberty) and further, how the age of consent from various statutes can be gathered as 18 years of age. What Exception Two does is that it recognises 15 years of age as the lower age of consent and permits forced sexual intercourse by the husband on a girl aged 15-18 years. The case questioned this arbitrary classification of minor girls based on marital status, thereby violative of Article 14 and violating bodily integrity and dignity under Article 21. The exception is violative of the fundamental rights of girls under the Constitution and the international obligations of India as a party of the Convention of all Forms of Discrimination against Women and the Child Rights Convention.

The case stated that the arbitrary classification was violative of Article 14 and the Exception was read down as "sexual intercourse or sexual acts by a man on his wife, not being under 18 years of age, is not rape". The case has positively protected young girls within a marital relationship. It has also been a beacon of hope for feminist efforts towards ending the protection of marital rape.

The constitutional validity of marital rape has been questioned in numerous instances. The wilful leaving out of marital rape from Section 375 has condoned and allowed rape within marriage. There has been a paradigm shift on the subject in recent years. With a series of petitions being heard around India recently, the Supreme Court in *Hrishikesh Sahoo vs the State of Karnataka*[24] will decide on the key issues.

(a) Does the Exception under Section 375 violate a married woman's right to equality? Does it denies married women the same legal remedy as an unmarried woman?

(b) Does the Exception deny married women the same status as men in a marriage?

(c) Does the Exception violate a married woman's right to privacy?

A woman filed a case against her husband, Hrishikesh Sahoo, accusing him of rape, cruelty and threats of causing harm. He was also charged with an offence under the POCSO Act for sexually assaulting his daughter. The petitioner invoked the marital rape exception; however, the Kerala High Court stated that "no exception under the law can be absolute, and become a licence to commit a crime against the society". On appeal, the Supreme Court granted an interim stay.

This was also followed by a petition filed by the RIT Foundation, Delhi, challenging the marital rape Exception in the Delhi High Court. A split verdict on the case was delivered, stating the Exception was discriminative to a woman's right to bodily autonomy. Meanwhile, recognising the institution of marriage, sexual relations are a legitimate expectation, whether consensual or not. The Centre's response to the case is pending. In effect, there has been judicial leniency towards marital rape due to the large-scale social ramifications.

There has been a generational shift post-Nirbhaya and CLAA. Looking forward, the criminal justice system has become more responsive to promoting women's rights. Having a more responsive system is a positive sign for the feminist movement in India.

So far, I have referred to the theoretical sphere where the criminal justice system has furthered women's rights. I will also discuss a landmark case that has assisted victims/survivors whilst interacting with the criminal justice system. The case of *Sampurna Behura vs. Union of India*[25] has been essential in enhancing court infrastructure. The tardy implementation of the JJ Act was brought out in the case, particularly concerning the special fast-track courts established under the PoCSO Act. The judgement mandated all High Courts and districts to establish child-friendly courts and vulnerable witness deposition courts. The case has been unique in recognising secondary victimisation. It recognised the need for vulnerable victims and witnesses to have access to a system of interacting with the court by recognising the principles of trauma-informed care.

From the procedural perspective, another aspect that has aided timely cognisance of cases is the 0-FIR. Under Section 154 of the Criminal Procedure Code, a First Information Report is recorded for a cognisable offence. The provisions of the Section are read along with the provision of territorial jurisdiction under Section 156 of the police station, which shall investigate the offence. On 16 December, 2012, when the Nirbhaya incident took place, the private bus where the gang rape of Jyoti Pandey took place, the offenders had injured her friend and thrown them out on a flyover where the victim lay naked and wounded. When the police eventually reached the crime scene, they reportedly spent forty-five minutes deciding where the jurisdiction lay. To eliminate such challenges, the concept of a 0-FIR has been introduced.

It allows the registration of an FIR at any police station, regardless of the jurisdiction. This move has ensured a timely and quick redressal is extended to the victim. Once a 0-FIR is registered, it has to be transferred to the concerned police station where the offence has been committed. Here, the term '0' implies there is no serial number and on investigation, when the jurisdiction is ascertained, the same has to be shifted to the rightful jurisdiction. The remedy ensures timely action and enforcement of law and order.

Judicial discourse has also strengthened post-sentencing rehabilitation and aid for victims. Section 357 A of the CrPC mandates the State government, in coordination with the Central Government, to prepare a scheme to disburse funds to victims of crime. One such scheme that exists at a policy level is the *Ujjawala* scheme,[26] dedicated to victims of human trafficking and sexual exploitation. It is a comprehensive scheme for the prevention of human trafficking, dedicated to the rescue, rehabilitation and reintegration of victims.

Similarly, Section 357B of the CrPC deals with compensation for victims of acid attacks. Under the provisions, the state government shall extend payment to the victim in addition to the fine. The scheme is disbursed with the help of the Legal Services Authority in judgements that ascertain a sum for compensation. In 2018, the National Legal Services Authority formulated a dedicated compensation scheme for women victims and survivors of sexual assault and other crimes.

For rehabilitation and reintegration of victims of sexual exploitation, the government has also created *Swadhar Grah.* These are shelter homes for women in distressed situations. These homes can play diverse roles in rehabilitation. These homes can take a step beyond providing safety, security and aid to the skill enhancement of the residents.

E-Governance

E-governance is an effective public instrument for promoting accessibility to government systems. This is particularly important, as women face traditional barriers, towards their inclusion in the governance and public participation. In India, lately, the focus has been on e-delivery of services, such as online registering of complaints (non-cognisable offences). There has also been an e-resources available for women such as NARI[27] portal (National Repository of Information for Women) at the initiative of Ministry and Child Development.

Initiatives, like the PENCIL[28] (Platform for Effective Enforcement for no Child Labour) portal and She-Box showcase efforts that streamline monitoring of labour exploitation cases of vulnerable population, like women and children.

On the corporate governance aspect, Mahila e-Haat[29] is an online platform for women entrepreneurs. It is part of GeM (Government e-Marketplace) to facilitate linkage for a market linkage for micro, small and medium enterprises.

Use of Information Technology has acted as a bridge to eliminate the digital divide. The government's comprehensive approach towards digital empowerment is also recognisable from efforts, like Digital India.

Political Sphere

Article 243(3)D of the Constitution of India extends affirmative action towards women in *panchayats* and municipalities. It reserves at least one-third of the total number of seats by rotation to different constituencies. Articles 243(4)D and 243 T(4) provide at least one-third of the office of the Chairperson to be reserved for women at each level. Local government bodies are extending a level playing field for women.

On 21 September, 2023, the Parliament of India took a historic step to bridge the divide in the upper house by passing the Women's Reservation Bill (*Nari Shakti Vandan Adhiniyam*). The Bill was unanimously passed by both the Lok Sabha and the Rajya Sabha. The Bill ensures a 33 per cent reservation in the state legislative assembly and the Lok Sabha. It was first introduced in 1996. The move is expected to add to the diversity by extending greater participation in public representation. At the moment, however, the legislation is scheduled to come into force after the next Census. The proposed system of rotation of reserved constituency every five years is also a significant hurdle. Female candidates will compete against other female candidates. In a bid for equality, it ends up restricting women from contesting against men.

As a law on paper, it is a step forward and back. The Bill has neglected lateral reservation for Scheduled Caste and Scheduled Tribe, highlighting the possible focus towards the privileged sections and ignoring intersectionality.

Sports and Athletic Events

The pay gap has been one of the most challenging hurdles towards equality and empowerment. In 2023, the Board of Control for Cricket in India, in a historic move, announced pay parity and inclusivity in cricket. This pay parity is towards equal prize money and match fees for men's and women's teams at the International Cricket Council Events[30]. The decision received unanimous approval from all the members of the Apex Council of BCCI.

The initiative is streamlined under the 'pay equity policy' under the sports governance umbrella. They are paving the path to the elimination of gender-based discrimination, empowering young female cricketers and enhancing the participation of women in sports and athletics. The average pay for men in sports and athletics is more significant than that for women. There are a multitude of factors contributing to this bridge, particularly, the lack of opportunities and the impact of motherhood on a sportswoman's career are the most common aspects.

Policy

With a plethora of legal provisions and case laws available for women to avail and within the policy framework, namely the following have played a vital role:

Schemes for young and adolescent girls:

i. *Beti Bachao Beti Padhao*[31]: The scheme has ensured that sex-selective elimination is prohibited. Further, young girls' future is secured by their education and empowerment.

ii. *Kishori Shakti Yojana*[32]: The scheme focuses on the health and nutrition of adolescent girls. The scheme is available to girls aged 11 to 18 years. The scheme helps improve awareness of health, hygiene, nutrition and family welfare.

Schemes for pregnant women and lactating mothers:

i. *The Pradhan Mantri Matru Vandana Yojana*[33]: The scheme provides a cash incentive in partial compensation for any wage loss incurred during the pregnancy period. This is extended so that the mother can seek adequate rest before and after the delivery of the child. The scheme has a PMMVY portal/mobile app. The app has new-age features, such as digital face recognition, UIDAI to verify eligible candidates and NPCI verification with beneficiary bank account to ensure a smooth transfer of Direct Benefit Transfer. It has highlighted the use of technology as an assistive tool.

ii. *Janani Suraksha Yojana*[34]: The scheme enables women from marginalised sections of society to access institutional delivery of children. The scheme has significantly reduced maternal and neonatal mortality. The scheme also extends conditional cash assistance to pregnant women giving birth in a government-run health facility. It also provides access to skilled birth attendants and emergency obstetric care.

Schemes and centees for response enhancement for women in distress and furthering women's rights:

i. *One-Stop Centres*[35]: Across states, centres have been set up to support women affected by violence. Distressed women can approach the centres that work in coordination with the counsellors of police-based support centres. It has been integrated with the 181 Women Helpline. These centres are centrally-sponsored under the Nirbhaya Fund. The Centre acts as a platform for extending emergency response, rescue services, immediate medical assistance, psycho-social support and counselling, assistance with the police to lodge an FIR, streamlining legal aid and access to shelter.

ii. *Mission Shakti*[36]: Gender budgeting scheme has comprehensively helped recognise the institutional challenges that women face, when it comes to accessing public forums, government systems. Gender impact assessments and audits have assisted in having budgetary allocations to streamline these challenges. The nodal authority for the creations of budgets at the central level is Ministry of Women and Child Development and at the state level, it is the Department of Women and Child Development.

iii. *State Resource Centre for Women*[37]: These centres extend technical expertise and assistance towards comprehensively implementing programmes. Its key focus areas are streamlining key stakeholders, research and development, training capacity building and awareness programmes. Gender Resource Centres- also contribute to issues on gender budgeting and funds.

iv. *Compensation Scheme for Women Victims/Survivors of Sexual Assault and other crimes, 2018*[38]: This scheme is both state and centrally-funded. The State Legal Services Authority, or the District Legal Services Authority is assists women in disbursement of funds for women who are victims. The scheme amount can also be granted to a dependent. The eligibility to avail of the fund is an application under Section 357 B of the CrPC.

Schemes for female entrepreneurs:

i. *Mudra Yojana Scheme*[39]: Under this scheme, women entrepreneurs can avail of funds to start small or micro-enterprises, the pre-requisite is that the enterprise should be a non-corporate or non-farm business. The funds limit that can be availed is up to Rs. 10 lakhs to start such an avenue.

   This financial assistance for eligible women has streamlined young entrepreneurs' access to funds.

ii. *Working Women Hostel*[40]: The objective behind the hostel is to provide young women who are leaving their homes access to a safe residential facility. Working women, single, widowed, divorced, separated, married women, whose husbands/family reside in some other city have access to this accommodation. There is also a lateral reservation for women with disabilities.

Challenges and Way Forward

Perhaps the best way is to highlight the hurdles women will face is the case of Dutee Chand (Indian athlete-sprinter). In 2014, she was barred from competing in the Commonwealth Games at Glasgow.[41] This was because of a test result which stated an escalated level of testosterone as the naturally occurring hormone in her body to the permissible level. She appealed against the decision at the Court of Arbitration, the highest court for sports-related appeals. The CAS gave a ruling supporting her. The decision suspended the International Association of Athletics Federation rule for two years. This also allowed her to compete for the title.

Several women questioned the decision to allow Dutee to compete. They argued that this jeopardises the level playing field for female athletes. The IAAF formulated a new rule restricting the athletic events to which such tests applied. The new ruling found that higher levels of naturally occurring testosterone did not add any advantage over those competing in a similar athletic event.

This incident highlighted the contentious issue of being a woman. What it means to be a woman, what is womanhood, is particularly relevant in the context of the transgender rights movement. This has added to the discourse on Trans- Exclusionary Radical Feminists. Trans-activists have coined the terminology. The term, lately, has been used as a weapon by those who advocate for trans-inclusion in female spaces.

The term is also weaponised by those who advocate and push for trans-exclusion from female-only spaces (such as bathrooms and changing rooms, which are single-sex spaces) on the grounds that men cannot change or completely transform into women. Therefore, allowing men who state they recognise themselves as women access to this space is unsafe.

Further, there are security-related threats which are unfair and unsafe for women. This exclusionary practice states that transwomen are not real women because the aspect of being feminine or womanhood is essentially related to the biological sex, also known as biological essentialism, highlighting the importance of biological sex. The famous author, J.K. Rowling, has been called a TERF[42] and has advocated for what sex essentialism is. This also comes with the stark contrast to the World Health Organisation and medical authorities that validate trans people in their authentic gender identity. This is coupled with the discrimination and exclusion that transgender people face at workplace, access to health care and housing.

The concluding aspect is that different forms of diversity go hand in hand. There is a need to have a systematic study of those transitioning and whether the women-only spaces are actually under threat. The scenario in India is governed by the Protection of Rights of Transgender Persons Act, 2019. The Act has a two-step process to have gender identity documentation.

Over the years, women have collectively pushed for a more excellent call for gender-equality. These movements today particularly, are aided by social media platforms. The best example of this is the tempest created by #MeToo. The internet has acted as a tool for women survivors of sexual assault, violence and harassment. No one in India has been spared of the allegations, be it the former Chief Justice of India or celebrities. The movement, however, eludes the position of domestic workers, factory workers and others employed in the informal sector. The PoSH legislation remains a significant step undertaken by the Indian government; the law remains only on paper. Poverty and the stigma of exclusion remain the biggest challenges. Within the lower economic strata, sexual harassment and sex-based discrimination remain trivial; something that must be ignored. Highlighting the cost of speaking up against harassment, this remains to be just one legislation that has captured the internet interests. In India, a comprehensive framework is needed to protect women's rights. The critical question to ask is whether women are disadvantaged due to their sex or also because of their caste, colour, religion, disability, age and sexual orientation. Hence, the aspect of women's rights to be progressive is the recognition of intersectionality; to improve the lives of all women, specifically, how it is impacted by the overlapping system of hurdles to disadvantages.

References

1. Feature based on Meena Gopal and Sabala's article, 'Body, Gender and Sexuality: Politics of Being and Belonging.' Available on - https://www.epw.in/engage/article/many-lives-womans-body
2. 2022 SCC OnLine SC 1321
3. '*Supreme Court rules all women entitled to safe, legal abortion*' by Raghav Ohri (Available at-https://economictimes.indiatimes.com/news/india/supreme-court-rules-all-women-entitled-to-safe-legal-abortion/articleshow/94542957.cms?from=mdr)
4. Online portal by the National Commission for Protection of Child Rights (Available at-https://pocso.ncpcrweb.in)

5. *'Justice-What's the right thing to do?'* by Michael J. Sandel
6. Lecture by Dr. M. Roa, *'Surrogacy in India'*, APU Colloquium Series (Available at-https://clpr.org.in/blog/apu-colloquium-series-surrogacy-in-india-lecture-by-dr-m-rao/)
7. (2017) 9 SCC 1
8. (2016) 226 DLT 647
9. (2020) 9 SCC 1
10. Manu Gupta vs. Sujata Sharma (CS (OS) 2011/2006)
11. AIR 1997 SC 3011
12. "Bhanwari Devi was raped for trying to stop 1992 child marriage. 'I curse her daily' says bride by Jyoti Yadav (Available at https://theprint.in/ground-reports/bhanwari-devi-was-raped-for-trying-to-stop-1992-child-marriage-i-curse-her-daily-says-bride/1765956/)
13. 'Bhanwari Devi: Justice eluded her, but she stands resolute for others' by Sachin Saini (Available at-https://www.hindustantimes.com/india-news/bhanwari-devi-justice-eluded-her-but-she-stands-resolute-for-others-101631811309362.html)
14. S.B. Civil Writ Petition No. 150/2021
15. SheBox (Availble at-https://shebox.nic.in)
16. 2009 VI AD
17. CWP No. 2955/2019
18. W.P.(C) 11016 of 2017
19. Beyond the glass ceiling: Why businesses need women at the top' (Available at-https://www.ilo.org/infostories/en-GB/Stories/Employment/beyond-the-glass-ceiling)
20. (2017) 6 SCC 1
21. [2011] 5 SCC 1
22. ILDC 868 (IN2004).
23. WP (C) 382/2013
24. SLP(Cr.) 4063-4064 of 2022
25. (2018) 4 SCC 433
26. Ujjawala a comprehensive scheme for Prevention of Trafficking and Rescue, Rehabilitation and Re-integration of Victims of Trafficking for Commercial Sexual Abuse (Available at https://wcd.nic.in/sites/default/files/Ujjawala%20New%20Scheme.pdf)
27. National Repository of Information for Women (Available at-http://www.nari.nic.in/.)
28. PENCIL Portal (Availabe at-https://pencil.gov.in)
29. Mahila E-haats (Available at-https://pib.gov.in/PressReleasePage.aspx?PRID=1695509)
30. 'ICC: Equal prize money for men's and women's cricket events' (Available at-https://economictimes.indiatimes.com/news/sports/icc-equal-prize-money-for-mens-and-womens-cricket-events/articleshow/101734760.cms?from=mdr#)
31. Beti Bachao Beti Padhao Scheme (Available at-https://wcd.nic.in/schemes/beti-bachao-beti-padhao-scheme)

32. Kishor Shakti Yojana (Available at https://wcd.nic.in/kishori-shakti-yojana)
33. Pradhan Mantri Matru Vandana Yojana (Available at https://pmmvy.wcd.gov.in
34. Janani Suraksha Yojana (Available at https://nhm.gov.in/index1.php?lang=1&level=3&lid=309&sublinkid=841https://nhm.gov.in/WriteReadData/l892s/97827133331523438951.pdf)
35. Mission Shakti- an integrated women empowerment programme (Available at shttps://wcd.nic.in/sites/default/files/Mission%20Shakti%20Guidelines%20-%20issued_1.pdf)
36. Mission Shakti – Gender Budgeting Scheme (Available at https://wcd.nic.in/sites/default/files/SoP%20for%20Gender%20Budgeting%20Scheme%20%28Final%29.pdf)
37. State Resource for Women (Available at-https://wcdhry.gov.in/schemes-for-women/state-resource-centre-for-women/)
38. NALSA's Compensation Scheme for Women Victims/Survivors of Sexual Assault/Other Crimes. (Available at-https://nalsa.gov.in/services/victim-compensation/nalsa-s-compensation-scheme-for-women-victims-survivors-of-sexual-assault-other-crimes---2018)
39. Mudra Yojana Scheme (Available at https://www.mudra.org.in)
40. Working Women's Hostel (Available Act https://wcdhry.gov.in/schemes-for-women/working-women-hostel/)
41. 'Family backs Dutee Chand to overcome doping ban' by Ashis Senapati (Available at-https://timesofindia.indiatimes.com/city/bhubaneswar/family-backs-dutee-chand-to-overcome-doping-ban/articleshow/102845878.cms#)
42. '*What is a Woman*?' by Michelle Goldberg (Available at https://www.newyorker.com/magazine/2014/08/04/woman-2)

□

13

Empowering Girls and Youth through Welfare Schemes in the Last Decade

—Dr. Richa Sahay

Master trainer (Smile Foundation), main trustee of NGO, motivational and life coach, author, spiritual teacher Entrepreneur)

Introduction

यत्र नार्यस्तु पूज्यन्ते रमन्ते तत्र देवता

The profound values embedded in the great Indian civilisation have long been a guiding force for leading a life enriched with principles. However, the past millennium bore witness to a significant deterioration, particularly in the treatment and respect accorded to females – a consequence of invasions and slavery. Even after India gained Independence, the plight of women remained largely unaltered. Confined within societal structures that restricted their freedom and identity, women lived in perpetual fear of insecurity due to their dependence. The patriarchal system further silenced their voices, denying them a platform for expression. The 2001 Census marked a stark decline in the child sex ratio, plummeting from 945 to 927 per 1,000 boys in the age group of 0-six years. This trend reached an all-time low of 918 girls for every 1,000 boys in 2011.[1] Unfortunately, little was done at the policy level to support women in claiming their rights and living a life of dignity, making the pursuit of a dignified existence seem like an unattainable dream for many.

Historical Context

When we look at history, we find that the past 1,000 years of Indian history was brutally marked by invasions and slavery and it witnessed a distressing degradation in the treatment and respect afforded to women. The societal structures that emerged perpetuated the confinement of women within the four walls of their homes, depriving them of freedom and a distinct identity. Even India's Independence from the British Raj failed to bring about any significant shift in the status of women and it only turned down the hopes of females for a better and dignified life. The patriarchal system, deeply ingrained in the fabric of society, ensured that women remained voiceless and relegated to the margins. The 2001 Census reflected the sombre reality of a declining child sex ratio, portraying the societal neglect and indifference towards the well-being and rights of the girl child.

Post-Independence Challenges

Despite gaining Independence, women in India found themselves ensnared within societal norms that curtailed their aspirations and potential. The absence of policies supporting their rights and dignity perpetuated a cycle of neglect. The 2001 Census data became an alarming indicator of the prevailing gender disparity, as it brought up a concerning decline in the child sex ratio. Furthermore, as per a report in April 2016, a depressing reality is that annually, an estimated 5,00,000 girls[2] were being lost to female foeticide. This troubling trend underscored the urgent need for transformative measures to uplift and empower the girl child. Apart from being an issue of female respect and dignity, this also triggered a 'bride crisis'[2] situation, forcing the sale of girls for sexual purposes. These victims endured extensive physical, mental, moral and emotional torment, facing the denial of even their basic rights.

The Transformative Decade

The past decade, however, has emerged as a turning point, bringing about transformative changes in the narrative of the girl child in India. Government initiatives, awareness campaigns and policy reforms have collectively worked towards dismantling the barriers that restricted the freedom and potential of women.

Government Initiatives

Initiatives like the Beti Bachao Beti Padhao (BBBP) scheme, launched in 2015, aimed at addressing the skewed child sex ratio and empowering girls through education. This scheme, along with others like Sukanya Samriddhi Yojana (SSY), educational empowerment programmes and healthcare initiatives, has contributed to the holistic development of the girl child.

Shift in Societal Paradigms

The focus on gender empowerment and the implementation of targeted schemes have gradually shifted societal paradigms. Awareness campaigns celebrating the girl child and environmental protection have played a pivotal role in building consciousness at various levels of society.

In conclusion, the past decade has witnessed a remarkable shift in the treatment and perception of the girl child in India. While historical challenges persist, the transformative measures implemented have kindled a sense of hope and empowerment. Government initiatives, awareness campaigns and changing societal norms collectively contribute to dismantling the age-old barriers that confined women to the shadows. The journey towards gender equality and empowerment continues, fuelled by the momentum gained in the past decade, offering a brighter and more equitable future for the girl child in India.

In this chapter efforts of the government have been highlighted through various schemes and their implementation vide elaboration of schemes and case studies of their impacts. The schemes which have been discussed are *'Beti Bachao, Beto Padao', 'Sukanya Samriddhi Yojana', 'Rashtriya Kishor Swasthya Karyakram',* National Child Labour Scheme, 'SABLA Scheme for Adolescent Girls', 'Protection of Children from Sexual Offences' and *'Ladli Laxmi Yojana'*. Girl child has been neglected by the previous government due to which there were foeticide and killing of girl child in the womb and torturing them while alive.

In a population exceeding 1.4 billion, crafting impactful policies is no easy feat, given the diversity of thought processes and the prevalence of self-serving motives in a democratic government. Implementing and executing these policies effectively presents an even greater challenge. However, over the last decade, a notable transformation has occurred. A robust political will, coupled with widespread and sincere implementation, has brought about significant changes. This chapter aims to provide insights into various aspects of this transformation, highlighting real-life success stories that instil confidence in the government's motives and its operational approach. The evolution in governance over the past 10 years reflects a commitment to positive change and a demonstration of effective administration amid the complexities of a vast and diverse population.

1. Beti Bachao, Beti Padhao

The male-to-female ratio, commonly referred to as the sex ratio, stands as a crucial socio-economic indicator with far-reaching implications for any country. This ratio plays a multifaceted role, influencing social harmony, family dynamics, cultural and social progress, as well as the overall health, well-being and economic development of a nation.

Beyond its numerical significance, the sex ratio serves as an indicator of societal attitudes and acceptance towards specific genders. A skewed sex ratio often reflects biased mindsets prevalent in society that manifest as preferences for one gender over another. This preference can contribute to the perpetuation of gender-based inequalities and discriminatory practices.

The consequences of a biased mindset extend beyond numerical disparities. They contribute to the degradation of society in terms of civilisation, fostering an environment where certain individuals or groups face unequal opportunities and treatment based on their gender. Such biases can hinder social progress, impede cultural evolution and create disparities that affect the overall well-being of a society.

Addressing and rectifying skewed sex ratios require not only numerical adjustments but also a concerted effort to dismantle biased mindsets deeply ingrained in societal norms. Promoting gender equality, challenging stereotypes and fostering an environment that values and respects all individuals regardless of their gender are essential steps toward building a more inclusive and equitable society. Recognising the interconnectedness of the sex ratio with various aspects of socio-economic development is crucial for formulating comprehensive strategies aimed at creating a balanced, harmonious and progressive society.

Taking the example of Haryana, which had a worrying sex ratio of 861 females per 1,000 males as per Census 2011[1], saw sharp degradation of female dignity. An article in *Hindustan Times*, dated 23 March, 2014, titled 'When Women Come Cheaper than Cattle'[2] stated, "The skewed sex ratio in Haryana, Punjab and western Uttar Pradesh has led to a flourishing trade in women from Assam, West Bengal, Jharkhand and Odisha, who are often bought for as little as Rs. 5,000." It underscored that the decline in the female population, coupled with entrenched feudalism, had led to the trafficking of women from impoverished villages in Assam, West Bengal, Jharkhand and Odisha. These women were compelled to work as bonded labour, coerced into forced marriages, or forced into prostitution.

An important reason for such a poor sex ratio was female foeticide wherein girl child would be aborted post confirmation via prenatal gender determination illegally. A girl child is considered a liability as spending on her upbringing and education was of no use as she has to be sent to the groom's house post marriage and marriage too also is not a cheap affair. In addition, the religious beliefs in many communities that the son only can be the medium of liberation of parents post death made a male child more desirable.

Desire of having a male child is not limited to just a few states but has been a national challenge.

To combat such a worrying scenario which would contribute negatively to the development of the country, a powerful, impactful and ambitious national scheme was launched by the Government of India in 2015, called as 'Beti Bachao, Beti Padhao' (BBBP)[3] which was unveiled by Prime Minister Narendra Modi at Panipat, Haryana, on 22 January, 2015, operated by the Ministries of Women and Child Development, Human Resource Development, and Health & Family Welfare. As the name suggests, the programme's primary objective is to protect girls from social problems, such as gender-based abortions and to promote girl-child education throughout the country.

The scheme is really ambitious and addresses the entire gamut of challenges faced by girl child that begins from its conception to healthy and empowered development.

The objectives[4] of the scheme are:

- The initiative seeks to address societal discrimination against girls and aims to shift the mindset of the country's citizens. Shift in mindset is always the best solution because it is not a superficial solution but a root treatment. Although it is not so easy and takes time, however once the mindset changes, the problem disappears forever.
- The programme aims to tackle a broad range of issues, encompassing the reduction of the child sex ratio (CSR), fostering women's empowerment, eliminating gender-based inequalities and ensuring the protection of girls. A change in mindset remains unattainable unless females are perceived as empowered. Therefore, addressing a wide array of issues related to female development is crucial.
- The programme also focuses on educating girls and promoting their active participation in society. Educated girls possess the ability to transform the culture within their families, consequently influencing society. When they engage actively in societal activities and contribute meaningfully, they cease to be marginalised.
- In addition, the initiative addresses the CSR issue through nationwide campaigns and implementation of multi-sectoral government interventions in 100 districts identified as gender-critical.

In order to achieve its humongous ambition, it charted a path that would lead to the desired result. These key features[3] of BBBP programme are:

- Establishing discussions and dialogues on the reduction of Child Sex Ratio (CSR) with the objective of raising awareness and facilitating improvement.
- Promoting community engagement and striving for enhanced development concerning the well-being and birth of female children.
- Implementing large-scale communication initiatives to disseminate information about the BBBP scheme.
- Providing training to local governing authorities and involving employees from government organisations and schools in the movement for societal change.
- Protect girl children and prevent inhumane practices, such as foeticide and female infanticide.
- Promoting women's involvement in education as a fundamental aspect and ensuring that each girl child receives appropriate access to education.
- Improving and enhancing the child gender ratio in states, such as Uttarakhand, Delhi, Punjab, Haryana and Uttar Pradesh.
- Preventing child marriage and ensuring the safety of girls from associated physical and mental harassment, as well as domestic violence.
- Promoting gender equality throughout the country.
- The BBBP scheme promotes financial security for girl children, aiming to ensure their future education, growth and development.

Accessing the scheme is not so simple for families. Any family with a girl child under 10 years can be benefitted from the scheme. The only qualification for the same is opening a Sukanya Samriddhi account in any Indian bank or Post Office (As per SSY requirement) in the girl child's name, provided the girl is a resident of India. This straightforward criterion ensures ease of participation in the programme.

The programme offers a huge array of benefits:

- An account can be opened for a girl child for financial security in the future. This account is completely tax-free and is exempted under the Act 1961 u/s 80C. In addition, the account has a decent rate of interest and withdrawal is only allowed for the girl child after she attains the age of 18 years.

- This facilitates easy savings for daughters via their parents or guardians and promotes generation of awareness regarding issues of girls and women, thereby improving delivery of welfare services for women.
- The programme also addresses declining CSR (child sex ratio) in critical states and regions and promotes better education and inclusion for women.

The sincerity of the government can be well understood by the way budget allocations year by year has been done. The following table shows the same:[6]

S. No.	Financial Year	Funds Allocated (Rs. in Crore)
1	2014-15	50
2	2015-16	75
3	2016-17	43
4	2017-18	200
5	2018-19	280
6	2019-20	280

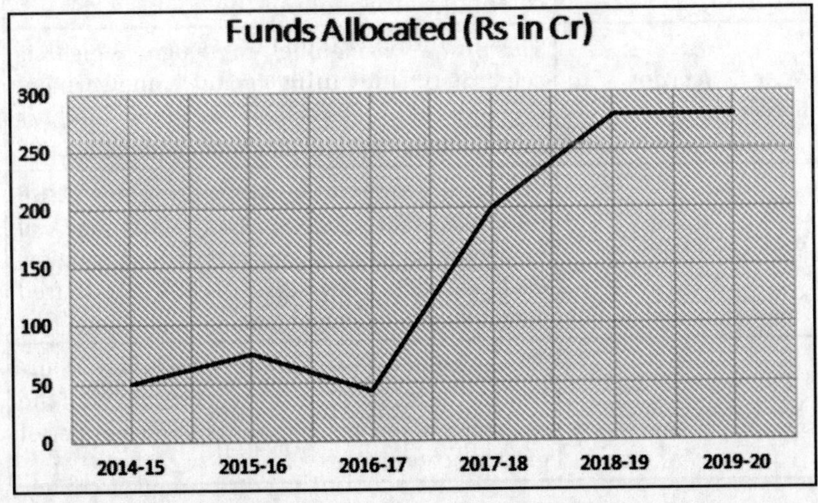

As the graph clearly exhibits, the budget has been significantly increased with the passing years, enabling better coverage of the scheme.

Under this scheme, districts have implemented various initiatives to create awareness among target groups and other stakeholders. The following Table[7] shows the initiatives:

Initiatives	Description
Digital Guddi-Gudda Board	This is a digital platform which has been established to showcase gender disparity in birth rates and disseminate information on schemes and programmes which are designed to safeguard the girl child.
Udaan - Sapne Di Duniya De Rubaru	This initiative has been taken with the objective to offer opportunities to girls to shadow professionals in the field of their choice for learning the skill in totality.
My Aim My Target Campaign	The programme facilitates recognition of top academic performances of girls in Higher Secondary Schools.
Lakshya Se Rubaru	This is an internship programme tailored for girl students in colleges, that aims to encourage them to make informed decisions about their careers.
Noor Jeevan Ka Betiyan	This is a week-long campaign which is celebrated by featuring gender empowerment theme-based interactive activities and is organised in Panchayat schools and colleges.
Bitiya and Birba	This is an awareness campaign under BBBP initiative that encompasses protection of environment as well. As a part of the campaign, each mother of a newborn girl child is honoured with a plant and celebrated.
Aao School Chalein	This is an enrolment campaign wherein door-to-door visits are done for registration with the objective to ensure 100 per cent enrolment of girls in schools.

Collector Ki Class	Under this initiative, coaching classes and career counselling are offered for free to underprivileged girls in public schools and colleges.
Bal Cabinet	This is a youth leadership initiative, wherein female students engage in simulated government cabinets and ministerial roles to deliberate and address various issues.

The scheme, despite many obstacles, has shown significant success.[5, 11] A few are pointed here:

- The BBBP scheme has defined quantifiable outcomes and indicators to track progress across 640 districts. Performance targets include improving the Sex Ratio at Birth in select gender-critical districts by two points per year, reducing gender differentials in the under-five child mortality rate metric by 1.5 points per year and providing functional toilets for girls in every school in select districts.
- There has been a 16-point improvement in Sex Ratio at Birth (SRB) from 918 in 2014-15 to 939 in 2021-2022, which indicates a positive trend in addressing gender disparities.
- Out of the 640 districts included in the BBBP initiative, 422 districts have demonstrated an improvement in the Sex Ratio at Birth (SRB) from the period of 2014-15 to 2018-19.[7]
- Gross Enrolment Ratio (GER) in secondary education has improved from 77.45 per cent in 2014 to 81.32 per cent in 2021 – an increase of 3.87 points in four years, which indicates more girls accessing education now.
- School dropout rates for girls in secondary education have come down to 12 per cent from 14 per cent in 2014, which is indicative of more girls completing their education now.
- The BBBP scheme has additionally emphasised the promotion of girls' higher education, aiming to foster sustainable development.

- The proportion of schools equipped with separate, functional toilets for girls increased from 92.1 per cent in 2014-15 to 95.1 per cent in 2018-19.[7]
- The first-trimester ANC (Antenatal Care) registration rate witnessed an increase from 61 per cent in 2014-15 to 71 per cent in 2019-20.[7]
- The rate of institutional deliveries experienced a significant increase, rising from 87 per cent in 2014-15 to 94 per cent in 2019-20.[7]
- The initiative has led to heightened awareness and increased sensitisation among the public regarding the prevalence of gender disparities.

Here are glimpses of a few of various initiatives taken by the government for BBBP:[8]

Glimpses of activities under BBBP at Cuddalore, Tamil Nadu

Photo courtesy: https://wcd.nic.in/bbbp-photo-gallery

Glimpses of initiatives undertaken by Department of Women & Child Development, Uttarakhand

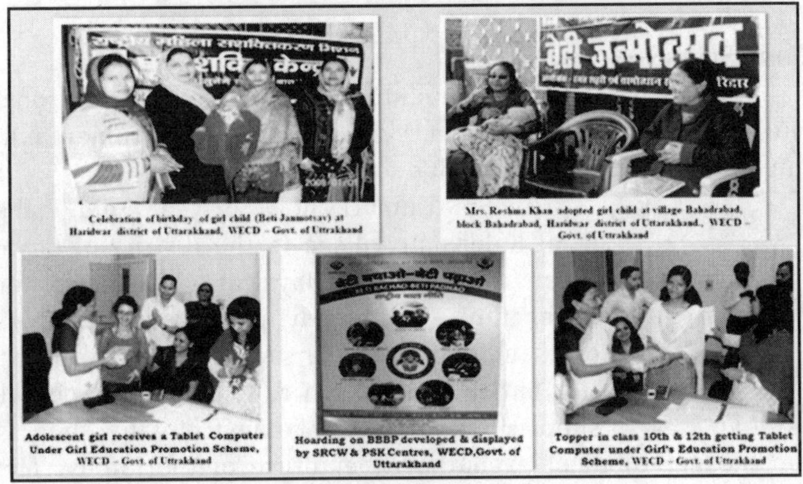

Photo courtesy: https://wcd.nic.in/bbbp-photo-gallery

Implementing a nationwide scheme in a country with a population exceeding 1.4 billion is a formidable task that requires extensive work at the grassroots level to yield results. It demands robust political will coupled with the requisite skills and capabilities for effective execution. Nevertheless, the government has demonstrated remarkable activity and noteworthy results, as highlighted above, have been achieved.

During the initial five years of implementation,[7] the BBBP scheme effectively enhanced crucial performance metrics specified in its target objectives. This has given confidence to the citizens of the country about the willingness to contribute significantly towards the girl child of the country. Government has been fast and observant at taking cognisance of the obstacles and to further enhance the success of the programme, the government intends to conduct an extensive district-level survey. This survey, facilitated by an independent agency in collaboration with Niti Aayog, aims to assess progress and identify obstacles to implementation. The primary objective is to devise strategies for reinforcing the execution of the scheme in states that exhibit lower performance.

What is very encouraging for the common man are the success stories of the people who have experienced the benefits and hence the change.

Case Story

Here is a real-life success story coming from a grassroots NGO called Vikalp Foundation,[13] which has been instrumental in implementing the government's scheme:

Kusum Kumari, now 22-years old, hails from Kaldaspur village in the district of Gaya, Bihar. Living with physical challenges, her lower limbs completely paralyzed, Kusum is eldest amongst her four sisters and one brother. Her father Kapil Mistri runs a small carpenter shop. However, the income from the shop is too meager to meet even the expenditure of the family. The challenging financial circumstances made it difficult for Kapil Mistri to provide education to his children. Kusum, who always dearly wanted to fulfill her dreams, too was deprived of higher education. Undeterred by the obstacles, she found a way and began offering home tuition to school children. This endeavour required her to travel, but the resilient young woman, refusing to succumb to challenges, commuted by using her tricycle, displaying unwavering determination to fund her higher studies.

Kusum's challenging life took a positive U-turn eight years ago when a survey team of Vikalp Foundation led by Chandrashekhar Azad in Gaya visited her village and identified her. Recognising her indomitable spirit, the Foundation decided to adopt Kusum. She received financial assistance for her higher studies and was also enrolled in computer training in the ongoing 'vocational education' at Vikalp Foundation which is supported by NABARD. Completing a six-month course in computer education, Kusum went on to establish her own computer training institute, offering typing, internet services and printing facilities. She also joined the DPO (Disabled People Organisation) network of Vikalp Foundation. Today, Kusum is thriving, surpassing the achievements of many normal youth. She is financially independent and supports the family too.

Kusum says that she is unable to express her feelings and gratitude towards the Foundation and Mr Azad. It is due to his kind support that she has been able to fulfil her dreams. Now she wants to get married and pledges to help physically challenged persons she would come across. She says that she would motivate them never to give up.

When the government demonstrates effective performance despite formidable obstacles, it instils confidence in its citizens, providing them with a sense of security, prosperity and happiness. Case studies, such as the one highlighted, serve as concrete examples of the positive impact of government initiatives, reinforcing the belief in a better, more promising future for the people.

2. Sukanya Samriddhi Yojana (Small Deposit Scheme for the Girl Child)

Yet another very powerful programme by Government of India, Ministry of Child and Women Development, Sukanya Samriddhi Yojana was launched on 22 January, 2015 as part of the BBBP programme.

In the context of India, the entrenched patriarchal culture has historically failed to provide sufficient encouragement for families to prioritise the education of their girls. The prevailing societal expectation revolves around the idea that girls will eventually move to their husband's household after marriage. This cultural norm, coupled with the deeply ingrained practice of demanding a dowry during the marriage ceremony, exacerbates the challenges faced by girls and their families.

The burden of dowry places immense financial strain on the parents of the girl child, particularly in the lower-middle-class and underprivileged communities, given their poor financial condition. Confronted with economic pressure, parents find themselves in a perpetual state of mental stress, struggling to meet substantial financial expectations associated with their daughter's marriage. The weight of this financial burden often acts as a demotivating factor, discouraging parents from prioritising their daughter's education and investing in her higher academic pursuits.

The result of these cultural and economic factors is the emergence of disempowered females, trapped in a cycle of limited opportunities and constrained life choices. Hindered by societal norms that prioritise marriage over education of girls, these individuals face challenges in asserting themselves in various aspects of life. The prevailing disrespect and subjugation become defining features of their existence, perpetuating a cycle of inequality and limiting their potential contributions to society.

Sukanya Samriddhi Yojana is a ray of hope and light for all such parents and girls. The scheme helps parents create a substantial fund for their girl child with assured high rate of interest of 8 per cent currently. The scheme has been framed in a way that it can be well utilised for her higher education and marriage purposes.

The simplicity and approachability of the scheme is such that one can get an account opened at any post office or a branch of notified authorised commercial banks.

The benefits[1] of the programme are:

- The programme offers a high interest rate.
- One can get tax benefit under Section 80C.
- Payment is done on maturity of girl child, ensuring that the fund is not used in between for any other purpose.

- Interest payment is made even after maturity, if account is not closed.
- The account is transferable anywhere in India.
- As soon as the girl child attains the age of 10 years, she too can operate the account.
- Contributions can be made to the account until the conclusion of a 15-year period from the date of its opening, as per the SSY scheme 2019 rules.

The scheme is witnessing a huge success and 1,42,73,910[1] new Sukanya Samriddhi Accounts have been opened by the citizens of the country from since 1 April 2018 to 31 October 2021.

Many such girls have been benefited under this scheme. Here are few real-life case studies:

Case Story 1[3]

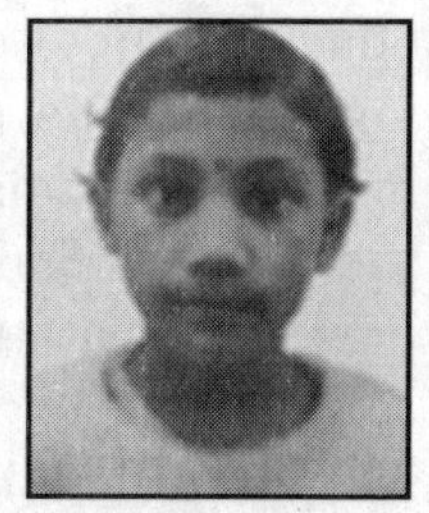

Rasta, an NGO, during a survey, identified Meghna Parveen as a school dropout in May 2023. Meghna resides with her grandparents in Noida, while her parents live in Ghaziabad. The family had migrated from West Bengal two years ago in search of employment opportunities. Given the financial constraints and lack of awareness about nearby schools, Meghna's grandparents, unable to afford her education, sought assistance from Rasta NGO. Consequently, Meghna was admitted to the gurukul centre run by the NGO. At this juncture, her grandparents were educated about the Sukanya Samriddhi Yojana, which could create a good corpus for Meghna's higher education needs as well as marriage requirements. This scheme was welcomed by her grandparents and they immediately got the SSY account opened for Meghna in the nearby post office. Meghna has now been successfully mainstreamed into the 3rd grade at the Government Primary School in Sarfabad. This transition marks a crucial step towards realising Meghna's academic aspiration as it brings a lot of hope for her bright future.

Case Story 2[3]

When Rasta NGO went to Sarfabad for survey of children's enrolment in their Rasta gurukul learning centre in June 2023, they met Shivani's family. Shivani and her younger brother

dropped out of school when they shifted from their village Sambhal with their parents two years ago to Noida, since earning a livelihood was challenging in their village. At Noida, Shivani's father works as a security guard while her mother works as a house help in the nearby society. Although they shifted for a better life, however it seemed destiny had some different plans for them. The roller coaster life was not allowing them to even manage their expenses due to which they could never think of their children's education. During the survey both the children were enrolled at Rasta Learning Centre as regular students. The mother was then educated about the Sukanya Samriddhi Yojana but she denied to join every time, even in the community meeting. A special group meeting was done with her after which she finally agreed and got the Sukanya Samriddhi account opened for her daughter in the post office with the help of Rasta's employees. Now she deposits some money every month in the account and is happy about her savings for her daughter's future.

Case Story 3[4]

The Smile Foundation team, during a scheduled home visit at Karoli, connected with Preeti and Mamta, the mother of a

Preeti with

three-year-old daughter Avni and seven-year-old daughter Bhumika, respectively. In their interaction, the team elaborated on their programmes, initiatives and the support they provide to the community. Following this, a one-on-one counselling session was conducted with Preeti. Subsequently, a group meeting was organised with the community to disseminate information about various government schemes, including Sukanya

Samriddhi Yojana that could bring manifold benefits to the community.

Both Preeti and Mamta were particularly interested in Sukanya Yojana and they received detailed insights from the Smile Foundation team regarding the scheme's requirements and comprehensive advantages.

Expressing her keen interest in securing her daughter's future and providing her with a better education, Preeti said she harboured the aspiration within herself but due to financial constraints, could not hope for a better and bright future for her daughter Bhumika. The Smile Foundation team played a pivotal role in clarifying the details of the Sukanya Samriddhi Yojana and today, Preeti and Mamta have taken a positive step forward by opening a Sukanya Samriddhi account for Avni and Bhumika and have initiated regular deposits. This not only fulfils Preeti's and Mamta's aspirations but also stands as a testament to how informed guidance and support can empower parents to shape a brighter future for their children, breaking the barriers posed by financial constraints.

Mamta with Bhumika

Such schemes showcase how breaking barriers becomes possible, thereby opening doors to education and a promising future for underprivileged children. Meghna, Shivani, Avni and Bhumika's stories are emblematic of the transformative impact that targeted interventions, such as the Sukanya Samriddhi Yojana, can have on the lives of marginalised children. Through holistic support, encompassing education, financial empowerment and community engagement, initiatives taken by various institutions and NGOs contribute to breaking the cycle of poverty and empower young minds to dream beyond their immediate circumstances. The journey of Meghna, Shivani, Avni and Bhumika exemplifies the potential for positive change when individuals and organisations unite to uplift the underprivileged and provide them with the tools to shape their destinities.

3. Rashtriya Kishor Swasthya Karyakram

Based on the 2011 Census data, there are 253 million adolescents aged 10-19 years,[1] constituting slightly over one-fifth of India's total population. This demographic encompasses individuals in a transitional stage of life, where nutrition, education, counselling and guidance is of key importance to facilitate their progression into healthy adults. Recognising the demographic potential of this group for substantial economic growth, it is imperative to invest in their education, health and overall development.

This age group undergoes significant hormonal changes that impact their thought processes, behaviours, and life choices. These formative years are crucial for their development, requiring proper guidance to navigate the challenges they face. Without adequate support, there is a significant risk that adolescents may deviate from the right path and engagein activities that could prove detrimental to both themselves and the society at large. This is particularly crucial in the present context, where the influence of social media is exceedingly high and a vast array of content is readily accessible to adolescents. This makes the need for proper guidance even more pressing as the abundance of information can shape their perspectives and decisions. The absence of suitable guidance could lead them astray, potentially causing harm to their well-being and negatively impacting the community.

Recognising the potential consequences, it becomes imperative to channel the energy and enthusiasm of adolescents in a constructive manner. The transformative phase they undergo can be a valuable asset for the country's growth, contributing to both economic and cultural advancements. Properly directed, their energy and creativity can lead to innovation, productivity and positive societal contributions. Conversely, if not provided with the necessary guidance and support, their energy may manifest in destructive behaviour, causing harm to themselves and others. The challenges posed by the contemporary digital landscape make it crucial to instil values, resilience and a sense of responsibility in adolescents, ensuring that they contribute positively to the collective progress of society.

Recognising the challenges and the need for holistic development of adolescent population, the Ministry of Health and Family Welfare launched the Rashtriya Kishor Swasthya Karyakram (RKSK) on 7 January, 2014 to reach these adolescents,[2] be they rich or poor; urban or rural; in school or out of school; married or unmarried with special focus on marginalised and undeserved groups.

It's important to take into cognisance that as per the national Census 2011 in the age group of 15 to 19, approximately 11.9 crore[3] are girls. This underscores a significant number of girls who have benefited from this scheme.

The programme broadens the scope of adolescent health programming in India. Previously confined to sexual and reproductive health, it now encompasses a wider range – nutrition, injuries, violence (including gender-based violence), non-communicable diseases, mental health and substance misuse. The programme's strength lies in its health promotion approach, signifying a shift from traditional clinic-based services to emphasise on promotion and prevention. It aims to connect with adolescents in their own environments, whether it be school, family, or community. Key components of the programme include community-based interventions, such as outreach by counsellors, facility-based counselling, social and behaviourial change communication and enhancement of adolescent -friendly health clinics at various levels of care.

The programme has set objectives to reduce malnutrition and iron deficiency anaemia among both adolescent girls and boys. It seeks to enhance knowledge, attitudes and behaviours related to sexual and reproductive health, with a focus on reducing teenage pregnancies. Additionally, the programme aims to improve birth preparedness, complication readiness and early parenting support for adolescent parents. Addressing mental health concerns among adolescents is another key goal. The programme also endeavours to promote positive attitudes to prevent injuries and violence among adolescents. Lastly, it strives to increase awareness of the adverse effects and consequences of substance misuse among adolescents.

It is well understood that adolescents lack the freedom to make their own decisions. Recognising this, the scheme actively involves parents and the community. The emphasis is on restructuring the existing public health system to better address the service needs of adolescents. This involves offering a comprehensive package of services, encompassing preventive, promotive, curative and counselling services. Routine check-ups are conducted at primary, secondary and tertiary levels of care during clinic sessions, catering to both married and unmarried adolescents, girls and boys.

Although the scope of the programme extends to both boys and girls of adolescent age, however a part of the scheme that benefited females especially are:

1. Adolescent-friendly Health Clinics (AFHCs), which provide a comfortable and friendly environment for adolescents to access healthcare services.
2. Weekly Iron Folic Acid Supplementation (WIFS), implemented in several districts, ensures the supply of iron and folic acid supplements to adolescent girls.
3. Menstrual hygiene programme, launched in 27 districts, aims to improve menstrual hygiene among adolescent girls.
4. Peer education is encouraged to create awareness and promote healthy practices among their peers.
5. Adolescent Health Day (AHD) is observed for outreach and community engagement.

Here are some case studies of the beneficiary girls who were impacted positively under the programme:

Case Story 1[5]

Chanda Jangir, a student of Class 12 in Bambor village, Rajasthan was identified by an NGO called Bal Sansar that is located in Jaipur, Rajasthan. Chanda's father is a blacksmith by profession. Bal Sansar named the programme 'Taiyari' for better local reach and under the project, Chanda who said that she lacked confidence to express herself, lacked awareness about social issues and was scared to speak in front of people benefited on various fronts.

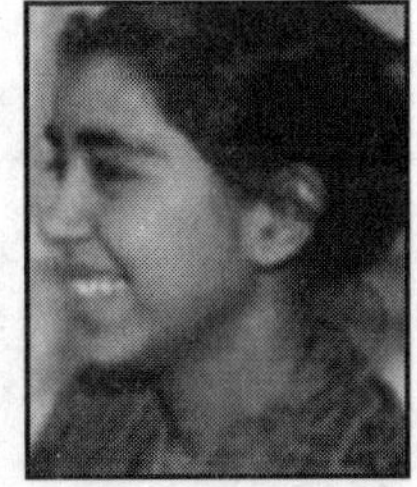

She joined the project where she got a platform to express her views without any fear. She understood the importance of eradication of social evils, like child marriage, female infanticide and dowry system and has been instrumental in spreading awareness about these. She says that for the first time she has understood the importance of haemoglobin test and iron capsules and under the programme, her haemoglobin has increased from 9g/dL. She also understood how healthy and nutritious food can help to increase the level of haemoglobin. In addition, she also became aware about different government initiatives taken for children and women.

Chanda now is a confident girl who is ready to take charge of her life.

Case Story 2[5]

Salma Banu, daughter of Bholu Khan, lives in Kayampura village, Rajasthan. Under the project Taiyari of Bal Sansar which was supported by UNICEF and was a part of RKSK, she got educated about the importance of girl child, education of girls, child marriage, personal health, dowry system and HIV and AIDS.

Salma was married to a man who worked as a driver and did not come home for long periods, when she was studying in Class 8 and was totally unaware about what child marriage meant. She was not sent to her in-laws' house because the tradition of '*gauna*' hadn't yet been completed. During the awareness meets at the Taiyari community programmes, she came to know about HIV, its causes and how it spreads. This really scared Salma since her husband did not come home for long periods. She says she will give all the information to her husband when she goes to her in-laws' house and has taken a pledge to prevent child marriage of her children and also spread awareness about why marriages should take place after the legal age only. She says that the Taiyari project has given a new meaning to her life and has opened her eyes on different issues of life.

It is truly heartening to witness the transformative impact of the Rashtriya Kishore Swasthya Karyakram, providing numerous girls with a new direction to their lives.

4. National Child Labour Scheme

Child labour has been a serious problem in India. With poverty increasing during the British Raj, the country had to provide for the uplift of the marginalised lot on receiving independence. Even as recent as 2009-2010, as per Suresh Tendulkar Committee report,[1] 29.6 per cent of the population was below the poverty line. There has been an amazing improvement in the statistics where the percentage of population living under poverty line had fallen to 15 per cent in 2019-21.

The biggest victims of such abysmal poverty are children, who instead of going to school and enjoying their childhood are pushed into laborious tasks, like rag picking, begging, and working at teastalls or in households to earn money. Children also become victims of child trafficking and prostitution.

Safeguarding the future of such children is one of the prime objectives of the government.

With this motive, the Government of India launched the National Child Labour Project in 1988[2]. The project has covered and benefitted many children since its inception. Launched in 12 child labour-endemic districts, today it benefits children under the age of 14 in 15 states.[2]

This serves as the foremost central sector scheme specifically designed for the rehabilitation of children. The scheme adopts a sequential methodology,[2] commencing with the survey of childrenengaged in hazardous occupations and processes. Subsequently, it involves the withdrawal of these children from such occupations, followed by their placement in special schools. The overarching objective is to facilitate their integration into the formal school system. The scheme places a significant emphasis on prioritising the rehabilitation of these children, ensuring that they are removed from hazardous work environments and provided with the necessary support for their education and overall well-being. This approach reflects a commitment to breaking the cycle of child labour and offering these children an opportunity for a better future through education and proper rehabilitation.

This initiative focuses on children aged nine to 14 years, aiming to eradicate child labour by withdrawing them from workplaces and enrolling them in NCLP Special Training Centres. Within these centres, these children receive comprehensive support, including education, vocational training mid-day meals, stipends and healthcare services, etc. The holistic approach prepares them for successful integration into the formal education system. Additionally, for children aged five to eight years, a direct connection to the formal education system is established through close collaboration with the Sarva Shiksha Abhiyan,[3] ensuring a seamless transition into mainstream education. This concerted effort not only addresses the immediate issue of child labour but also focuses on providing a well-rounded educational experience to these vulnerable children, fostering their overall development and creating a foundation for a brighter future.

In the year 2020-2021 alone, 58,286[4] children were rescued/ withdrawn from workplaces, rehabilitated and mainstreamed under NCLP scheme.

Needless to say, while the scheme caters to all children, it has undeniably proven to be particularly beneficial for numerous girls, allowing them to lead lives of dignity. While specific statistics regarding the number of girl beneficiaries are not readily available, my personal survey has revealed the positive impact on a number of girls who have availed the benefits under the scheme. The anecdotal evidence from this survey highlights the tangible improvements in the lives of these girls, showcasing the scheme's effectiveness in empowering and providing opportunities for them. Although precise figures may be lacking, the qualitative evidence underscores the significant strides made in enhancing the well-being and prospects of girl children through the implementation of this scheme.

Two of such real-life case stories are shared below:

Case Story 1[5]

Nisha, now 19 years old, was adopted by Gurugram-based non-governmental organisation, Maxvision, when she was around

sevenyears of age. Coming from a family of five siblings, Nisha's father, employed as a peon in a bank, struggled to meet the financial demands in the sub-urban locality where they lived. Nisha became a beneficiary under the National Child Labour Programme, marking the beginning of her transformative journey.

Demonstrating exceptional academic prowess, Nisha flourished during her years at the Maxvision NCLP centre, progressing from Class 1 to Class 5. Subsequently, she seamlessly transitioned to a government school in Class 6, successfully completing her education up to 12th standard. Beyond academics, Nisha actively engaged in various activities at the Maxvision Education Centre and took on the responsibility of teaching her two younger brothers at home.

Driven by a sense of responsibility and aware of the family's challenging financial circumstances, Nisha aspired to support her father and actively took on household responsibilities while growing up. Presently, Nisha has become a teacher at Sanskaar Public School, contributing significantly to improving the family's living conditions. Her journey serves as an inspiring example of resilience and determination.

Nisha extends her impact beyond her immediate surroundings. She passionately advocates for not keeping children out of school, emphasising that lack of financial resources should not be a barrier. She actively engages with her community, raising awareness about available policies and institutions that facilitate education without imposing any financial burden. Nisha's story epitomises the transformative potential of education and underscores the crucial role of individuals like her in creating a positive change within their community.

Case Story 2[5]

Anshu, daughter of a *gol-gappe* seller and a factory worker (mother), embarked on her journey with NGO Maxvision Education Centre in Class 5. The financial struggles of her parents, with a composite income that barely exceeded four figures, coupled with three siblings, exposed Anshu to the challenges of financial instability. Despite these hardships, she actively supported her mother in household chores so that her mother could go to work on time and also balanced her academic commitments.

Anshu, recognised for her creativity, harboured the dream of becoming a beautician. However, financial constraints hindered her pursuit of formal training and certification in the field. Fortunately, the Maxvision Education Centre proved to be a pillar of support. Drawing inspiration, Anshu decided to take charge of her life. She began private tuition classes and utilised the income generated not only for household expenses, but also for her parlour training.

Through determination and resourcefulness, Anshu successfully completed a six-month parlour coaching programme. Today, she stands as a certified beautician, realising her dream of working in the field. Not only does she contribute to the family income as a beautician at Salu Beauty Parlour, but also demonstrates her resilience and the transformative power of educational support. Her journey underscores the importance of empowerment through education and the positive impact it can have on individuals striving to overcome financial constraints and pursue their aspirations.

Anshu expresses profound happiness as she stands on her own feet and pursues her dream career, giving credit to Maxvision and the NCLP programme for shaping her life.

Many Nishas and Anshus are eager to share their success stories on a larger platform. The stories are tales of a committed Bharat and committed government towards recreating a country of 21st century. These stories embody the commitment of both the people of India and the dedicated efforts of the government collectively striving to transform the nation into a progressive and resilient country. The narratives of Nisha and Anshu exemplify the positive impact of government initiatives in uplifting lives and fostering a brighter future for individuals across the country.

5. SABLA – Scheme for Adolescent Girls

In the demographic landscape of India, adolescent girls, aged between 11 and 18 years, constitute a significant segment, making up approximately 20 per cent of the total female population, which stands at 58.646 crores.[1] This demographic analysis, translating to around 11.98 crores individuals (adolescent girls),[2] faces multifaceted challenges, primarily stemming from suboptimal educational opportunities, limited healthcare access and insufficient nutritional support.

The educational disparity is stark, with the female literacy rate of merely 64.63 per cent.[3] This underscores a critical gap in ensuring that these adolescent girls are equipped with the necessary knowledge and skills for personal and societal advancement. This educational deficit not only hampers their individual development but also has broader implications for the overall progress of the nation.

Furthermore, a staggering 55.6 per cent[4] of these adolescent girls are grappled with malnourishment (47.0 per cent underweight, 5.9 per cent overweight and 2.7 per cent obese),[4] constituting a distressing approximately 33 per cent of the total demography. This nutritional inadequacy not only jeopardises their immediate well-being but also has long-term implications for their health and productivity.

The National Family Health Survey-3 (NFHS-3)[6] brings to light another concerning aspect – approximately 56.2 per cent of women in the age group of 15-49 suffers from anaemia. This prevailing health issue among adolescent girls accentuates the need for targeted health services tailored to address the unique requirements of this group.

The challenges faced by these adolescent girls are further compounded by deep-seated gender discrimination prevalent in society. This discrimination acts as a barrier, impeding their access to essential health services and perpetuating an environment where their rights are curtailed.

Moreover, the persistence of early marriage and childbearing practices adds an additional layer of vulnerability, placing adolescent girls and their offspring at an increased risk of adverse health outcomes. This complex interplay of factors underscores the urgency for strategic interventions and affirmative measures to bridge these gaps, as enshrined in the constitutional principle of gender equality. The Constitution of India, recognising the intrinsic worth and dignity of every individual, mandates the State to proactively eliminate discrimination against girl children, adolescent girls and women, thereby fostering an inclusive and equitable society.

It was also recognised by the government[6] that the phase of adolescence marks a crucial juncture in the journey of mental, emotional and psychological development. This transitional period serves as a pivotal window of opportunity to lay the foundation for a robust and healthy adult life. Within this timeframe, it is possible to address and partially rectify nutritional issues that may have originated in the earlier stages of life, while simultaneously tackling those that are currently prevalent. The unique characteristics of adolescence, with its malleable nature and transformative potential, allow for targeted interventions to promote overall well-being and set the stage for a healthy adulthood.

To address this challenge and to ensure a physically and psychologically healthy adolescent girl population, the Government of India launched yet another powerful scheme, SABLA, on 1 April, 2011, under the Ministry of Women and Child Development[7] which was aimed at empowering adolescent girls.

SABLA literally means enabled, empowered one and is used for feminine gender. The programme is run in 200 selected districts of all the states and UTs in the country.

The fundamental goals of the initiative are to foster self-development and empowerment of adolescent girls, enhance their health and nutrition, raise awareness about health, hygiene, nutrition, as well as adolescents' reproductive and sexual health, family and child care. Additionally, the programme seeks to enhance their home-based life skills and vocational skills. The project also encompasses the reintegration of out-of-school adolescent girls into formal and non-formal education. These girls will also receive guidance on accessing various public services, including primary health centres, post offices, banks, police stations and others.

The programme has two major components:[5, 7]

1. Nutrition component for out-of-school girls in age group of 11 to 14 years and all the girls in age group of 14 to 18 years, wherein complete nutrition is provided to them.
2. Non-nutrient component for out-of-school adolescent girls belonging to age group of 11 to 18 years which encompasses health education, counselling/guidance on family welfare, adolescent reproductive and sexual health, child care practices and home management. It also provides life skills education and education for accessing public services. In addition, there is vocational training for girls aged 16 and above under National Skills Development Programme.

The objectives of the programme are as follows:[5, 8]

Enabling young girls to lead a more productive and empowered life.

- Emphasising comprehensive well-being by addressing both nutritional and non-nutritional needs.
- Encouraging skill development to foster self-reliance among adolescent girls.
- Enhancing their current skill set and collaborating with the National Skill Development Programme.

- Leveraging the potential of anganwadis, schools and panchayat buildings to reach every vulnerable girl.
- Advocating for Adolescent Reproductive and Sexual Health (ARSH), providing counselling and encouraging child care practices among girls.
- Facilitating the integration of out-of-school girls into the education system.

Reaching out to such a vast population, especially when a good percentage of them are unapproachable due to their conservative lifestyle of staying in the four walls of the house, is not an easy task. However, the commendable on-the-ground positive outcomes stand as a testament to the government's dedicated efforts, underscoring its commitment to overcoming challenges in reaching these communities.

The following case story would make readers proud of the government's achievements:

Case Story[9]

Naima Basak, a beneficiary of Sabla Kanyashree programme,[10] belongs to a family consisting of parents, disabled elder brother and three elder sisters, who are married now and a paternal aunt, residing at Alipurduar district, West Bengal. The family is financially poor with the father being the only earning member of the family, and disabled brother needs to be taken care of. None of the sisters could finish education, which the father regrets and hence encourages Naima to continue with her education. She says, she hopefully would be the first one to complete education in her family. In order to arrange some finance, she used to work three days as agricultural labour and attend school for three days. The income from her work helped her to buy books, pay for tuition fees and buy clothes.

She came to know about the Sabla Kanyashree Convergence programme through her paternal aunt who is an *anganwadi* worker of the village and Naima started attending meetings. There she learnt about the effects of early marriage, nutrition, asset creation and the importance of financial securities. She bought two pigs and eight hens from the scheme money she received and now sells eggs. She wishes to receive more training regarding rearing animals and taking care of them, etc. as she wants to start a pig farm in future. She says that the most significant change by attending the Sabla sessions was learning about asset creation and that as a girl, she is able to help her family financially and is also able to continue her education. She was also awarded by the district Kanyashree department for her efforts to obtain financial security and complete education in August 2017, which she says has given her confidence.

6. Protection of Children from Sexual Offences (POCSO)

India, with its vast population of over 44 crore[1] children, grapples with an alarming and persistent issue – child sexual abuse. Incidents of sexual assault against minors are reported regularly across the country, shedding light on the gravity of the situation. Studies emphasise the profound impact of such abuse, leading to myriad psychological and emotional disorders that can hinder a child's overall development. The trauma inflicted upon victims can have lasting consequences, creating barriers to their well-being and potential.

One significant challenge in addressing this problem is the underreporting of incidents.[1,2] Children and parents often refrain from reporting due to the fear of social stigma, the prospect of indignity, communication gaps within families, community denial and the daunting nature of legal procedures. This silence perpetuates the suffering of the victims, hindering their access to support and justice. It is crucial to foster an environment that encourages open communication, awareness and a supportive system to empower children and parents to break the cycle of silence surrounding child sexual abuse and thereby ensuring a safer and healthier future for the nation's youth.

The Constitution of India stands as a guardian of various provisions aimed at safeguarding the rights of children. Additionally, India has actively participated in international initiatives by signing pivotal agreements, including the Convention on the Rights of the Child and the Protocol to the Convention on the Rights of the Child on the Sale of Children. Despite these commendable steps, the nation lacked a specific legal provision addressing the grave issue of child sexual abuse.

Historically, cases of child sexual abuse were prosecuted under diverse sections of the Indian Penal Code, revealing a systemic inadequacy in dealing with this heinous crime. IPC 375,[4] under which rape criminals were prosecuted, does not provide specific protection for male victims or individuals facing sexual acts involving penetration other than the 'traditional' peno-vaginal intercourse. IPC 354 that deals with outraging the modesty of a woman does not include a statutory definition of 'modesty'. The offence carries a relatively weak penalty and is considered a compoundable offence. Additionally, it does not extend protection to the 'modesty' of a male child. And IPC 377, addressing unnatural offences, lacks a specific definition for 'unnatural offences'. The provision focuses on cases where the victim is subjected to the perpetrator's non-consensual sexual acts and it is not explicitly designed to address the criminalisation of child sexual abuse. The glaring need for a dedicated legal framework became evident in the 1990s when a child sexual abuse racket was exposed in Goa.[3] In response to this, the state government took a pioneering step by enacting a legislation in 2003, explicitly focusing on promoting child rights. This marked a significant stride towards addressing the legal gaps concerning child protection.

Simultaneously, the Special Expert Committee under the guidance of Justice V.R. Krishna Iyer took substantial measures to address the void in legislation related to child rights. The committee presented a comprehensive draft code, known as the Children's Code Bill,[3] in 2000. This proposed legislation aimed at consolidating and strengthening legal provisions for the protection of children's rights in India.

These developments underscored the imperative for a specific legal framework to combat child sexual abuse comprehensively. The legislative efforts at both the state and national levels signalled a collective acknowledgment of the urgency to address this critical issue and reinforced the commitment to providing effective legal safeguards for the rights and well-being of children in the country.

These two pivotal initiatives laid the foundation for dedicated legislation against child sexual abuse. Recognising the urgent need for comprehensive legal measures, the Department of Women and Child Development took a significant step in 2005 by preparing a draft bill. This proposed legislation aimed to specifically address various offences targeted against children. The draft bill marked a crucial milestone in the journey towards establishing a robust legal framework tailored to combat child sexual abuse.

The 2007 report titled *The Study of Child Abuse*,[3] published by the Ministry of Women and Child Development, encompassed 13 states and involved a sample size of 12,447 children, 2,324 young adults and 2,449 stakeholders. Examining various forms of child abuse, the study revealed that 50.76 per cent of the surveyed children reported experiencing one or more forms of sexual abuse.

In September 2010, the Ministry of Women and Child Development drafted the Protection of Children from Sexual Offences Bill, 2010. After undergoing several rounds of revisions, this bill was enacted as the POCSO Act on Children's Day, which falls on 14 November 2012.[2] This was a very bold step taken by the government in order to safeguard all children below the age of 18 years from sexual crime.

A disproportionate number of victims are girl children aged between 13 to 18 years and they often face challenges in receiving timely help and support, particularly during and after pregnancy. This difficulty is exacerbated by the social stigma attached to their plight due to which a large number of such cases remain unreported, thereby denying justice to victims.

The POCSO, 2012 was introduced to establish a comprehensive legal framework for safeguarding children from sexual assault, harassment and pornography. The Act prioritises the well-being of the child throughout the judicial process by incorporating child-friendly reporting mechanisms, evidence recording and ensuring swift trial proceedings. Special courts have been designated to handle these offences, emphasising a child-centric approach in the implementation of the Act. Additionally, the Act introduces procedural reforms aimed at simplifying the trial process for children in India. By adopting a child-friendly approach, the objective is to reduce the trauma experienced by the victim, prevent revictimisation and offer protection against intimidation during legal proceedings.

As stated in the letter released by the Government of India MWCD,[2] '*the main objective of the scheme is to provide integrated support and assistance to minor pregnant girl child victims under one roof and to facilitate their immediate, emergency and non-emergency access to a range of services for long-term rehabilitation in terms of access to education, police assistance, medical (also comprising maternity, neo-natal and infant care), psychological, mental health counselling, Non-institutional care support, place of stay in CCI/aftercare facilities and health insurance cover for the girl child victim and her new-born under one roof to enable access to justice and empowerment of such girl child with victims.*'

The implementation of mandatory reporting provisions in the POCSO Act has led to a notable rise in reported cases. One report[1] says that, as per the NCRB (National Crime Records Bureau's) data, there has been a surge of over 30 per cent in POCSO cases between 2016 and 2020. The years 2019 and 2020 alone witnessed more than 47,000 reported cases each, averaging 129 cases daily under this Act. Notably, from 2017 to 2020, with available data, girls consistently accounted for 97.1 per cent to 97.6 per cent of the victims each year. This alarming rise in reported cases emphasises the critical need for effective measures to address and prevent child sexual abuse, particularly targeting the safety and well-being of girls, who constitute a predominant majority of the victims. The graph below shows the number of cases filed under POCSO Act, 2012 from 2014 to 2020 and the increase in number of cases registered has been on an increasing trend.

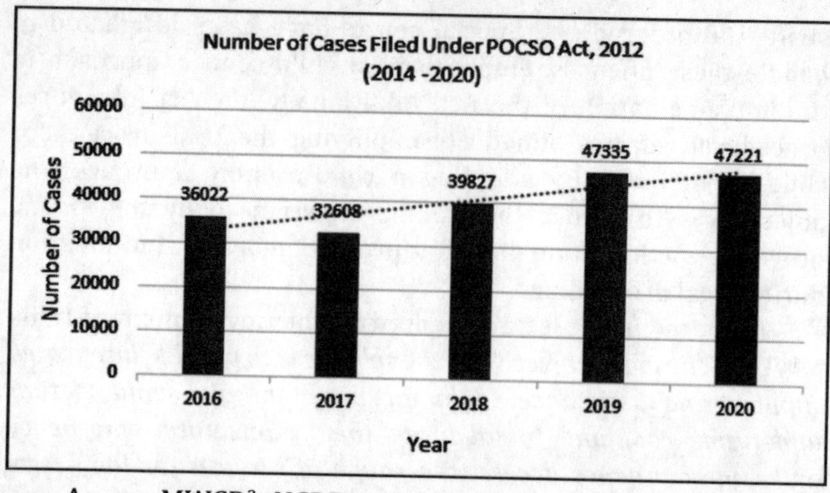

As per MWCD[2], NCRB reports indicate that during the last three years (November 2020-November 2023), an average of 29,472 cases have been registered under Sections 4 and 6 of the POCSO Act, 2012.[2] Within this statistics, an average of 29,188 cases specifically pertain to girl children as victims. The increase in reported cases sheds light on the effectiveness of the mandatory reporting mechanism in addressing and bringing attention to instances of child sexual abuse, particularly emphasising the prevalence of such cases involving girls as victims. This data underscores the significance of the POCSO Act in prompting awareness and action against child sexual offences in the country.

Case Stories in News

Delta Meghwal Rape Case: The tragic incident involving Delta Meghwal occurred on 29 March, 2016 when a 17-year-old Dalit girl was discovered lifeless at her college in Nokha, Bikaner district, Rajasthan. Her body was found in a water tank at the Jain Adarsh Teacher Training Institute for Girls, where she was a student. The First Information Report (FIR) filed by her parents indicated that on 28 March, she had informed them of being raped by a teacher who allegedly took her life afterwards.[4]

A POCSO court in Bikaner sentenced a Physical Training Instructor (PTI) of a college to life imprisonment, while the school principal and the warden received six years of imprisonment.[5] The court's decision reflects the legal consequences for individuals involved in cases related to sexual offences against children, emphasising the severity of such crimes and the commitment to justice for the victims.

POCSO represents a significant stride in safeguarding the rights of children, particularly addressing the vulnerabilities faced by girl children, as indicated by data. This governmental initiative has fostered compassion and recognition of the challenges faced by girl children. It sends a powerful message about the government's commitment to ensuring the protection of girls across the country.

7. Ladli Laxmi Scheme

The Government of India has implemented numerous policies and schemes over the years, aiming to uplift and empower women. These initiatives often involve collaboration with state governments.

The Ladli Laxmi Yojana,[1] a noteworthy social welfare scheme initiated by former Chief Minister Shivraj Singh Chauhan as a state government initiative, holds paramount significance in addressing the status of women in India. As detailed earlier, this scheme is designed to empower and uplift female citizens, particularly those belonging to economically disadvantaged backgrounds.

This policy stands as a testament to the government's commitment to promoting gender equality and combating the challenges faced by women, including child marriages, trafficking and maternal mortality. By focusing on providing enhanced education and healthcare, Ladli Laxmi Yojana aims to break the cycle of gender-based disparities, offering a pathway for the holistic development of young girls.

The Ladli Laxmi Yojana aligns with the broader national objective of women's empowerment, acknowledging their pivotal role in societal development. It exemplifies efforts to provide enhanced education and healthcare to female citizens, especially those from low-income backgrounds. This scheme underscores the commitment of the state government to address gender-based disparities and uplift the socio-economic status of women. The following details elaborate on the Ladli Laxmi Yojana and the benefits it extends to eligible female children, contributing to their overall development and well-being:

Launched on 2 May, 2007,[1] the Ladli Laxmi Yojana is a Madhya Pradesh government initiative that gained widespread acceptance. Appreciated by citizens, it later inspired other states, showcasing its positive impact and relevance in fostering socio-economic development in the states. These states are:

- Uttar Pradesh
- Delhi
- Bihar
- Chhattisgarh
- Goa
- Jharkhand

The Ladli Laxmi Yojana extends its benefits[2] to all female orphans born after 1 January, 2006 and who fall within the non-tax-paying bracket. This inclusive approach aims to provide support and empowerment to vulnerable girl children, recognising their specific needs and circumstances.

Objectives[2]

The primary goal of the scheme is to provide coverage for school and marriage-related expenditures. By addressing these essential aspects, Ladli Laxmi Yojana aims to alleviate financial burdens and promote the educational and marital well-being of eligible girl children.

The other objectives that the Yojana aims to achieve are:

- Improvement of the sex ratio of girl children by encouraging states to celebrate the birth of a girl child. This celebration is intended to alleviate stress related to education and marriage finances, fostering a positive environment that promotes the well-being of the girl child.
- Improvement of overall health and education status of girl child in the respective state, fostering comprehensive development and well-being.

- Securing a bright future for the girl child and foster self-reliance by offering financial assistance for education and marriage expenses.
- Discouraging child marriages by addressing education expenses, ensuring that girls can pursue their education without financial constraints, thus promoting a more informed and empowered approach towards marriage.
- The scheme also contributes to population control by encouraging families to limit their size to two children, irrespective of the gender, promoting family planning and sustainable population growth.

The Yojana offers multiple benefits, thereby widening the scope of a brighter future for girl children.

- The Ladli Laxmi Yojana provides an Assurance Certificate of INR 1,18,000/- to the girl child which is issued in the name of the girl child by the government.
- Besides, on various stages, the girl child who is covered under the scheme receives support from the government. INR 2000/- is offered to her on her admission in Class 6; INR 4000/- is offered on her admission in Class 9; INR 6000/- on her admission in Class 11 and INR 6000/- on her admission in Class 12. This beautifully ensures that at no stage would the girl child experience any blockage in her education due to financial constraints.
- Furthermore, under the Yojana, girl children receive an incentive amount of INR 25,000, given in equal instalments during the first and last year of their graduate course after admission.
- The government bears the tuition fee for higher education under this scheme.
- In addition, a final payment of INR one lakh is made upon the child reaching 21 years of age, adulthood, under this scheme. This substantial sum serves as a powerful tool, empowering the girl child to chart her path towards a brighter and more secure future.

However, the benefits cease in case the girl child stops her formal education or drops out of school, or gets married before the legal age of 18 years; or the family planning option is not exercised by parents after the birth of the second child.

The scheme is intricately crafted to foster the education and empowerment of girl children, instilling a sense of responsibility among parents regarding the country's population. It comprehensively addresses all stages of financial needs, offering holistic support for the education of the girl child.

Words would not be enough to define the sense of hope and assurance and the feeling that parents get because of this scheme. One such real-life story is shared below:

Case Story[3]

The story belongs to a family living in Delhi, comprising three members – parents and one daughter named Kiara. During the

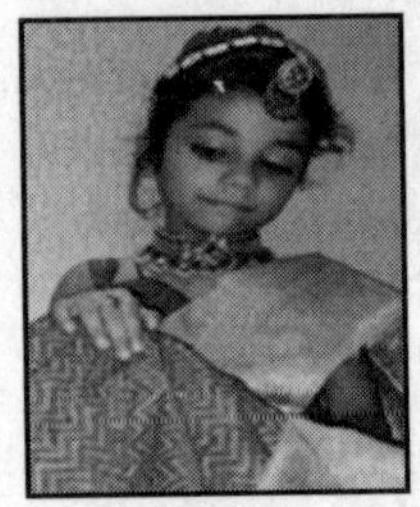

survey by the Mahila Panchayat team of Rasta, Kiara was seven-year old then. The parents, despite working in a private firm (father) and as a house help (mother), struggled to make ends meet due to insufficient income. Despite coming from a lower middle-class background, they cherished their daughter dearly. Their sentiment is encapsulated in their words as "*Hamari ek hi beti hai; hum uske liye sab karenge* (we have only one girl child and we will do everything for her).

The Rasta team took the initiative to inform and educate the mother about various government policies related to women and social security schemes. They specifically highlighted the Ladli Laxmi Yojana and explained its functioning. The newfound knowledge about this Yojana brought a sense of hope and optimism to Kiara's mother. Recognising that the aspirations they had for their daughter could be achieved with the help of this scheme, the parents were convinced. With the assistance of the Rasta team, they opened a bank account for their daughter Kiara, who has already started receiving funds under the scheme.

The parents expressed deep gratitude to the Rasta team for their invaluable support at every step.

Stories like Kiara's symbolise the progress and advancement of a nation.

Conclusion

The commitment and effectiveness of the government in empowering every girl child in the country are evident through a comprehensive range of initiatives and schemes. As BBBP spans across the nation to secure a balanced sex ratio, eradicate gender-based disparities, promote women's empowerment and safeguard the girl child, Sukanya Samriddhi Yojana bestows essential financial freedom upon the daughters of the country. From Rashtriya Kishore Swasthya Karyakram (RKSK) focusing on the health promotion approach to Ladli Laxmi Yojana emphasising education and financial support, the government has taken significant strides to uplift the status of girls across the nation. Each scheme addresses specific needs, contributing to the holistic development of the girl child by enhancing her physical, emotional, financial and health aspects in a distinctive manner.

The initiatives like the Beti Bachao, Beti Padhao (BBBP) campaign highlight the government's determination to improve the status of girls in society. By addressing issues like the declining child sex ratio, promoting education for girls and encouraging awareness campaigns, BBBP underscores the multifaceted approach needed to bring about positive change. Not only that, the government's commitment is clearly visible with increasing budget for BBBP from Rs. 50 cr in 2014-15 to Rs. 280 cr in 2019-20.

The RKSK, with its paradigm shift from clinic-based services to health promotion and prevention, stands out as a groundbreaking initiative. By reaching adolescents in their own environments, such as schools, families and communities and incorporating community-based interventions, like outreach programmes and counselling, RKSK addresses the unique needs of this age group. The involvement of parents and communities is a key feature, recognising the limited autonomy and agency adolescents often face in decision-making.

Additionally, schemes like Ladli Laxmi Yojana exemplify the government's dedication to eradicating gender-based discrimination. Launched with the intent to counter female foeticide and alleviate the financial burden associated with the birth of a girl child, this scheme is a beacon of change. Providing financial empowerment, educational support and ensuring the overall well-being of the girl child, Ladli Laxmi Yojana reflects a holistic approach to address societal issues.

Furthermore, the government's focus on rehabilitation is evident in the National Child Labour Project (NCLP) and its sequential approach. By withdrawing children from hazardous occupations, providing education, vocational training and linking them to formal education systems, the scheme aims to break the cycle of child labour.

The commitment to safeguarding the rights and well-being of children is further emphasised in schemes like the Protection of Children from Sexual Offences (POCSO) Act. The enactment of dedicated legislation against child sexual abuse and the subsequent increase in reporting cases showcase the government's dedication to addressing and preventing such heinous crimes.

The well-being and status of the girl child and young girls demand ongoing empathy and unwavering attention, particularly as they were largely overlooked and neglected prior to the last decade. The recent decade has witnessed remarkable transformations in the status of the girl child, exemplified by substantial improvements in sex ratios, notably in regions like Haryana. This positive shift is encouraging and should be sustained. Education is a crucial aspect for the girl child, but equally important is the transformation in societal perceptions towards them. The societal mindset needs to evolve, fostering an environment where girls are regarded with dignity, respect and equality. The efforts made in recent years to address these issues must persist, promoting a holistic transformation that not only encompasses educational opportunities but also aims at eliminating deep-rooted biases and discrimination against the girl child. By nurturing a more inclusive and supportive society, we can ensure that every girl has the opportunity to thrive, contribute and fulfil her potential.

In conclusion, the stories of transformation, like those of Kusum, Meghna, Shivani, Chanda, Salma, Nisha, Anshu, Naima, Kiara and many unmentioned ones, serve as testimonials to the effectiveness of government initiatives in empowering girls. The concerted efforts to address health, education and social issues demonstrate a commitment to creating an environment where every girl can thrive. These initiatives not only break barriers but also set the stage for a more equitable and inclusive society, where the potential of every girl child is recognised and nurtured. The government's unwavering dedication to empowering girls is a testament to its vision for a progressive and gender-equal nation.

References

1. https://wcd.nic.in/sites/default/files/FinalBBBPReport06042015.pdf
2. https://www.ncbi.nlm.nih.gov/pmc/articles/PMC5084599/#:~:text=Since%201991%2C%2080%25%20of%20the,are%20lost%20to%20female%20feticide

(1) Beti Bachao, Beti Padhao

1. https://www.census2011.co.in/sexratio.php
2. https://www.hindustantimes.com/india/when-women-come-cheaper-than-cattle/story-EJD38cJ4kaTGVn03LJzUkJ.html
3. https://groww.in/p/savings-schemes/top-10-government-girl-child-schemes-in-india
4. https://groww.in/p/savings-schemes/beti-bachao-beti-padhao
5. d: https://www.ibef.org/government-schemes/beti-bachao-beti-padhao
6. https://data.gov.in/search?title=beti%20bachao%20beti%20padhao%20
7. https://www.ibef.org/government-schemes/beti-bachao-beti-padhao (f, g)
8. https://wcd.nic.in/bbbp-photo-gallery
9. https://www.ispp.org.in/evaluation-summary-beti-bachao-beti-padhao-2015-2022/30283/
10. https://pib.gov.in/PressReleaseIframePage.aspx?PRID=1691725
11. https://sundayguardianlive.com/news/beti-bachao-beti-padhao-showing-significant-results
12. https://www.downtoearth.org.in/news/governance/reversal-of-gains-

haryana-a-state-with-historically-poor-sex-ratio-is-fast-losing-its-hard-won-gains-in-recent-years-92763

13. Vikalp Foundation is a non-profit, voluntary organisation, working at grassroot level and addressing poverty stricken rural populace in six blocks of Gaya district in Bihar with focus on gender justice and goal of changing the region's development perspectives from needs to rights. In was founded by Dr. Chandrashekhar Azad and other volunteers on 2 October, 1998 and is registered under the Indian Societies Registration Act on 3 August, 2001 at Patna. The case story has been shared by Vikalp Foundation. Know more: www.vikalp.org.in

(2) Sukanya Samriddhi Yojana (SSY)

1. https://static.pib.gov.in/WriteReadData/specificdocs/documents/2022/jan/doc20221207101.pdf)
2. https://en.wikipedia.org/wiki/Sukanya_Samriddhi_Account
3. Rasta is a non-government organisation, functioning since 1994 for empowerment of the vulnerable sections of society in Delhi, Uttar Pradesh, Uttarakhand and Haryana and enjoying national jurisdiction. Their main areas of intervention are education, community health, women empowerment and skill development. So far, they have educated more than 30,000 children, of whom 10,000 have been admitted in formal schools. They have developed their own, need-based teaching and learning material in Hindi, Maths and English for Class 3 and Class 4. The case study has been shared by Rasta NGO. Know more: https://rasta.org.in/
4. Smile Foundation is one of the top 10 NGOs in India, initiated in 2002 by Santanu Mishra and his four friends. Smile Foundation works in the field of education, health, livelihood, women empowerment, disaster response and empowering grassroot NGOs. It reaches out to over 15,00,000 underprivileged children, youth and women through various development projects across India with presence in 24 states of the country. The case studies have been shared by Smile Foundation. Know more: https://www.smilefoundationindia.org/

(3) Rashtriya Kishor Swasthya Karyakram (RKSK)

1. https://nhm.gov.in/index4.php?lang=1&level=0&linkid=152&lid=173
2. https://vikaspedia.in/health/nrhm/national-health-programmes-1/rashtriya-kishor-swasthya-karyakram-rksk
3. https://www.rksk.in/
4. https://www.ncbi.nlm.nih.gov/pmc/articles/PMC9891055/
5. Bal Sansaar is a registered, non-profit voluntary organisation established in 1992, headquartered in Jaipur, Rajasthan. Their objective is to build effective responses on the issues of child rights, education and development; skill-entrepreneurship development for adolescent and youth; community health and development; women development and gender issues; Research & Documentation; capacity building; networking and advocacy. Know more: https://balsansarindia.com/

(4) National Child Labour Scheme

1. https://en.wikipedia.org/wiki/Poverty_in_India
2. https://labour.gov.in/childlabour/nclp
3. https://pib.gov.in/Pressreleaseshare.aspx?PRID=1593410
4. https://labour.gov.in/sites/default/files/pib1849795.pdf
5. Maxvision Social Welfare Society is a non-profit organisation functioning since 24 February, 2004. It is based at Gurugram and is registered under the Society Registration Act 1973 dated 24 February, 2004. Their core focus areas are educational support for the underprivileged children, vocational training programmes for the youth, women empowerment programmes, health camps for children, parents and the elderly population, awareness programmes on health, environment, hygiene and pollution and legal aid to poor. Know more: https://www.maxvisionsws.org/

(5) SABLA Scheme for Adolescent Girls

1. https://pib.gov.in/newsite/PrintRelease.aspx?relid=71383#:~:text=The%20population%20of%20the%20country,Chandramouli
2. https://www.rksk.in/
3. https://mospi.gov.in/sites/default/files/reports_and_publication/statistical_publication/social_statistics/WM16Chapter3.pdf
4. https://www.ncbi.nlm.nih.gov/pmc/articles/PMC6293888/#:~:text=The%20present%20study%20revealed%20that,%2C%20and%202.7%25%20obese)
5. https://wcd.nic.in/sites/default/files/1-SABLAscheme_0.pdf
6. https://en.wikipedia.org/wiki/Sabla_(India)
7. https://timesofindia.indiatimes.com/city/patna/SABLA-scheme-for-adolescent-girls/articleshow/7927855.cms
8. https://testbook.com/ias-preparation/sabla-scheme#:~:text=The%20Sabla%20scheme%20aims%20at,community%20buildings%2C%20schools%2C%20etc.
9. https://cdn.landesa.org/wp content/uploads/Landesa 2018 SABLA Kanyashree-Evaluation-Scaling-Phase-2015-2018.pdf
10. https://www.wbkanyashree.gov.in/readwrite/notice_publications/SABLA-KP_Convergence_Assessment_2018.pdf
    (SABLA Kanyashree programme was a result of integration of SABLA (Government of India initiative) with Kanyashree Prakalp programme (Government of West Bengal initiative) which was done on recognising that the overall aim, objective as well as target group of both the programmes are same.)

(6) Protection of Children from Sexual Offences (POCSO)

1. https://factly.in/data-pocso-cases-increased-by-30-in-5-years-while-pendency-rate-in-courts-crossed-94/
2. https://wcd.nic.in/acts/scheme-care-and-support-victims-under-section-4-6-protection-children-sexual-offences-pocso-act

3. https://indianexpress.com/article/explained/explained-law/10-years-of-pocso-an-analysis-of-indias-landmark-child-abuse-law-8276030/
4. https://en.wikipedia.org/wiki/Protection_of_Children_from_Sexual_Offenses_Act
5. https://timesofindia.indiatimes.com/city/jaipur/delta-meghwal-case-life-term-for-teacher-six-year-jail-for-principal-warden/articleshow/86978536.cms

(7) Ladli Laxmi Scheme

1. https://www.creditmantri.com/ladli-laxmi-yojana/
2. https://www.policyx.com/life-insurance/articles/ladli-laxmi-yojana/
3. Rasta is a non-government organisation, functioning since 1994 for empowerment of the vulnerable sections of society in Delhi, Uttar Pradesh, Uttarakhand and Haryana and enjoying national jurisdiction. Their main areas of intervention are education, community health, women empowerment and skill development. So far, they have educated more than 30,000 children, of whom 10,000 have been admitted in formal schools. They have developed their own need based, teaching/learning material in Hindi, Maths and English for Class 3 and Class 4. The case study has been shared by Rasta NGO. Know more: https://rasta.org.in/

□

14

Towards Self-reliance and Sustainability: A Journey of Women Empowerment through Ecofriendly Measures

—Dr. Shivani Jha

As India moves into a new era of development and awareness, it is beset with challenges that have continued to plague it since time immemorial – the condition of women in rural areas particularly being an important concern. Over a period of time, the fate of the girl child has metamorphosed from that of a completely marginalised one to one with promise. However, this has not been the case uniformly across the nation. There is a prevalence of gender discrimination and the need for empowerment of women, particularly in developing countries as women in developing countries are assessed to be lower and are treated differently from their male counterparts. Such discrimination deprives them of their rightful education, job opportunities, vistas for awareness and political responsibility. Coupled with fewer job opportunities, low wages for women and the responsibility of running the household particularly as the male members of the family leave for greener work pastures, the dependency of the women on menfolk increases and the resources at their disposal decrease, impoverishing the household further. "In many countries, women still do not have legal ownership rights to land and manage property, conduct business or even travel without the consent of the husband. The number of women falling within the poverty cycle is increasing at a faster rate than that of men" (Parsuraman and Somaiya, 2016).

The situations prevalent in such societies have created the need for developing policies and programmes for empowering women. Economic empowerment includes helping women to acquire skills, improve the enabling and institutional environment enabling them to make decisions for their growth and development. Women in India have learnt to live with challenges and make most of the situation they find themselves in, by persevering and overcoming. This article aims to study the empowerment of the marginalised, particularly women, through eco-friendly and sustainable means.

The handloom sector in India is one of the largest cottage industries, with 23.77 lakh looms and also one of the biggest unorganised Indian economic activities, representing and reflecting India's vibrant culture. The handloom weavers of the nation have carved a niche for themselves internationally due to their unique ways of weaving and printing. The trade is followed in families for generations by these artisan families usually based in small towns and villages. The handloom sector is also one of the second largest employment-generating sectors in the rural region, providing employment to more than 3 million people directly or through associated activities. According to the handloom Census 2019-20, the industry provides employment to 3,522,122 handloom workers, out of which 72.29 per cent (amounting to 25.46,285) are primarily women. Additionally, there are approximately 16,87,534 women handicraft artisans registered with the Office of the Development Commissioner (Handicrafts).

Given the fragile global economy and the impact of climate emergency on nations across the world, sustainable development goals are a major aspect for any nation to factor in, in its individual quest for growth and development. The conventional methods of indigenous art and craft in India have eco-friendly leanings which add to the promise of sustainable growth. The Batik painting imported to India from Indonesia by the Nobel laureate Rabindranath Tagore is one such art, apart from the Madhubani paintings of Mithila.

Although, the Khatri community of Gujarat were known to be the original artisans of Batik printing, the technique was dispersed to other regions and cultures of India over time. It was revived around a century ago, when Rabindranath Tagore travelled to Java (Indonesia) in 1927 and fascinated with the exquisite dyeing technique, brought back several pieces of the fabric with the hope of reviving this traditional printing technique in India. With his efforts, the study of Batik was thus introduced at the Vishwabharati University in Santiniketan. Here, Batik flourished as a part of the academic course curriculum in Kala Bhavan and the skill development study of Shilpa-Bhavan. Practised primarily on leather and fabric, the revival of the art spread from Santiniketan to Calcutta and other parts of India. One of the pioneers who explored Batik design in Santiniketan was Gauri Bhanja, the renowned artist and principal of Kala Bhavan whose craftsmanship took the practice of Batik to a much higher level than previously. Throughout her teaching career in Kala Bhavan in Santiniketan, Bhanja worked extensively on it. Other prominent, primarily female artists of Santiniketan to enrich the Batik design include Rani Chanda Haimanti Chakravarty, Jamuna Sen, Kshoma Ghosh, Ila Ghosh, Arundhuti Thakur, Indusudha Ghosh and Bani Bose, etc.

In the book, *Sharing the Dream – The Remarkable Women Artists of Santiniketan*, Tapati Mukherjee highlights the significance of the women's presence in the academic space of Santiniketan and their innovations in the field of design. Haimanti Chakravarty, a Santiniketan artist, provides a detailed account of the history and techniques of Batik design in her book, *Batik: Decoration of Fabric as Practised in Java and South Asia*.

At Santiniketan, Batik became an essential female craft, maintained and sustained by women. Where earlier textile work only entailed sewing and mending for women, Batik brought on a revolution, providing them with the scope for expressing their inherent creativity and desire for expression, attracting women from various backgrounds and providing them economic independence, enabling even those women artists who could never afford to attend an art school, instilling in them the courage to practice this craft with minimum affordable materials. It also gave them the opportunity of connecting the culturally embedded practice of *alpana* making in the domestic sphere with that of Batik printing. The Batik art currently is mainly produced in various centres of Gujarat (Mundra and Mandvi), West Bengal (Santiniketan), Tamil Nadu (Injambakkam) and Madhya Pradesh (Indore, Bhairavgarh), among others.

The creation of Batik work follows an intricate process. The first step is designing, followed by waxing, then dyeing and finally, eliminating the wax. Waxing and dyeing involve further stages especially if the artist desires to get more than one colour. The final process is removing the wax to get an overall finished Batik print. Dyeing is a method where a patterned area is blocked with wax. Batik can be dyed with many types of dyes. For instance, in the dyeing process, the cloth is placed in an indigo vat several times until the correct shade of blue is obtained. However, as contrary to the earlier Batik work where natural dyes from vegetable sources were used, after the advent of synthetic dyes, Batik printing technique became highly commercialised. Internationally, Batik work switched to the use of naphthol, a chemical and solubilised vat dye; the waxed fabric first soaked in the dye-bath of the first colour, with darker colours requiring longer periods or numerous immersions. The fabric was then placed into cold dyeing. When the desired colour had been achieved and the fabric had dried, the wax was reapplied over the areas. The number of colours in Batik represented the number of times it was immersed in the dye-bath.

In the Indian context, Batik is often made by using natural materials and traditional techniques, making it a sustainable option in the fashion industry. As the fashion industry continues to prioritise sustainability, Batik is becoming an increasingly popular choice for eco-conscious designers and consumers. The most common and traditional colours included in the Batik material are indigo, dark brown and white as indigo and brown are the most commonly available natural dyes. Natural dyes are renewable and a sustainable resource with minimal environmental impact, low toxicity and allergic effect.

The rise of Madhubani women artists is also steeped in history. In the 1960s, during the severe drought in north Bihar, men left their villages to look for work or business in towns, whereas women and children had to stay back and face the wrath of the natural calamity. Many starved. Under this demanding and devastating situation, the enterprising women started to transfer the wall paintings of their houses on paper. Earlier confined to the four walls of their houses, they came out and sold their Madhubani pictures, often with the help of dealers and earned their families' livelihood. The role of the government in providing the desired impetus to the Madhubani artists is noteworthy. In the 1960s, the Government of India decided to distribute free paper in these villages of Mithila facing drought but not shy of talent. This initiative provided the rural women with an opportunity to paint on paper rather than on walls. With the change in the medium, the scale and scope of the art also broadened. The paintings, which were confined like their creators, the Mithila women, to the four walls of the houses now gained currency at the global scale. The commercialisation of Madhubani paintings began in 1962 CE, when a foreign artist travelling through this town was attracted by the murals. He persuaded the women to paint those same drawings on paper, so that he could take them and show them in his country. The idea was a great success and thus began the commercialisation of Madhubani paintings.

Traditionally practiced in the Mithila region of Bihar and the adjoining parts of what is known as the Terai in Nepal, Madhubani art has an important tradition in the form of paintings and is known and appreciated worldwide today. Madhubani paintings (also known as Mithila paintings) have been practised by the women of the region through the centuries and are considered as a living tradition of Mithila, with women decorating the floors of huts (the floor paintings called aripana) and freshly plastered mud walls (*kohabar*) for ceremonies. However, they are now also done on cloth, handmade paper and canvas. Characterised by vibrant colours made of natural vegetable dyes and mineral oxides, utilising a mix of tools the artist uses her fingers, brushes, twigs, nib pens and matchsticks to etch the paintings of the popular art of Mithila that displays the creativity and sensitivity of its people. Like any folk-art, it also highlights the psychology of the society it is rooted in, reflecting the morals, values and customs of Mithila. The Madhubani art boasted of depictions on themes ingrained in religion, ideas of love and fertility, with paintings for each occasion, ranging from birth to marriage and extending to various festivals.

Over the years, the Madhubani women have taken the baton in their hands with the added responsibility of "selling their paintings at markets throughout India, travel to foreign countries, create pictures there and become important ambassadors of Indian culture." (Frenz, 2020) The creativity of women like Ganga Devi was greatly encouraged and many became celebrated artists. Today a tour of any crafts exhibition has the Madhubani art on display, on paper, canvas and textile. The recognition and adulation to the art is much more than giving a fresh life to the fading folk tradition of painting; it is a means of employment. Albrecht notes the change in their financial and familial position since then as he writes, "Today their paintings have a global market and are the basis for income of many families in the villages of north Bihar. It is amazing to observe that within a few decades, Mithila women of Brahmin, Kayastha and Harijan castes alike emancipated themselves from the role as an indoor housewife into public life."

At present, the Office of the Development Commissioner (ODC) (handicrafts) under the Union Ministry of Textiles is working closely with the Bihar state government to provide an opportunity to local artisans to showcase their art on different platforms. The prime objective of the learning centres being established all over Bihar is to inculcate the required skill sets among artisans, to provide financial assistance and organise awareness-cum-training workshops and seminars for them. A training centre, Upendra Maharathi Handicrafts Institute at Patna has been set up to offer short-term vocational courses on Madhubani painting to encourage younger generations to take up this skill as an employment-generating avenue.

The art as practiced in India is eco-friendly in nature with the artisans of Madhubani paintings using colours procured directly from nature. For these enterprising artists, lamp soot served as a source of black, white was created from powdered rice, green was made from the leaves of the apple tree and tilcoat blue from the seeds of *sikkot* and indigo, yellow was drawn from the parts of *singar* flower or the jasmine flower, bark of *peepal* was to be boiled to make a part of saffron colour, red was made from *kusum* flower and red sandalwood. To make the painting last long as well as take vividness, they mixed gum with colour. Flowers and leaves of *Euphorbia pulcherrima* (Lalpatia leaf), red *Cannabis sativa* (*bhang* leaf), green *Labalab purpureusi* (Sem leaf), Green *Lawsonia inermis* (mehendi leaf), *Clitoria ternatea* (Aparajita flower), *Argemone mexicana* (Kataiya flower), *Helianthus annus* (*Suryamukhi*) were used widely. The symbolic motifs in Mithila paintings also indicated the close linkages among man, his immediate surroundings, his mind, environment, plants and animals. Several indigenous plants as listed above are being used as dye in the traditional Mithila painting. It is not surprising to find paddy and *makhana* (*Euryle ferox*) symbolised in the painting as Goddess of Wealth and Prosperity as they are grown extensively in this region and are a source of livelihood for the rural people of this region.

It has been noted that that there is a great demand for indigenous dyed products in the textile and craft industries worldwide, with this sector emerging as a strong economy that must be considered with rational management of renewable natural resources. The cultivation of dye-yielding plants could also be part of alternative farming. However, a disturbing trend nowadays is that many of the artisans have switched over to cheap and ready to use chemical dyes that act as a threat to the traditional practice of dye extraction from natural sources for the traditional painting. This development underscores the power and importance of nature in the life of mankind, thereby emphasising the need for the protection of plants, animals and the natural environment. Artist Shanti Devi observes that the use of synthetic colour and modern round brushes have replaced the cotton-tipped bamboo sticks and stiff twigs that used to serve as brushes a few years back.

From paper, the art form moved on to textiles and fashion. Hand-painted Madhubani sarees, stoles and scarves became extremely popular in cities and in turn, helped in the economic development of the region. Companies like Urban Medley collaborate with Madhubani artists from Bihar to promote the art through silk, with each scarf comprising a complete painting in itself. Hand-painted Madhubani sarees and stoles are also greatly appreciated by the connoisseurs of arts and looked upon as slow sustainable fashion items.

The apparel and accessory designers take inspiration from the lively, mythological and colourful motifs of Madhubani art and use them extensively for design and development of a gamut of high-end artifacts, apparels, home textiles and accessories. Accordingly, designers have been working in close association with local artisans that serve both alike. Revival and promotion of this traditional textile craft by incorporation in latest apparel and accessory merchandise come with the promise of boosting the traditional folk-art on national and international platforms. Today, the Madhubani prints, both hand-printed or simulated using screen-printing technique, are gaining widespread acceptance among teenagers and young professionals. A range of apparels, embellished with Madhubani paintings from sarees, draperies, stoles, *dupattas*, *kurtis*, tops and accessories like umbrellas, footwear, handbags, jewellery, watches are greatly sought after, particularly in crafts *melas*, artisan markets and handicraft exhibitions.

In a concentrated effort to promote the sector, the government has approved the launch of Production Linked Incentive (PLI) scheme for textiles and Pradhan Mantri Mega Integrated Textile Region and Apparel (PM-MITRA) scheme. Other schemes already supporting the industry are the Amended Technology Upgradation Fund Scheme (A-TUFS), schemes for the development of the powerloom sector (Power-Tex), Silk

Samagra, National Handloom Development Programme, National Handicraft Development Programme, National Technical Textile Mission, Scheme for Integrated Textile Parks (SITP), SAMARTH - The Scheme for Capacity Building in Textile Sector, Jute (ICARE-Improved Cultivation and Advanced Retting Exercise) to name a few.

Handloom weaving or production is inherently an integral part of the Make-in-India programme. The Government of India has announced a special economic package, viz. Atmanirbhar Bharat Abhiyaan for boosting the economy of the country with a simultaneous movement towards self-reliance. Relief and credit-support measures have been announced for various sectors, including MSMEs. The weavers and artisans have the option to avail the benefits of these relief and credit support measures to revive their businesses.

Apart from the above special economic package, the Ministry of Textiles has taken steps to enable the artisans to sell their products directly to various government departments and organisations. To promote e-marketing of handloom products, a policy framework was designed under which any willing e-commerce platform with good track record could participate in online marketing of handloom products.

Accordingly, 23 e-commerce entities were engaged for online marketing of handloom products. A social media campaign, #Vocal 4 handmade, was launched on the 6th National Handloom Day by the government, in partnership with all stakeholders, to promote the handloom legacy of India and to ensure people's support for the weaving community. The social media campaign has also resulted in renewed interest of the Indian public in handlooms and several e-commerce players have reported increase in sales of Indian handloom products. In the face of the unprecedented Covid-19 pandemic, the government endeavoured to provide online marketing opportunities to the weavers and handloom producers.

Taking a step towards realising 'Atmanirbhar Bharat', the Handloom Export Promotion Council also made noteworthy efforts to virtually connect the handloom weavers and exporters from different corners of the country with the international market. With more than 200 participants from different regions of the country showcasing their products with unique designs and skills, an Indian Textile Sourcing Fair was organised on 7, 10 and 11 August, 2020. The show has attracted considerable attention of the international buyers.

Additionally, Design Resource Centres are also being set up in Weavers' Service Centres (WSCs) through NIFT with the objective to build and create design-oriented excellence in the handloom sector and to facilitate weavers, exporters, manufacturers and designers for creating new designs. To enable the handloom agencies and weavers to withstand their profession, the Ministry of Textiles is implementing many schemes through the office of the Development Commissioner for Handlooms across the country as the National Handloom Development Programme (NHDP); Comprehensive Handloom Cluster Development Scheme (CHCDS); Handloom Weavers' Comprehensive Welfare Scheme (HWCWS) and Yarn Supply Scheme (YSS, which provides financial assistance for raw materials, purchase of looms and accessories, design innovation, product diversification, infrastructure development and skill upgradation and other amenities and loans at concessional rates. For the weavers and consumers alike, it is the dawn of a New Bharat.

References

1. Frenz, Albrecht, 2020, *The Parur Songs Reflections on the Role of Women*, vol. I, Issue 3, Final New 2.pmd, www.tapasam.com
2. https://www.fibre2fashion.com/industry-article/8682/revival-of-madhubani-painted-textiles
3. https://www.kmgcbadalpur.org/wp-content/uploads/2019/10/3.3.4-138.pdfhttp://wcd.nic.in/sites/default/files/Final%20Report-TISS-%20Skill%20in%20slums.pdf
4. Handloom Industry, www.indiantradeportal.in
5. Halder, Ram Prasad Das, Arundhuti *et. al. A Detailed Study on Madhubani Art of Mithila, Bihar* © 2018 JETIR, January 2018, volume 5, Issue 1, www.jetir.org
6. https://www.researchgate.net/publication/297564600_Traditional_practices_of_natural_dyes_for_mithila_painting_of_Bihar

7. https://urbanmedley.com/how-madhubani-evolved-from-murals-to-wearable-art/
8. https://www.worldhistory.org/article/1527/madhubani-paintings-peoples-living-cultural-herita/
9. Indarti, Surabaya *et. al.*, Sustainable Batik Production: Review and Research Framework, *Advances in Social Science, Education and Humanities Research*, vol. 390 67 Microsoft Word - proceeding.docx
10. Parsuraman, S and Somaiya, Medha, 2016, *Economic Empowerment of Women: Promoting Skill Development in Slum Areas.*
11. *'Make-In-India' Programme for Weavers*, Press Information Bureau, pib.gov.in
12. Mukherjee, Esha, *Batik in Santiniketan, Emami Art.* www.emamiart.com
13. Women's Indispensable Role in the Handloom Industry, *The Statesman*, www.thestatesman.com

□

15

Empowering Indian Women through Financial Inclusion: A Policy Review of Select Government Initiatives

—Dr. Geetanjali Batra, Shabana Noori & Anjali R. Meena

Abstract

Financial inclusion is a crucial indicator of the economic growth and development of a nation. Making basic financial services available to citizens has become the priority of several developing economies. The Government of India has initiated several programmes, such as the Pradhan Mantri Jan Dhan Yojana (PMJDY), Pradhan Mantri Mudra Yojana (PMMY), Stand-Up India, Atal Pension Yojana (APY), Pradhan Mantri Jeevan Jyoti Bima Yojana (PMJJBY) and Pradhan Mantri Suraksha Bima Yojana (PMSBY). These financial inclusion programmes stand as a crucial strategy in nurturing gender equality and progressing women's empowerment. This study emphasises the impact and effectiveness of these financial programmes initiated by the Government of India to empower women through financial inclusion. The results show that these programmes have positively influenced the lives of people. Some steps in the direction of raising financial literacy, organising awareness campaigns and offering technology education tailored to women will further enhance the effectiveness of such programmes.

Keywords: Financial inclusion, women empowerment, PMJDY, PMMY, Stand-Up India, APY, PMJJBY, PMSBY.

Section I

Introduction

India's developmental strategy has recognised the inherent positive relationship between economic growth, financial expansion and financial inclusivity. The conversation about finance and economic growth has evolved with a greater emphasis on the role of finance in alleviating poverty, reducing inequality and empowering individuals by enhancing their capabilities. Financial inclusion is about the systematic facilitation of providing access to financial services at a reasonable cost to vulnerable and weaker sections of society including low-income groups and women (Rangarajan, 2008). It is the economic condition in which individuals are not excluded from obtaining essential financial services as a result of inefficiencies in infrastructure available for accessing public goods and services within a well-functioning society (Sharma, 2016). Financial inclusion is a step towards reducing poverty and inequality by allowing people to invest in the future, maintain stable consumption patterns and effectively navigate financial risks (Demirgüç-Kunt & Singer, 2017). Financial inclusion is likely to result in increased savings, reduce income disparity and poverty, increase employment rates, support educational progress, allow households to make more informed decisions about their economic affairs and simplify the start-up of new businesses (Guiso *et al.*, 2004). Good governance is essential for advancing financial inclusion due to its focus on building a globally competitive financial market by reducing transaction costs through innovation and competition (Claessens & Rojas-Suarez, 2016). Women make up roughly half of the global population. Women's empowerment signifies a transformative approach aimed at reshaping power dynamics in favour of the female gender and is deemed fundamental for global advancement. Empowering women is consistent with the belief that they deserve equal opportunities in all aspects of life (Chant, 2016). Empowerment comprises numerous dimensions and refers to expanding one's ability to choose and act freely across social, economic and political spheres, allowing individuals to shape their own lives. It also entails having authority over resources and making decisions (Pal, *et. al.*, 2022). Women empowerment includes social, educational, economic, political and psychological empowerment. Small and medium-sized enterprises owned by women usually face difficulties in access to financial services (Shetty & Hans, 2018). Financial inclusion programmes have a history of focusing on women and empowering them, even when they are not explicitly designed for them. Certain types of digital financial services have produced positive outcomes, particularly for women, by facilitating independent savings (Hendriks, 2019). The Indian government has initiated numerous programmes to improve the status of women. This study discusses the role of financial inclusion programmes, like PMJDY), PMMY, Stand-Up India, APY, PMJJBY and PMSBY in nation building and influencing lives of women.

Section II

Literature Review

Financial inclusion involves giving citizens access to credit services provided by established financial institutions, allowing them to participate in educational and entrepreneurial endeavours and making formal insurance products more accessible, thereby improving an individual's ability to manage and reduce financial risks (Demirguc-Kunt, 2017). The decision-making process for financial investments is influenced by economic, sociocultural and psychological factors. There is a significant and positive correlation between the level of financial literacy and the intelligence with which investors make their investment choices, resulting in higher returns (Bellofatt *et al.*, 2018). Financial inclusion in any country is influenced by several factors. Level of financial innovation, poverty, stability of the financial sector, economic conditions, levels of financial literacy and the various regulatory frameworks that exist across the country influence financial inclusion (Ozili, 2021). Financial inclusion stands as a fundamental strategy employed to accomplish the Sustainable Development Goals under the global development agenda as suggested by the United Nations (Sahay *et al.*, 2015); contributes to greater social inclusion across different communities (Bold *et al.*, 2012); helps in reducing poverty rates (Neaime and Gaysset, 2018), provides additional socioeconomic benefits (Sarma & Pais, 2011). It underlines the role of women's access to finance as an indispensable condition to ensure gender equality and empower women as well as young girls, thereby contributing to sustainable development and encouraging pro-poor growth (Aziz *et al.*, 2022). Women are unable to access the benefits offered by various programmes due to a lack of awareness about available schemes and challenges, such as illiteracy (Singh & Lamba, 2012). Women's empowerment will remain obscure unless women actively participate in and contribute to their self-empowerment (Tomar, 2020). Women entrepreneurs have experienced a notable shift in empowerment following the acquisition of loans. A considerable number of them continue to encounter discomfort or challenges when making decisions regarding personal matters, familial concerns, relationships, financial choices and societal involvement (ViggKushwah *et al.*, 2021). The administration and banking industry have the opportunity to improve existing policies and initiatives aimed at increasing access to the scheme so that a variety of training programmes can help to create a welcoming environment and assist borrowers in the early stages of their endeavours. The government should strive for gender equality in educational access, encourage women's economic participation and facilitate a more comprehensive approach to development (Ndoya & Tsala, 2021). Women with improved literacy, expertise and intra-household negotiation skills have more control over their earnings and savings (Arnold & Gammage, 2019). Persistent discriminatory socialisation continues to be a major contributor to gender inequality. Education is critical in empowering women, as is aligning financial products with the specific needs of women

(Kaur & Kapuria, 2020). Self-help groups for women have positively influenced women's political empowerment, mobility and control over family planning. These groups reduce domestic violence or improve psychological empowerment (Brody *et al.*, 2015). In countries where religious restrictions make it difficult for women to pursue professional careers, they are less likely to have a bank account than men; as a result, countries that promote gender equality in the workplace and implement strong regulatory frameworks to support these efforts tend to have higher levels of women actively involved in financial matters (Aziz *et al.*, 2022). Households led by women exposed a reduced predisposition to utilise formal financial channels and displayed a higher inclination towards informal finance so that women encountered limitations stemming from both the demand for and availability of financial services, hindering their access to and utilisation of formal financial systems (Ghosh & Vinod, 2017).

Section III

Objective of the Study

This study presents a review of financial inclusion programmes initiated by the Government of India, with a particular emphasis on the performance of these initiatives on the empowerment of women. This study is descriptive and is based on secondary data obtained from a range of sources, such as books, journals, newspapers, reports from government agencies and official websites of the Indian government.

Section IV

Government Schemes for Financial Inclusion and Women Empowerment

Pradhan Mantri Jan Dhan Yojana (PMJDY): Pradhan Mantri Jan Dhan Yojana was announced in 2014. This initiative aims to provide for financial inclusion by providing access to banking services. Within this framework, individuals can open savings accounts without the requirement of maintaining a minimum balance. Even if the beneficiary does not have official documents typically needed for opening a bank account, they can still open an account. The beneficiary gets accidental insurance cover of Rs. 2,00,000, life insurance cover of Rs. 30,000 and an overdraft facility of up to Rs. 10,000. Preference is given to female members of the household. The beneficiary is provided with a RuPay ATM-cum-Debit Card. The PMJDY initiative creates a comprehensive platform for accessing financial services for all Indian citizens. It encourages financial inclusion for Indian women, promotes their financial literacy and strengthens their economic and social capacities. Female participants use the Jan Dhan Yojna to start their banking (Jyothi, 2019). Since the emergence of PMJDY accounts, Self-Help Groups (SHGs) have presumed a more significant role as compared to moneylenders (Singh & Naik, 2018). PMJDY provides convenient access to banking facilities. Financial literacy initiatives are undertaken from time to time to impart knowledge about financial products. Furthermore, the beneficiary gets a RuPay debit card. The PMJDY was formulated as an inventive and ambitious endeavour. The drive to establish PMJDY accounts received widespread acceptance across India, aiming to make banking accessible to a large segment of the Indian populace. The inclusivity of this initiative is accentuated by the fact that more than two-third of PMJDY accounts are situated in rural regions and over 55 per cent of the account holders are women. Over time, there has been considerable growth in the deposit volume in PMJDY accounts in terms of the cumulative deposit balance in PMJDY accounts amounts as well as the average deposit per account (Maity & Sahu, 2020).

Table 1: Pradhan Mantri Jan Dhan Yojana Beneficiaries as on 06.12.2023 (All Figures in Crore)

Bank	Female Beneficiaries	Total Beneficiaries	Percentage of Female Beneficiaries
Public Sector Banks	21.96	39.90	55.03
Regional Rural Banks	5.52	9.55	57.80
Private Sector Banks	0.77	1.47	52.38
Rural Cooperative Banks	0.10	0.19	52.63
Total	**28.36**	**51.11**	**55.47**

Source: Progress-Report Pradhan Mantri Jan-Dhan Yojana (2022-23)

Pradhan Mantri Mudra Yojana (PMMY): The PMMY is a microfinance programme designed for small-scale industrial units run in both rural and urban areas. The programme was launched in 2016. It promotes economic empowerment by way of Self-Help Groups (SHGs). It was designed with the objective of 'funding the unfunded' and increasing women's participation in the entrepreneurial landscape (Kadaba *et al.*, 2022). Under the aegis of PMMY, there are three sub-schemes. Under the sub-scheme 'Shishu', a loan of up to Rs. 50,000 is provided. Under the sub-scheme 'Kishore', the beneficiary may get a loan between Rs. 50,000 to Rs. 5 lakhs. Under the sub-scheme 'Tarun', the beneficiary may get a loan between Rs. 5 lakhs to Rs. 10 lakhs. There is no requirement to provide collateral security for the disbursement of loans. These measures are aimed at encouraging young, first-generation entrepreneurs. Entrepreneurs of any ongoing business may also get financial support for the expansion of their business activities. By providing affordable credit for initiating entrepreneurship ventures, the scheme promotes sustainable livelihood practices and provides employment opportunities. It significantly empowers women economically, socially, psychologically and politically (Agarwala *et al.*, 2022). By extending loans under the MUDRA Yojana to the targeted 'bottom of the pyramid' group, the goals of employment generation and social empowerment can be simultaneously achieved. This programme serves millions of unfunded micro-borrowers in the country by providing them with much-needed loans to pursue their business. The scheme has benefited the grassroots economy of the country to contribute to the overall economic growth of the nation. It empowers women as the majority of the beneficiaries are women (Mahajan, 2019).

Table 2: MUDRA Loans and Beneficiaries during FY 2021-22

Category	Number of Female Beneficiaries	Total Beneficiaries	Percentage of Female
Number of Accounts	3,84,29,259	5,37,95,526	71%
Amount Sanctioned (in crores)	1,66,422	3,39,110	49%
Amount Disbursed (in crores)	1,64,442	3,31,402	50%

Source: *Mudra Annual Report (2021-22)*

Stand-Up India Programme

Stand-Up India programme was launched in 2016 to provide bank loans ranging from Rs. 10 lakh to Rs. 1 crore to at least one borrower from the Scheduled Caste (SC) or Scheduled Tribe (ST) category and at least one female borrower per bank branch. These funds are provided to launch new businesses. This programme assists businesses that are involved in agriculture, trading, manufacturing, or providing services. The programme is being run by all scheduled commercial banks. With the help of the Stand-Up India initiative, many job seekers have successfully transitioned into job creators, particularly providing a prosperous platform for women entrepreneurs (Kaur & Arora, 2022). This programme encourages women, members of Scheduled Tribes (ST) and Scheduled Castes (SC) to start entrepreneurial ventures. These populations face significant barriers as a result of inadequate guidance, as well as difficulties associated with inadequate and delayed availability of credit. By engaging with these underprivileged populations, the programme seeks to support them in starting new businesses through the use of institutional credit framework. Credit requirements of both seasoned as well as inexperienced borrowers are catered to. Consultancy and assistance to potential borrowers is also provided in the Stand-Up India scheme. The outlook report states that by 31 March, 2023, the sanction amount was Rs. 40,710 crore. Among these, 1.44 lakh accounts held by women have received a total of Rs. 33,152.43 crore. About 80 per cent of loan disbursements since the programme's founding in 2016 have gone to female entrepreneurs. The Stand-Up programme is a long-term approach towards increasing the potential of female entrepreneurs, promoting economic growth and creating resilient societies worldwide (Kaur, 2018). Using the loan funds, women have joined productive activities and have been able to enhance their participation in decisions relating to their family finances (Vigg Kushwah *et al.*, 2021). Growing governmental support in providing financial assistance and raising awareness is likely to motivate aspiring entrepreneurs from economically disadvantaged backgrounds (Lande, 2019).

Table 3: Women Borrowers Benefited under the Stand-Up India Scheme as on 28.11.2022

Category	Female Beneficiaries	Total Beneficiaries	Percentage of Female
Numbers of Accounts	127165	158437	80.26
Sanctioned Amount (in crore)	29297.69	35886.94	81.63

Source: Annual Report, Department of Financial Services, 2022-23

Atal Pension Yojana (APY): Launched in 2015, APY provides a fixed pension for subscribers. The beneficiary should start the subscription between the age-group of 18 to 40 years. However, the beneficiary will get a pension only after attaining the age of 60 years. The amount of pension is in the range of Rs. 1,000 to Rs.

5,000 per month. It depends on the amount of contribution and the age at the time of starting a subscription to the programme (Sudindra, 2016). The beneficiary must have a bank account under PMJDY. It is a promising programme for those individuals who are willing to contribute a small sum of money but for a longer duration. It is a breakthrough move for encouraging workers from the unorganised sector to willingly save for their retirement and marks a transition from a pension-less society towards a pensioned society. It provides the beneficiary with financial security in old age (Yadav, 2016). In case the main account holder of the APY programme passes away during the duration of the scheme, the spouse can either claim the contributions or complete the duration of the scheme. This scheme is more popular among workers in the unorganised sector as they get old age security using very low investment (Bhattacharjee, 2020).

Pradhan Mantri Jeevan Jyoti Bima Yojana (PMJJBY): PMJJBY was introduced in 2015, under the aegis of PMJDY to provide financial support and increase the reach and density of insurance coverage in India for inclusive growth (Shukla, 2017). The motto of the scheme is 'jan dhan se jan suraksha'. The beneficiary is required to pay an annual premium of Rs. 330 for an insurance cover of Rs. 2,00,000. People in the age group of 18–50 years may join the scheme. It is necessary to have a bank account under PMJDY (Katoch, 2016). PMJJBY is attractive as an economical term-insurance service due to its flexibility, easy and clear process and reliable claim process (Vyas, 2019). To enhance the coverage and reach of the scheme, it is suggested that some revisions may be considered in the entry age of the beneficiary and sum assured (Sharma, 2017).

Pradhan Mantri Suraksha Bima Yojana (PMSBY): PMSBY was launched in 2015. It requires the subscriber to pay a premium of Rs. 12 per annum for an insurance cover of Rs. 2,00,000 in case of accidental death or full disability and an insurance cover of Rs. 1,00,000 in case of partial disability. People in the age group of 18 to 70 years having wa bank account under PMJDY may subscribe to the programme (Katoch, 2016).

Section V

Conclusion

This study emphasises the crucial role of financial inclusion programmes in achieving comprehensive and inclusive growth, particularly concerning the empowerment of women. To provide women with financial services that are accessible and convenient, service providers must understand their requirements, as well as social and economic limitations. These insights should be integrated into the design of financial programmes (Sabherwal *et al.*, 2019). Improving women's financial inclusion, gauged through their access to bank accounts and credit facilities, yields a favourable influence on economic advancement. Financial and technical training to effectively cultivate entrepreneurial qualities and skills will allow the beneficiaries to adapt to changing global markets and navigate local economic landscapes for long-term viability and success as entrepreneurs (Dutta, 2018). Consequently, concerted endeavours involving governments and financial institutions are essential to narrow the gender disparity in financial inclusion. Empowering women in this realm stands as a pivotal stride towards fostering enhanced economic growth. The PMMY scheme will significantly benefit individuals involved in small-scale industries, consequently fostering positive economic strides on a broader scale (Shahid & Irshad, 2016). The PMJDY scheme has demonstrated significant success, particularly among women residing in slum areas (Bhatia & Singh, 2019). In the case of PMMY, approximately 81.63 per cent of the sanctioned amount benefits women and under Stand-Up India, around 80 per cent of the beneficiaries are women. These initiatives significantly contribute to the empowerment of women. In conjunction with financial and entrepreneurship support programmes, the government has the potential to organise awareness programmes on empowerment in educational institutions, *panchayats* and other relevant platforms.

References

- Agarwala, V., Maity, S. and Sahu, T.N. (2022), Female entrepreneurship, employability and empowerment: impact of the Mudra loan scheme, Journal of Developmental Entrepreneurship, 27(01): 2250005.
- Arnold, J. and Gammage, S. (2019), Gender and financial inclusion: The critical role for holistic programming, Development in Practice, 29(8): 965-973.
- Aziz, F., Sheikh, S.M. and Shah, I.H. (2022), Financial inclusion for women empowerment in South Asian countries, Journal of Financial Regulation and Compliance, 30(4): 489-502.
- Bellofatto, A., D'Hondt, C. and De Winne, R. (2018), Subjective financial literacy and retail investors' behaviour, Journal of Banking & Finance, 92: 168-181.
- Bhatia, S. and Singh, S. (2019), Empowering women through financial inclusion: A study of urban slum, Vikalpa, 44(4): 182-197.
- Bhattacharjee, R. and Rengma, S.S. (2020), Attitude towards Atal Pension Yojana scheme, Indian Journal of Health and Wellbeing, 11(1-3): 40-42.
- Bold, C., Porteous, D. and Rotman, S. (2012), Social cash transfers and financial inclusion: Evidence from four countries, Population (in millions), 193(46): 109.
- Brody, C., De Hoop, T., Vojtkova, M., Warnock, R., Dunbar, M., Murthy, P. and Dworkin, S.L. (2015), Economic Self-Help group programmes for improving women's empowerment: A systematic review, Campbell Systematic Reviews, 11(1): 1-182.
- Chant, S. (2016), Women, girls and world poverty: empowerment, equality or essentialism? International Development Planning Review, 38(1): 1-24.
- Claessens, S. and Rojas-Suarez, L. (2016), Financial regulations for improving financial inclusion, Centre for Global Development, 2(3): 44-53.
- Demirgüç-Kunt, A. and Singer, D. (2017), Financial inclusion and inclusive growth: A review of recent empirical evidence, World Bank Policy Research Working Paper, (8040).
- Dutta, J. (2018), Women Entrepreneurs and Stand-Up India Scheme: A Critical Evaluation, International Journal of Advanced Scientific Research and Management, 3(7): 67-73.
- Ghosh, S. and Vinod, D. (2017), What constrains financial inclusion for women? Evidence from Indian microdata, World Development, 92: 60-81.
- Guiso, L., Sapienza, P. and Zingales, L. (2004), The role of social capital in financial development, American Economic Review, 94(3): 526-556.
- Hendriks, S. (2019), The role of financial inclusion in driving women's economic empowerment, Development in Practice, 29(8): 1029-1038.
- Hung, A., Yoong, J. and Brown, E. (2012), Empowering women through financial awareness and education.
- Jyothi, A. (2019), Empowering women through banking innovation with the knowledge of innovation, a special reference to a Self-Help Group, International Journal of Social and Economic Research, 9(3): 156-194.

- Kadaba, D.M.K., Aithal, P.S. and KRS, S. (2022), Role of MUDRA in Promoting SMEs/MSE, MSMEs, and allied Agriculture Sector in the Rural and Urban Area to Achieve 5 Trillion Economy, International Journal of Management, Technology, and Social Sciences (IJMTS), 7(1): 373-389.
- Katoch, R. (2016), An analysis and critical evaluation of Pradhan Mantri Jan Suraksha Yojna in India, International Journal of Research in Social Sciences, 6(10): 130-144.
- Kaur, L. and Arora, J. (2022), Women Entrepreneurs and Stand-up India Scheme in Punjab: A Critical Review, Gyan Management Journal, 16(1): 53-60.
- Kaur, S. (2018), Challenges and future prospects of women entrepreneurship in India: An analysis, Asian Journal of Multidimensional Research (AJMR), 7(3): 207-215.
- Kaur, S. and Kapuria, C. (2020), Determinants of financial inclusion in rural India: Does gender matter? International Journal of Social Economics, 47(6): 747-767.
- Lande, G. (2019), Providing Financial Support to Emerging Entrepreneurs in India: A Study of Stand up India Scheme, International Education and Research Journal, 5(8): 32-35.
- Mahajan, Y. (2019), A study and review of Pradhan Mantri Mudra Yojana (PMMY) in the state of Maharashtra, International Journal of Advance and Innovative Research, 6(2): 1-7.
- Maity, S. and Sahu, T.N. (2020), Role of public sector banks towards financial inclusion during pre- and post-introduction of PMJDY: A study on efficiency review, Rajagiri Management Journal, 14(2): 95-105.
- Ndoya, H.H. and Tsala, C.O. (2021), What drives the gender gap in financial inclusion? Evidence from Cameroon, African Development Review, 33(4): 674-687.
- Neaime, S. and Gaysset, I. (2018), Financial inclusion and stability in MENA: Evidence from poverty and inequality, Finance Research Letters, 24: 230-237.
- Ozili, P.K. (2021, October), Financial inclusion research around the world: A review. In: Forum for Social Economics, 50(4): 457-479), Routledge.
- Pal, M., Gupta, H. and Joshi, Y.C. (2022), Social and economic empowerment of women through financial inclusion: Empirical evidence from India, Equality, Diversity and Inclusion: An International Journal, 41(2): 294-305.
- Rangarajan, C. (2008), Report of the Committee on Financial Inclusion, Ministry of Finance, Government of India, 155-167.
- Sabherwal, R., Sharma, D. and Trivedi, N. (2019), Using direct benefit transfers to transfer benefits to women: A perspective from India, Development in Practice, 29(8): 1001-1013.
- Sahay, M.R., Cihak, M., N'Diaye, M.P., Barajas, M.A., Mitra, M.S., Kyobe, M.A. and Yousefi, M.R. (2015), Financial Inclusion: Can It Meet Multiple Macroeconomic Goals? International Monetary Fund.

- Sarma, M. and Pais, J. (2011), Financial inclusion and development, Journal of International Development, 23(5): 613-628.
- Shahid, M. and Irshad, M. (2016), A Descriptive Study on Pradhan Mantri Mudra Yojana (PMMY), International Journal of Latest Trends in Engineering and Technology, 3(5): 121-125.
- Sharma, M.K. (2016), Financial inclusion: A prelude to the economic status of vulnerable groups, International Journal of research-Granthaalayah, 4(12): 147-154.
- Sharma, S. (2017), Analytical View on Pradhan Mantri Jeevan Jyoti Bima Yojana, Journal of Management Engineering and Information Technology (JMEIT), 4(5): 15-18.
- Shetty, S. and Hans, V. (2018), Women empowerment in India and financial inclusion barriers, International Journal of Management Sociology and Humanities, 9(3): 344-352.
- Shukla, U.N. (2017), Pradhan Mantri Jeevan Jyoti Bima Yojana – Advocating Penetration in Indian Life Insurance Industry for Inclusive Growth: An Empirical Study, IIMS Journal of Management Science, 8(2): 130-137.
- Singh, C. and Naik, G. (2018), Financial inclusion after PMJDY: A case study of Gubbi Taluk, Tumkur, IIM Bangalore Research Paper, (568).
- Singh, I. and Lamba, P. (2012), Women welfare schemes in Haryana, Asian Journal of Multidimensional Research (AJMR), 1(2): 101-111.Sudindra, V.R. (2016), Feasibility analysis of Atal Pension Yojana, International Journal of Advanced Research, 4(3): 1652-1655.
- Tomar, T.S. (2020), The Overview of Women Empowerment in India, International Journal of Management (IJM), 11(12).
- ViggKushwah, S., Singh, T., Das, M.S. and Sharma, A. (2021), The role of government initiatives on women empowerment: The case of women entrepreneurs in India, Annals of the Romanian Society for Cell Biology, 11522-11535.
- Vyas, M.N. (2019), A Study on Pradhan Mantri Jeevan Jyoti Bima Yojana, Paripex Indian Journal of Research, 8(8): 176-178.
- Yadav, R.K. and Mohania, S. (2016), A Case Study with Overview of Pradhan Matri Jan Dhan Yojna (Atal Pension Yojana), World Scientific News, (29): 124-134.

□

16

Rural Women: A Decade of Upliftment, Empowerment and Societal Change

—**Dr. Ritu Saraswat, Sociologist**

A decade ago, when India began its journey towards a new horizon, the sky was glowing with the golden aura of Atmanirbhar Bharat. It is not just a model of economic development; it was a successful attempt to awaken the dormant self of India.

Atmnirbhar Bharat or a self-reliant India is not only a dream, but it is like an artery carrying blood and nutrients to the sacred land; it is a life force that takes our nation from being dependent to being self-reliant.

It is not that the journey towards self-reliance has been undertaken in the last decade, but it was dreamt of and initiated many decades ago to take India towards self-reliance. Thus, it is not a new concept, but it has blossomed and flourished in the last decade.

In October 1919, Gandhiji delivered a speech at Bhagini Samaj in Mumbai. In his address, he stressed the need to make India *atmnirbhar*. He said, "Hindustan must learn to be self-reliant." The question arises: When a self-reliant India was envisioned back then, why didn't it materialise in the form that was expected?

Another important question is: Is it possible to achieve it without involving or including half the population? These are a few of the questions that need to be addressed and answered. The main reason for the non-realisation of the concept of self-reliant

India, or Bharat, despite being envisioned a few decades ago, was the lack of policies required for its implementation at ground level. This is sure and there are no doubts that to achieve the goal that was dreamt of – to become a self-reliant and developed nation, a systematic framework of a definite work system and policies were to be prepared. Although earlier governments made budgetary provisions and some other measures were taken to implement the planning, those proved insufficient because they lacked the effort to amalgamate self-reliance with self-respect among the citizens and thus, it was altogether left behind.

An answer to the second question, which asks: Can the dream of a self-reliant India be realised without the involvement of half the population of our country? The answer is loud and clear: No.

The beginning of the journey towards making Bharat self-reliant started with a giant stride. The foundation was laid by the Hon'ble Prime Minister on 14 September, 2014, with the launch of the 'Make in India' mission as part of a wider set of nation-building initiatives. Devised to transform India into a global design and manufacturing hub, 'Make in India' was a timely response to a critical situation.

By 2013, the much-hyped emerging market bubble had burst and India's growth rate had fallen to its lowest level in a decade. The promise of the BRICS nations (Brazil, Russia, India, China and South Africa) had faded and India was tagged as one of the so-called 'Fragile Five'. Global investors debated whether the world's largest democracy was a risk or an opportunity. India's 1.2 billion citizens questioned whether India was too big to succeed or too big to fail? India was on the brink of severe economic failure, desperately in need of a big push.[1]

Then 'Make in India' was launched, which has not only set up economic goals for the country but also infused an emotional connection for the people with tremendous planning and on-the-ground implementation. 'Make in India' focuses on 27 sectors and involves almost all ministries, departments and Central and state governments. All the necessary steps were taken by the government to encourage a balanced thrust for local as well as foreign business with the policy reforms that have not only encouraged foreign investment but have also developed an ecosystem for local businesses to flourish. This has infused confidence and reliability, which proved catalysts in the growth of the Indian manufacturing and marketing sector at global levels.[2] The objectives with which 'Make in India' was started in 2014 were backed by a strong will to overcome all the obstacles and challenges to achieve the goals set. This has led to results that are highly encouraging and have given impetus and momentum to the Indian economy, which has put all the doubts raised by the critics to rest.

Since its launch, less than a decade has passed and the *World Investment Report 2023* has reported India as an FDI powerhouse, as India has secured the third highest foreign investment in the years 2021-22. The total FDI inflow received during the last decade was about 614 billion dollars, with more than 101 countries having invested across the country.[3] Amidst the encouraging results, it becomes imperative to dwell on the policies that have strengthened India's economy during the last decade. Policymakers in the country have focused on and ensured that the planning should be village-centric, as it was evident from past experiences and failures that the Indian economy cannot stand strong without strengthening the economic structure of villages. Here, it is natural to raise the question of whether the rural economy was not given attention after Independence? Were the policies not formulated for their self-reliance and economic improvement? The answer to both of these questions is that, although after Independence, various schemes for the growth of the rural economy were proposed in the policies and plans of the Central and state governments and worked upon at various levels, the participation of women from rural areas was either lacking or negligible and the reasons for this were clear. There were many challenges to the direct economic participation of women. Amidst the rigid structure of patriarchal society, a lack of capital and traditional social and cultural values that don't allow women to take the initiative, this has forced them to live within the narrow confines of the four walls of the house.

The biggest challenge for women to overcome these obstacles was a lack of self-respect, or rather a loss of self-respect, which in turn deeply affects the self-confidence of any person and a lack of self-confidence forces one to live within the perimeters of shackles of dependency. It percolates deep down and hampers the growth of individuals as well as that of groups socially and economically. Barring a few exceptions, women's economic participation as a group has been dismally low. There is no doubt that lack of self-esteem is closely linked with incompetence and apathy. Indian rural women were facing similar situations, which is why the earlier schemes for the empowerment of rural women did not succeed as expected.

After almost seven decades of Independence, on 15 August, 2014, an iconic clarion call was given by the Hon'ble Prime Minister regarding the restoration of self-respect and uplifting the self-esteem of women in the country through his address to the nation, which proved to be an indelible chapter in the history of women empowerment. On 15 August, 2014, Prime Minister Narendra Modi focused on setting up more toilets across the country, unconventionally taking up the issue of cleanliness among all Indians. On the occasion, the Prime Minister urged parliamentarians to use constituency funds to build toilets in every school. "Can we not create proper toilet facilities? I don't know whether people will appreciate my talking about dirt and toilets from the Red Fort, but I come from a poor family. I have seen poverty and the attempt to give dignity to the poor starts from there," he said.[4] The PM also appealed to corporations to join hands with the government as part of their social responsibility to build toilets. "There should be separate toilets for girls. Next year, when we stand here, every school should have toilets for girls and boys. If 125 crore people resolve not to dirty our surroundings, no force on earth can come and dirty our country," he said, emphasising 'clean India'.[5] This moment opened the doors of self-respect for the women of India. There is no doubt that open defecation is the biggest cause of mental anguish and embarrassment for women.

Researchers have reported and have come up with the results indicating the health risks of women's sanitation experiences. They have reported feeling ashamed if witnessed by someone, abstaining or not eating food and not drinking water to limit and control excretion, avoiding or delaying in going for Nature's call as because of non-conducive surroundings, may it be physical or social environment, not relieving themselves due to social hesitation, at a risk of violence physical or sexual while venturing long distances to look for a safer place or space during addressing the need, most of the time the conditions of sanitation has been well beyond their control and they are helpless,[6] Studies also suggests that women suffer from psychosocial stress after such dreadful sanitation-related experiences. Factors concerning the physical and social environment, personal constraints, safety, sexual violence and finances have all been reported to contribute to women's experiences of stress from sanitation.[7] Before the ambitious Swachh Bharat Mission-Grameen (SBM-G) was launched in 2014, the state of sanitation in the country was abysmal. Only around 40 per cent of households had access to a toilet. The mission, with its exclusive focus on behaviour change communication (BCC), women's involvement and social acceptance have turned out to be a tremendous success. Yet for the construction of a toilet, improved convenience was not the main driving force behind the survey, which was a collaborative effort between UNICEF, Bill & Melinda Gates Foundation (BMGF) and Sambodhi Research and Communications Private Limited with assistance from the Department of Drinking Water and Sanitation. The Ministry of Jal Shakti showed many positive outcomes that has brought more physical comfort and made their lives easy after the construction of toilets in their homes. They don't have to travel long for defecation; thus, they are able to save up to an hour. Further they can use the toilet any time instead of waiting till dark or late evening. They are no longer afraid of going to the toilet in the dark of the night, which in comparison is a very big difference as it was only 12 per cent in the pre-toilet construction stage. Men also felt lots of comfort after toilet construction asthey no longer traverse difficult terrains looking for secluded place such as hills, ditches, near water bodies, etc. to ease themselves. They too have been freed of the discomfort because of insects and flies at open defecation sites. With no access to a private toilet, women used to either deliberately restrict their intake of water and other liquids so that they wouldn't need to go out to heed to Nature's call. But, 93 per cent of the women reported no longer hesitate or check food and water intake to control the urge to defecate or urinate after getting the household toilet. This has proved to be a major relief for the women in rural areas in their daily routine and has reduced the risk of catching any infection or disease. They no longer have to rely or look for others to take care of their dependents while they go for defecation. Before the construction of toilets, they were afraid or embarrassed while going and defecating in the open. About almost half of the surveyed subjects reported that they avoided their relatives and neighbours as they felt embarrassed at not having toilets in their homes and felt shame as they were judged by the others of their community. Most of the young unmarried women and almost all the men felt a sense of pride when they got toilets in their homes. About three-quarters of surveyed women said they felt stress-free as it proved an added help during menstruation needs. The majority of women, especially unmarried young women, said they were proud to own a toilet.

The report '*Access to Toilets and the Safety, Convenience and Self-Respect of Women in Rural India*' states that many of the women surveyed spent a significant amount of time in reaching the open defecation site. At times, especially given the strict social norms, some women had to walk half a kilometre or more. Nearly 91 per cent women stated that they had to trudge for one hour or so to reach a toilet, while 98 per cent said that they would travel up to a kilometre. This is not the case anymore.[8]Prime Minister Narendra Modi, in the Lok Sabha on 7 February, 2108, said, "The Clean India Mission has boosted the self-confidence of women. It has become one of the reasons for their liberation from great pain. Swachh Bharat Abhiyan made an unprecedented contribution to women's empowerment. On the one hand, it freed them from embarrassment by getting rid of going for open defecation, while on the other hand, they also participated by being a part of this campaign."

Lakhs of champion women contributed to the success of this programme. SBM-G became a great employment opportunity for those who not only took on the role of masons for constructing toilets, but also working as '*swachhagrahis*'.[9]

It was the first chapter on women's self-respect which was written in 2014 and proved to be an important signature of women's empowerment. A further addition to this chapter was Prime Minister Modi's speech at the historical Red Fort on 15 August, 2020 when he deliberated at length upon the physiological dimension of women's health which covered menstruation. It reflected his concern for the women of India and his commitment toushering in a new era of women's empowerment. He underlined that his government has managed to provide affordable sanitary napkins to poor women through Jan Aushadhi centres for just one rupee each. "This government has been persistently concerned about better healthcare for poor sisters and daughters. We have done a huge job of providing sanitary pads at one rupee each in Jan Aushadhi Kendras.[10] India's commitment to achieving the Sustainable Development Goals (SDGs) has been confirmed, particularly concerning Goal 3 on good health and well-being, Goal 4 on quality education, Goal 5 on gender equality and Goal 6 on clean water and sanitation. Additionally, the policy will serve as a catalyst in creating awareness by challenging societal norms and fostering a society that embraces menstrual hygiene as a natural and normal part of life.[11] In terms of location, 73% of rural women and 90% of urban women use a hygienic method of menstrual protection. These findings highlight the need for targeted efforts and initiatives to improve menstrual hygiene practices in these regions.[12] Menstrual health is an integral part of the health and well-being of a person and is a determinant of the quality of life, which includes mobility, work participation, access to education, dignity and freedom. Such steps lead to gender equality, education and overall development.[13]

During the last decade, every step taken towards women's empowerment has been successful in touching upon and ameliorating the issues that were earlier hardly considered serious enough. One such aspect touches on the most universally accepted truth that water and clean drinking water have been the primary needs of every living being. The task of collecting and fetching clean drinking water was considered the women's duty but now with the announcement of 'Jal Jeevan Mission, Prime Minister Modi announced on 15 August, 2019, "And so I declare from the Red Fort today that in the days to come, we will take forward the Jal Jeevan Mission. The Central and state governments will jointly work on this Jal Jeevan Mission. We have promised to spend more than Rs. 3.50 lakh crores on this mission in the coming years. In the next five years, we have to do more than four times the work that has been done in the last 70 years." Jal Jeevan Mission (JJM) has been launched and it aims to provide Functional Household Tap Connection (FHTC) to every rural household by 2024. The programme focuses on service delivery at the household level, i.e. water supply regularly in an adequate quantity prescribed and of quality. This necessitates the use of modern technology in the planning and implementation of water supply schemes, the development of water sources, the treatment and supply of water, the empowerment of the *Gramin Panchayat* and local community, a focus on service delivery, partnerships with other stakeholders, convergence with other programmes, methodical monitoring of the programme and capture of service delivery data automatically for ensuring the quality of services. . From 1951 to 2019, efforts were focused on providing a safe drinking water supply to rural populations either through hand pumps, protected wells, or piped water supply with public standposts as delivery points. In the last few decades, as reported by states, viz. Gujarat, Goa, Haryana, Himachal Pradesh, Punjab, Sikkim, Telangana, etc., they have focused on providing tap connections to rural households. Of late, many states are making concerted efforts to provide all rural households with piped water supply.[14]

The Jal Jeevan Mission (JJM) has marked a milestone, as 70 per cent of rural households have been provided tap water connections till now. Regular access to tap water frees individuals, particularly women and young girls, from having to carry heavy bucket loads of water to satisfy their daily needs and which reduces the arduous labour that has been done for centuries. The time saved by not having to collect water is directed towards earning money, developing new skills and assisting in the education of children. Teenaged girls no longer need to quit school to assist their mothers in fetching water. It greatly aids in educating and empowering girls.[15]

Women are given a pivotal role under the 'Har Ghar Jal' as they are the primary stakeholders and are involved in the programme since the very beginning. They are part of planning, monitoring and also receive training to undertake water quality testing from time to time. It is a move to empower women and reduce their drudgery.[16] Savita Kaushik from Manguwa, district Lalitpur, Uttar Pradesh shares her story of how the mapping of 'Women Time Use Analysis' facilitated by UNOPS was an eye-opener. The village women were divided into two groups and each group had to prepare a comparative chart of the kind of work done and the time taken from morning to evening and how much water the other group spent on what kind of work? Both the groups wrote on the chart paper and gave a presentation. "From this, we realised that it takes more time to fill water. If there is a tap connection in our homes, then we can do other more productive work in that time," said Savita.[17]

'Jal Jeevan Mission' proved instrumental in changing the lives of thousands of 'Savitas'. This campaign connected lakhs of women in the country with various schemes for economic self-reliance and took them from incapability to empowerment. As it was discussed earlier, since the country's Independence, women empowerment has been at the centre of many schemes of the Central and state governments. Despite this, half the population was left behind and was unable to join the mainstream. Women's empowerment is a very broader concept with many minute and finer aspects associated with it. It is not possible to empower women through any single scheme or budgetary provision; in fact, the biggest challenge is the question of self-confidence which cannot attained by just waving a magic wand. Instead, it is a long and continuous journey to achieve self-confidence and self-respect. Unfortunately, for decades, no attention was paid to this. Neither enough research was conducted on the role of women involved in the socio-cultural sphere, nor was there any deep thinking and reflection at the government or non-government levels. Most painful was the fact that the physical and mental sufferings of women were not of anyone's concern. The past decade has been like that golden period where initiatives were taken to protect and maintain the self-respect of women. This would not have been possible if the initiative had not been taken up by the Prime Minister. It has given confidence and empowerment to the women of India and, in turn, is ready to touch new heights. 'Jal Jeevan Mission' has also paved the way for rural women to move firmly towards economic self-reliance.

Amidst all these efforts, the powerful contribution of the Ujjwala Yojana cannot be forgotten. Prior to the revolution brought about by the scheme, traditional cooking fuels like firewood, coal and cowdung cakes were used.. It was common for Indian women to cook meals in smoky kitchens, coughing and struggling to breathe throughout the day. This not only impacted their health but also contributed to environmental concerns. However, the Government of India launched the Pradhan Mantri Ujjwala Yojana (PMUY) in May 2016 to make clean cooking fuel like LPG available to rural and deprived households. This initiative marked a liberating experience for Indian women who had endured generations of hardship, finally realising the dream of a smoke-free kitchen.[18] During the Viksit Bharat Sankalp Yatra, several women shared the transformation in their lives that has occurred after getting access to an LPG cylinder under the PM Ujjwala Yojana. During one month of the Yatra itself, about 3.77

lakh women have enrolled for the scheme, adding to the crores who have already benefited under this scheme since its launch in 2016.[19] Women no longer need to go to forests to collect firewood or face sexual harassment.[20]

The Ujjwala Yojana, Jal Jeevan Mission, and Swachh Bharat Mission established the groundwork for rural women to step forward and move towards economic security and as stated by Prime Minister Modi, "When women prosper, the world prospers." The most effective way to empower women is through a women-led development approach. India is making strides in this direction.[21]

The scheme called the Development of Women and Children in Rural Areas (DWCRA), a sub-scheme of the Integrated Rural Development Programme, was launched in 50 village districts in 82-83 to help rural women become financially independent by helping them open bank accounts, buy assets and take loans from the bank instead of moneylenders. According to a study released by the National Council for Applied Economic Research Centre for Macro Consumer Research in 2011, interest on loans from moneylenders is highest (44 per cent) against 12.6 per cent from banks.[22]

This model of economic empowerment only had a few successes in small pockets of India, such as Andhra Pradesh, Gujarat, Maharashtra, and Tamil Nadu, because the rural credit networks in most areas were poorly understood and not effective. Following these schemes, micro-credit schemes like Self-Help Groups (SHGs) were introduced, which partnered with the local banks in the area. This scheme was successful since it imparted financial knowledge as well as financial discipline, thereby enabling a significant decrease in payment defaults. As opposed to the earlier schemes, this model encouraged women to take up different economic activities at their own pace since they had access to a dependable source of credit.[23]

Besides, in the past few years, a number of initiatives were taken for the holistic development and empowerment of women. The Government of India implements various schemes and programmes for the welfare of women and girls, in which community participation plays an important role. Under the National Rural Livelihoods Mission (NRLM), nearly 9 crore women have been connected with around 83.5 lakh women's Self-Help Groups that are transforming the rural socio-economic landscape in several innovative and socially and ecologically responsible ways, also availing governmental support, including through collateral-free loans. The Mahatma Gandhi National Rural Employment Guarantee Act, 2005 (MGNREGA) mandates that at least one-third of the jobs generated under the scheme (MGNREGS) should be given to women. The National Agriculture Market, or e-NAM, an online trading platform for agricultural commodities, is helping women overcome or compensate for the barriers they face in accessing markets. The National Cooperative Development Corporation (NCDC) is playing a significant role in uplifting women's cooperatives, as a large number of women are engaged and involved in cooperatives dealing with activities related to foodgrain processing, plantation crops, oilseed processing, fisheries, dairy and livestock, spinning mills, handloom and power-loom weaving.[24] A women-farmer empowerment scheme was launched, under which training has been imparted to more than 33 lakh women farmers. In addition to this, more than 25,000 community livelihood resource persons were selected who have been providing 24x7 support at the rural level. Today, the farmers of the country understand the importance of value addition. They are adopting it and are reaping its benefits. In some states, this value-chain approach has been adopted for some particular crops, like corn and mangoes, in the horticulture and dairy sectors, etc. More than two lakh members of Self-Help Groups have received support for this.[25] The Ministry of Agriculture and Farmers' Welfare and the Ministry of Rural Development have been encouraging the participation of rural women farmers through various schemes. The Mahila Kisan Sashakti Karan Pariyojana (MKSP) is one of the major initiatives for skill training rural women farmers. MKSP was introduced as a subcomponent of DAY-NRLM (Deendayal Antyodaya Yojana).[26]

Members of Self-Help Groups have been appointed as Bank Mitra and Bank Sakhi in order to provide banking and financial services in rural or remote areas. Today, nearly 2,000 Self-Help Groups have been working as Bank Mitra or Bank Sakhi throughout the country and transactions worth Rs. 350 crore have taken place through them.[27]

The lives of Indian rural women have radically changed in the last decade. The pain, which they could not express, was understood by recognising and fulfilling their basic needs, and by providing them help, it has guarded their self-esteem and opened new doors for living a life full of' self-respect.

The extent to which Self-Help Groups have been helpful in achieving the goal of self-reliance for rural women can be seen at Nighsan, a village in Kheri district of Uttar Pradesh. In the heart of Nighsan, lives a rural entrepreneur named Meera, who faced severe financial struggledue to limited agricultural land and absence of her husband since he was away, looking for better work. But instead of wallowing in her difficult circumstances, she turned the support of her Self-Help Group (SHG) into a catalyst for change. In 2022, Meera completed her entrepreneurship development training and started her business of selling cattle feed, a high-demand product in her area. She also diversified her income streams through advanced farming techniques, like oyster and mushroom cultivation. This not only ensured her family's financial stability but also transformed her into a key player in the local agricultural landscape. But Meera was not satisfied with her own empowerment. Her vision extended beyond her own household. She established a button mushroom demonstration unit at her home with the help of Krishi Vigyan Kendra (KVK), where she encouraged other women in her SHG to learn and earn. This move created a network of financially independent women who, like Meera, became decision-makers in their families. Her endeavours not only improved her community's financial well-being but also elevated the identity of women in the village.[28]

There are thousands of women like Meera who are writing new chapters of self-reliance and empowerment every day. The story of self-reliant India is incomplete without the contribution of these rural women.

References

1. https://www.makeinindia.com/about
2. https://ddnews.gov.in/business/make-india-increases-record-breaking-fdi-inflows-manufacturing-sector%C2%A0%C2%A0
3. https://www.indiaingreece.gov.in/page/fdi/
4. https://www.icis.com/chemicals-and-the-economy/2014/08/nodie-highlights-toilets-indias-independence-day-speech/
5. https://www.indiablooms.com/news-details/N/3452/modi-pledges-to-set-up-more-toilets-on-i-day.html
6. Caruso, B.A., Clasen, T., Yount, K.M., Cooper, H.L., Hadley, C. and Haardörfer, R. (2017), Assessing women's negative sanitation experiences and concerns: The development of a novel sanitation insecurity measure, International Journal of Environmental Research and Public Health, 14(7): 755.
7. Bisung, E. and Elliott, S.J. (2017), "It makes us really look inferior to outsiders": Coping with psychosocial experiences associated with the lack of access to safe water and sanitation, Canadian Journal of Public Health, 108(4).
8. https://swachhbharatmission.gov.in/sbmcms/writereaddata/Portal/Images/pdf/Safety-security-and-dignity-of-women.pdf
9. Ibid.
10. https://www.google.com url?sa=t&source=web&rct=j&opi=89978449&url=https://static.pib.gov.in/WriteReadData/specificdocs/documents/2021/sep/doc202191721.pdf&ved=2ahUKEwiyt4XTrP-DAxXWzjgGHVpBAhkQFnoECDAQAQ&usg=AOvVaw3epGNEfyofrAx7Gq01QVMY
11. https://www.google.com/amp/s/indianexpress.com/article/trending/trending-in-india/independence-day-2020-pm-modi-sanitary-pads-remark-in-speech-reactions-6555977/lite/
12. https://main.mohfw.gov.in/sites/default/files/Draft%20Menstrual%20Hygiene%20Policy%202023%20-For%20Comments.pdf
13. Ibid.
14. https://jalshakti-ddws.gov.in/sites/default/files/JJM_Operational_Guidelines.pdf
15. https://planet.outlookindia.com/news/11-crore-rural-families-in-india-have-access-to-water-connections-jal-shakti-ministry-news-414766
16. https://www.google.com/amp/s/www.news18.com/amp/news/opinion/empower-a-woman-and-change-her-story-how-jal-jeevan-mission-is-changing-womens-lives-4871735.html
17. Ibid.
18. https://pib.gov.in/PressReleaseIframePage.aspx?PRID=1988087
19. Ibid.

20. https://www.google.com/amp/s/www.livemint.com/opinion/online-views/opinion-how-clean-burning-fuel-has-empowered-women-in-india/amp-1549981726903.html
21. https://pib.gov.in/PressReleseDetail.aspx?PRID=1944922
22. https://www.orfonline.org/expert-speak/assessing-the-empowerment-of-women-in-rural-india-today
23. Ibid.
24. https://pib.gov.in/PressReleaseIframePage.aspx?PRID=1941360
25. https://pib.gov.in/Pressreleaseshare.aspx?PRID=1538468
26. https://pib.gov.in/Pressreleaseshare.aspx?PRID=1538468
27. https://pib.gov.in/Pressreleaseshare.aspx?PRID=1538468
28. https://www.villagesquare.in/rural-entrepreneur-empowers-other-women-in-up/

□

Government of India Schemes for Women

Beti Bachao Beti Padhao

The trend of decline in the Child Sex Ratio (CSR), defined as number of girls per 1,000 boys between 0-6 years of age, has been unabated since 1961. The decline from 945 in 1991 to 927 in 2001 and further to 918 in 2011 is alarming. The decline in the CSR is a major indicator of women disempowerment. CSR reflects both pre-birth discrimination manifested through gender biased sex selection and post-birth discrimination against girls. Social construct discriminating against girls on the one hand, easy availability, affordability and subsequent misuse of diagnostic tools on the other hand, have been critical in increasing Sex Selective Elimination of girls leading to low Child Sex Ratio. Since coordinated and convergent efforts are needed to ensure survival, protection and empowerment of the girl child, the government has announced Beti Bachao Beti Padhao initiative. This is being implemented through multi-sectoral intervention in all the districts of the country. This is a joint initiative of Ministry of Women & Child Development, Ministry of Health & Family Welfare and Department of School Education & Literacy, Ministry of Education.[1]

The objectives of this initiative are:

- Prevention of gender-biased sex selective elimination
- Ensuring survival and protection of the girl child
- Ensuring education and participation of the girl child

1 https://wcd.nic.in/bbbp-schemes

Mahila Shakti Kendra

MSK scheme is envisaged to provide an interface for rural women to approach the government for availing their entitlements and for empowering them through training and capacity building.

Objective : The new scheme MSK is envisaged to work at various levels. While, national level (domain-based knowledge support) and state level (State Resource Centre for Women) structures will provide technical support to the respective governments on issues related to women, the district and block level centres will provide support to MSK and also give a foothold to women empowerment schemes, including BBBP in 640 districts to be covered in a phased manner. Community engagement through student volunteers is envisioned in 115 most backward districts as part of the MSK block-level initiatives. Student volunteers will play an instrumental role in awareness generation regarding various important government schemes/ programmes as well as social issues that have an impact on the lives of women in a given block (or equivalent administrative unit, when such blocks are not in place).[2]

---

2 https://wcd.nic.in/schemes/mahila-shakti-kendras-msk

'Mission Shakti'

Ministry of Women and Child Development has issued detailed guidelines for 'Mission Shakti' scheme. The Government of India has launched 'Mission Shakti', an integrated women empowerment programme as an umbrella scheme for the safety, security and empowerment of women for implementation during the 15th Finance Commission period, 2021-22 to 2025-26. The norms of 'Mission Shakti' will be applicable with effect from 1 April, 2022.

'Mission Shakti' is a scheme in mission mode aimed at strengthening interventions for women safety, security and empowerment. It seeks to realise the government's commitment for 'women-led development' by addressing issues affecting women on a life-cycle continuum basis and by making them equal partners in nation-building through convergence and citizen-ownership.

The scheme seeks to make women economically empowered, exercising free choice over their minds and bodies in an atmosphere free from violence and threat. It also seeks to reduce the care burden on women and increase female labour force participation by promoting skill development, capacity building, financial literacy, access to micro-credit, etc.

'Mission Shakti' has two sub-schemes – 'Sambal' and 'Samarthya'. While the 'Sambal' sub-scheme is for safety and

security of women, the 'Samarthya' sub-scheme is for empowerment of women. The components of 'Sambal' sub-scheme consist of erstwhile schemes of One Stop Centre (OSC), Women Helpline (WHL), Beti Bachao Beti Padhao (BBBP) with a new component of Nari Adalats – women's collectives to promote and facilitate alternative dispute resolution and gender justice in society and within families.[3]

Mudra Yojana

The Mudra loan scheme is a government initiative aimed at promoting entrepreneurship, with a special focus on women entrepreneurs. It provides financial support to micro and small enterprises, offering loans up to Rs. 10 lakhs with easy terms and conditions. Notably, no collateral is required for loans within this limit and women entrepreneurs benefit from lower interest rates.[4]

- **One Stop Centre and Universalisation of Women Helplines:** One Stop Centres (OSCs) are intended to support women affected by violence, in private and public spaces, within the family, community and at the workplace. Women facing physical, sexual, emotional, psychological

3 https://pib.gov.in/PressReleaseIframePage.aspx?PRID=1841498

4 https://ssnifound.in/2023/09/28/empowering-women-entrepreneurs-through-government-funding-schemes/#:~:text=The%20Mudra%20loan%20scheme%20is,with%20easy%20terms%20and%20conditions.x

and economic abuse, irrespective of age, class, caste, education status, marital status, race and culture will be facilitated with support and redressal. Aggrieved women facing any kind of violence due to attempted sexual harassment, sexual assault, domestic violence, trafficking, honor-related crimes, acid attacks or witch-hunting and who have reached out or been referred to the OSC will be provided with specialised services.

In Haryana state, initially one stop centre was set up in district Karnal on 31 August, 2015. Currently a total of 22 one stop centres are running in the state (Table 1.2). It's 100% centrally-sponsored scheme under the Nirbhaya fund.

Objectives: The objectives of the scheme are:

- To provide integrated support and assistance to women affected by violence, both in private and public spaces under one roof.
- To facilitate immediate, emergency and non-emergency access to a range of services including medical, legal, psychological and counselling support under one roof to fight against any forms of violence against women.[5]

Pradhan Mantri Matru Vandana Yojana

From 1 January, 2017, the Maternity Benefit Programme was implemented in all the districts of the country in accordance with the provisions of the National Food Security Act, 2013. The programme is named as 'Pradhan Mantri Matru Vandana Yojana' (PMMVY).

Under PMMVY, a cash incentive of Rs. 5000/- is provided directly in the account of pregnant women and lactating mothers

5 Reference : https://wcdhry.gov.in/schemes-for-women/onestop-centre/

(PW&LM) for first living child of the family, subject to their fulfilling specific conditions relating to Maternal and Child Health.

The eligible beneficiaries would receive the remaining cash incentives as per approved norms towards maternity benefit under Janani Suraksha Yojana (JSY) after institutional delivery so that on an average, a woman will get Rs. 6000/- .

Objectives:

1. Providing partial compensation for the wage loss in terms of cash incentives so that the woman can take adequate rest before and after delivery of the first living child.
2. The cash incentive provided would lead to improved health seeking behaviour amongst the pregnant women and lactating mothers (PW&LM).[6]

Pradhan Mantri Ujjwala Yojana

Pradhan Mantri Ujjwala Yojana (PMUY, translation: Prime Minister's Lightning Scheme) was launched by Prime Minister Narendra Modi on 1 May, 2016 to distribute 50 million LPG connections to women of Below Poverty Line (BPL) families.[1][2][3] A budgetary allocation of Rs. 80 billion (US$1.0 billion) was made for the scheme. The scheme was replaced by the Ujjwala Yojana 2.0 in 2021. The first year of its launch, the connections distributed were 22 million against the target of 15 million. As of 23 October, 2017, 30 million connections were distributed, 44% of which were given to families belonging to Scheduled Castes and Scheduled Tribes.[7]

6 http://it.delhigovt.nic.in/writereaddata/Odr2017841095.pdf
7 https://en.wikipedia.org/wiki/Pradhan_Mantri_Ujjwala_Yojana

Ujjwala 2.0: Additional allocation was made of 1.6 crore LPG connections under PMUY scheme with special facility to migrant households. Target number of connections under Ujjwala 2.0 was achieved during December, 22, thus taking overall connections under the scheme to 9.6 crore.[8]

Stand-Up India Scheme

The Stand-Up India scheme is a government scheme that aims to promote entrepreneurship among women and other marginalised communities. It provides bank loans to at least one Scheduled Caste (SC) or Scheduled Tribe borrower and at least one woman per bank branch for the establishment of a greenfield business. In the case of non-individual firms, a SC/ST or woman entrepreneur must possess at least 51 per cent of the ownership and majority stake. Under this scheme, women entrepreneurs can get a loan ranging from Rs. 10 lakh to Rs. one crore to start or expand their small business.

8 https://www.pmuy.gov.in/about.html

- **Swadhar Greh Scheme:** The Ministry of Women and Child Development is implementing the Swadhar Greh Scheme which targets the women victims of difficult circumstances who are in need of institutional support for rehabilitation so that they could lead their life with dignity. The scheme envisages providing shelter, food, clothing and health as well as economic and social security for these women.
- **Beneficiaries:** The benefits of the component could be availed by women above 18 years of age in the following categories:

  Women who are deserted and are without any social and economic support; women survivors of natural disasters who have been rendered homeless and are without any social and economic support; women prisoners released from jail and who are without family, social and economic support; women victims of domestic violence, family tension or discord, who are made to leave their homes without any means of subsistence and have no special protection from exploitation and/or facing litigation on account of marital disputes; and trafficked women/girls rescued or run away from brothels or other places where they face exploitation and women affected by HIV/AIDS who do not have any social or economic support. However, such women/girls should first seek assistance under Ujjwala scheme in areas where it is in operation.[9]

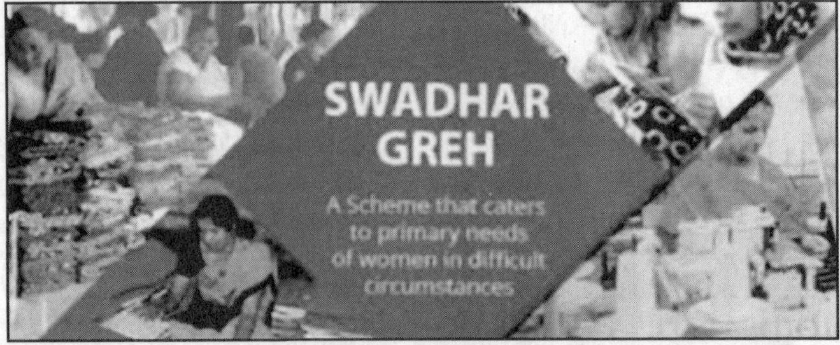

9 https://www.myscheme.gov.in/schemes/sg

The Sukanya Samriddhi Yojana

The Sukanya Samriddhi Yojana (SSY) is a small deposit scheme by the Ministry of Finance exclusively for the girl child. SSY was launched by the Hon'ble Prime Minister on 22 January, 2015 as a part of the Beti Bachao Beti Padhao campaign. The scheme is meant to meet the education and marriage expenses of the girl child. Notified by the Government of India on 14 December, 2014, this scheme encourages parents to build a fund for the future education and marriage expenses of their female child. One can apply for SSY through Post Offices or through the branches of public sector banks and three private sector banks, viz. HDFC Bank, Axis Bank, and ICICI Bank. The account can be opened by a parent or legal guardian of the girl child. The girl child must be below the age of 10 years. Only one account is allowed for a girl child. A family can open only two SSY accounts. The minimum investment is Rs. 250 per annum; The maximum investment is Rs. 1,50,000 per annum. The maturity period is 21 years. For the period 01.04.2023 to 30.06.2023, the rate of interest is 8.0%. The principal amount deposited, interest earned during the entire tenure, and maturity benefits are tax-exempt. The principal amount is deductible under section 80C up to Rs. 1,50,000. Since the inception of the scheme, around 2.73 crore accounts have been opened under the scheme, having nearly Rs. 1.19 lakh crore deposit[10]

10 https://www.myscheme.gov.in/schemes/ssy

Ujjwala Scheme

Ujjwala: A comprehensive scheme for prevention of trafficking and rescue, rehabilitation and re- integration of victims of trafficking and commercial sexual exploitation[11]

Objective of the Scheme

- To prevent trafficking of women and children for commercial sexual exploitation.
- Through social mobilisation and involvement of local communities, awareness generation programmes, generation of public discourse through workshops/ seminars and such events and any other innovative activity.
- To facilitate rescue of victims from the place of their exploitation and place them in safe custody.
- To provide rehabilitation services both immediate and long-term to the victims by providing basic amenities/ needs, such as shelter, food, clothing, medical treatment including counselling, legal aid and guidance and vocational training.

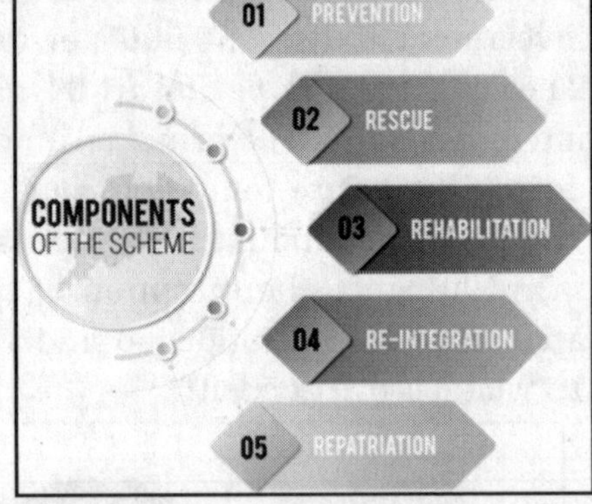

- To facilitate reintegration of the victims into the family and society at large.
- To facilitate repatriation of cross-border victims to their country of origin.

□

11 https://wcd.nic.in/sites/default/files/Ujjawala%20New%20Scheme.pdf

Notes on the Contributors

Dr. Anamika Sinha is a teacher, trainer and a coach. She has deep level knowledge on human processes having been a member of ISABS (Indian Society for Applied Behaviour Sciences) and pursuing T group process labs. Recently, she has also completed OKR Certification Level 2 as well.

A Ph.D. in Organisational Behaviour from University of Lucknow, she has over 22 years of experience in teaching, training and consulting, of which 18 years have been with management institutes of repute, like Goa Institute of Management, Nirma University, Defence Services Staff College and Amity. She actively consults organisations in the area of HR audit, competency mapping, PoSH training and IC capability building and organisational restructuring etc. She has written cases and research papers in journals of repute, including Harvard Business Case studies.

Prof. Vijita Singh Aggarwal has worked towards establishing herself as a distinguished academician, dedicated social worker, prolific writer and an accomplished researcher. With a multi-dimensional approach to her work, she combines her expertise in academia, research, writing and social work to create a significant impact in society at large. Currently working as a Professor of Management at GGS Indraprastha University, she is ever curious, socially conscious and entrepreneurial in her academic and

professional journey. With a genuine dedication to social causes, she actively engages with marginalised communities and helps in their upliftment by advocating for justice. One such community she has worked along with is the vulnerable voices of Kashmir and Bengal. Prof. Vijita has authored numerous scholarly articles, research papers and book chapters, contributing valuable insights to the academic community. She has further been a recipient of numerous prestigious offers, such as the Erasmus Mundus Scholarship for European Research Masters at University of London and has additionally been associated with institutions like IIT, Jammu, Delhi University, IIT Roorkee, IIIT Kota and NLU Shimla as a visiting/adjunct faculty.

Prof. Richa Sawant is a professor at the Centre of Russian Studies, School of Language, Literature and Culture Studies, Jawaharlal Nehru University, New Delhi. Her areas of interest are contemporary Russian language, culture and area studies. She has a number of articles and has co-authored two textbooks. She takes a keen interest in pedagogy and student development.

Dr. Manorama Tripathi holds a doctorate in Library and Information Science from Banaras Hindu University, Varanasi. At present, she is working as Librarian at Jawaharlal Nehru University, New Delhi. Prior to joining JNU, she served Indira Gandhi National Open University as a Documentation Officer, New Delhi and as afaculty member, University of Delhi, Delhi and Banaras Hindu University, Varanasi.

Dr. Shipra Awasthi is working as an Assistant Librarian at Dr. B.R. Ambedkar Central Library, Jawaharlal Nehru University, New Delhi. Prior to this, she worked with NIT, Rourkela, Odisha, as Assistant Librarian. Her areas of interest include open access, anti-plagiarism software, electronic theses and dissertations,